Theater of Capital

SERIES EDITORS This series publishes books in theater and performance studies,
Patrick Anderson and focused in particular on the material conditions in which
Nicholas Ridout performance acts are staged, and to which performance itself
might contribute. We define "performance" in the broadest sense,
including traditional theatrical productions and performance art,
but also cultural ritual, political demonstration, social practice,
and other forms of interpersonal, social, and political interaction
that may fruitfully be understood in terms of performance.

Theater of Capital

Modern Drama and Economic Life

✦

Alisa Zhulina

NORTHWESTERN UNIVERSITY PRESS
EVANSTON, ILLINOIS

Northwestern University Press
www.nupress.northwestern.edu

Copyright © 2024 by Northwestern University. Published 2024 by
Northwestern University Press. All rights reserved.

Printed in the United States of America

10 9 8 7 6 5 4 3 2 1

Library of Congress Cataloging-in-Publication Data

Names: Zhulina, Alisa, author.
Title: Theater of capital : modern drama and economic life / Alisa Zhulina.
Other titles: Performance works.
Description: Evanston, Illinois : Northwestern University Press, 2024. |
 Series: Performance works | Includes bibliographical references and index.
Identifiers: LCCN 2023036633 | ISBN 9780810146341 (paperback) |
 ISBN 9780810146358 (cloth) | ISBN 9780810146365 (ebook)
Subjects: LCSH: Drama—19th century—History and criticism. | Drama—
 20th century—History and criticism. | Capitalism in literature.
Classification: LCC PN1643 .Z48 2024 | DDC 809.293553—dc23/
 eng/20230808
LC record available at https://lccn.loc.gov/2023036633

For Martin and Mathilda

CONTENTS

Acknowledgments — *ix*

Introduction — *3*

Chapter 1
Finance Capital: Henrik Ibsen and the Invisible Hand — *43*

Chapter 2
The Dowry versus Erotic Capital: The Drama of Courtship in Strindberg, Shaw, and Benedictsson — *83*

Chapter 3
Casino Capitalism: Anton Chekhov and Gambling — *143*

Chapter 4
Labor and Strike: Gerhart Hauptmann's *The Weavers* and Its Legacy in German Expressionism — *175*

Coda — *201*

Notes — *213*

Bibliography — *259*

Index — *283*

ACKNOWLEDGMENTS

I am deeply thankful to all the friends and colleagues who have made this project possible over the years. At Harvard University, Martin Puchner guided my work with care, kindness, and encouragement. His outstanding scholarship, intellectual generosity, and dedicated mentorship of students taught me how an academic life should be led, and I will always be grateful. William Todd has read my prose and shared his wisdom with me since my undergraduate years. His legendary course Literature as Institutions influenced the methodology of this book and how I think about culture. David Damrosch always gave me invaluable suggestions and asked critical questions that helped expand the scope of the project. D. N. Rodowick first sparked my interest in philosophy. I owe my fascination with the nineteenth century to Stephanie Lin Carlson. Carrol Statom nurtured my love for the theater. Brian L. Blank taught me how to write. The late Svetlana Boym advised me early in my graduate work, and I am fortunate to have learned from her that the life of the mind can be full of surprises, humor, and joy.

I am grateful to Nicholas Ridout and Patrick Anderson for their support and enthusiasm for this project. To be published in their superb series is an honor. As I indicate in the book, Ridout's work has been a great inspiration for my own thinking. I also thank everyone at Northwestern University Press, especially Faith Wilson Stein, who has been an exemplary editor. For their assistance in the final stages of the project, I thank Jessica Hinds-Bond, Maia Rigas, and Christi Stanforth.

The book attained its final form when I joined the Department of Drama at the Tisch School of the Arts at New York University. I am indebted to many wonderful colleagues who supported and encouraged my scholarship. Carol Martin has been a marvelous mentor, role model, and friend. Her wise advice and guidance have helped me immeasurably. I am also thankful to Edward Ziter, who assured me in the early stages that writing about *The Weavers* was, in fact, important and interesting and who has continued to champion this project ever since. Stefanos Geroulanos introduced me to the vibrant community of intellectual history and kindly offered several opportunities to develop my ideas, providing crucial feedback. Anne Lounsbery welcomed me to the community of Slavic Studies and invited me to present material from the manuscript on numerous occasions. Many influential conversations with colleagues helped shape this book. I especially thank Gwendolyn Alker, Awam Amkpa, Sebastián Calderón Bentin, Elizabeth Bradley, Una Chaudhuri, Rossen Djagalov, Laura Levine, Erin Mee, Rubén Polendo, Mauricio Salgado, Tomi Tsunoda, Jay Wegman, Lauren Whitehead, and Brandon Woolf for sharing with me their important insights, questions, and experience. For their unparalleled institutional support, I thank J. M. DeLeon, John Dietrich, Carrie Meconis, and Joe McGowan. I want to express my gratitude to Allyson Green and Karen Shimakawa for supporting my junior colleagues and me in our endeavors to combine scholarship with artistic practice. Finally, my students are the most gifted and intellectually curious young people I know. Our discussions enabled me to look at the material with fresh eyes and to think through many issues in the book.

Numerous scholars whose work I deeply admire helped me along the way. I thank Minou Arjomand, David Bruin, Tarryn Chun, Jason Fitzgerald, Ian Fleishman, Matthew Franks, Jacob Gallagher-Ross, Julia Jarcho, Nicole Jerr, Rebecca Kastleman, Debra Levine, Derek Miller, John Muse, Elizabeth Phillips, Magda Romanska, Susanah Romney, Alexandra Vazquez, Susanna Weygandt, and Joshua Williams for many illuminating conversations. Leonardo Lisi is one of my most important interlocutors. I am very grateful for his astute and vital feedback at different stages of the project. I owe a special debt to Martin Harries, who has generously read several versions of the manuscript, and whose challenging questions and brilliant suggestions pushed me to refine my argument and made this a better book.

Thanks to kind invitations, I had the opportunity to rehearse ideas from the book at decisive stages of the writing process. The Centre for Ibsen Studies at the University of Oslo has hosted me on two occasions, both times transformational. I am indebted to Narve Fulsås, Kristin Gjesdal, Frode Helland, and Tore Rem for their insightful comments. I want to thank Fiona Bell for inviting me to the Yale Slavic Colloquium and Edyta Bojanowska, Molly Brunson, and Katerina Clark for their warm hospitality and critical engagement with my chapter on Chekhov. The participants of the "Chekhov in the World" conference at NYU—Rodrigo Alves do Nascimento, Carol Apollonio, Michael Finke, Jeanne-Marie Jackson, Radislav Lapushin, Matthew Mangold, and Cathy Popkin—offered me invaluable remarks and encouragement. I also want to thank Annie Baker, Clare Barron, and Sam Gold for giving me the opportunity to translate *Ivanov* and *Three Sisters* and for our stimulating conversations about Chekhov.

This book would not have been possible without the generous and timely support of the Goddard Junior Faculty Fellowship, the Provost's Global Research Initiative at NYU Florence, Mrs. Giles Whiting Fellowship in the Humanities, the Krupp Foundation, and the École Normale Supérieure Exchange Fellowship. I want to express my deep gratitude to

Acknowledgments

Ulrich Baer, Molly Rogers, and the fellows of the 2019–2020 cohort at the NYU Center for the Humanities for an extraordinary year of riveting talks and fruitful conversations. Many thanks are also due to the archivists and librarians at the Harvard Theatre Collection at Houghton Library, the New York Public Library for the Performing Arts, the Bibliothèque nationale de France, and Elmer Holmes Bobst Library at NYU.

The Mellon Summer School for Theater and Performance writing workshops, led by Jennifer Buckley and Andrew Sofer, provided much-needed advice about style, revision, and publishing. I also want to thank all the participants for carefully reading early drafts of the manuscript, asking the right questions, and offering me generative feedback.

The editors of *Modern Drama*, *Modernism/modernity*, and *Theatre Survey* provided me with many helpful suggestions for revision when they published early versions of sections of the book. I especially want to thank Alan Ackerman, Julia Cosacchi, Anne Fernald, and Michael Gnat for their exceptional assistance. Two anonymous readers for Northwestern University Press were extremely generous and insightful, and I thank them for their time and suggestions.

Special thanks go to friends whose kindness and humor have sustained me throughout some difficult years: Rich Angle, Melody Brooks, Jillian Crawford, Sara Gorman, Tess Howsam, Olivia Jampol, Robert Kohen, Yaël Levine, Conan Liu, and Ashley Simpson. Something more than a thank-you goes to Julia Sun Choe, whose friendship I have cherished for the past two decades.

My parents, Irina and Igor, have sacrificed so much for me that only now, after becoming a parent myself, am I beginning to fully appreciate their gifts. Despite all the hardships, they gave me the kind of education few could hope for in our economic circumstances.

This book is dedicated to Martin Hägglund. Martin has truly lived with this book, reading every word, discussing its central ideas, and reminding me of its stakes. Our life together is a testament to the kind of partnership possible between the free and the equal. The book is also dedicated to our daughter, Mathilda.

Theater of Capital

INTRODUCTION

What Is Capital?

During the 2015 Venice Biennale, a team of performers would stage daily marathon readings of the three volumes of Karl Marx's *Capital* (1867). This was not a protest by activists, but a commissioned work directed by artist and filmmaker Isaac Julien. The late curator Okwui Enwezor took Marx's magnum opus as an inspiration for the entire Biennale under the title "All the World's Futures." The challenge that he faced was how to present ideas from a text that is, in the words of Lorena Muñoz-Alonso, "as liberally quoted within art circles as it is seldom actually read."[1] Performance became the medium through which Enwezor attempted to convey Marx's thought. In addition to the live readings, Enwezor included a series of "annotations"—a selection of performances that commented on *Capital*—such as a film featuring Isaac Julien's interview with David Harvey, a batch of nineteenth-century ballads curated by Jeremy Deller, and Maja Bajevic's *Arts, Crafts and Facts*.[2] The latter, with its unmistakable nod to textile designer and socialist William Morris, is a video installation featuring a choir of workers inside a textile factory singing about price fluctuations in global markets. The audience was invited to sit on pillows made by those very same workers.

The paradox of performing Marx's words on the site of one of the world's most opulent exhibitions was not lost on the critics. Many were quick to point out the myriad contradictions: the sponsorship of Rolls-Royce, collector billionaires leisurely strolling among artworks depicting the exploitation of labor, and—an event that elicited perhaps the greatest delight from the media—a dock collapsing under the weight of A-listers on their way to a party at Fondazione Prada. No one was harmed. The soaked guests laughed off the minor mishap.

The incident was a farcical and perverse echo of a real tragedy that had taken place a few weeks before the opening. On the night of April 18, 2015, a fishing boat carrying migrants sank between Libya and the Italian island of Lampedusa, ending more than nine hundred lives. In 2019, this very same boat would reappear at the Venice Biennale as an exhibit by Swiss-Icelandic artist Christoph Büchel under the title *Barca Nostra (Our Boat)*. Although Büchel maintains that the transported boat was meant as a somber reminder of Europe's refugee crisis, many critics have lambasted

3

the piece, noting that visitors were often oblivious to its story, mingling as they did in a nearby café or taking selfies next to the boat.[3]

The interpenetration of art and global capital is nothing new and goes back at least to the Medici family's patronage of artists. The stark difference, however, lies in the unnerving fact that the contemporary art world, which now allows the 1 percent to store its wealth in acquired artworks held in tax-free storages, has rendered institutional critique particularly challenging. As Ryan Hatch eloquently puts it, "Contemporary art is implicated in the very machinery of neoliberal violence that many writers allege the artwork exists to contest, or at least reveal."[4]

How does one, then, critique a system of which one is, to borrow Bruce Robbins's term, "a beneficiary" without falling into the trap of hypocrisy, self-righteousness, or handwringing?[5] Robbins defines the "beneficiary" as "the relatively privileged person in the metropolitan center who contemplates her or his unequal relations with persons at the less-prosperous periphery and feels or fears that in some way their fates are linked."[6] Although Robbins's focus is on the contemporary global situation of beneficiaries (with a nod to earlier examples in the cases of Adam Smith, George Orwell, George Eliot, and others), his definition is pertinent to the position of the playwrights described in this book. These modern dramatists engage in what Robbins calls the "discourse of the beneficiary." As Robbins emphasizes, such a discourse is inherently "contradictory" because it belongs to someone who is "denouncing a system that he finds intolerable but to which he nevertheless continues to belong, from which he continues to derive certain benefits and privileges, from which he may have no possibility of making a clean break—and which he can only denounce to others who also continue to belong to it."[7]

According to Marx, internal contradictions are inherent to capitalism.[8] And, as Boris Groys has recently noted in his defense of contemporary art, "only self-contradictory practices are true in a deeper sense of the word."[9] This was precisely Enwezor's point when he tried to justify what many were calling a pretentious and politically problematic curatorial vision: "Beyond the distemper and disorder in the current 'state of things,' there is one pervasive preoccupation that has been at the heart of our time and modernity. That preoccupation is the nature of Capital, both its fiction and reality. Capital is the great drama of our age."[10] If the fascination with the nature of capital is one of the defining features of modernity, when and how did it develop over time? And how can theater and performance deepen our understanding of the workings of capital?

This book investigates "the great drama of capital" by focusing on the European drama of the late nineteenth century, when the notoriously difficult-to-define term "capital" animated public discussion and when the word "capitalism" entered debates about economic systems in the wake of the publication of the first volume of *Capital* (1867). In fact, the term "capitalism" is more recent than the economic and political system that it describes. Emerging in the second half of the nineteenth century in the context of socialist critique, "capitalism" was from the onset a polemical term. The French socialist Louis Blanc is often credited as the first thinker to use "capitalism" in this critical sense, defining it as "the appropriation of capital by some, to the exclusion of others."[11] Soon after, Pierre-Joseph Proudhon explicitly linked the overthrow of capitalism to socialism, emphasizing that socialism was not just "the extinction of misery, abolition of capitalism, transformation of private property" but also "the universalization of the middle class."[12] Marx rarely used the word "capitalism," preferring the phrase "capitalist mode of production."[13] Gradually, the awareness of capitalism as a system of production and of capital as its driving force became more widespread due to the institutionalization of modern social sciences, including economics, through the work of Marx, Émile Durkheim, Max Weber, and many others.

This turbulent time coincided with the birth of modern drama. As I will argue, theater as an institution and artistic practice is particularly adept at staging the social implications of the relentless drive for capital accumulation and the internal contradictions of capitalism. *Theater of Capital* traces how theater represented capital, explored economic issues, and engaged in an immanent critique of capitalism at a time when three historical transitions were underway: neoclassical economics was emerging as a separate social science committed to abstract thinking; speculation and investment were becoming legitimate economic activities distinct from gambling; and questions about how to run the economy, especially those raised by socialist thinkers, galvanized public debate. This was also a time when theater was trying to gain ground as a reputable artistic medium and social institution: living off capital and helping to reproduce capitalist society while simultaneously critiquing it.

This study focuses on the bourgeois playwrights of modern drama, exploring not only their dramatic texts but also, most importantly, the representation of capital through performance inside the institution of late nineteenth-century theater. Hence the title: *Theater of Capital*. The modern dramatists at the center of this book thought deeply about the material conditions and economic constraints of their place of work, whether it was Ibsen drawing on his experience of running a theater to write about power, or Shaw checking the box office receipts to learn more about the audience frequenting his productions. They wrote not in a vacuum but for the stage, which always needs infrastructure, machinery, and the labor of people.[14] Their texts often contain the challenge of their staging and acknowledge in a metatheatrical way the space of the theater, especially when it bears an uncomfortable resemblance to the stock exchange, the brothel, or the factory. They wrote with an eye toward performance. As Marvin Carlson once noted, theater practitioners "have long developed their work with an intuitive understanding" of "the concept of the supplement," privileging neither performance nor the written text.[15] Rather, this particular "text-performance dynamic" encourages "an adjustment of perception in both directions."[16] Modern playwrights were acutely aware of how the material conditions of theatrical performance in a capitalist society, ripe with contradictions, influenced their writing, and how their writing could potentially challenge and change those very same conditions.

"Theater of capital" thus means a number of things in this book. It is first and foremost a theater that makes capital one of its main subjects. It is also an institution that needs capital to survive, even as its beneficiaries (artists, producers, and audiences) engage in a critique of capitalism. Moreover, it is a theater that itself operates—however precariously and unevenly—as a form of cultural capital.[17] In and through all of these aspects, it is a theater that finds its inspiration in the internal contradictions of life under capitalism.

Only in the late nineteenth-century theater do we begin to hear the words "capital" and "capitalism" spoken aloud. The widespread awareness of capitalism spilled into the theater. While, in the twentieth century, capitalism would primarily be associated with Wall Street and the United States (this is certainly true of the mythical America of Bertolt Brecht's plays), during the fin de siècle it was the United Kingdom that still dominated as the world's largest industrial power. Hence, in Anton Chekhov's *The Cherry Orchard*, the invisible hand of the market is personified by offstage English investors. The United States would overtake the United Kingdom as the world's largest economy by World War I.[18] This is why this book, which focuses on late nineteenth-century theater and capital, does not feature Wall Street as prominently as European stock markets. Nevertheless, by the final chapter, which discusses Emanuel Reicher's 1915 English-language production of Gerhart Hauptmann's *The Weavers* (*Die Weber*, 1892), we will arrive on the American stage, mimicking the movement of global capital.

The broad meaning of "capital"—namely, "wealth employed in carrying on a particular business"—dates from the 1640s, but its specific use as that part of a person's stock which she "expects to afford ... revenue" comes from Adam Smith's *An Inquiry into the Nature and Causes of the Wealth of Nations* (1776), the magnum opus that launched the study of political economy in modern Europe.[19] The word "capital," for example, never appears in George Lillo's *The London Merchant* (1731), even though the play certainly deals with issues of money and capital. It appears only once in Bernard Shaw's first play, *Widowers' Houses* (1892).[20] A decade later, *Major Barbara* (1905) would feature the word "capital" six times, and "capitalist" three. Put simply, however imprecise or nebulous their use of these terms might be, modern playwrights, their dramatic characters, and audience members begin to talk about capital, capitalists, and capitalism. Yet do we fully understand what capital is and how it works? In his interview with Isaac Julien, which played at the 2015 Venice Biennale, David Harvey explains capital as follows: "It's a bit like gravity. It's a very powerful force; it's a relationship which makes things happen. . . . You can really only intuit that capital exists by its effects."[21] In this respect, theater, a medium that specializes in the boundary between the visible and the invisible, is exceptionally well equipped to represent capital and explore its social effects. As Jane Moody notes, the "instability of the relationship between the actual and the imaginary lies at the heart of theatrical illusion."[22] Nevertheless, it is important to highlight a few crucial and concrete definitions of capital that will appear in this book.

Different definitions of capital were in circulation in the nineteenth century, and this variety of meanings shows up in the speeches of characters and in the dramatizations of the movement of capital onstage. In August Strindberg's *Miss Julie* (*Fröken Julie*, 1888), when Jean claims that his "expertise" and "incredible experience" are "sufficient capital" to start a hotel business, he anticipates the French sociologist Pierre Bourdieu's concepts of embodied cultural and social capital.[23] For Bourdieu, capital is "accumulated labor (in its materialized form or its 'incorporated,' embodied form) which when appropriated on a private, i.e., exclusive basis by agents or groups of agents, enables them to appropriate social energy in the form of reified or living labor."[24] When Shaw's Mrs. Warren confesses that, in her youth, all she had at her disposal to support herself were her "appearance and . . . a turn for pleasing men," she inadvertently anticipates what British sociologist Catherine Hakim would call, in the twentieth-first century, "erotic capital."[25] Although I disagree with Hakim, I justify my engagement with her theory of erotic capital because it is the culmination of "economism," or "the tendency to interpret all phenomena in market terms."[26] This tendency began to take root during the marginal revolution (about which more later) and the rise of neoclassical economics in the late nineteenth century. Thus, we can notice this historical transition in the fin-de-siècle theater in the myriad ways that dramatic characters try to embrace an economic approach to their lives and in the ways this approach fails them. Still another definition of capital comes from Fabian socialists. For Shaw and members of his Fabian circle, capital was first and foremost "spare money" made from differential rent.[27] As we will explore in chapter 2, this "spare money" is at the core of the economic problem in Shaw's *Mrs. Warren's Profession*. Fabians' focus on circulation instead of production mirrors Shaw's own interest in dramatizing the lives of capitalists rather than those of workers.

Marx's most referenced definition of capital is found in chapter 4 of the first volume of *Capital*, titled "The General Formula of Capital," where he defines capital as money used to buy commodities to sell those commodities to make more money (i.e., profit). This transformation of money into capital is captured in the formula M-C-M, in contrast to C-M-C, in which commodities are sold to make money that can then be used to purchase other commodities.[28] But this is not the whole story: it only describes circulation, not production. According to Marx's more fundamental definition in *The Grundrisse*, capital "itself is the moving contradiction, [in] that it presses to reduce labor time to a minimum, while it posits labor time, on the other side, as sole measure and source of wealth."[29]

In Marx, surplus value is not generated through circulation or rent, both of which are zero-sum games, since when one person or group loses money, another person or group gains it. While surplus value is realized in exchange (what Marx calls the "valorization of value"), its source lies in production—only living beings can *produce* surplus value.[30] As Martin Hägglund explains, living beings generate a surplus of time "by virtue of their own activity of self-maintenance."[31] After a living being (a human being or an animal) has spent time ensuring survival, there is free time left to engage in other activities, whether leisure or work. This is why human beings can, in fact, enjoy repose, engage in political activities, or make art. They have the time to do so. But this is also why, Hägglund argues, their labor can be exploited. Because living beings generate more "lifetime" than "it 'costs' to keep them alive," capitalists can use them as means to generate profit for themselves.[32] For the surplus value of human labor to be transformed into profit, they must not only sell their labor for wages but also buy commodities—the products of others' labor. The profit that results from this cycle is the source of capital growth.[33]

To survive competition, capitalists must try to maximize their profits. According to Marx, the measure of value in a capitalist society, what he calls "socially necessary labor time," is the length of time it takes for an average worker to make a commodity.[34] As Hägglund points out, socially necessary labor time is not fixed once and for all; rather, it depends on the technological means of production and labor efficiency.[35] For example, if a worker makes commodities faster and more efficiently than the social average, then she will increase her employer's profit margins. Capitalists are always trying to raise their relative surplus value, which is the difference between the wage they pay their workers (i.e., one hour of labor) and the value their workers generate during the same hour of labor. Machinery, according to Marx, "is the most powerful means of raising the productivity of labor, i.e., of shortening the working time needed to produce a commodity," but "it is also, as a repository of capital, the most powerful means of lengthening the working day beyond all natural limits."[36] As Hägglund notes, because in capitalism technological innovation is carried out primarily for the sake of profit instead of our collective well-being, the capitalist exploits the fact that the machine reduces the labor time required to produce a commodity. Now the capitalist can make the workers produce even more value in a shorter time while also keeping the wages low. Of course, technology can also be created for our collective well-being. For example, in a different socioeconomic system, it is conceivable that, by reducing the time of work, technology could free up time for us to make art, take better care of one another, enjoy more leisure, and so on. But under the capitalist mode of production, where the main economic motive is profit, machines only enable the further exploitation of the working class. As technological innovation increases, fewer laborers are needed to operate the machinery. As a result, there is a rise in unemployment, and those workers who still have jobs are exploited even more and for even lower wages. Now we have a crisis of overproduction. There are many commodities on the market, but the population does not have the means to buy them. So, what does capital do? It extends credit and emboldens unbridled speculation. Marx elaborates in volume 3 of *Capital*:

> Concentration grows at the same time, since beyond certain limits a large capital with a lower rate of profit accumulates more quickly than a small capital with a higher rate of profit. This growing concentration leads in turn, at a certain level, to a new fall in the rate of profit. The mass of small fragmented capitals are thereby forced onto adventurous paths: speculation, credit swindles, share swindles, crises.[37]

Marx's socioeconomic analysis of capital growth finds an intriguing parallel in the change in the aesthetic representation of capitalism that took place in the transition from melodrama to modern drama. Just as Marx's distillation of how capitalists try to increase their relative value abandons simplistic moral outrage and shows that capitalists cannot behave in a different way (if they want to survive the ruthless competition and stay financially afloat *as* capitalists and not become wage earners), so too did modern drama move away from melodramatic representations of capitalists as greedy and corrupt villains. In Marx's drama of capital, capitalists are rational agents who cannot act in any other way but to try to maximize their profits: "The capitalist is just as enslaved by the relationships of capitalism as is his opposite pole, the worker, albeit in a quite different manner."[38] Marx, of course, is in no way justifying or promulgating the capitalists' worldview; he is simply showing its logic. This allows him to study the internal contradictions of capitalism. In this respect, Marx was one of the main thinkers of the nineteenth century to promote the notion of capitalism as an economic and political system that puts pressure on every member of society (albeit to a different degree). Even if not every playwright had read or even been exposed to Marx's theories, the general idea that capitalism is a "system" in which everyone is interconnected and fighting for their economic survival became more widespread in the nineteenth century. Consequently, instead of justifying its values or merely decrying its injustices, more and more works of modern drama began to explore the internal contradictions of capitalism on a deeper level.

It is worth stressing that I am not interested in reading works of modern drama as mere illustrations of the economic developments of its time. In recent years, theater scholars who are interested in economic issues have shifted their attention away from what happens onstage to how theater fits into the process of capitalist production by studying questions of infrastructure, the organization of theatrical labor, the circulation and consumption of theatrical products, and theater's ability to awaken the class consciousness of its audience.[39] This move is in part motivated by the sober insight that neither the content nor the formal characteristics of a given performance, however radical, precludes it from participating in the accumulation of capital or promoting capitalist values.[40] I, too, take on the question of theater's material conditions throughout the book, and particularly in chapter 4, where I look at specific productions of Gerhart Hauptmann's *The Weavers* and analyze the organized labor of the actors and various attempts to rouse the working class. However, I am also interested in the internal contradictions of works of modern drama that critique capitalism while participating in and profiting from it, contradictions many modern dramatists were aware of, just as many of today's playwrights and theater practitioners are.

The recent call to re-embed theater's economic questions into the social and the political was not something the European playwrights of the late nineteenth and early twentieth centuries had to be asked to do. They already treated the economy as "embedded in social relations," for "the great transformation" of the modern market society that Karl Polanyi famously describes had not yet been fully realized.[41] In fact, it is a common misconception that Polanyi's central argument is that in the nineteenth century, the "economy was successfully disembedded from society and came to dominate it."[42] Rather, Polanyi insists that a fully self-regulating market economy can never be achieved, for just "as the consequences of unrestrained markets become apparent, people resist," and a strong countermovement always arises to protect society against the dangers of laissez-faire capitalism.[43]

Economics beyond the Profit Principle

The playwrights covered in this study do not treat the economy as a separate sphere; rather, they see it as an integral part of human existence that involves fundamental questions of social morality and social organization. The emergence of economics as a separate discourse and science was a historical process, and so too was the transformation of the business world into "a closed compartment with laws of its own," to borrow R. H.

Tawney's turn of phrase.⁴⁴ Throughout most of the nineteenth century, economics, as Sheryl Meyering points out, "had a larger significance than it does now," with intellectuals as diverse as John Stuart Mill, John Ruskin, Thomas Carlyle, Herbert Spencer, and many others taking on economic questions in the context of biology, culture, and philosophy.⁴⁵ These economic questions were not divorced from moral or political concerns.

Writing in 1862, Ruskin lamented that the science known in his time as "political economy," which originated in the eighteenth century and which dealt solely with the "investigation of the phenomena of commercial operations," had nothing in common with the philosophy of "the great thinkers of past ages" such as "Plato, Xenophon, Cicero, and Bacon."⁴⁶ The Ancient Greek *oikos*, which lends its root to the English word "economics," means "family," "family property," and/or "family home." As Cheryl Anne Cox reminds us in her reading of Xenophon's *Oeconomicus*, the *oikos* was simultaneously "a unit of production, a unit of consumption, and . . . a unit of reproduction."⁴⁷ For Aristotle, the *oikos* was important not only because it generated wealth but also because it promoted health and *philia* within its walls and among its members. *Philia* was friendship, "described as 'some sort of excellence or virtue'" that connected the household (*oikos*) to the *polis*.⁴⁸ For Ruskin, in the same way that ancient domestic economy managed the "acts and habits of a household," so political economy should mean first and foremost the state's "support of its population in healthy and happy life." The goal of economics, argued Ruskin, should be not the mere accumulation of wealth but the "extension of life."⁴⁹ Similarly, as the authors of the recent "Marxist Keywords for Performance" remind us, Marx's entire critique of political economy "targeted the separation of politics from economics that defines bourgeois ideology."⁵⁰

This book spans from the 1870s to World War I and its aftermath, a time when the political imagination was more adventurous and diverse than it is today; when a great variety of socioeconomic models and futures were up for negotiation that the supposed triumph of capitalism and the collapse of Soviet socialism have since obscured. From the Paris Commune of 1871 to the Bavarian Soviet Republic of 1919, Europe was in the grip of revolutions and socioeconomic experimentations. The fin de siècle was a time of mass action in the name of socialism and anarchism, labor strikes, and unionism. Although the Paris Commune was stifled by the regular French army on May 28, 1871, it continued to serve as a prefiguration of a communist society and a model for participatory democracy in the imaginations of Mikhail Bakunin, Lenin, Marx and Engels, and many others. The Second International (1889–1916) declared the first of May an annual event of workers' demonstrations and festivities to commemorate the 1886 Haymarket Affair, during which workers in Chicago began to strike for an eight-hour workday. The one hundred thousand dock workers of the London Dock Strike of 1889 were victorious in establishing the Dock, Wharf, Riverside and General Labourers' Union and garnering support for the British labor movement in general. Demanding an eight-hour workday and an increase in wages, almost one hundred thousand German miners (86 percent of the workforce) went on strike in the Ruhr Valley. Although the strikers did not manage to secure any lasting deals, tension between the miners and their employers persisted over the next two decades. By 1890, 289,000 workers had participated in 715 strikes across Germany.[51] At the strike movement's peak (1889–93), 3.4 million laborers took part in strikes in Europe.[52] The general strike of the textile workers of St. Petersburg in May 1896 reverberated throughout the Russian Empire, galvanizing other mass strikes and setting into motion events that would lead to the Russian Revolution of 1905. World War I had a deeply debilitating effect on the labor movement, and after the establishment of the Soviet Union in 1922, as news of famine and political repression spread, disillusionment and political cynicism quickly took over. But during that brief historical interlude, things could have been different.

Even as economics was becoming a separate science and profession, this historical process was not yet complete by the end of the nineteenth century. Even the founder of English neoclassical economics, Alfred Marshall, whose influential *Principles of Economics* (1890) helped popularize the use of the supply and demand graph, defined economics in a capacious manner that went beyond the profit principle:

> Political Economy or Economics is a study of mankind in the ordinary business of life; it examines that part of individual and social action which is most closely connected with the attainment and with the use of the material requisites of wellbeing. Thus it is on the one side a study of wealth; and on the other, and more important side, a part of the study of man. For man's character has been moulded by his every-day work, and the material resources which he thereby procures, more than by any other influence unless it be that of his religious ideals; and the two great forming agencies of the world's history have been the religious and the economic.[53]

Instead of focusing on the mere drive for capital accumulation, Marshall takes an interest in the well-being of humanity. Even as Marshall concedes that a person's character is formed by work, he does not exclude other influences (e.g., religious, military, or artistic).

The late nineteenth century was also witness to the marginal revolution, which was a reaction both to the classical political economy of the previous century and to the burgeoning socialisms of its time.[54] Focusing on consumer desire, marginalists argued that people make economic decisions "on the margin." In other words, the value of a product or a service depends on how much additional utility an extra unit of that product or service offers an individual. Spearheaded almost simultaneously by William Stanley Jevons, Carl Menger, Léon Walrus, and Marshall, the marginalist school of economics developed a model of value that deprioritized labor, material conditions, and social relations and instead turned its attention to the individual consumer. In this way, marginalism shifted attention away from production to consumption, postulating that personal desire, rather than property, was the marker of individualism. As Regenia Gagnier has persuasively shown, the choice of the consumer "ceased to be a moral category: it did not matter whether the good desired was good or bad, just that the consumer was willing to pay for it." Consequently, value "ceased to be comparable across persons: it became individual, subjective, or psychological."[55] The marginal revolution took place between the mid-1860s and the mid-1870s and was part of a larger historical transition to economic individualism. It also marked the beginning of the narrow field known today as neoclassical economics.

Although late nineteenth-century economics was transforming into an increasingly abstract and insulated social science, with its own laws and exclusory jargon, it expanded its field of interest to include all human affairs and sought to explain the world outside itself in purely mercantile terms. It sold, cajoled into accepting, and, when necessary, violently imposed its abstract and commodified vision onto the rest of the world. Thus, what Gary Becker, one of the leading thinkers of the Chicago school of economics, calls the "economic approach," which according to him is the only sound way to study human behavior, developed at the end of the nineteenth century.[56] Gagnier calls this "tendency to interpret all phenomena in market terms" "economism,"[57] echoing Bourdieu, who defines "economism" as a "partial view" that maintains that every form of capital "is reducible in the last analysis to economic capital" and "ignores what makes the specific efficacy of the other types of capital."[58] According to Bourdieu, the "universe of exchanges" of human communication cannot be reduced to "mercantile exchange, which is objectively and subjectively oriented toward the maximization of profit."[59] Thus, it is important to bear in mind that even if mainstream media today tend to associate neoclassical economics with economics *tout court* (because it is the dominant version), that is not the only way economic questions can be framed, posed, and explored. The sheer diversity of economic models and theories at the end of the nineteenth century points to a broader and richer vision of what economics could have been and still can be.

How often and what kind of economic thought were modern European dramatists exposed to? Although the extent of their study of political economy varied, their interest in economic ideas and their investment in testing economic models were strong across the board. Although Henrik

Ibsen never seriously studied economics, he respected the discipline. In a letter asking King Oscar II to grant his son, Sigurd Ibsen, permission to continue his legal studies at the Royal Frederik's University (Det kongelige Frederiks Universitet) in Kristiania, Ibsen lists many eminent nineteenth-century European economists that Sigurd had studied when pursuing a law degree in Munich and Rome, including Gerolamo Boccardo, John Ramsay McCulloch, Michel Chevalier, Frédéric Bastiat, and others. Although Ibsen himself had not read them in depth, he understood how important the study of the "principles of political economy" was for an aspiring jurist.[60] As a young journalist, Chekhov covered the most notorious bank fraud in the history of the Russian Empire, an event that continued to inspire his fiction and drama throughout his career. Hauptmann read Darwin, Saint-Simon, and Marx.[61] Strindberg too read Marx and was an avowed socialist. In addition to his commitment to Fabian socialism, Bernard Shaw was one of the founders of the London School of Economics. Most importantly, since economics was still in the process of developing as a social science and a profession, even the most influential thinkers wrote for a general audience.[62]

As the nineteenth century wore on, neoclassical economic theory continued to treat consumer behavior and the supply and demand curve as primary economic order, relegating social relations, power dynamics, material conditions, labor exploitation, and the persistent importance of property to the background. Modern drama sheds light on these neglected areas. One way that modern drama registered the excitement of its time was by posing economic questions and presenting them not as separate issues but as part and parcel of broader moral, social, and political concerns and by engaging in an immanent critique of capitalism (about which more later). While marginalism gained traction in newly founded economics departments across western Europe and the United States, resulting in the establishments of the Austrian school, the Cambridge school, and the Lausanne school of economics, among others, the late nineteenth century was also a fervid time for the development of various socialisms as well as heated debates within the socialist opposition to capital.

The Rise of the Bourgeoisie and the Immanent Critique of Capitalism

One crucial question of the epoch was the relationship between critique and political practice. Could socialist critique raise the consciousness of audience members (whether capitalists or laborers), agitate workers for future uprisings, or at the very least help make sense of past revolts? Another question concerned the legacy of Marx. This issue was at the center of the debate between Eduard Bernstein—the executor of Engels's estate and the chief ideologue of the SPD (the Social Democratic Party of Germany), who was influenced early in his career by Fabian socialists in London—and Rosa Luxemburg, a Polish German revolutionary Marxist and antiwar activist. Bernstein was one of the first socialists to undertake a "revision" of orthodox Marxism in the articles he wrote for *Neue Zeit* in 1897–98. In those essays, he contends that because capitalism has the capacity to adapt and is supposedly subject to a natural evolution, focusing on revolutionary action is no longer necessary. Instead, according to Bernstein, socialists should push reforms that ameliorate "the condition of the working class within the existing order."[63] In other words, socialism would now be built by "means of the progressive extension of social control and the gradual application of the principle of cooperation."[64] By contrast, in *Reform or Revolution* (1908), Luxemburg argues that far from solving crises like overproduction and mass unemployment, Bernstein's proposed "means of adaptation," such as the credit system, cartels, and the "new, perfected means of communication," render the internal contradictions of capitalism "sharper and more aggravated."[65] Crises, Luxemburg underscores, are not just "derangements of the economic mechanism" that can be fixed but are "'derangements' without which capitalist economy could not develop at all."[66] According to Luxemburg, only revolutionary action undertaken by workers armed with the "keen and dependable weapons of scientific Socialism" could lead to a real social transformation.[67]

The debate concerning reform versus revolution animated modern drama as well. Yet it is important to stress that the plays discussed in this study, even those that fall under the rubric of the drama of ideas,[68] do not simply regurgitate arguments that the socialist writings of the period articulate. Modern drama became the site of potent immanent critique not only because it tackled the bourgeois schools of economics but also, most importantly, because it put on trial the various strands of socialism. As T. J. Clark notes, socialism "occupied the real ground on which modernity could be described and opposed; but its occupation was already seen at the same time (on the whole, rightly) to be compromised—complicit with what it claimed to hate."[69] Indeed, as several examples in this book highlight, whatever socialist positions the playwrights may have defended in the public realm, these were not unproblematically reflected or enthusiastically promulgated in their drama. For example, the plays of Shaw, who was an avowed Fabian socialist, are not mere dramatizations of Fabianism but are often more radical critiques of the "parliamentary road" that moderate socialism had taken.[70]

The socialist leanings of dramatists like Ibsen and Strindberg were complicated by their affinities with other social and political movements. Like Marx, Ibsen saw the Paris Commune of 1871 as a premonition of the eventual end of the bourgeois state. As Evert Sprinchorn points out, however, Ibsen focused more on the "spiritual enhancement of humanity" than on its material conditions.⁷¹ While Ibsen acknowledged that "without consciously aiming at it," simply by "depict[ing] human character and human destinies," he may "have arrived at some of the same conclusions as the social-democratic moral philosophers had arrived at by scientific processes,"⁷² his plays often flaunt "aristocratic individualism"⁷³ and even anarchism, which are difficult to reconcile with socialism's calls to solidarity and collective action. Whatever socialist beliefs the young Strindberg may have held were intermingled with Strindberg's later embrace of the Nietzschean idea of the intellectual superman. Drama—which allows multiple and competing voices to be heard in the most concrete way—became the channel through which these playwrights attempted to work through their own and their era's inherent contradictions. They did so through immanent critique—a method of locating intrinsic contradictions "between the avowed ideals of an institution or an ideology and the actual practical form it legislates for itself," a method that emerged from the dialectic of Hegel and evolved through Marx's challenge to the supposedly natural laws of the science of political economy.⁷⁴

In recent years, the efficacy of critique has been challenged, most notably by Bruno Latour, Jacques Rancière, and Rita Felski.⁷⁵ The fatigue and disillusionment with critique stem in part from what Hal Foster identifies as critique's "self-regarding posture."⁷⁶ It is important to bear in mind, however, the difference between critique, broadly defined, and immanent critique: a crucial distinction that is barely mentioned in recent reassessments.⁷⁷ Equally important is to distinguish between the awareness that immanent critique has limits (in that it can encourage but not guarantee political action) and the hypocritical "embrace of self-reflexivity and knowingness as the ultimate good"—an accusation cast by critics of critique.⁷⁸ In what follows, I will trace the emergence of immanent critique with the rise of the bourgeoisie, its relationship to capitalism, and its role in the theater of the late nineteenth century.

Once theater becomes divorced from ritual, it becomes bound up with capital, and spectacularly so.⁷⁹ What can theater, with its ineluctable stain of commerce, say or do about capitalism? This question resonated with modern dramatists and continues to animate public discussion today. In the wake of the 2008 financial crisis, theater's contradictory imbrication in capital has palpably come to the fore, as the most commercially successful shows both denounce the status quo and inadvertently end up celebrating the core values of capitalism through their economic infrastructures and/or ideological messages. Tickets for Stefano Massini's *Lehman Trilogy*, chronicling the rise and fall of the Lehman brothers, sold for over $2,000 on StubHub, ensuring that it was mostly the haves who were in the seats. Wall Streeters could be heard gushing in the lobby of the Park Avenue Armory: "Finally, a show that gets us." The *New York Times* succinctly summarized the show's contradictions in the title of its review—"'The Lehman Trilogy'

Criticizes Capitalism, at $2,000 a Seat." According to Ginia Bellafante, the show reinforces in the spectator "a sober skepticism about the complexities of modern finance that you probably already had before the curtain rose."[80]

Similarly, one of the most profitable musicals in recent history, Lin-Manuel Miranda's *Hamilton*, not only tells the story of the first secretary of the treasury of the United States but has also enabled scalpers to earn up to $6 million annually from the resale of tickets.[81] What is more, *Hamilton* was housed in a Broadway theater owned by the Nederlander Organization, which consistently bankrolls conservative political candidates who actively support white supremacy. Through the allocation of funds and their ownership of 20 percent of Broadway venues, the Nederlander family, as Chelsea Whitaker points out, can decide and "police what BIPOC narratives get produced."[82] As several scholars have argued, Miranda's championing of diverse stories and inclusive casting comes at the price of promoting the capitalist creed of pulling oneself up by one's bootstraps, or what Donatella Galella has aptly described as "nationalist neoliberal multicultural inclusion."[83] Even theater that is not blatantly commercial, such as the experimental Off-off-Broadway, depends on outside funding to survive and thus also reveals theater's intimate relationship to capital.

One approach to dealing with theater's entrenchment in monetary relations is to simply accept its commercial side as a necessary evil and to trust that as long as profit-making does not overrule aesthetic considerations, theater is in the clear as far as artistic integrity goes. This acquiescence, however, echoes the "reflexive impotence"[84] that Mark Fisher calls "capitalist realism," namely, the pervasive ideology that "not only is capitalism the only viable political and economic system, but also that it is now impossible even to imagine a coherent alternative to it."[85] By contrast, the theater of capital of the late nineteenth and early twentieth centuries investigated the very interpenetration of art and capital, including its own contradictory position in the culture of capitalism. Many theater artists today, such as the German director Thomas Ostermeier and the American Pulitzer Prize–winning playwright Ayad Akhtar, continue this legacy by pursuing an immanent critique of capitalism. What I mean by "the culture of capitalism" is a set of social practices, norms, and habits that are attributed to the capitalist socioeconomic system, such as the work ethic, competition, efficiency, self-reliance, protection of private property, division of labor, heightened professionalization, and a system of values organized around wage labor, profit, and economic growth. Treating aesthetic concerns separately from the business side of theater reinscribes the very ideology by which economics has sealed itself off as a separate sphere of influence. Bypassing the economic side of theater as its least interesting and most annoying aspect, scholars will often focus on topics supposedly worthier of critical attention, or—if they do turn their attention to economic issues—find that they have to justify their interest in the way Bernard Dukore does in the introduction to his excellent *Money and Politics in Ibsen, Shaw, and Brecht* (1980).[86] While asserting that the socioeconomic themes he addresses have been "among the major but often neglected concerns of these three writers," Dukore finds it necessary to defend his intellectual interest by assuring his readers that he is "alert to the poetic beauties of Shaw and Brecht as well as those of Ibsen" and that he is also "aware that their plays deal with subjects other than money and politics," as if the mere focus on money and politics would somehow trivialize or vulgarize the aesthetic merits of those playwrights or put into question his own critical prowess.[87]

There is an intriguing parallel here with Chekhov's dramatic characters, who often become embarrassed and eschew the subject of money, deeming it beneath the higher purposes of art and intellectual work. Yet, as Beth Holmgren observes, when skewering the Russian intelligentsia, Chekhov always makes sure to lay bare the "material base of their 'antimaterialist' life style."[88] Although Leon Trotsky was a fan of neither Chekhov nor the Moscow Art Theater, excoriating the first for his supposedly "passive realism" and the latter for its outdated "moribund cast," Trotsky's pronouncement about the relationship between art and economics finds resonance in Chekhov's oeuvre and is important for this study. "Culture," writes Trotsky, "feeds on the sap of economics, and a material surplus is necessary, so that culture may grow, develop, and become subtle."[89] Or, as Tracy Davis, whose scholarship has been crucial to understanding the connections between the business side of British theater and its aesthetics, puts it: "Culture, broadly wrought, permeates all business decisions, just as business matters permeate all pertaining to culture, more narrowly defined."[90]

Another way to reckon with theater's blatant commercialism is to search for visions of a different political future despite theater's reliance on capital. Jill Dolan calls "utopian performatives" those "small but profound moments in which performance calls the attention of the audience in a way that lifts everyone slightly above the present, into a hopeful feeling of what the world might be like if every moment of our lives were as emotionally voluminous, generous, aesthetically striking, and intersubjectively intense."[91] This fruitful definition speaks to how audiences are able to experience moments of hope even in the most unapologetically profit-making of shows or to discern "a utopian performative" in "even the most dystopian theatrical universe."[92] Another approach is to argue, as Nicholas Ridout persuasively does, that "it is precisely in theater's failure, our discomfort with it, its embeddedness in capitalist leisure, its status as a bourgeois pastime that its political value is to be found."[93] For Ridout, theater is "a good (because perverse) place to go looking for communist potential" because of the ways that it dramatizes the relationship between work and leisure under industrial capitalism.[94] Thus, both Dolan and Ridout see theater as a site for envisioning different political possibilities. For Dolan, utopian potentials exist despite theater's dependence on capital; for Ridout, it is precisely theater's entrenchment in the culture of capitalism that makes it politically valuable.[95]

One aim of my book is to show that attending to the economic context of theater and the economic questions raised in modern drama is not a reductive gesture but, rather, opens new meanings in a given work as well as in the study of economics. Thus, it is important to note that theater scholars are not the only ones susceptible to a dismissive or disparaging view of economic questions. This bias permeates the humanities in general. As Elizabeth Hewitt remarks in reference to American literary studies, even as the scholarship of the past three decades has investigated the importance of the market, "the field has not entirely erased its essentially antagonistic attitude toward the economic world that is so fundamental to the production of the archive it studies."[96] In part, this hostile attitude is due to the fact that economics has become a members-only club with its own rules and exclusory jargon. For example, Martin Bodenham, a contemporary writer of financial thrillers, describes how the mere mention of finance tends to elicit, at best, boredom and, at worst, annoyance from readers: "Mention the words equation, percentage, fraction, and multiplication to most people I know and their eyes glaze over. I get much the same reaction from friends when I tell them my first career was in private equity and investment banking. Instinctively, they flinch and quickly move the conversation on to another subject."[97] In a similar vein, Leigh Claire La Berge identifies a tendency among humanities scholars to simply refer to finance as "abstract" without explaining what they mean by it.[98] According to Akhtar, there is a price to be paid for neglecting the economic world, as the public's ignorance is precisely what allows the business elites to grab and hold on to power. In *Junk* (2017), a finance drama with Ibsenian undertones, Akhtar has Robert Merkin, his antihero, express the following insight: "That's how they get you. It's how they get everyone. The system's speaking a different language, a language that they know people don't understand. The second anyone tries to explain it, their eyes glaze over. That's by design."[99] Cultural economy has tried to rectify this oversight by illuminating the critical role of "'cultural' factors in the functioning of financial systems," and so has economic criticism (about which more later).[100]

It is important to remember that the prevalent economic myopia is historically contingent—it is a product of the development and domination of neoclassical economics. What passes today as "economics" in general parlance, disparaged as an abstract and insular science focused on the supply and demand curve, is only one (even if predominant) version of the study of economic questions. By contrast, the playwrights covered in this book were passionately interested in the economic questions of their day. They were committed to studying and trying out a variety of different economic ideas and models onstage. They were also fascinated by the very nature of money. As Nicky Marsh has recently noted, although scholars of modernist studies have paid increasing attention to market relations and to socioeconomic questions in the last two decades, the chief preoccupation "has been with what money does rather than with what money *is*."[101] Money is indeed a strange subject to tackle. It is one of the most symbolic, mythical, one might even say magical objects. At the same time, it is also incredibly prosaic, an object all of us handle, one way or another, in our everyday lives. Even as most of us spend a lot of time worrying about money, we rarely think deeply about its ontology. As this book will show, modern dramatists were committed to exploring what money *is*.

This study will argue that there is political value to be found in the theater made by bourgeois playwrights of the late nineteenth and early twentieth centuries, as they dramatized the internal contradictions of capitalism, including their own place in history, and traced the myriad ways that the forces of capital were transforming European society. Despite all the bad press the word "bourgeois" would receive throughout the nineteenth century, it is essential to remember that Marx and Engels claimed that "the bourgeoisie, historically, has played a most revolutionary part."[102] In *The Communist Manifesto* (1848), they observe that "the weapons with which the bourgeoisie felled feudalism to the ground are now turned against the bourgeoisie itself" and have "called into existence the men who are to wield those weapons—the modern working class—the proletariat."[103]

In fact, the very term "bourgeois" was hotly debated at the turn of the century. Although German playwrights like Georg Kaiser and Ernst Toller condemned so-called bourgeois values and called attention to the dire conditions of the working class, they could not be at peace with the undeniable fact that, as artists and intellectuals, they themselves embraced values that potentially could be described as "bourgeois." As Ridout has recently suggested, using the term "bourgeois" is "an act of *disidentification*."[104] It is a way for the subject to reject "the terms by which they are named by the institutions and the social order in and through which they live."[105] And, as Roy Pascal remarks, the ambivalent term "bourgeois" reveals "a deeper social malaise than most writers were aware of," so that "self-criticism on the part of the bourgeoisie" was probably the most salient characteristic of fin-de-siècle culture.[106] Indeed, self-criticism suffuses the plays of Ibsen, Strindberg, Shaw, Chekhov, and other playwrights of the theater of capital. It is precisely their socioeconomic position as the beneficiaries of capitalism that allowed them both to dramatize the internal contradictions of capitalism onstage and to explore the limits and potentials of their own critique.

Moreover, even before Brecht, many theater theoreticians and practitioners saw the theater as an important "weapon for raising political awareness" among both the working class and the bourgeoisie.[107] In 1897, the Russian anarchist and writer Emma Goldman lectured on Bernard Shaw in a Welsh coal mine.[108] In 1914, when speaking about modern drama at New York's Berkeley Theatre, she insisted that it was not just the proletariat "which makes revolutions" but "also those who wield the brush or pen."[109] In *The Social Significance of Modern Drama* (1914), Goldman argues that because "political pressure has so far affected only the 'common' people" through exploitation, persecution, and imprisonment, a different "medium is needed to arouse the intellectuals . . . to make them realize their relation to the people, to the social unrest permeating the atmosphere."[110] Enter the theater of capital and its immanent critique of capitalism.

Several economists and sociologists have noted capitalism's unique relationship to critique. Simply put, the critique of capitalism is challenging precisely because capitalism has a way of co-opting critique, repackaging it for commercial entertainment, and rendering it null. In the *New Spirit of Capitalism* (1999), French sociologists Luc Boltanski and Eve Chiapello discuss the "waning of critique at a time when capitalism was undergoing significant restructuring whose social impact could not go unnoticed."[111] Here is the overarching question of their study of the management discourse after 1968: Why has social critique become powerless, beyond expressing moral indignation, at a time when social conditions are deteriorating?[112] Boltanski and Chiapello define "the spirit of capitalism" in broader terms than Max Weber (for whom "the spirit of capitalism" evolved from the Protestant work ethic), as the "ideology that justifies engagement in capitalism."[113] The most signal feature of this ideology is its ability to address threats to its hegemony by inventing new justifications for "the insatiable character of the capitalist process."[114] Since "capitalist accumulation is amoral," it is not tied to any specific creed.[115]

Other thinkers, like economist Joseph Schumpeter, have seen the relationship between critique and capitalism in a different light. Instead of viewing critique as outside artillery aimed at the fortress of capitalism that the latter manages to capture and subdue, Schumpeter echoes Marx and Engels's *Communist Manifesto*, arguing that critique is *intrinsic* to the capitalist process, which has produced "that atmosphere of almost universal hostility to its own social order." "Capitalism," writes Schumpeter in 1942, "creates a critical frame of mind which, after having destroyed the moral authority of so many other institutions, in the end turns against its own; the bourgeois finds to his amazement that the rationalist attitude does not stop at the credentials of kings and popes but goes on to attack private property and the whole scheme of bourgeois values."[116] No wonder Schumpeter concluded that capitalism would ultimately fail.

By contrast, even as German historian Jürgen Kocka underscores that critique is intrinsic to capitalism, he arrives at a different conclusion—that the development and "triumph of capitalism have taken place in an intellectual and mental climate of pronounced *Kapitalismuskritik*, or criticism of capitalism."[117] This leads Kocka to ponder why critique has not "hindered or handicapped the real rise of European or European-sponsored capitalism more."[118] Echoing Bernstein, Kocka suggests that the "widespread criticism of capitalism has contributed to its permanent change and reform—as well as indirectly and inadvertently to its survival and success."[119] Yet, as the earlier Bernstein-Luxemburg debate demonstrates, not all socialist critique is immanent. Bernstein lambasted many aspects of capitalism, but he ultimately believed it could be perfected to be a more just and equitable system. Luxemburg's immanent critique, by contrast, insists that capitalism is characterized by internal contradictions and crises like mass unemployment and overproduction, which can only be resolved by overcoming capitalism. As Brazilian theater director and political activist Augusto Boal once put it, capitalism "is fundamentally immoral because the search for profit, which is its essence, is incompatible with its official morality, which preaches superior human values, justice, etc."[120] This pronouncement makes it sound as though the ideas of equality, freedom, and justice are a mere façade in a capitalist society. Yet the discrepancy between liberal ideals and capitalist reality is a matter not simply of hypocrisy but of transition.

Immanent critique—the method of locating contradictions between society's own ideals and their practical forms, including the aforementioned self-critique on the part of the bourgeoisie—becomes possible only with the rise of the bourgeoisie. This is what Marx and Engels mean when they call the bourgeoisie "revolutionary."[121] As Hägglund observes, the "historical emergence" of the "liberal ideals of equality and freedom" is "inseparable from the capitalist mode of production." Yet these ideals can be fulfilled only "through the overcoming of capitalism."[122] To put it another way, immanent critique is a necessary but insufficient (on its own) step in the revolutionary transformation of society. The nineteenth-century bourgeoisie, then, is a *transitional* class whose critical disposition eventually turns in on itself. In Marx's account, the proletariat too is a transitional class, just like the "dictatorship of the proletariat" (the form of production during which the workers hold political power) is a transitional phase. What comes next depends on one's interpretation of Marx. In his reading of Marx, for example, Hägglund argues that the purpose of the revolutionary transformation of society is the overcoming of a division of classes in favor of a "cooperative participation in society" and "a democratic form of collective self-legislation."[123]

What members of the bourgeoisie do with their self-awareness—their understanding of themselves as a historical class formed by specific material conditions—is an open question. They can and should (according to Marx) join the proletarian revolution. But that outcome, of course, is not a given. The bourgeois can also turn against the workers in distrust or fear (as it happens in a few early twentieth-century German expressionist dramas), engage in sham allyship, or fall into the "reflexivity trap," namely what cultural critic Katy Waldman has recently called, in reference to Sally Rooney's fiction, the "implicit, and sometimes explicit, idea that professing awareness of a fault absolves you of that fault."[124] Although Waldman has in mind the "disaffected millennial[s]" from the upper middle class or those aspiring to become them, and not the nineteenth-century bourgeoisie, her description of the "reflexivity trap" as "cast[ing] self-awareness as a finish line, not a starting point" is a helpful way to think of the problematic gesture of self-awareness on the part of the beneficiaries of capitalism, whether the bourgeois of a bygone era or today's millennial hipster.[125] According to Waldman, neither authors nor readers should be applauded merely for the "moral work of feeling bad" or for their self-hatred as members of the ruling class.[126]

This self-critique on the part of the beneficiaries of capitalism can help us understand how nineteenth-century bourgeois theater has political value. Immanent critique is an indispensable step in the revolutionary struggle, but it is not sufficient in and of itself. According to Ridout, there is a crucial connection to be drawn between the bourgeoisie's gaining an awareness of itself as a class that directly benefits from the exploitation and suffering of others (women, the proletariat, colonial subjects) and bourgeois theater's "contain[ing] the seeds of its own defeat."[127] In fact, the possibility of bourgeois theater overcoming itself—both by transforming itself into a more emancipatory art form and by discovering new (democratic) ways of engaging with others—stems, in Ridout's view, "from the ever-present possibility that it will reveal to its spectators-subjects that their lives, as spectators, are a matter of historical contingency rather than tragic inevitability."[128] Ridout's *Scenes from Bourgeois Life* (2020) thus offers an important way to understand bourgeois subjectivity and the role that theater has played in shaping that subjectivity and the role theater might play in overcoming it.

In general, the political rise and socioeconomic dominance of the bourgeoisie have been studied in relation to the eighteenth- and nineteenth-century novel, so much so that theater scholars, like Jane Moody, have long bemoaned the fact that "the novel's position as the definitive genre of capital remains undisputed."[129] The novel, of course, played a significant part in providing the bourgeoisie with the blueprint and justification for their ascendancy (as I go into more detail in chapter 2). But the lack of critical attention to theater's role and the kind of spectatorial modes it generated and encouraged is surprising given that, before the advent of cinema, theater was second in popularity only to the newspaper as a medium of communication. In this way, Ridout provides an essential contribution not only to the study of spectatorship but also to the historical understanding of bourgeois subjectivity in general. Analyzing the daily eighteenth-century publication *The Spectator* (1711–12) and the concurrent bourgeois theater, Ridout argues that from the eighteenth century onward, theater helped produce a "view of the world that has been chosen by and for the bourgeoisie, which places at a spectatorial distance the world in which its own hegemony is the source of suffering."[130] But this very same theater can also, claims Ridout, reveal to its spectators their own historically contingent role in perpetuating the injustices of capitalism. This was, after all, Brecht's hope. Ridout's argument is a brilliant corollary to and reworking of Cavell's reading of Shakespeare's *King Lear* in "The Avoidance of Love." While Cavell suggests that in unveiling to its spectators the world's theatricality and their own passive acquiescence to the state affairs, *King Lear* "arouses a kind of ethical desire to move beyond the condition of being a spectator,"[131] Ridout emphasizes that this experience is not only *not* unique to *King Lear* but also exemplary of much of theater, which "always contains within it the capacity to undermine or cancel the effects of its own theatricality."[132] On the one hand, yes, theater is perhaps one of the most powerful ideological tools, what Terry Eagleton calls a "moral technology" for the production of complacent bourgeois subjectivity.[133] On the other hand, as Ridout points out, by referencing Althusser's "little theoretical theater," theater does not always work in this way.[134] Members of the audience might not be looking where the playwright or director wants them to.[135] Instead, spectators can, as Ridout himself does throughout his study, pay close attention to colonial subjects erased from theater history and to products of colonialism that appear onstage (most notably coffee and tobacco) and thereby consider "the conditions of their own production."[136]

What emerges from Ridout's incisive argument is that bourgeois theater grapples with its internal contradictions. In the same way that the capitalist mode of production gave rise to the ideals of equality and freedom and created the possibility of a critical frame of mind that could eventually turn on capitalism itself, so bourgeois theater (having originated in capitalist culture) is equally capable of producing the tools for its own overcoming. Even as theater creates a spectatorial colonial distance between its spectators-subjects and the rest of the world they subjugate, it also creates a potential for immanent critique, which, while not sufficient in and of itself, is a necessary step in understanding the conditions of one's production as a bourgeois subject in order to overcome those conditions. Put simply, just because I might become painfully and anxiously aware that as a theater spectator and professor of theater studies, I am a beneficiary of capitalism, colonialism, and white supremacy—namely, that I directly benefit from the exploitation and suffering of others—does not mean that I will take political action or even want to change the world. But self-awareness does increase that possibility, compared with a situation where I am completely oblivious to the historical conditions of the production of my subjectivity, or with the feudal system, where I might believe that my position is appointed by God and therefore just. Of course, I might also, like a self-aware character in a Sally Rooney novel, exchange lots of texts about Marx with friends, do a lot of handwringing, find the whole political apparatus insurmountable, and engage in cynicism and self-loathing, while simultaneously trying to drown out all that cynicism and self-loathing with alcohol, drugs, and/or sex. Nevertheless, reading about or watching such characters onstage—who do nothing about their self-awareness as beneficiaries of capitalism but indulge in decadent or disaffected nihilism—might inspire me *not* to be like them. In this book, I will argue that what I call the theater of capital not only invites its spectators (who primarily are beneficiaries of capitalism) to attend to their own historical position but also dramatizes the internal contradictions of capitalism while testing different economic ideas and models onstage.

Many of the playwrights in this study display a marked hostility toward capitalism and their complicity as members of the bourgeoisie (Hauptmann, Kaiser, Toller). Some even stage humanity's self-destruction (Kaiser, Čapek). Most importantly, modern drama constantly questions the effect and purpose of its own critique. I do not disagree that the nineteenth-century drama of social reform, for example, sought to ameliorate social conditions (and, in some cases, was successful), but it is not the only theoretical work being done in this drama, which at the same time puts on trial the theoretical weapons of left-wing intellectuals: irony, satire, dark humor, moral outrage, and, yes, self-critique. For instance, one may undoubtedly read Shaw's *Major Barbara* as an illustration of Shaw's politics, namely the Fabian belief in the advancement of socialism through gradualist and reformist means, eventually resulting, as Dukore puts it, in the fusion of "money and morality."[137] Yet an interpretive problem arises when Adolphus Cusins discovers that Andrew Undershaft, the powerful arms dealer, has built a William Morris Labor Church in his would-be capitalist utopia of Perivale St. Andrews. Discerning the dark humor and perversity of the situation, Cusins immediately exclaims: "Oh! It needed only that. A Labor Church!"[138] The socialist ideas of William Morris, who was friends with Shaw for twelve years and gave regular lectures at the Fabian Society, are mangled and recycled in Undershaft's domain to make workers, in Undershaft's own words, "most economical," "unselfish," "indifferent to their own interests," "conservative," "with their thoughts on heavenly things," and "not on Trade Unionism or Socialism," so that Undershaft's "profits are larger" (98). Capitalism has found a way to superficially address the concerns of Fabian socialists regarding the working conditions of laborers and to carry on its quest for capital accumulation. Any "reform whatsoever," warns the Austrian-French philosopher André Gorz, "may be emptied of its revolutionary significance and re-absorbed by capitalism."[139] While Shaw may have been a Fabian socialist in the public arena, his drama questions the efficacy of reformism and the integrity of revisionism.

Fin-de-Siècle Capitalism, Financialization, and Tainted Theater

What was distinctive about the late nineteenth-century European theater's relationship to capitalism? After all, the first manifestations of capitalism can be discerned as early as the Middle Ages, and money matters feature prominently in medieval and Renaissance drama. In early modern Europe, professional theater companies were already protocapitalist joint-stock corporations that depended on large-scale credit that the 1571 usury statute made available. No wonder many of William Shakespeare's plays, such as *The Merchant of Venice* (1596–97) and *Timon of Athens* (1605–8), dramatize the uncertainties of credit and debt.[140] The last four decades in particular have witnessed significant scholarly attention paid to economic issues in early modern English drama, a time when drama faced little competition from prose fiction.[141] As Jean-Christophe Agnew has shown, theater of the "long sixteenth century" functioned "as a proxy form of the new and but partly fathomable relations of a nascent market society."[142] During the Restoration and early eighteenth century, morality plays about the perils of avarice and unbridled speculation were popular with audiences. Thomas Shadwell's *The Volunteers, or The Stockjobbers* (1692) predicted the crash of the South Sea Bubble that came in 1720. (Caryl Churchill includes a scene from Shadwell's play at the top of her *Serious Money* [1987], which chronicles the financial crimes of the London International Financial Futures and Options Exchange.) George Lillo's *The London Merchant* was an early dramatic attempt at a bourgeois tragedy. In the early nineteenth century, Goethe already satirized paper money in the second part of his closet drama, *Faust* (1832), where Mephistopheles saves the Emperor's finances by issuing paper money as a substitute for gold. The ghost of Goethe's Mephistopheles would go on to haunt Ibsen's *Peer Gynt* (1876), *The Master Builder* (*Bygmester Solness*, 1892), and *John Gabriel Borkman* (1896).

The Victorian stage too brimmed with plays about money and capital, as evinced by the success of such comedies as Edward Bulwer-Lytton's *Money* (1840), Dion Boucicault's *London Assurance* (1841), and George Henry Lewes's *The Game of Speculation* (1851; adapted from Balzac's *Mercadet*), among many others.[143] Kristen Guest identifies a marked shift already present in late Victorian melodramas in their representation of the individual versus the market. If early Victorian plays emphasize the "hero's merit, effectiveness, and respectability," then, in the second half of the nineteenth century, these individual positive traits are replaced by "anxious depictions of male victims' struggles within an impersonal and abstract economy."[144] Guest relates these changes to a more general turn in "economic discourse away from confirmations of individual, moral control over the marketplace" to the embrace of the elusive and illusionary concept known today as "the market."[145] In France, the social-problem melodramas of Émile Augier and Alexandre Dumas fils took on the world of high finance. Toward the end of the century, Émile Zola's play *Thérèse Raquin* (1873) and Henry Becque's *The Scavengers* (*Les corbeaux*, 1882) helped establish the genre of *comédie rosse* (cynical or bitter comedy), in which the "conventional happy" resolution is replaced with a sardonic ending where "dilemmas [are] resolved by a sexual or financial accommodation."[146]

The nineteenth century was witness to several pivotal financial innovations and attendant legal reforms that fundamentally changed the face of capitalism, such as the introduction of limited liability by the state of New York in 1811, the legalization of futures trading by the Chicago Board of Trade in 1863, and the transformation of speculation into an economic activity apart from gambling. This phase of financialization provoked public anxiety about who was responsible for the boom-and-bust cycles of capitalist modernity and about the differences (if any) between honest and corrupt businesses. In the *Supplement and Addendum* to the third volume of *Capital*, which Engels prepared in 1894, he suggests that although Marx highlighted the importance of the stock exchange to capitalist production in chapter 27 of the first volume, a crucial change had taken place since 1865 that

> gives the stock exchange of today a significantly increased role, and a constantly growing one at that, which, as it develops further, has the tendency to concentrate the whole of production, industrial as well as agricultural, together with the whole of commerce—means of communication as well as the exchange function—in the hands of stock-exchange speculators, so that the stock exchange becomes the most pre-eminent representative of capitalist production as such.[147]

According to Engels, all industries were transforming into joint-stock undertakings, so much so that even colonization was becoming a "pure appendage of the stock exchange."[148]

The fin de siècle was a veritable age of speculation. More people than ever now participated in investment activities, even as the stock exchange provoked much anxiety. One source of public concern was the element of luck. As Thorstein Veblen remarks in *The Theory of the Leisure Class* (1899), "The belief in luck" was "incompatible with the requirements of the modern industrial process, and more or less of a hindrance to the fullest efficiency of the collective economic life."[149] Even if industrial capitalists played on the market and benefited from their laborers' false hopes that the capitalist system would one day pay off, they also wanted their laborers to focus on hard work, not on lotteries or speculation. The other source of collective apprehension was the epistemological crisis that late nineteenth-century speculation caused in the speculators' ability to discern between an actual project and a scam—between a truth and a lie. While manias and crashes indeed occurred in the early modern period (take, for example, the Tulip Mania or the South Sea Bubble), the invention of the telegraph in 1837 and the stock price ticker in 1867 enabled the rapid transmission of financial information across great distances, making the modern economy more volatile and vulnerable to radical contingency.

What would begin as a bona fide endeavor to raise capital for the construction of public infrastructure could quickly veer into chicanery if a company found itself in economic trouble and tried to cover it up by performing success in order to keep raising capital so that it could return to a sound financial footing. This is essentially the plot of Ibsen's *An Enemy of the People* (*En folkefiende*, 1882), which will be examined in chapter 1. And this is exactly what happened in the real-life financial scandal at Skopin's bank, which Chekhov chronicled during his days as a young journalist and which is the subject of chapter 3. It is important to stress that Skopin's bank started as a real enterprise for the common good of the town and that it was the financial stress of surviving in the capitalist economy that pushed it into the murky waters of corruption. Starting in 1825, international financial crises occurred almost every decade.[150] It is not surprising, then, that Marx concluded that periodic cyclical crises were endemic to the capitalist system.[151]

Speculation became a general metaphor for moral relativism, opportunism, and the abandonment of political ideals. In Oscar Wilde's *Lady Windermere's Fan* (1892), the titular character laments to Lord Darlington that "now-a-days people seem to look on life as a speculation."[152] In *An Ideal Husband* (1895), Lady Chiltern tells her husband that he is not like those other "men who treat life simply as a sordid speculation."[153] For Wilde, speculation was not just a metaphor, for he composed *An Ideal Husband* in the midst of the public scandal surrounding the abysmal failure of the Panama Canal project. Although undertaken in the wake of the successful completion of the Suez Canal, the construction of the Panama Canal was fraught from the start with fraud and bribery rumors as well as engineering and labor problems, especially when it became clear that a sea-level canal was unfeasible. In 1889, the Compagnie Universelle du Canal Interocéanique de Panama, led by Ferdinand de Lesseps (who had been in charge of the triumphant Suez Canal), went bankrupt, and its financial collapse was a major scandal in France. Lesseps and his son were tried for offering bribes to ministers in exchange for the permission to keep issuing stock even though the company was struggling financially (their sentences were eventually revoked). Over five hundred members of the French Parliament were accused of taking bribes from the Panama Canal Company.[154] The Americans under the leadership of Theodore Roosevelt took over the property in 1904, so not all the initial efforts were in vain. Still, in 1893, when Wilde sat down to write *An Ideal Husband*, the project was deemed an embarrassing and colossal fiasco on the part of the French government. Wilde alludes to it by making up a completely fictitious enterprise in his play—"the Argentine scheme" (240). This imaginary name of the scheme echoes the financial make-believe that went on in the Panama Canal Company.

By the end of the nineteenth century, European theater was in the perfect position to explore the impact of capitalist culture: it was at the zenith of the economic hierarchy of the arts and at the nadir of the aesthetic hierarchy. Before the advent of film, millions of people frequented the theater each year. In 1865, the London theater scene drew around twelve million spectators a year. And by the end of the century, London and Paris each boasted over one hundred theaters.[155] Still, even with the serious drama of Ibsen and Chekhov, theater could not entirely purge itself of the tinge of commerce. It is easy to forget how uneasy the founders of modern European drama initially felt about their attraction to an art deemed low by their contemporaries. "A play is a pension," writes Chekhov in a letter to his brother, as he advises the latter to start writing for the stage because it does not require much talent.[156] Yet the stage offered two promising potentials—an opportunity for profit and a platform for serious intellectual content.[157]

While nineteenth-century poets and novelists could still entertain the Romantic notion that aesthetic values were above commercial values, theater artists could not ignore the relationship between the artistic choices that they made every day and the economic world at large. As Sarah J. Townsend eloquently notes, "Because it unfolds over time, and because its realization requires a material stage as well as the presence of a collective audience, the 'art' of theater is more difficult to disentangle from the process of its production and its sociopolitical and economic stakes."[158] To be sure, the writing, circulation, and reception of novels and poems are also embedded in the capitalist mode of production. But theater tends to expose its own mode of production in front of a collective body of people in a more direct and immediate way, so that the attention of spectators can wander to the context of a performance, including its socioeconomic and political underpinnings. Of course, when a reader spends time alone with a novel, she too might think of the laborers who have printed the pages of the book that she now holds in her hands or wonder about the author's advance payment. But in a theater, the spectator is confronted with a social situation where, as Ridout puts it, "one group of people" often pays "to sit for hours to see others be paid to perform for them,"[159] where collective labor is necessary to make scenic effects happen, and where the whole commercial business of the theater is persistently on display (from the ushers escorting the spectator to her seat to the lines for the café during intermission); and this set of circumstances encourages the spectator to think about socioeconomic questions even if she tries not to.

Theater explicitly relies on the risks of speculation and investment. Producers must raise capital and often go into debt in hopes of reaping a financial return or, at the very least, breaking even. And theater's vertical architecture (albeit one that is inverted, as the upper balcony houses the cheapest seats) signals class hierarchies. Thus, when theater artists express moral outrage over an economic system that provides them with their bread and butter, they often come across as either naive or hypocritical. Akhtar makes this exact point when he explains the rationale behind his play *Junk*:

> What I wanted to do was tell the story of how finance became the dominant philosophical ideology of our culture. It's easy to criticize capitalism and it's even easier to enjoy its benefits. This is how we live. These are the values. Rather than criticizing them, let me explore them in very complicated ways that make audiences not entirely sure how they feel about any of it.[160]

This does not mean that Akhtar's play embraces capitalist values. His financial dramas explore the culture of finance with all its internal contradictions. For Akhtar, the economy is not a separate bubble, and money is not simply a medium of exchange. Instead, as he elaborates in the preface to his play *The Invisible Hand* (2015), titled "Finance and the Figure of Now," money is "the metonymic complement of personal will itself" and is "at the root of art's ultimate pursuit: the most hidden, the most human, the most primal."[161]

The Novel of Capital versus the Theater of Capital

In the context of nineteenth-century literature, there is a difference between the representations of capitalism that appear in narrative prose (the novel and the short story) and those that occur in modern drama. In this study, I will briefly look at novels and short stories written by the theater artists that I cover, for two main reasons. First, because many modern dramatists continued to write narrative prose and because modern drama was invested in solidifying its reputation as a high literary object, the nineteenth-century novel and modern drama share an archive of tropes, character types, and narratives. The two genres did not develop in isolation.[162] For example, Victoria Benedictsson's novel *Money* (*Pengar*, 1885), with its considerable amount of dialogue, showcases Benedictsson's talent for writing drama. It is also a direct response to Ibsen's *A Doll's House* (*Et dukkehjem*, 1879). Second, as I will argue, the representation of the relationship between aesthetic and commercial values is often a more complicated affair in the theater, with its material stage and overt reliance on capital, than it is in the novel and the short story, even though the latter too can and do expose the internal contradictions of capitalism. For example, while Chekhov tends to elevate aesthetic and spiritual values above material values in his short stories, in his mature drama he displays a more profound anxiety about the interpenetration of aesthetic and commercial values.

During the last two decades of the nineteenth century and the first decade of the twentieth, we find an array of novels depicting speculative bubbles, financial panics, and the circulation of money that critics have called "the novel of the stock exchange."[163] To name but a few examples, these include Zola's *The Kill* (*La curée*, 1871) and *Money* (*L'argent*, 1891), Anthony Trollope's *The Way We Live Now* (1875), William Dean Howells's *The Rise of Silas Lapham* (1885), Frank Norris's *The Octopus: A Story of California* (1901) and *The Pit: A Story of Chicago* (1903), Upton Sinclair's *The Moneychangers* (1908), Joseph Conrad's *Chance* (1913), and Theodore Dreiser's *The Financier* (1912) and *The Titan* (1914).[164] These novels grapple with the culture of capitalism, financialization, and collective anxieties over new ways of managing and manipulating public and private capital. Despite the realistic psychological portrayals of characters, what these novels have in common is their reliance on melodramatic conventions that make moral accountability in the new economy intelligible by laying the blame for crises and panics on identifiable villains of the business world. Melodrama, defined by Peter Brooks as "express[ing] the anxiety brought by a frightening new world in which the traditional patterns of moral order no longer provide the necessary social glue," reigned supreme on the page and on the stage until Ibsen took a more ambivalent and sober look at capitalist modernity.[165] In this regard, Ibsen foreshadows contemporary playwrights like Akhtar, who reject simplistic moral outrage and self-righteous critique of the system from which they directly benefit. Ibsen shows not only how members of society are complicit in the socioeconomic structure from which they profit but also how the whole community performs the cover-up of capitalism's crimes and contradictions, including the separation of economic behavior from moral conduct.

What is more, the naturalist novel of the turn of the twentieth century often portrays the ups and downs of economic cycles as natural and thus inevitable occurrences. For example, in William Dean Howells's *The Rise of Silas Lapham*, the decline in the popularity of Lapham's paint and his eventual bankruptcy are punctuated by the start of a dull, droughty summer. The business cycle is equated with seasonal changes. In Norris's *The Pit*, the global wheat market is described as an uncontrollable "ocean" with "gigantic pulses of . . . ebb and flow."[166] In Zola's *Money*, the persistent desire to make money from money (Marx's M-M) is associated with libido and is compared to the sexual instinct.[167] In short, on the surface these novels might criticize corporate greed and corruption, but they end up reinscribing capitalist ideology by *naturalizing* its social effects and crises. By contrast, in the last chapter of *The Bourgeois: Between History and Literature* (2013), Franco Moretti takes on the drama of Ibsen and underscores some of the advantages that drama might hold over the novel in representing capital. In particular, drama can capture the frenzy, fervor, and futuristic outlook of speculation:

> The realistic bourgeois is ousted by the creative destroyer; analytic prose, by world-transforming metaphors. Drama captures better than the novel this new phase, where the temporal axis shifts from the sober recording of the past—the double-entry book-keeping practiced in *Robinson* and celebrated in *Meister*—to the bold shaping of the future which is typical of dramatic dialogue. In *Faust*, in the *Ring*, in late Ibsen, characters 'speculate', looking far into the time to come. Details are dwarfed by the imagination; the real, by the possible. It's the *poetry* of capitalist development.[168]

Throughout its history, the stock exchange has been compared to the theater.[169] Part of the association of speculation with theatricality has to do with the architecture of stock exchanges, which were often built like theaters, with galleries from which onlookers could observe the daily spectacle of trading (see fig. 1). As in the theater, where the gallery is reserved for the holders of low-cost tickets, so the gallery of the stock exchange, while not explicitly a space for only the lower classes, is for those who are not the direct players of the financial game but are mere spectators. And it was in the late nineteenth century, as Steve Fraser points out, that Wall Street became "a spectacle, an object of mass fascination."[170] Indeed, stories of the enormous fortunes amassed by the likes of Gould and Vanderbilt captured the public's imagination.

The opening and closing of *The Pit* by Frank Norris establish a parallel between the theater and the wheat exchange by showing the same set of characters avidly participating in both worlds. Likewise, most of the action of Zola's *Money* takes place not at the Bourse but at the Coulisse, the plural form of which (*coulisses*) means in French "the wings of the theater." The official Paris Bourse remained a market chiefly for *rentes* (government securities) and railway securities until the 1890s. The buying and selling of futures happened at the Coulisse, that is, on the outside wings of the Bourse, in the building known as Palais Brongniart. There bankers and financiers could

Fig. 1. Interior view of the Paris Bourse. From Edmond Texier, *Tableau de Paris*, vol. 2 (Paris: Paulin et Le Chevalier, 1853), 158. Louis Bertrand / Alamy Stock Photo.

bypass government regulation. Near the Paris Bourse was the notorious Théâtre des Variétés (in Zola's *Nana*, Monsieur Bordenave insists on referring to it as his "brothel"): indeed, the market and the theater were facing each other.[171] Before the construction of Palais Brongniart was completed to house the Bourse, the trading of stocks and bonds took place behind the Paris Opera until the 1820s.[172] The parallels between the two worlds went beyond architecture.

In 1882, Edmond Benjamin and Henry Buguet published a journalistic and satirical account set in the world of the theater and the world of the Bourse whose title, *Coulisses de bourse et de théâtre*, played on the dual meaning of *coulisse*. In the preface, dramatic critic Francisque Sarcey slyly assures the reader that the theater and the Bourse have nothing in common, yet the anecdotes that follow illustrate how the two worlds often share a similar lexicon and are frequented by the same crowds. For instance, *souffler aux nigauds*, or "to prompt the dummies," was a common phrase among seasoned speculators hoping to persuade the more naive participants to buy or sell stocks to the speculators' advantage.[173] The novel of capital often associates financial speculation with the world of the theater so that its critique of corrupt businesses relies on what Jonas Barish calls "the antitheatrical prejudice."[174] Speculation, like theatricality, has the potential to sway and swindle an audience. At the end of the nineteenth century, the novel and drama are locked in a fierce competition for audiences, so the antagonism is not altogether surprising. Writing in the mode of financial melodrama, both novelists and dramatists joined a public discourse that equated financial crises with scripted melodramas staged by powerful financiers. In the conspiracy theories of the day, influential capitalists were said to spur panics for their own monetary gains.[175] By contrast, Ibsen, a self-professed capitalist and avid investor, would show in *An Enemy of the People* how, under capitalism, the financial stability of an entire community depends on it being continually performed and how each member is complicit in this performance (albeit to a varying degree). In fact, modern playwrights across the political spectrum drew freely from capitalist culture for financial and aesthetic purposes. For example, the socialist-inclined German expressionists may have criticized the dehumanizing aspects of machines and management, but they too, paradoxically, found stylistic inspiration in capitalist modernity's new sights and sounds, generating an artistic Taylorization of the stage. In this manner, the modern stage became a testing ground for the central ideas of capitalist culture, including the work ethic, competition, and the relentless drive for capital accumulation.

Theater Studies, Economic Criticism, and the *Oikos*

Theater and performance can help us understand economic questions on a deeper level. One methodology that has attempted to bridge economics and the humanities (particularly literary studies) is economic criticism and, later, new economic criticism.[176] However, economic criticism often assumes a division between the two disciplines, which has not always been the case.[177] As Kurt Heinzelman notes, by the time William Jevons's *The Theory of Political Economy* was published in 1871, literary studies and economics had already become separate discourses.[178] Martha Woodmansee attributes the rift between economics and the humanities to "Romantic ideology, which defined literature (and indeed the arts generally) in opposition to commerce, and to the belief in the separation of aesthetic value from monetary value that endures to this day."[179] Some scholars argue that the split between literary and economic discourses happened earlier—in the eighteenth century—with the emergence of the science of political economy and the novel, when each, in its way, attempted to make capitalism legible.[180]

Introduction   35

Keeping these historical transformations in mind, new economic criticism has shown how the two spheres profoundly influenced one another.[181] As Mary Poovey has argued, by the end of the seventeenth century, one of the ideological goals of "imaginative writing in general was to mediate value—that is, to help people understand the new credit economy and the market model of value that it promoted."[182] It bears noting, however, that many of the assumptions made by new economic criticism about the diverse interactions between economics and literature are based predominantly on the novel. Woodmansee and Mark Osteen make almost no reference to drama. Only Marc Shell reminds us of the ancient connection between economy and theater: the use of the word *economy* in dramatic theory begins with Aristotle's *Poetics*, where he distinguishes between a household (*oikos*) appropriate for representation in comedy and one suitable for tragedy.[183]

Thus, theater is perhaps the oldest art form to expose how the economy relates to broader collective decisions. From this perspective, theater is not *mired* in commerce; rather, it refuses to treat the economy as a separate sphere, revealing instead how economic questions are at the center of our collective life. Indeed, as Hägglund has recently argued,

> the fundamental questions of economy—the questions of what we prioritize, what we value, what is worth doing with our time—are thus recognized as being at the heart of our spiritual lives. How we organize our economy is inseparable from how we live together (how we make our shared home, our *oikos*), since the way we organize our economy is ultimately how we express our priorities and our conception of value.[184]

As we will see, when characters ask economic questions in the theater of capital, what they are often dealing with are moral and spiritual issues. In these plays, to borrow Akhtar's turn of phrase once again, money gets "at the root of art's ultimate pursuit: the most hidden, the most human, the most primal."[185] As riveting as Akhtar's exploration of the ideology of finance is, it is not new but places him in a genealogy of dramatic writers interested in a serious examination of capitalist modernity that goes beyond moral outrage and that includes studying the language, ideas, and rules of the financial world. In Europe, this lineage begins with Ibsen, whose theater of capital not only presents a critique of capitalism (that is easily done, according to Akhtar) but also educates its audience about the sleights of hand inherent to economics as a discourse.

Theater of capital—which includes playwrights influenced by Henrik Ibsen, such as Anton Chekhov, Bernard Shaw, Oscar Wilde, Harley Granville-Barker, David Mamet, Ayad Akhtar, Caryl Churchill, Lucy Prebble, and many others—acknowledges its own complicity in sustaining the capitalist mode of production, taking perverse inspiration from the very fact that theatrical production, as Michael Shane Boyle notes, "exemplifies the capitalist production process, even though the actual theatrical commodity behaves in rather exceptional ways."[186] Thus, in the preface to *Major Barbara*, Shaw denounces "railway shareholders" who "kill and maim shunters by hundreds to save the cost of automatic couplings, and make atonement by annual subscriptions to deserving charities," but right after "shareholders," he adds in parentheses: "I am one."[187] In the same preface, Shaw famously states that "all money is tainted."[188] Shaw is not being defeatist here. Rather, he suggests that until the system of capitalism is overcome, it is impossible to earmark money from supposedly clean and ethical sources. One of the inspirations behind the play's antihero, capitalist Andrew Undershaft, was the Krupp family, a German ammunition dynasty that became the world's largest industrial company by the end of the nineteenth century. During the Third Reich, the Krupps supported the Nazi regime and the use of forced labor. In an ironic twist of fate, the Krupp Foundation has also funded research for this book, proving Shaw's point.[189]

Still, the very act of exposing the internal contradictions of theater and, by proxy, the capitalist mode of production makes theater worth making. Economic constraints and the conditions of production (what kind of theater can be made at a given historical moment) do not always restrict artistic freedom: they can also become a source of inspiration and aesthetic innovation.[190] As we will observe in chapter 1, Ibsen's *John Gabriel Borkman* acknowledges, in a metatheatrical manner, that a theater's repertoire is dependent on capital and the demands of its patrons but then transforms that constraint into an opportunity for immanent critique. Economic theory, as Judith Butler notes, is "one of the processes that performatively bring about the market, or what we might call 'the market presumption.'"[191] If economic structures are "performatively produced" and reproduced, then theory can expose the irresolvable contradictions of those very same structures.[192] So can theater.

This study is not an account of how modern drama was funded, as there are already several excellent studies devoted to this topic.[193] Nor is it meant as an exhaustive exposé of all the theatrical instances in which money appears onstage, for almost every play has some reference, however indirect, to money, capital, or value, though I will examine some significant moments of money appearing onstage, such as when Nora tips the porter at the start of *A Doll's House*, or when Jean throws a silver coin in Julie's direction in *Miss Julie*. Instead, *Theater of Capital* traces how modern playwrights attempted to elucidate economic concepts and try out economic models and theories in the theater. In other words, theater became a space for artists to experiment and play with the economy.

To be sure, modern drama was a diverse and heterogeneous movement and is thus challenging to define. As Martin Puchner notes, it is difficult to pinpoint "what was 'modern' about modern drama" besides its rupture with inherited dramatic conventions and institutions of nineteenth-century drama and theater.[194] Moreover, modern drama produced a wide range of critical responses to the culture of capitalism, from Ibsen's idea of the spiritual improvement of humanity to Brecht's outright championing of communism. The theater of capital is one vital current that performs the work of immanent critique of political economy: it exposes the rhetorical strategies and ideological constructions of economics, lays bare the process of theater's own productive apparatus and commodification, and explores the dynamic relationship between capitalism and critique. Theater, I will argue, offers a space for testing economic concepts, ideas, and models. In fact, theatrical thinking can provide something that economic theory explicitly does not—experimentation and play. For example, socialist thought, like capitalist ideology, often betrays dogmatism and an emphasis on certainty and inevitability. As philosopher Axel Honneth has observed,

> Regardless of whether socialists favored reform or revolution, both sides excluded experimentation as a historical-practical method. Even those who assumed that socialist organizational principles could only be established gradually were not content to experiment with various possibilities and potentials, but pretended to possess total certainty. The divide between socialism and an experimental understanding of historical action was categorical and not gradual: Due to socialists' belief in the inevitable course of history, they were certain right from the start about the next step of social change, obviating any need for situational experimentation with various possibilities of social organization.[195]

Theater offers a space for precisely such a "situational experimentation with various possibilities of social organization" that includes both cautionary tales and utopian potentials. For example, according to Strindberg, role-playing in the theater was "what the experimental method was to science."[196] Many of the issues that we are grappling with today, such as the conflict between labor and capital, heightened financialization, and staggering economic inequality, were all being debated at the end of the nineteenth century. What if automation could replace human labor? This question informs Karel Čapek's 1920 sci-fi play *R.U.R.* (*Rossum's Universal Robots*), which invented the word *robot* from the Czech word for slave labor (*robota*). What if Andrew Carnegie's *Gospel of Wealth* was carried out to its full conclusion and all public services became privatized? This is the question behind the neoliberal model town of Perivale St. Andrews in Shaw's *Major Barbara*. What is the difference between gambling, speculation, and investment? This question animates many of Chekhov's plays.

In this way, the theater of capital does not merely illustrate the economic theories of its time in an instrumental fashion but actually participates in the process of experimental thinking.

For the same reason, this study is not invested in one single economic theory, for example, that of Marxism. There are, of course, many productive Marxist readings of nineteenth-century literature and drama.[197] The aim of this study, however, is to highlight the range of economic ideas and models that were debated on the stage. And because theater deals with real bodies in real time and not with the unrealistically rational and self-interested *Homo economicus*, the works of the theater of capital produce crucial knowledge about how human beings might interact with one another and what choices they might make when managing their time and collective *oikos*, thereby shedding light on the blind spots of neoclassical economics.

The first chapter of the book focuses on how Ibsen's drama reveals the invisible hand of the market to be a theatrical construction, a repurposed hand of Providence in the age of capital, at a historical juncture when Norway was embracing modernization. Although Ibsen may not have read Adam Smith, the invisible hand was a well-known literary trope by the time Smith employed it. Ibsen suggests that the invisible hand of capital is not immaterial but always that of labor. In the case of *A Doll's House*, that labor is the hidden and erased work of women both inside and outside the capitalist household. Ibsen's investment activities provided him with the necessary experience and expertise to convey the workings of finance to his audience and to test in the theater whether the free market worked the way it was supposed to and whether the bourgeois household really was the safe haven from the outside economic world that it alleged to be. I then look at contemporary artists, like Ostermeier and Akhtar, who continue Ibsen's legacy of trying out economic ideas by drawing their own logical (and violent) conclusions.

The second chapter—"The Dowry versus Erotic Capital: The Drama of Courtship in Strindberg, Shaw, and Benedictsson"—goes deeper into the bourgeois household and the alienated intimate relationships forged through marriage and prostitution. Engels's *The Condition of the Working Class in England* (1845) and *The Origin of the Family, Private Property, and the State* (1884) posit prostitution as the central metaphor for bourgeois marriage and labor exploitation to call attention to the internal contradictions of the love marriage under capitalism. But prostitution was also a profitable and booming industry in the nineteenth century with ties to the stock exchange and the theater. Reading Strindberg's *Miss Julie*, Shaw's *Mrs. Warren's Profession*, and Benedictsson's *Money* and *The Enchantment* (*Den bergtagna*, 1888) in relation to nineteenth-century economic writings about the dowry as well as Hakim's theory of erotic capital, I investigate and untangle the vicious intertwinement of the discourses of money and sex. I do this by paying close attention to the forms of capital that money takes in the circulation of sex at the end of the nineteenth century. This circulation involved courtship, marriage, and prostitution.

The third chapter traces a rarely discussed but pivotal episode in the early journalistic career of Chekhov. Twenty-four-year-old Chekhov covered the most notorious bank fraud in the history of nineteenth-century Russia, the Rykov affair, aspects of which would continue to reverberate throughout his fiction and drama. The blurry boundary between gambling, speculation, and investment that characterized the burgeoning capitalist economy of Imperial Russia provided Chekhov with the temporal structure of the near win, which creates dramatic tension in many of his plays. Chekhov experimented with various scenarios that unbridled speculation could spur, finally mastering the representation of casino capitalism in *The Cherry Orchard* and exposing the underlying power dynamics of the economic game.

Finally, the fourth chapter discusses the radical exploration of labor in Hauptmann's *The Weavers* in the context of Marx's writings and the play's legacy in theater history. The staging of the weavers' revolt and the destruction of private property in front of a bourgeois audience has proven to be a subversive act, provoking riots in the theater and encouraging actors to fight for their labor rights. It was so incendiary, I argue, that the German expressionist playwrights who wrote in Hauptmann's wake curtailed his play's championing of the working class, betraying their doubts and fears concerning the rise of the proletariat.

The present study also aims to show how theatrical metaphors imbue economic theory so that an intriguing paradox emerges. On the one hand, neoclassical economic theory wants to posit the laws of supply and demand and the business cycle as akin to the natural laws and processes studied by the natural sciences. On the other hand, economics reverts to metaphorical language in moments when it stumbles upon something it cannot fully explain by the would-be laws of nature.[198] The theater of capital exposes theatrical constructions that attempt to naturalize and mask capitalist ideology: concepts like "the invisible hand," "the work ethic," "the market," and so on. In their treatment of economics, the playwrights of the theater of capital resemble the authors of science plays, who, as Kirsten Shepherd-Barr has shown, "seem paradoxically attracted to some of the scientific and mathematical principles that seem most mysterious and unstable."[199]

A brief note on the selection of texts is in order. First, most of the works featured in this book are realist dramas. As many of its theorists have noted, realism is the "aesthetic mode most intimate to capitalism."[200] For its detractors, then, realism is already a compromised endeavor, "producing the very subjects and objects that the mode claims to document."[201] According to W. B. Worthen, the "rhetoric of realism" cannot adequately engage with the Woman Question because its strategies of representing women onstage are part of "the social machinery the plays attempt to criticize."²⁰² Defenders of realism (among whom I count myself) argue that, on the contrary, it is precisely its intimacy to capital that gives realism its ability to engage in immanent critique.

Second, this book does not cover Brecht. It stops, one might say, at the threshold of Brecht's arrival onto the theater scene. This choice is deliberate. In many ways, the topic of theater and capitalism is almost synonymous with Brecht's drama, and the scholarship on it is extensive and rich.²⁰³ I hope to show that far from constituting a decisive break from the theatrical tradition that came before him, Brecht was, in fact, the logical continuation and culmination of the kinds of developments that were percolating in the bourgeois drama of the late nineteenth century. The self-critique and self-awareness of the bourgeois playwrights as beneficiaries of capitalism who preceded Brecht paved the way for his critique of dramatic theater. As many have pointed out, Brecht's own theater can still be considered thoroughly bourgeois.²⁰⁴

Third, most of the works covered in this study are part of what one might call the European "classical dramatic canon."²⁰⁵ In no way am I suggesting that modern drama was a predominantly European phenomenon.²⁰⁶ I am interested in problematizing this heritage by looking at its erasures (the work of women, including that of Victoria Benedictsson) and vestiges of colonial exploitation (which we see, for example, in Ibsen's bourgeois drawing rooms). This study also looks at contemporary artists, like Ostermeier, who are invested in weaponizing the classical canon by seemingly catering to their audience but, in reality, presenting them with "Trojan horses."²⁰⁷ The contemporary beneficiaries of capitalism are thus confronted with works created by the beneficiaries of capitalism of a bygone era, with all of that world's injustices only intensified. Other theater artists revisit and approach these well-known dramatic works of the nineteenth century as "repository[ies] of cultural memory,"²⁰⁸ bringing to light their latent violence, as when Inua Ellams rewrites Chekhov's *Three Sisters* as a family saga set in Nigeria, in 1967, with the sisters now surrounded by a brutal military, on the brink of the Biafran Civil War, or when Yaël Farber transports Strindberg's *Miss Julie* to today's Karoo, South Africa, where race and the question of land ownership now intersect with Strindberg's original helix of class and gender. Finally, the examples chosen for this book are meant not to be exhaustive but to highlight some of the central preoccupations and questions that animate the theater of capital.

Theater has long been criticized for its unapologetic and unbreakable ties to commerce and finance. Yet what if theater got it right all this time? As Aristotle suggests, drama and *oikos* are intimately connected in that both ask pressing questions about how we manage our time, what we prioritize, and what we ultimately value. Looked at this way, the theater of capital has enormous political worth in refusing to treat the economic world as a separate sphere of influence with its own laws, special treatment, and exclusionary vocabulary. This book is a journey back to a time when economics had not yet been fully institutionalized as a separate discipline and when theater took on the challenge of experimenting with different socioeconomic models and envisioning different futures, some more desirable than others. By the same token, the book seeks to show how the nineteenth-century theater of capital can shed light on the theater of capital today, which continues to treat economic questions as moral, political, and spiritual concerns.

Chapter 1

✦

Finance Capital

Henrik Ibsen and the Invisible Hand

The Rise of Financialization in Norway and Ibsen's Career

"Theater is not political action. Political action happens in the streets." This is how the German director Thomas Ostermeier addressed the audience in a conversation with American playwright Branden Jacobs-Jenkins at the Brooklyn Academy of Music on October 12, 2017. All theater can do is make us realize the "lies we tell ourselves." Ostermeier made a name for himself staging the socially conscious dramas of Sarah Kane and Mark Ravenhill. After becoming the artistic director of Berlin's Schaubühne, Ostermeier turned to Ibsen in hopes that the Norwegian author's bourgeois world would appeal to the patrons of the Schaubühne: "Characters in Ibsen constantly worry about money."[1] Perhaps this was also the reason behind Ostermeier's desire to bring his acclaimed production of Ibsen's *An Enemy of the People*, adapted into English by Branden Jacobs-Jenkins, to the patrons of Broadway in the fall of 2018.[2] It's a Trojan horse. Get the haves into the theater and make them see their complicity in perpetuating the injustices of capitalism.

Ostermeier's version of *An Enemy of the People* interpolates a long passage from *The Coming Insurrection* (2007), a French anarchist manifesto by the Invisible Committee, into Thomas Stockmann's assembly speech and then breaks the fourth wall during the play's town hall meeting to invite members of the audience to share their thoughts about capitalism and democracy. In the United States, *An Enemy of the People* has become popular once again since the 2016 presidential election, with eight different versions produced in 2017, compared with only two in 2015.[3] Recent productions of note include Brad Birch's 2018 adaptation for the Guthrie Theater and the 2017 site-specific *Public Enemy: Flint* directed by Purni Morell in Flint, Michigan, in a gymnasium of a former school. Although Ibsen's drama eerily foreshadowed Flint's water crisis and the spread of fake news, the continued relevancy and urgency of his play go deeper than its plot, as Ibsen illuminates the contradictions of capitalist modernity and the culture of rampant financialization.

Ibsen's oeuvre exposes the historical constructions and ideological assumptions that economic discourse, which emerged as a separate discourse and social science by the second half of the nineteenth century, attempts to naturalize as supposedly scientific facts, such as the laws of supply and demand, the invisible hand, and the ubiquitous "market."[4] In Norway, the rapid development of finance during the nineteenth-century railway boom and the lax laws governing it resulted in a surge of financial scandals and general uncertainty about the ethics of business. It is not surprising, then, that both the material conditions and the content of Ibsen's work show a preoccupation with capital and money. Expanding domestic and European literary markets helped elevate Ibsen to a preeminent position in world drama, while his oeuvre tackled such prominent features of nineteenth-century economic life as debt, speculation, and the invisible hand of the market.[5]

The financial hardship of his father left a mark on the young Ibsen. Since, in the middle of the century, there was still no literary market in Scandinavia to support a professional writer without a family fortune, Ibsen turned to the theater for regular income. From 1851 to 1857, he served as a stage manager at the National Theater in Bergen. In 1857, he became the head of the Norwegian Theater in Kristiania, which went bankrupt in the summer of 1862. Ibsen's 1865 play *Brand* earned him public acclaim and an annual state grant. During the 1870s, burgeoning book markets and successful theater productions set Ibsen on the road to economic security. In 1870, Ibsen began to keep an account book, painstakingly tracking every single investment and expense, a testament to the careful attention he paid to the financial side of his authorship. Given Ibsen's own pecuniary struggles, it is no wonder that financial uncertainty is the sword of Damocles that hangs over the heads of his characters, generating dramatic tension in plays like *Pillars of the Community* (*Samfundets støtter*, 1877), *A Doll's House* (1879), *Ghosts* (1881), *An Enemy of the People* (1882), *The Wild Duck* (*Vildanden*, 1884), *Hedda Gabler* (1890), and *John Gabriel Borkman* (1896).

This chapter will trace how Ibsen's modern drama exposes the market to be a theatrical construction by showing both its visible social effects and the hidden structures of alienated labor. To begin with, many of Ibsen's plays unveil the illusion of the free market by showing that the invisible hand of the market, which originated in the religious concept of Providence, operates like the hackneyed theatrical device of the deus ex machina. Put simply, both the deus ex machina in the theater of capital and the invisible hand in liberal discourse are illusions that uphold the market logic as the only viable option. The former does so in the interest of dramatic closure; the latter, for the promotion of the free-market enterprise. The economic fiction of the invisible hand stifles the political imaginary. The aesthetic repurposing of the deus ex machina in modern drama, however, has the potential to stimulate the political imaginary and even, perhaps, to inspire political action. Friedrich Nietzsche famously criticized Euripides for relying on the deus ex machina and thereby flattening tragic dissonance and substituting "the cheerful optimism of the theoretical man" for tragedy's metaphysical consolation.[6] Ibsen's deus ex machina can, indeed, be described as what Nietzsche dubs the new "god of machines and crucibles" called upon "in the service of a higher egotism."[7] What is represented at the end of many Ibsen's plays is the arbitrary power of and deification of capital. Andrew Sofer proposes the term "dark matter" to signal "*whatever is materially unrepresented onstage but un-ignorable.*"[8] This is a generative term to apply to such an immaterial concept as the invisible hand and to capital, which is notoriously difficult to define. It might as well be the "dark matter" of economics. Yet just as the movement of the deus ex machina is possible in the theater because of the labor of stagehands, so the invisible hand of capital is revealed to be the hand of labor. As we will soon see, this insight is foregrounded in *A Doll's House*. Ibsen's political lesson is as pertinent today as it was in the late nineteenth century: even as financialization invades every aspect of social life, human beings are still exploited through their labor, even if that labor is not immediately visible. While *Pillars of the Community*, *An Enemy of the People*, and *John Gabriel Borkman* explore the movement of financial capital, *A Doll's House* brings to light the labor behind it by focusing on Nora's hidden labor—manual, emotional, and sexual.

Before delving into Ibsen's oeuvre, it is crucial to consider the unstable legal landscape of nineteenth-century European finance and Norway's late modernization. Although "financialization" is a twentieth-century neologism tied to the rise of neoliberalism,[9] the process is not new if "financialization" is defined as the process by which financial institutions and elites gain control over economic policy. Referencing Fernand Braudel's *Civilization and Capitalism*, Giovanni Arrighi argues that finance capital is not a new phase of capitalism; rather, it is "a recurrent phenomenon which has marked the capitalist era from its earliest beginnings in late medieval and early modern Europe."[10] Features of financialization can be traced back to the boom of railway construction in Europe in the early nineteenth century and to the beginning of legalized futures trading by the Chicago Board of Trade in 1863. Economist Alessandro Vercelli identifies a "secular tendency towards financialization" originating in ancient civilizations, and David Graeber notes that ancient Egyptian and Mesopotamian texts show "that credit systems . . . *preceded* the invention of coinage by thousands of years."[11]

In contrast to neighboring Sweden, the Norwegian economy was characterized more by the small-scale and local character of early industrial capitalism than by the "organized capitalism" developing in other parts of Europe by the end of the century. There were no nationwide corporate banks or industrial companies, and although there were many limited-liability companies, no corporate law existed until the Companies Act of 1910. Oslo Børs, the Norwegian stock exchange, was founded in 1881 but continued to be unregulated, so that "warnings against Norwegian companies were issued abroad."[12] New financial instruments sparked collective unease about the ethics of business. For instance, the railroad monopoly in *Pillars of the Community* and the poisonous baths in *An Enemy of the People* reveal how large-scale public development projects rely on a complicated network of competing private and public interests. Ibsen highlights how the use of theatricality, the strategic performance of spurious financial success in front of the public, could attract more shareholders and thus more capital. In particular, futures trading triggered public anxiety about the very meaning of truth. If future profits could atone (at least in financial terms) for the past crimes that generated them, then the very definitions of crime and truth become unstable. As Mayor Peter Stockmann puts it in Brad Birch's version of *An Enemy of the People*, "Appearances are all that matters when you're asking for a kroner of people's hard-earned money."[13] Moretti dubs this uncertain legal status of financial maneuvers in Ibsen the "grey area."[14] To put it another way, the "grey area" includes new economic activities that the law has not caught up to yet.[15] Ruthless businessmen and other opportunists exploit the legal loopholes, producing an intrabourgeois conflict that is "ruthless, unfair, equivocal, murky—but seldom actually illegal."[16] Ibsen thus represents for Moretti the fall of the honest bourgeois and the rise of the visionary capitalist: "Recognizing the impotence of bourgeois realism in the face of capitalist megalomania: here lies Ibsen's unforgettable political lesson."[17]

Ibsen himself took part in the culture of investment and speculation. As a young man, he worked as an apothecary's apprentice in the town of Grimstad, the socioeconomic structure of which might have inspired "the microcosmic framework" of *Pillars of the Community* and *An Enemy of the People*. As Robert Ferguson points out, most male citizens of Grimstad, "regardless of class, were small investors in the shipping trade" and shared the risks of the enterprise.[18] Ibsen wrote *Peer Gynt* (1867) during the construction of the Suez Canal, and in the fall of 1869 he attended the grand opening as Norway's representative. *Peer Gynt* captures the transition from industrial capitalism to the beginnings of financial capitalism. When (in act 4) the titular character is fleeced and discarded by his companions on the shore of Morocco, he does not turn into an industrious Robinson Crusoe. Instead, Peer speculates. He looks at the desolate desert in front of him and immediately imagines an oasis, urban development, and global trade. Peer's vision is Eurocentric colonization.[19]

Ibsen's publisher, the prominent Frederik Hegel, not only managed the selling of his books but also supported Ibsen's investment activities. In fact, Ibsen's income from his authorship was often directly linked to his investment activity, as he preferred to invest part of his royalties in bonds. In a letter to Hegel, Ibsen writes: "I have now, of course—thanks to you—become a capitalist!"[20] Ibsen took the fee for the revision of *Catiline* (1850, rev. ed. 1875) in the form of shares in the Zealand (Sjælland, Denmark) railway. At the time, Ibsen was writing *Pillars of the Community*, which he finished in 1877, at the height of the railroad boom in Norway, when the Røros Line (Rørosbanen) connected central Norway to its capital. Ibsen continued to keep an eye out for investment opportunities throughout his life, especially when he came into prosperity. When *Little Eyolf* (1894) was published simultaneously in Kristiania, Berlin, and London, Ibsen informed his wife, Suzannah, that he was buying stock for them worth "10,000 kroner" from the royalty.[21] Ibsen even got into a monetary dispute with his main advocate in Sweden, actor and theater director August Lindberg. Ibsen declined to give Lindberg the rights to *The Master Builder* if he did not pay the royalty in advance. In a letter to the Swedish director, Ibsen curtly explained his reasons: "I sent a large sum of money last week to Copenhagen for the purchase of bonds, with the result that I am now very short of cash."[22]

A Bankruptcy: Bjørnstjerne Bjørnson's Financial Melodrama and the Fantasy of the Honest Bourgeois

Ibsen was not the first playwright to write bourgeois drama or to document the financial scandals that shook Norway in the 1870s. To appreciate Ibsen's innovations, it is generative to compare his theater of capital to a genre that predominated before it—financial melodrama, a genre that attempts to rein in "capitalist megalomania" and to bring back the good, honest bourgeois.[23] Bjørnstjerne Bjørnson, Ibsen's friend, rival, and winner of the 1903 Nobel Prize in Literature, satirizes financial speculation in one of his most popular plays, *A Bankruptcy* (*En fallit*, 1875).[24] Even when Ibsen attained early success with his *Pillars of the Community*—which, by the end of its first year, had been produced by twenty-seven theaters in Germany alone—his play still did not match the popularity of *A Bankruptcy*.

A Bankruptcy tells the story of brewer Henning Tjælde, who faces financial ruin because of his penchant for speculation. After lawyer Berent confronts Tjælde about his practice of cooking the books, Tjælde undergoes a moral conversion and foreswears speculation. Bjørnson's play exposes the collective anxiety about the new world of high finance and corporations, where moral responsibility is dispersed among many shareholders and customers, who knowingly or unknowingly perpetuate the injustices of capitalism with their wallets. But it also behaves like a melodrama, which, in Peter Brooks's definition, "demonstrates over and over that the signs of ethical forces can be discovered and can be made legible."[25] Because "melodramatic good and evil are highly personalized," the melodramatic mode allows Bjørnson to assign blame to individual agents in the context of the morally ambiguous economic forces of the market.[26]

Resorting to melodrama, Bjørnson associates irresponsible speculation with a sham spectacle (both "speculation" and "spectacle" stem from the Latin *spectāre*, meaning "to look") and with theatricality, so his critique of corruption relies on what Barish calls "the antitheatrical prejudice."[27] In order to balance his budget and achieve liquidity, Tjælde needs the financial support of a powerful banker, Mr. Lind from Christiania. With Mr. Lind's capital, Tjælde can cover up his deficit and pass Mr. Berent's audit. But in order to gain Mr. Lind's capital, Tjælde must first win his trust by showing him that his company is on sound footing, which he does by means of an elaborate performance of success and wealth.

The dinner party that Tjælde throws in honor of Mr. Lind, which takes up the entire first scene of act 2, is rendered as a metatheatrical escapade of fake-it-till-you-make-it. Tjælde refers to his comportment at the dinner as his "last pretense" meant to capture Mr. Lind's capital (60). For this purpose, Tjælde acts as a kind of theater director, making sure his set includes lavish food and drinks, orchestrating cannon salutes, and prompting other guests to speak on his behalf as though they were actors in a theater production. For example, Tjælde encourages his employee, the brewery manager Jakobsen, to raise a toast and tell the story of how Tjælde allegedly "pulled him out of the gutter" by giving him his first job (70). While some of the guests at the dinner, like Tjælde's business competitors, see through his Potemkin village, Mr. Lind initially believes the performance and places his trust (and capital) into Tjælde's teetering firm. In this way, *A Bankruptcy* presents theatricality as a calculating craft meant to impress and swindle an audience.[28] This distrust of theatricality in business affairs lingers today in the term "success theater"—a vanity practice by which entrepreneurs use "the appearance of growth" to make their businesses appear more profitable than they really are. By attracting more investors, they can often turn their success theater into a self-fulfilling prophecy.[29] Mr. Berent, however, who becomes the personification of Tjælde's moral conscience, refuses to take the bait and confronts Tjælde in private about his theatrical duplicity.

The scene between Tjælde and Berent that immediately follows the spectacular dinner party takes on the form of a religious confession, where Berent acts as a priest, demanding that Tjælde acknowledge his wrongdoings and repent: first in private to him and then in public. At first blush, the solemn tone of the episode seems to offer a stark contrast to the metatheatrical exuberance of the previous scene's banquet. Instead of hyperbolic toasts, words of flattery, and the roar of cannons, we witness Berent read off to Tjælde a litany of his assets and liabilities. Berent claims he can correctly measure the actual worth of Tjælde's business based on the present market situation rather than on speculation about future growth. In this scene, we seem to have left the public space of the theater for the semiprivate space of the confessional booth. The spectators are construed as voyeurs of Tjælde's would-be conversion from an inveterate speculator to a virtuous bourgeois and investor who learns how to handle his clients' money responsibly. But what does it mean to be a virtuous and responsible investor in practice? *A Bankruptcy* dodges this question by relying on vague definitions of speculation and investment while at the same time trying to maintain a distinct boundary between these two (often overlapping) economic activities. Berent demands that Tjælde abandon all pretense at financial responsibility and own up to his sins: "I have known several speculators in my days and have received many confessions" (101). In return for Tjælde's confession and public declaration of bankruptcy, Berent promises him a life of honest work, a clear conscience, and a good night's sleep. Later on, the play will offer us a specious example of such a moral businessman who can restrain both his ambition and his drive for capital accumulation.

Berent not only takes on the role of the confessor but also acts as the play's would-be realist who can tell Tjælde the *real* values of his assets and liabilities. Yet this supposedly sensible exchange soon turns into the most melodramatic scene of the whole play: repressed theatricality returns as a full-blown farce. In his initial phase of resistance, Tjælde locks the door, pulls out a revolver, and threatens to first shoot the messenger of morality (Berent) and then himself if he is not allowed to continue his business as usual. Tjælde objects to Berent's evaluation of his accounts by noting (not unconvincingly) that if Berent plans to assess every business in his overscrupulous manner, "everybody in this place will have to go bankrupt" (81).[30] According to Tjælde, financial values (such as property rates and stock prices) are perpetually in flux, and all financiers are engaged in some sort of swindling to survive on the market. The only way to endure is to beat the competition. According to Moretti, one of Ibsen's main political lessons is that "the good *Bürger* will never have the *strength* to withstand the creative destruction of capital; the hypnotic entrepreneur will never yield to the sober Puritan."[31] By contrast, Bjørnson's *A Bankruptcy* entertains the fantasy of converting a megalomaniac capitalist into a conscientious and honest bourgeois. When Tjælde remarks that every business will go bankrupt under Berent's rigid and fixed system of values, Berent is prepared to risk that. In other words, if need be, the likes of Berent will launch a whole crusade against speculators. At this moment in the play, one may be tempted to ask who, in fact, is the play's *real* realist: Berent, who dreams of appealing to the collective conscience of capitalists on a global scale, or Tjælde, who knows what it takes to run a business? At the time of the play's publication, Bjørnson underwent a spiritual crisis and eventually abandoned hope in institutionalized religion. But the Lutheran ideology concerning money and commerce still permeates his play. The traditional doctrine of Luther, as expressed in his *Long Sermon on Usury* in 1520 and *On Trade and Usury* in 1524, insists that prices are to be fixed by public authorities and that sellers cannot deviate from these figures in order to accumulate capital beyond what is necessary to maintain their station in life. Merchants are not to manipulate scarcity to raise prices, corner the market, or trade in futures.[32]

A Bankruptcy promotes its antispeculation message by bringing tangible money onstage. Virtue triumphs when young Sannaes, Tjælde's faithful clerk, offers his bankrupted boss a lump sum of tangible money earned by looking out "for such business that would not be affected by major trading" (134). With this supposedly clean money, the hardworking Sannaes and Tjælde's daughter, whom Sannaes marries, rebuild the family business on a sound and honorable foundation beneficial to the entire community. It is unclear, however, what types of businesses are not influenced by the fluctuations of major trading. How does Sannaes manage to restrain greed and the drive for capital accumulation in his company? When his daughter compares his business to a lottery, Tjælde protests: "You evidently don't understand what business is. Down today, up tomorrow" (21). He then compares himself to a visionary and a poet: "You don't understand how a businessman can have hope from one day to the other, a constantly renewed hope. This doesn't make him a swindler. He is sanguine, a poet, if you like, living in an imaginary world—or he is a real genius, who sees land ahead when no one sees it" (24). That values—financial, moral, and aesthetic—are fluctuating and that the entire community might be complicit in this new culture of speculation are troubling thoughts that *A Bankruptcy* evades. These questions are left unanswered by Bjørnson's drama, which, in wishing to exorcise speculation from its own internal economy, ends up perpetuating the ideology of unbridled capitalism. After all, the search for supposedly safe investments that Sannaes claims to have discovered is one of the staple dreams (and delusions) of the capitalist.

The fantasy of financial melodrama—that an honest business could restrain the drive for capital accumulation or, at the very least, curb greed—reappears in myriad nineteenth-century texts both on the page and on the stage. For instance, in Honoré de Balzac's novel *César Birotteau* (1837), the titular speculator should have been content with his business in cosmetics but instead ventures into the world of property speculation and, as a result, goes bankrupt. The cautionary moral tale concludes when César pays back his debt and dies happy, having restored his reputation.

Pillars of the Community: From the Invisible Hand of Providence to the Invisible Hand of the Market

Ibsen read *A Bankruptcy* in March 1875, and the final version of *Pillars of the Community* is in dialogue with Bjørnson's work.[33] While Bjørnson's *A Bankruptcy* is a financial melodrama that places the blame for an economic crisis on one irresponsible merchant's illegal act of cooking the books, the central plot of *Pillars of the Community* hinges on the drama of insider trading, which, at the time, hovered in a legally "grey area" in Norway.[34] Ibsen revolutionizes the genre of bourgeois drama by disposing of the strong moralizing impulse of melodrama in favor of a more nuanced representation of capitalist modernity. Karsten Bernick, the shipping magnate of a small coastal town, is planning to launch an inland railroad branch that will connect his town to the mainline. As the play unfolds, we learn a few of Bernick's dark secrets. First, he had once prevented the construction of a coastal railway line, and it soon becomes evident that this project would have competed with his shipping empire. Second, he has been secretly buying out the land adjacent to the future inland railroad. In other words, Bernick is trying to secure a monopoly on transportation.

Ibsen's careful use of language highlights a changing moral landscape shaped by the turbulent culture of financialization. When, in the very first scene, Bernick's wife remarks that her husband had once helped prevent the construction of a coastal railway, schoolmaster Rørlund quickly corrects her that it was "Providence" (*forsynet*) that curbed the project, not Bernick, who was only a tool in a higher hand (*redskab i en højeres hånd*; 12). Throughout the play, most characters throw around the expressions *forsynet* (Providence; 12, 40, 151, 166) and *forsynets hånd* (hand of Providence; 148, 151). These words have the advantage of masking greed and placing economic motives under the domain of Providence. Bernick, however, uses a slightly different expression to explain how he stumbled upon the valley where the idea for the inland branch first came to him. Ibsen's early English translators, William Archer and R. Farquharson Sharp, interpret, through their translations, the invisible force guiding Bernick to be Providence.[35] Their choice is justifiable given how frequently this phrase appears in the play, albeit spoken by other characters. Bernick himself, however, does not use *forsynet*, a word steeped in religious connotation. Instead, Bernick goes with *styrelse*, a much broader term, which includes Providence but can also refer to a range of other phenomena, such as steering, agency, administration, management, or corporation (41). It stems from the noun *styre*, meaning "rule, government, management."[36] To put it another way, Bernick suggests that it was some kind of agency or management that was steering his business trip when he stumbled upon the natural resources of the valley. The question that is left open by Bernick's ambiguous use of language is whether it was divine management (Providence) or the management of Bernick & Co. that ultimately *steered* Bernick to consider an inland railway project. This is not an isolated incident. In contrast to his business partners, who hypocritically invoke divine order, Bernick's vocabulary brims with words like "luck" (*lykke*) and "accident" (*uheld*), which he does not immediately link to divine order.

We might compare the way rumor moves in this play to an invisible hand. Joseph Roach metaphorically connects Adam Smith's "invisible hand" to the system of gossip at work in Ibsen's *A Doll's House* (1879) and Sheridan's *The School for Scandal* (1777). Like the invisible hand, argues Roach, "the exchange of information at each transaction adds up to a total effect far larger than the sum of its parts, pooling into ever-deepening truth-effects—celebrity, notoriety, urban legends, ethnic stereotypes."[37] In *Pillars of the Community*, the invisible hand has a direct connection to the economics of the play. Bernick permits the circulation of the rumor that his wife's younger brother stole money from his company. He knows that this is a lie and that his business simply went bankrupt because of bad luck, but in order to placate his creditors and uphold the trust of his community, he does not contradict the rumor. Bernick needs both private and public funding: individual subscribers as well as the backing of the municipal corporation. This dramatic setting realistically captures how public railways were financed in Norway during Ibsen's time. The capital for Norway's first public railroad, which opened on September 1, 1854, was raised by issuing two million shares. Half the capital came from British shareholders, and the other half was provided by Norwegian subscriptions, of which the state owned more than half.[38]

There is no direct evidence that Ibsen ever read Adam Smith or that he was familiar with Smith's invisible hand. In any case, the influential economic principle of the invisible hand of the free market as we know it today—that is, the self-regulating nature of the market by which individuals act in their own self-interest and end up benefiting society as a whole—is a modern concept dating from the mid-twentieth century. Economists have long bemoaned its imprecise use and attribution to Adam Smith, who used the phrase only three times in all his writings.[39] By the time Adam Smith began to write *An Inquiry into the Nature and Causes of the Wealth of Nations* (1776), "the invisible hand" was already a common literary trope. It appears as "the mighty hand" of Zeus in Homer's *Iliad*; Caeneus's "invisible hand, inflicting wound within wound" in Ovid's *Metamorphoses*; Augustine's "hand of God," "which moves visible things by invisible means"; "Thy Bloody and Invisible Hand" in Shakespeare's *Macbeth*; William Leechman's "the silent and unseen hand of all wise Providence," and elsewhere.[40] The prevalence of this literary trope leads Gavin Kennedy to dismiss Smith's use of it: "The metaphor of an invisible hand is just a metaphor and modern wonder over its meaning is, well, meaningless."[41] Taking Smith's invisible hand seriously, R. H. Tawney argues in *Religion and the Rise of Capitalism* (1926) that, by alluding to "an invisible hand," Smith sees "in economic self-interest the operation of a providential plan."[42] Peter Harrison concurs that "by far the most common" use of it "involved reference to God's oversight of human history and to his control of the operations of nature."[43] Thus, Ibsen's *Pillars of the Community* captures in its language the turbulent transformation of the invisible hand of Providence into the invisible hand of the market and reveals the sheer difficulty of choosing sides between Carl Schmitt's and Hans Blumenberg's views on modernity and the place of religion within it. Although their debate is outside the purview of this project, suffice it to note that Schmitt proclaimed that "all significant concepts of the modern theory of the state are secularized theological concepts,"[44] while Blumenberg, who critiqued the very term "secularization," insisted that the transition to the modern era involved a complete break from the theological framework.[45] Indeed, Bernick steers away from theological explanations of his political and economic motives, choosing instead to follow the new rationale of the market though his business partners still rely on religion.

Ibsen's drama thus chronicles a modern world in transition, where elements of Christian ethics coexist with new secular values of capitalism. For example, insurance appears simultaneously as the supernatural force of Providence and as a financial instrument. Ibsen's characters navigate between the old system of morality, which once contained economic conduct, and the laws of the market, where economic appetite becomes the guiding principle. At times these social systems of morality clash, as in *Ghosts* (premiered 1882; *Gengangere*), when Pastor Manders declines to insure Mrs. Alving's orphanage lest their community think that they do not have faith in Providence. At other times, Christian ethics and the business code of conduct work in perverse harmony, as in *Pillars of the Community*, when Bernick & Co. sends its ships out into the storm. If the shipping corporation chooses to wait out the inclement weather, it risks losing money from competition. If the ships sail and sink, however, the corporation will still profit from the insurance claim. Either way—the consideration of human lives notwithstanding—sailing in the storm is the rational business choice. This commercial decision conveniently supports the tradesmen's alleged faith in Providence. In this respect, Ibsen echoes the insight of his contemporary Friedrich Engels, who noted that, in its early development, the stock exchange "confirm[ed] the Calvinist principle that divine election, alias accident, is already decisive in this life as far as bliss and damnation, wealth (pleasure and power) and poverty (renunciation and servitude) are concerned."[46] More important, *Pillars of the Community* unveils the theatrical construction that is both the market and the dramatic device of the deus ex machina. On a formal level, Ibsen's drama stages the social consequences of the "unrepresentable" and invisible force that Martin Harries calls "the phantom heart of the economy," revealing "the surprising traces of the supernatural in works of political economy and social thought."[47]

At first glance, Bernick's change of heart at the end of *Pillars of the Community* echoes the moral conversion of Tjælde in *A Bankruptcy*. Bernick delivers a speech to the constituents of his town in which he announces that he will disband his monopoly: "I have tonight come to the decision that these properties should be offered as a company of which the ordinary shares shall be offered for public subscription; anyone who wants them will be able to get them" (201). In doing so, Bernick throws his three business conspirators under the train and simultaneously offers an advertisement for Bernick & Co. shares. The project will go on, and it will be financed with the money of the town's citizens. Bernick might not gain as much as he initially had hoped, but he no longer faces a colossal loss. Let us not forget that Bernick has invested his whole fortune into the railway, so his entire livelihood is on the line. This ending has been interpreted both as a genuine moral lesson that "the spirits of truth and freedom should become the real pillars of society" and as a hoax that makes Bernick no better than a "television evangelist" who manipulates his followers to give him money.[48] But instead of condemning and punishing his lead capitalist as Bjørnson does in *A Bankruptcy* or as Arthur Miller would in *All My Sons* (1947), Ibsen allows Bernick to remain onstage with all the contradictions of his personal and financial decisions. The point is that Bernick stands neither for melodramatic villainy nor for its transformation into virtue; rather, he emerges as a modern capitalist.

In Ibsen's theater of capital, Bernick looks after his private interests *and* believes that in doing so he is acting in the best interests of his beloved community. His decision to confess his past greed is at once a partial moral transformation *and* the smartest business choice in the given circumstances. The financial health of Bernick & Co. determines the prosperity of the entire town, thus making Bernick too big to fail. Ibsen does not tell us whether Bernick's moral transformation at the end of *Pillars of the Community* is a genuine change of heart or a theatrical trick meant to sway the public to buy shares for his company. The boundary between the two is blurred. In the brave new world of capitalist modernity, the public image of corporations and public trust are matters of spectacle. In other words, a company's success depends on how well it can perform its would-be financial health, thereby making it a self-fulfilling prophecy by attracting more shareholders. Just like Marx abandons moralizing in *Capital* for an in-depth analysis of why capitalists cannot act any differently than continue to accumulate more capital, so Ibsen's drama refuses to condemn Bernick in order to illuminate his economic motives in the capitalist society in which he lives. In this light, studying the economic issues at the heart of Ibsen's play, including Bernick's economic rationale, does not reduce our analysis to the narrow approach of economism but instead enriches our understanding of Bernick's complex humanity, living as he does under capitalism.

John Gabriel Borkman: The "Icy, Iron Hand" and the Comedy of Capital

Another example of an invisible hand appears in *John Gabriel Borkman*.[49] "An icy, iron hand" moves John Gabriel Borkman in his relentless pursuit of capital and ultimately to his death (242). In the final scene, Ella Rentheim and John Gabriel Borkman take a walk in the freezing cold up to a slope from which Borkman takes in the expansive landscape. Looking down, Borkman tells Ella that in the far-off mountains lies his "deep, endless, inexhaustible kingdom" (*dybe, endeløse, uudtømmelige rige*; 237). It remains ambiguous whether Borkman refers here to all the natural resources that he envisions unearthing in the future or whether he intuits that he is close to death. The enigmatic atmosphere of the scene intensifies when Borkman collapses and pronounces: "It was an ice hand that grabbed my heart" (239). Borkman's last words correct his previous statement, however: "No—no ice hand. An iron hand it was" (240). From his very first appearance onstage, Borkman emphasizes that he is "a miner's son" (*en bergmands søn*), and his insatiable desire for more capital is linked to his idea of excavating iron in the mountain ranges (76). Surveying the wintry landscape around him, he tells Ella: "The air acts like a breath of life on me. The air comes like a greeting from underground spirits. I sense them, the buried millions; I feel the ores stretch out their curving, branching, luring arms to me" (237). Borkman then adds that he saw the iron arms before him like "living shadows" (*levendegjorte skygger*) in the vault of the bank when he was speculating with his clients' securities (237). This is a strange and paradoxical remark given that in his machinations Borkman was using not metal but intangible forms of money—securities. The reference to iron hands and Borkman's desire to unearth metal may indicate his desire for liquid capital. The living shadows of the iron arms projected onto the walls of the vault also echo Plato's allegory of the cave, as Borkman is so entranced with the illusions of capital that he does not see the reality of his situation.[50] An intriguing parallel can be drawn between Borkman's study of these "living shadows" and how the cave prisoners in Plato's parable assign credit and prestige to those who can quickly remember the shadows that came before and predict which shadows will follow. The image of the hand reappears at the very end when Mrs. Borkman asks Ella about the cause of her husband's death: "Then not by his own hand?" (242). Ella tells Mrs. Borkman that her husband did not commit suicide; instead, "an icy, iron hand" (*en isnende malmhånd*) seized his heart, thus bringing the images of the different hands together (of ice and of iron). Each character interprets the meaning of the invisible hand in a different way. For Ella, it is primarily "an icy hand" that kills the capacity to love, that congeals love into a commodity for sale. For Mrs. Borkman, "the cold" that Ella blames for Borkman's death evokes his tarnished reputation and fall from grace (244). For Borkman, it is "an iron hand" (240) that lures him to expand capital in order to achieve what he calls "the kingdom—and the power—and the glory" (*for rigets—og magtens—og ærens skyld*), with its inescapable allusion to the Lord's Prayer (238).[51] Thus, it might stand for Borkman's hubris and the capitalist megalomania of relentless expansion.

In trying to figure out what the final metaphor of the "icy, iron hand" means, the reader and spectator engage in a kind of speculation. To be sure, this speculation—in the contemplative sense of the word—is different from Borkman's financial speculation, yet there are intriguing parallels worth considering. As Marc Shell has argued, metaphor is itself an exchange, and language and thought internalize money into what he calls "money of the mind."[52] In *The Economy of Literature*, Shell traces the shared historical origins of both philosophy and coined money to show how linguistic products often interiorize aspects of the political economy.[53] Focusing primarily on nondramatic literary texts, however, Shell's analysis privileges material forms of money (such as coins and paper notes) and the written word. As a result, money and language are associated in his account because both are mediums of exchange. Ibsen's drama, most of which was written for performance onstage, intuits something else about the meaning of money: that it might not merely be a medium of exchange.[54]

When we scan Ibsen's dramatic oeuvre, we quickly discover an arresting paradox. For all the discussions centered on money, money itself, whether in the form of coins or banknotes, rarely appears as a prop onstage. Ibsen's stage directions rarely indicate the presence of—or exchange of—money as a tangible object. This is also what differentiates Ibsen from Bjørnson, who makes it an ideological point to bring out tangible money onstage in *A Bankruptcy* to mark the honest, nonspeculating bourgeois. In Ibsen, money appears largely in intangible forms: as financial instruments of the market (debt, bonds, stocks, securities), as metaphors, and as topics of conversation. To be sure, at the beginning of *A Doll's House*, Nora tips the porter with fifty øre and Torvald hands Nora forty banknotes to manage their Christmas household. Yet the appearance of this physical money onstage only highlights the larger, invisible sums that loom over the characters' lives in the form of past debts and hopes for future profits. Nora still needs to supplement the pocket money that Torvald occasionally gives her by secretly taking on odd jobs, such as crocheting or embroidering, so that she can meet the payments on the loan (1,200 speciedaler, or 4,800 kroner) that she took out to save his life. And both Nora and Torvald stake their financial future on Torvald's forthcoming promotion at the bank. Ibsen's capitalist drama thus offers us a way to rethink the meaning of money as performing the trace of the relationship between the debtor and the creditor. The credit theory of money posits that money is not actually a "thing"—"a commodity chosen from amongst the universe of commodities to serve as a medium of exchange"; rather, it is "the social system of credit accounts and their clearing."[55] Ibsen promoted this theory in this own household, as he frequently drew "imitation banknotes" for family celebrations as gifts "to be cashed when sufficient funds" became available. These often featured drawings of a cat or an eagle—Ibsen's nicknames for Suzannah.[56]

Reading Adam Smith with Ibsen highlights the oscillation between the providential meaning of the invisible hand and its secular sense relating to the free market. More important still, the metaphor of the invisible hand points to the sheer challenge of understanding and representing the nature of economic forces of the marketplace. Characters in Ibsen, just like his readers and spectators, have to pause and speculate about the meaning of the invisible hands that are motivating the characters and moving the dramatic plot along. What steers Bernick to discern the potential for urban development in the valley that he has stumbled upon? After all, he was not being a flâneur; he was on a business trip. Bernick cannot identify the exact nature of that impetus, so he too reverts to metaphor. Despite Gavin Kennedy's dismissal of metaphor, metaphor is doing theoretical work both in Smith's writings and in Ibsen's drama. It is productive, then, in the given context to remember sociologist Robert Nisbet's seminal explanation of metaphor:

> What is a metaphor? Much more than a simple grammatical construction of speech. Metaphor is a way of knowing—one of the oldest, most deeply embedded, even indispensable ways of knowing in the history of human consciousness. It is, at its simplest, a way of proceeding from the known to the unknown. It is a way of cognition in which the identifying qualities of one thing are transferred in an instantaneous, almost unconscious, flash of insight to some other thing that is, by remoteness or complexity, unknown to us.[57]

Victor Turner agrees with him, underlining that metaphor is "metamorphic."[58] Ibsen's characters and spectators have to use metaphor to think about the economic forces in their lives and to work out what they might be. Bernick and Borkman do not revert to metaphorical language to simply cloak their private interests. The movement from the known to the unknown, which Nisbet identifies, mirrors the characters' speculation. They speculate in order to accumulate capital, literally moving from known territories to unknown territories (Bernick's valley; Borkman's buried millions in the mountains). But they also speculate in the contemplative sense of the word as they struggle to understand the nature of their economic activity and its relation to moral conduct. Finally, Bernick's ambiguous intentions suggest that the economy is not a separate sphere of influence. When Bernick thinks about economic questions, he is, in fact, thinking about the most pressing issues in his life—the future of his son, the well-being of his family, the prosperity of his town.

As R. H. Tawney has argued, up to the Protestant Reformation, economic activity was thought to be "one among other kinds of moral conduct."[59] Economic egotism and desire for financial power were curbed and branded as immoral. The modern, secular doctrine silenced moral scruples with the ideology of economic expediency and the focus on profit and capital growth. The business world no longer seeks moral guidance outside its own bubble. The laissez-faire market takes economic efficiency, economic appetite, and private property as nonnegotiable moral values. Tawney's aim in *Religion and the Rise of Capitalism* is to trace the change from the view of economic activity as one kind of moral conduct to "the view of it as dependent upon impersonal and almost automatic forces; to observe the struggle of individualism, in the face of restrictions imposed in the name of religion by the Church and of public policy by the State, first denounced, then palliated, then triumphantly justified in the name of economic liberty."[60] Tawney himself often reverts to metaphor in reference to the economic forces of the market, using phrases like "impersonal and almost automatic forces"; "the infallible operations of the invisible hand"; "the ebb and flow of economic movements"; "the sport of social forces which they could neither understand, nor arrest, nor control," and so on.[61] In this, he echoes Adam Smith, who reverts to "an invisible hand" at moments where he tries to identify the origin and nature of economic impulses. What Ibsen's drama ultimately foreshadows is the deification of the market, in which economic expediency has the last word.

The deus ex machina at the end of *John Gabriel Borkman* highlights the dependency of art, and of theater in particular, on capital. The exchanges between Borkman and his friend, poet Foldal, begin the play's metatheatrical commentary on the institution of theater. Foldal tries to show his tragedy to Borkman in order to get his attention, echoing the way an artist might attempt to persuade his would-be producer to sponsor a project: "Good god, if I could only get it staged—! *(He eagerly opens and leafs through the folder.)* Look! Let me show you something that I've changed—" (92). But Borkman remains uninterested and tells Foldal that his tragedy will have to wait till another time. But another time will never come, because there is no demand for tragedies in the modern world, at least not according to Borkman.[62] Still, this does not mean that theater must blindly cater to popular taste. Instead, it can find aesthetic inspiration in economic constraints without becoming a slave to the law of supply and demand. Richard Halpern has recently traced the waning of tragedy and political action precisely to Adam Smith's "great innovation" in "argu[ing] that public happiness results not from action, and certainly not from sovereign action, but from production."[63] Consequently, the invisible hand, claims Halpern, "is not the agent of tragic irony but rather of something that looks more like comic (or more properly, Stoic) Providence."[64]

Indeed, *John Gabriel Borkman* flirts with the tragic mode but swerves into the comic register by way of the relentless expansion of capital. In his conversation with Foldal, Borkman comments on his own life story in metatheatrical terms. When Borkman's rival, Mr. Hinkel, rose to great heights in his career, Borkman plunged into the depths of misery. On hearing this, Foldal describes the events of Borkman's life as "a terrible tragedy" (*frygteligt sørgespil*; 102). Borkman first agrees with Foldal but then laughs and adds that "it is really a kind of comedy" (*er det virkelig en slags komedie*; 103). Borkman refers to the capitalist fiction that one person's tragic fall is always another's triumphant rise. Human destinies oscillate like stock market quotes, or, as Bjørnson's protagonist in *A Bankruptcy* puts it: "Down today, up tomorrow" (21). Borkman discerns a comedy in the way that his son, Erhart, and Foldal's daughter, Frida, attend parties hosted by the man who ruined him: "My son is down there in the dance row tonight. Isn't that, as I say, a comedy?" (105). Similarly, Ibsen's *John Gabriel Borkman* plays out not as a banker's tragedy but as a dark comedy of capital.

By the end, the unremitting expansion of capital will subsume all the characters. The beginning of the play sets up the struggle between the twin sisters, Mrs. Borkman and Ella Rentheim, over Erhart's direction in life. Such an exposition may initially suggest the structure of a Greek tragedy, as defined by Hegel, which depends on the collision and the reconciliation between two opposing and valid forces, each making an exclusive claim.[65] But the conflict between the two women is ultimately carried out in vain. Neither wins, and their reconciliation—the final stage picture is of the two women joining their hands over Borkman's dead body—is futile. They lose both Borkman and his son, becoming, in Ella's words, themselves only "two shadows" (*to skygger*; 245), just like the shadows projected onto the walls of Borkman's bank vault (237). Borkman's son falls victim to a kind of icy, iron hand personified by Mrs. Wilton, a wealthy, older woman who seduces him. Instead of choosing either his mother or aunt, Erhart leaves them both for Mrs. Wilton, who takes Frida and him away in her sledge of silver bells. The silver bells of Mrs. Wilton's sledge serve as a fetishistic object for the play's characters. Mrs. Borkman can tell the nearing of Mrs. Wilton's sledge just by the ringing of the bells alone. (Ibsen's stage directions indicate the hypnotic sound of the bells offstage.) And Borkman's obsession with metal carries to these silver bells as he comments on their genuineness.

In a way, Ibsen here is subtly rewriting the Danish writer Hans Christian Andersen's famous fairy tale *The Snow Queen* (*Snedronningen*, 1884). In the original tale, the Snow Queen casts a spell over a boy named Kai and keeps him away in her palace until, after many trials and tribulations, Kai's childhood friend Greda finds him and melts his frozen heart with her tears. Mrs. Wilton even compares her seduction of Erhart to a kind of spell that makes him do her bidding. In Ibsen's version, however, Mrs. Wilton is no fairy sorceress but, rather, figures as a personification of capital, as she carries away the progenies of the play, Erhart and Frida, promising to support them. Unlike brave Greda in the fairy tale, Frida cannot resist Mrs. Wilton's spell, as the latter takes Frida abroad to help launch her music career. So, while John Gabriel Borkman is knocked down by "an icy, iron hand," his son falls prey to a modern-day Snow Queen. When Mrs. Borkman taunts Mrs. Wilton that Erhart may one day grow tired of her and turn his attention to the younger Frida, Mrs. Wilton remains unfazed: "Men are so variable, Mrs. Borkman. And so are women" (203). Mrs. Wilton maintains that she knows how to arrange for herself and that she will be fine. Again, there is no tragic end in sight, only the inconstancy of human sentiments. The comic register of *John Gabriel Borkman* reinscribes the status quo in the sense that the deus ex machina of capital ties up loose ends and drives the play to its finale. But it is a dark comedy—a modern tragicomedy. The expansion of capital, epitomized in the deification of economic expediency, proves to be a congealing and destructive force that leaves living beings frozen and dead or turns them into shadows. Just as Adam Smith, in Halpern's view, "degrades sovereignty itself" by shifting power from sovereign action to production, so does Ibsen's deus ex machina lose its ancient meaning of Olympian "god from the machine."[66] If this old theatrical trick resolves anything onstage, it does so only by reinscribing the same market logic that got the characters into their current predicament in the first place.

An Enemy of the People: Fake News and Capital as Deus Ex Machina

In *Anatomy of Exchange-Alley* (1719), the English writer and trader Daniel Defoe was one of the first historical figures to predict that the expanding culture of financialization would lead to the plight of fake news: "[Stock-jobbing] is founded in Fraud, born of Deceit, and nourished by Trick, Cheat, Wheedles, Forgeries, Falsehoods, and all sorts of Delusions; Coining false News, this way good, that way bad; whispering imaginary Terrors, Frights, Hopes, Expectations, and then preying upon the Weakness of those, whose Imagination they have wrought upon, whom they have either elevated or depress'ed."[67] *An Enemy of the People* stages this influence of financialization on the proliferation of fake news and the destabilization of scientific truth. The play presents a panorama of a small coastal town in Norway, where things have been looking up since the public development of the Baths: "Buildings and landed property are rising in value every day" and "the unemployment rate is diminishing" (5–6).[68] The town has invested a large amount of public and private capital into the project, and now all that is needed is "a really good summer" and "lots of foreign visitors—lots of sick ones" to establish it as a tourist getaway and finally get returns on the investments (6). The mayor's brother, Doctor Thomas Stockmann, has agreed to write a scientific article about the salubrious conditions of the waters for the *People's Messenger*, crowning the marketing of the Baths with his the-doctor-recommended review. And then Thomas Stockmann makes the inconvenient discovery that the waters are poisonous. What is more, the worst pollution comes from the tanneries of Morten Kiil, the adoptive father of Stockmann's wife.

To idealist Thomas, there is a straightforward solution. The Baths project must be stopped immediately, and the town must build a sewer to draw off the impurities from the tanneries at Molledal. Initially, the liberal press, headed by Hovstad, and the Householders' Association, chaired by Aslaksen, offer their support, until they find out the price they will have to pay: the financial burden will fall hardest on the small taxpayers. The journalists of the liberal-minded press, struggling to stay afloat during financially unstable times, switch sides when they learn that Thomas has no capital. It is neither simple greed nor the reluctance to pay higher taxes that causes the entire community to turn against Thomas and brand him "an enemy of the people" (168). Rejecting melodrama, Ibsen gives us a nuanced scenario of how it is possible for a community to believe in truth and freedom in principle and to act otherwise in practice. As mentioned in the introduction, the capitalist mode of production gave birth to the ideals of freedom and equality for all, but only the overcoming of capitalism can realize those ideals. In the meantime, the citizens of Ibsen's fictitious spa town, like his spectators, find themselves in a historical transition between the emergence of emancipatory ideals and their still-to-come material fulfillment.

An Enemy of the People shows how the ideals of freedom and equality have little chance in a world completely dominated by the profit motive, where everything is done for the accumulation of capital. Peter Stockmann thus makes a persuasive claim that even if the town were to make the sacrifice, raise the necessary capital, and re-lay the water pipes, their future would still be doomed. It is not only the present investment loss that the mayor has in mind but the town's future reputation as well. During the time it would take for the town to turn the whole project around, "other neighboring towns with conditions for bathing places" would promote their spa resorts by besmirching their small community (67–68). The good intentions of the town would have been in vain. The mayor proposes that he and Thomas reach a compromise. If Thomas gives his scientific stamp of approval now, then later "the management, in principle, will not be disinclined to consider whether it would be possible to provide some improvements with a reasonable expense" (69). In other words, Peter asks his brother to be *realistic* in the capitalist sense of the word. Shunned by the entire community, Thomas Stockmann shows up to the town hall meeting and delivers an impassioned speech, the gist of which is that "the most dangerous enemy of truth and freedom amongst us is the compact majority" (154). The play ends with Dr. Stockmann professing that he will continue the fight alone (219). The success of Thomas's revolt, however, is uncertain, given the tempting proposition that he receives at the end of the play and the way Ibsen's drama is framed.

The exposition and the denouement of *An Enemy of the People* are punctuated with the arrival of Morten Kiil, Thomas's wealthy father-in-law and the owner of the tanneries at Molledal. Kiil thus figures as the personification of capital and the play's deus ex machina. He is the source of Thomas's wife's future inheritance and of the town's ongoing business. When Kiil first appears onstage, he insinuates that Thomas's discovery about the poisonous waters is an opportunistic fiction meant to ruin the board of the Baths, which had expelled Kiil. So Kiil advises Thomas to keep up this game (47). Thomas disregards this remark as a sign of dotage, though later it is revealed to be a speculator's careful assessment of the financial climate. Kiil cares not about the facts—whether or not the waters are actually polluted—but only about what the official announcement regarding the water supply can do for his business. At the end, Kiil uses the entire inheritance meant for Thomas's wife as capital to buy all the shares of the Baths, which he then offers to Thomas. They are worth nothing at that point, but if Dr. Stockmann were to change his stance on the quality of the waters and announce that the Baths are safe after all, the shares would skyrocket. After Kiil's departure, Hovstad and Aslaksen show up apologizing profusely for their conduct toward Thomas at the town hall meeting. Now that word has spread that Thomas's father-in-law has been acquiring all the shares of the Baths, Hovstad and Aslaksen suspect that his claim about the water supply was part of a ploy to drive down the prices of stocks. They are thus willing to accept Thomas more as a savvy speculator than as an idealist who upholds the integrity of scientific research; they offer to represent him and his family in the best light to the public. Essentially, the two blackmail Thomas and ask for a percentage of his profits. As Hovstad reminds Thomas, "This case of the shares can be represented in two ways" (209). Ibsen chooses to end his drama with Thomas utterly appalled at the society in which he finds himself, as he chases Hovstad and Aslaksen out of his house and tells his wife that he is prepared to fight alone.

It bears noting that the vision that Ibsen's original leaves us with at this end is that of radical individualism—what is often referred to as Ibsen's anarchist streak, or what Ivo de Figueiredo calls Ibsen's "aristocratic individualism."[69] There is no call for collective action to overhaul the system that puts economic pressure on each and every citizen of the town. It is Thomas Stockmann against everyone else. Ironically, this spirit of radical individualism (which emerges at the end of *A Doll's House* as well) is characteristic both of bourgeois subjectivity and of capitalist ideology. At the same time, Ibsen does put this capitalist self on trial in *Peer Gynt*, where the "Gyntian self" of the "*filthy* rich capitalist," as Branislav Jakovljević dubs him, "makes a prophet of himself" in order to embrace his capitalist megalomania and "obsessive imperial desire."[70] Still, by dramatizing the inherent contradictions of the capitalist world that he was chronicling (in particular, all the ways that his characters genuinely try to uphold the ideals of freedom and equality and try to do the right thing but end up succumbing to the profit motive and to capital accumulation), Ibsen left a potential space for productions to push the immanent critique even further.

Thomas Ostermeier's *An Enemy of the People* and Capitalist Realism

Thomas Ostermeier's 2012 production of a radically transformed adaptation of *An Enemy of the People* by Florian Borchmeyer for the Schaubühne am Lehniner Platz cast a shadow of doubt over Thomas Stockmann's ability to resist Morten Kiil's Faustian bargain.[71] Instead of emphasizing Thomas's strength of will, this contemporary version chose to highlight the lure of capital latent in Ibsen. In the last stage picture, Thomas (Stefan Stern) and his wife Katharina (Eva Meckbach) are at the end of their rope. Shunned by their community, fired from their jobs, and given notice of eviction, they sit on their living room couch drinking beer. A baby is heard wailing in the background. They pick up the document for the shares left by Morten Kiil (Thomas Bading), read the numbers, and exchange looks. The lights go out, and the audience is left in the pitch dark to contemplate whether the decision to go ahead with Kiil's plan is an unforgivable weakness or whether the decision not to is an act of insanity. Ostermeier's production focused on the family as the most potent unit of socialization and the strongest pull that society exerts on individuals to concede and to comply with the status quo. The almost incessant crying of Stockmann's baby throughout the production drove this point home.

Borchmeyer and Ostermeier do away with the last vestige of idealism in Ibsen—the belief in the integrity of scientific research and scientific fact.[72] In the original text, when Morten Kiil mentions that if Thomas sticks with his "mad idea," he stands to lose everything, Thomas briefly entertains the idea that "it might be possible for science to discover some prophylactic . . . or some antidote" for the toxic waters (201). Yet he quickly abandons this hypothesis as nonsense, and Ibsen does not venture into the cynical place of imagining what would happen if scientific research were to go corporate and bend its results to fit the demands of the market. Marx hints at this possibility when he writes that "invention becomes a business, and the application of science to direct production itself becomes a prospect which determines and solicits it."[73] For Ostermeier's version, Borchmeyer added a few disturbing lines to Morten Kiil's selling pitch to show how seductive capital can be. Instead of trying to win Dr. Stockmann over with promises of financial security and wealth, Kiil reminds Thomas that no scientific discovery is 100 percent accurate. What if he made a computation mistake somewhere along the lines? What if the waters are not as detrimental as the first tests had shown? Maybe, Kiil speculates, Thomas took his samples on a day when the level of pollution was way off because of some natural aberration. In other words, Kiil tries to seduce Thomas with the language of science by offering him a scientific justification for accepting the shares. He invites the scientist to speculate in the contemplative sense of the word, that is, to imagine a variety of possible scenarios in the future so that the meaning of truth itself becomes relative and up for grabs.

What is more, Kiil suggests that if Thomas were to gain control of the Baths, he would have the power to use science for good and even discover an antidote for the waters if the subsequent tests still show that they are dangerous. Here again, we see the capitalist ideology of optimism that takes hold of Ibsen's protagonists who hope the market will eventually swing in their favor. Kiil encourages Thomas to view the process of scientific discovery itself as a financial speculation, inviting him to bet on the future possibility of an invention that will eventually make the Baths a safer place and atone for the present cover-up. All that Thomas would be agreeing to is letting the Baths function in their current condition for the time necessary for the investments to pay off.

Ostermeier describes his directing "work as based on 'capitalist realism'"—"where every reading and interpretation is allowed . . . where the self-determination of an essential kernel within a subjective individual no longer exists, when all can be deconstructed."[74] Ostermeier's use of "capitalist realism," with its ironic nod to socialist realism,[75] finds an echo in Mark Fisher's use of "capitalist realism" to describe the "pervasive *atmosphere*" and ideology that makes it "impossible even to imagine a coherent alternative" to capitalism.[76] According to Fisher, capitalist realism is characterized by the fantasy of the infinite expansion of capital and by "reflexive impotence." That is, people "know things are bad, but more than that, they can't do anything about it."[77] As a theatrical aesthetic, however, capitalist realism is different from its ideology. The intellectual impasse at the end of Ibsen's plays discussed in this chapter and his resort to the deus ex machina of capital might be a call to action outside the theater. Ostermeier seems to gesture to such a call to action by opening up the play's town hall meeting to his audience and by asking the spectators to engage in a public conversation about what is to be done. Of course, this is all still talk. But at least, in a Brechtian manner, it points to the fact that there is political work to be done outside the theater.

In the original text of *An Enemy of the People*, Ibsen's way out of the stalemate of a corrupt system is to end the play with a cry of despair. We hear one lone man's voice of reason defying the whole system that he faces. Written in the wake of the public outcry over his scandalous *Ghosts*, *An Enemy of the People* was Ibsen's challenge to his audience. When *Ghosts* was published in 1881, theaters across Europe refused to touch the script. Even Frederik Hegel, Ibsen's publisher, thought his client "had gone too far" after the latter made him lose a considerable amount of money.[78] Through the voice of his protagonist, the playwright declares that he will continue to speak the truth no matter how vehemently his audience protests.

The capitalist realist playwrights who wrote in the wake of Ibsen, such as Shaw, Wilde, and Granville-Barker, would turn the critical blade onto themselves. Instead of singling out paragons of resistance, their plays would highlight the complicity of each and every member in perpetuating the social order through the motifs of "tainted" money and toxic inheritances.[79] Rather than imagine a way out of the irresoluble contradictions of the political economy, these playwrights made the intellectual dilemma and the political gridlock the very source of dramatic tension in their works. Despite the conflict onstage, very little gets done, and the status quo is reaffirmed. Yet this troubling reaffirmation is a perversely happy ending meant to leave the audience with a sour aftertaste, as capital takes the form of a deus ex machina that artificially and perfunctorily takes care of the plot and the unsolvable moral problem at the end. In Ibsen's modern drama, capital has expelled the god from the machine, along with his or her divine justice, and replaced it with the relentless logic of the market, echoing Hans Blumenberg's argument that in modernity "the position of transcendence was reoccupied by the element of postponement."[80] The invisible hand of the market makes its material grasp felt onstage through either the sudden arrival of a wealthy capitalist who decides the fate of the rest of the characters (Mrs. Wilton in Ibsen's *John Gabriel Borkman*) or a business deal (Shaw's *Widowers' Houses*), a reference to the stock exchange (Shaw's *Mrs. Warren's Profession*), a reference to the corporation (Shaw's *Major Barbara*), a nod to invisible shareholders (Galsworthy's *Strife*), accounting (Elmer Rice's *The Adding Machine*), or the appearance of financial shares (Ibsen's *An Enemy of the People*).

In an unsettling way that is meant to leave the audience with rotten food for thought, economic efficiency often has the last word. This is how the theater of capital performs the task of immanent critique of political economy. The main economic question that these capitalist realist works test is whether the free market works in the way that liberalism claims it does, namely, that the free market self-regulates by means of a fair competition established between free agents pursuing their own interests. Even if many critics of capitalism argue that it does not, theater can show exactly *how* the free market fails. Thus, in Ibsen's *Pillars of the Community* and *An Enemy of the People*, we witness how the desires for efficiency, economic prosperity, and return on investment are taken too far—to the detriment of the community.

Ayad Akhtar's *The Invisible Hand*: War and the "Free" Market

One contemporary example of the theater of capital that puts the free market on trial in the spirit of Ibsen is Ayad Akhtar's *The Invisible Hand* (2014), which presents its audience with a covert lesson in economics, explaining various concepts: a future, an option, a put, insider trading, Bretton Woods system, and, of course, the invisible hand. Akhtar puts to the test Adam Smith's famous claim from *The Wealth of Nations*, which also serves as the play's epigram: "It is not from the benevolence of the butcher, the brewer, or the baker that we expect our dinner, but from their regard to their own interest. We address ourselves not to their humanity but to their self-love."[81] Like Ibsen, Akhtar has a solid grasp of economics. Before turning to playwriting, he read the *Wall Street Journal* daily and *Barron's* on the weekend. Akhtar's father had struck a deal with him—he promised to pay Akhtar's rent if the latter read the *Wall Street Journal* every day.[82]

The Invisible Hand is a financial thriller that captures and maintains its audience's attention by means of suspense. Nick Bright, an investment banker, finds himself kidnapped for ransom in Pakistan and strikes a deal with his captors: he will make his own $10 million ransom by playing the market. In the process, Nick ends up teaching his guard Bashir the American way of finance. The pedagogical setup is not forced but makes perfect sense given the plot. Re-creating the fervid energy of the stock market, Akhtar's theater of capital turns finance into a thrilling spectacle, mimicking the excitement and anxiety experienced by those who trade stocks. Will Nick earn money for his ransom? Will luck be on his side? In between the trades, Nick shares his liberal ideas regarding the efficiency and fairness of the market: "The free market is guided by the confluence of everyone's self-interest, like an invisible hand moving the market" (60). This is the theory that the play will put into practice, experimenting with some of its potential outcomes. How far can one take this view? In Akhtar's drama of ideas, Bashir serves as a raisonneur who pokes holes in Nick's free-market ideology, especially regarding Nick's belief in the information advantage.[83] Bashir begins to wonder if there is a difference between finding out information that no one has figured out yet and instigating events in order to manipulate the market—precisely the kind of scenario that Morten Kiil suggests to Doctor Stockmann at the end of *An Enemy of the People*. In *The Invisible Hand*, we witness Bashir transform, thanks to Nick's lessons, from a man who once believed that keeping an interest-paying bank account is against Allah's will into a man who blows up Pakistan's state bank along with all the members of its board to drive down the rupee. In this light, the market is revealed to be not some mysterious, dispassionate entity, some invisible hand that autocorrects human greed, but the economic, physical, and systemic violence of war. When Bashir finally releases Nick into the war zone where blood is "flowing in the streets," Nick's "freedom" turns into an indictment of liberalism and laissez-faire capitalism (112). While the play certainly presents a trenchant critique of capitalism, especially the way that American liberalism forces the ideology of the free market onto the rest of the world, this critique is arrived at only after a serious and in-depth exploration of the core ideas and entrenched values of capitalism. The invisible hand of the market conceals violence and the exploitation of labor. Like Marx, Akhtar suggests that the invisible hand is not that of capital but that of labor.[84] This is also Ibsen's insight.

Moretti argues that Ibsen's realist plays mainly focus on the bourgeoisie and that there are "no workers in the experiment—even though the years of the cycle, 1877–1899, are those when trade unions, socialist parties and anarchism are changing the face of European politics."[85] Yet there *are* workers in Ibsen whose labor is hidden and erased precisely because it was not represented in the trade unions of the time. Ibsen's drama sheds light on the invisibility of the labor of women, the process of its erasure, and its connection to the larger economy and culture of financialization in *A Doll's House*.

Nora's Backhand: *Hygge* and the Hidden Labor of Women

A dollhouse is an apt metaphor for theater as a space to experiment with economic ideas and models. Not only is a dollhouse a three-dimensional model, its history is also bound up with pedagogy, class politics, colonialism, and women's labor. Before they were toys, dollhouses had two purposes: an exhibition of wealth and education. Because they were traveling without women, English colonists regularly brought along with them dolls and other toys (such as hobbyhorses) to communicate with Indigenous peoples by means of what D. B. Quinn calls "musical diplomacy"—a musical theater involving humans and puppets. The colonists aimed to show that they, too, had women back home and to "delight the savage people, whom [they] intended to win by all Faire meanes possible."[86] The term "Dutch wife," which today means a body-length pillow, was one of the earliest sex dolls made from cloth, which Dutch sailors took with them on their long voyages of colonial expansion. As we will soon see, this historical fact finds an echo in the theme of sexual exploitation in Ibsen's *A Doll's House*. And in sixteenth-century Germany, "Nuremberg kitchens" were popular instructional tools for socializing girls. Mothers would use them to teach their daughters how to manage their future households and servants.

The nineteenth-century market economy transformed the definition of childhood by emphasizing the importance of play. With the advent of the Industrial Revolution and the proliferation of mass-produced objects, dollhouses became toys.[87] Tellingly, at the start of *A Doll's House*, Nora comes home after her Christmas shopping having bought a doll and a doll's cot for her daughter. The mass production of dollhouses, marketed for the consumption of little girls, increasingly relied on the labor of women and children. Yet this labor was not immediately visible. As the poet Susan Stewart notes, the toy dollhouse becomes a symbol of the "erasure of labor" in modernity, as play becomes a "celebration of the mechanism for its own sake" and "a promise of immortality, the immortal leisure promised by surplus value."[88] Yet this "immortal leisure" was available to some classes and denied to others.

The main economic question that drives *A Doll's House* is Nora's first question at the top of the play: "How much?"[89] The question is addressed to the porter, but it also broadly applies to Nora's entire home, her *oikos*, displayed onstage. How much does it cost to maintain a household like the Helmers', and whose labor does it depend on? And most importantly, what *is* money in the play? As Elizabeth Hardwick puts it, "*A Doll's House* is about money, about the way it turns locks."[90] Many critics concur, ably tracing the play's various economic metaphors.[91] Little attention, however, has been paid to *what* the play shows money actually to be. Exploring *A Doll's House* as an economic world where what is at stake is not just the fate of one woman, Nora, but the management of an entire household (*oikos*) offers a more nuanced panorama of capitalist modernity and the play's dramatization of the nature of money. In the 140 years since *A Doll's House* premiered on December 21, 1879, at the Royal Theatre in Copenhagen, Denmark, critics have focused almost exclusively on the character of Nora and the play's resounding end. Thus, feminist interpretations of *A Doll's House*, most notably the excellent analyses of Toril Moi and Joan Templeton, center on Nora, who understandably tends to steal the spotlight.[92] It is not hard to see why. The greatest actors of their generations have interpreted the role. Marx's youngest daughter, Eleanor, famously played Nora in a private performance in her living room alongside Bernard Shaw as Nils Krogstad, May Morris (the daughter of William Morris) as Kristine Linde, and Eleanor's husband, Edward Aveling, as Torvald Helmer.[93] Nora, especially when she dances the tarantella, is the very personification of theatricality onstage.[94]

Since its premiere, audiences have wondered: What happens to Nora after she slams the door? Already during Ibsen's lifetime, many sequels were penned attempting to answer this very question, even though the play offers plenty of hints about what Nora might do, indeed, what she has been doing all along to survive. If we turn our attention to the question of women's work, then, surely we would do well to pay attention to all the women in the play, including Kristine Linde and Anne-Marie, as well as to the relationships forged between them, taking into consideration the intersections of gender and class.

The Norwegian title, *Et dukkehjem*, is Ibsen's spin on a term that literally translates as a "doll home"—in other words, "a small, cozy, neat home."[95] The word "home," *hjem*, appears twenty-nine times in the text. All the characters bring up the idea of home at one point. Nora and Torvald stress how lovely and comfortable their family home is. Rank repeatedly refers to their home as beautiful. The nanny, Anne-Marie, had to leave her home and daughter because she had no other means of economic survival but to accept employment as Nora's nanny and then to stay on to help Nora raise *her* children. Historically, theater productions have often cut the scenes between Nora and Anne-Marie for the sake of time, but recent shows have instead highlighted the economic subjugation of Anne-Marie. For example, Alfredo Castro's 2006 production for Chile's Teatro Nacional in Santiago drew attention to the scenes between Nora (Amparo Noguera) and Elena (Mireya Moreno), as the nanny is called in this version, to show the significant presence of the maid in the middle-class household of post-Pinochet Chile.[96] Likewise, in Thomas Ostermeier's 2002 *Nora* for Berlin's Schaubühne, the nanny and maid were morphed into one character, Monika (played by Agnes Lampkin), a housekeeper from an unidentified country in Africa. The production took the relationship between Nora (Anne Tismer) and Monika as an opportunity to broach issues of immigration and racism in the yuppie household of reunified Germany.

Just as important as references to Helmers' home is the word used to describe it—*hyggeligt*, which is in fact the very first word of the play. Ibsen's directions indicate that his marital drama opens in "a cozy and tasteful but not expensive-looking living room" (2). Unfortunately, the English word "cozy" does not do justice to the Dano-Norwegian *hyggeligt*, which comes from the noun *hygge*, a cultural concept that, by the mid-nineteenth century, already conjured up an entire bourgeois atmosphere. Perhaps the English expression "home and hearth" comes closest to capturing its meaning. Thanks to global capitalism, the Anglo-American world today too can enjoy *hygge*, which was a finalist for the *Oxford English Dictionary*'s word of the year in 2016.[97] *Hygge* is a Danish and Norwegian term that evokes feelings of coziness, safety, and togetherness. The joy of spending time with friends and loved ones. A perfect winter day. A fireplace. A delicious cup of hot chocolate or mulled wine. A good conversation. It stems from the old Nordic and originally meant "seeking refuge, protection, and shelter from the raging of the outside elements."[98] It came into use in the eighteenth century and was already a thoroughly bourgeois bromide by the time Ibsen put it on trial in the first scene of *A Doll's House*. Although the Helmers' living room has often been viewed as the epitome of realist drama, it is essential to keep in mind the extent to which their living room is chock-full of clichés associated with *hygge*, including books in handsome bindings, a Christmas tree, a rocking chair, an array of porcelain art objects, and a fireplace that is keeping the house warm in the winter.[99] In a way, *A Doll's House* opens on a note of exaggeration. Ibsen is laying it on thick. Here the stove is still the epicenter of comfort. Ibsen will later recycle the stove in *Hedda Gabler*, where it becomes an instrument of destruction.

Almost all the characters in *A Doll's House*—Nora, Torvald, Dr. Rank, and Kristine—refer to the Helmers' home as a source of *hygge*. Dr. Rank tells Nora he will miss the lovely, cozy evenings at the Helmers. Nora emphasizes that Torvald really knows how to conjure up that good *hygge*. Kristine thanks Nora for a *hyggeligt* evening. During their reconciliation scene, Kristine tells Krogstad that what she desires most in her life is a home (*hjem*) into which she can bring some *hygge*. *A Doll's House* is thus a story about what it takes to achieve and upkeep such a cozy, safe home, free from anxiety, which is another important aspect of *hygge*—there should be no unpleasant sentiments, only joy and happiness. This is not a space to receive a friend who is showing signs of a terminal illness. Hence, when Dr. Rank realizes that he is dying, he shuts himself off and stops going to the Helmers'. Most importantly, *hygge*, in principle, means freedom from financial worries. This is why it is so vital to Torvald that the upkeep of their home does not depend on debt. In short, while *hygge* costs money to maintain, it should not show it.

A Doll's House is not simply a moral tale about bourgeois complacency and complicity, however. To condemn Nora and Torvald in this way is to distance them from us and to miss the illusions of the economic world that they, along with us, often buy into. As Marx points out, the commodity has a "mysterious character" because it "reflects the social relation of the producers to the sum total of labour as a social relation between objects, a relation which exists apart from and outside the producers."[100] To put it another way, commodity fetishism misrepresents social relations between people—who are employing whom, under what conditions, and for how long—as objective economic relations among commodities exchanged on the market. *A Doll's House* adds yet another dimension to this reification because Marx did not predict lifestyle branding through which commodities would be bundled and sold together specifically to conjure up a feel-good atmosphere that creates the illusion of still another level of social relations, as in the case with *hygge*. After all, one needs to purchase a whole host of objects to achieve that desired effect of shared warm feelings—from the wool socks to the scented candles. In this light, a relationship between the exploited and the exploiter might appear instead as a different social relation, such as friendship, collegiality, marriage. This is where theater can help expose and untangle the complexity of multi-layered social relationships. But although Ibsen might have criticized his countrymen's obsession with *hygge*, he was not above participating in it if it meant more income for himself. Ibsen requested that his plays be published in November to catch the "Christmas market"—this way, his plays in beautiful bindings could be wrapped up as presents and put under the tree.[101]

How is the economy managed within the Helmers' *hyggeligt* home? What is happening in plain sight, and what is hidden? The background of the play that most readers and spectators tend to focus on is the moment when Nora forged her father's signature to take out a loan. The borrowed money allowed Nora and Torvald to travel to Italy to improve his health. Nora spends the next eight years paying off the loan by saving money from the allowance that Torvald gives her and by taking on a variety of odd jobs—"sewing, crocheting, embroidery, and things like that" (9). This fixation on Nora's crime, however, reinscribes and reenacts the very mechanism of misogyny that Ibsen's play critiques. Nora is not the first person to set off the chain of financial misconduct. To fully appreciate Ibsen's incisive representation of the capitalist economy and the social relations it produces, it is imperative to follow the money. To do this, we would do well to move beyond Nora and to study the entire economic microcosm of the play. As discussed earlier, Ibsen's plays offer a way to rethink the meaning of money beyond a medium of exchange. *Pillars of the Community*, *An Enemy of the People*, and *John Gabriel Borkman* highlight the credit theory of money. *A Doll's House* inadvertently dramatizes Marx's labor theory of money.

One winter, Nora is fortunate to get some copying work. When she shuts herself in her room to do the copying, Torvald believes she is occupied making paper flowers to decorate their Christmas tree. Nora's secret labor is not housework but work directly connected to the larger economy outside their bourgeois home. When Torvald asks Nora what she wants for Christmas, she asks for money and suggests wrapping the money in gilt paper and hanging it on the tree. On both occasions, Christmas decorations are made of paper representing Nora's unseen labor. The difference is that money is paper "with encrypted print" recognized by the government.[102] According to Marx, whose *Capital* (1867) was published the same year as Ibsen's *Peer Gynt*, "Money as a measure of value is the necessary form of appearance of the measure of value which is immanent in commodities, namely labour-time." Put simply, the need for a unified appearance of abstract labor led Marx to the conclusion that that form of appearance must be money.[103] Similarly, as Leonardo Lisi observes, the character of Peer Gynt, whose last name rhymes with *mynt* (coin), circulates like money in the play that bears his name, connecting all the other characters.[104] Although there is no direct evidence that Ibsen ever read Marx, Ibsen had plenty of practical experiences with money, banking, and investment, and, as Lisi points out, both Ibsen and Marx were influenced by Goethe's *Faust*.[105]

A Doll's House reveals a more nuanced picture of labor performed by women. Although many feminist scholars have had, at best, an ambiguous relationship with Marxism, from the late 1960s to the 1980s scholars like Margaret Benston, Mariarosa Dalla Costa, Silvia Federici, and Wally Seccombe all revalued housework.[106] The point they all agree on is that women's housework is not compensated and is thus invisible because of its removal from the wage relation. All the while, women are also responsible for reproducing the reserve army of labor through childbirth and domestic caregiving. *A Doll's House* shows that by the nineteenth century, bourgeois women were already on triple duty—housework, caregiving, and the odd job outside the house.[107] Ibsen's play also suggests that mere compensation for women's invisible labor is not enough to do away with exploitation. In a sense, Torvald is already paying Nora for the management of their home: we see him give her money for Christmas household expenses and something for herself. These payments are problematic because they establish a coercive sex-bartering economy within their household.

Nora's predicament in *A Doll's House* reflects the historical reality of both Norwegian and British working- and middle-class women in the nineteenth century, who had to work in order to help cover their families' expenses. Some of the sectors they joined included the factory, family business, and domestic service. Women's work, however, was not always recorded by sources that historians study because much of women's work, like Nora's, was sporadic, part-time, home-based, or within a family business. It was only in the 1860s that women in Norway "were allowed to support themselves through handicraft and craftsmanship on the same conditions as men."[108] Moreover, women's wages were considered secondary income and not as important as their husbands' income, even though they were necessary for the family's economic survival. Census documents from the early nineteenth century often leave blank spaces for the occupation column under women's names—even though we now have proof from sources dating from the 1850s that women performed a diverse range of paid labor.[109] As Pat Hudson points out, women may have preferred to keep their work outside the home and other "money-raising activities" secret because they did not see such supplementary work "as a centrally defining characteristic of their lives" in the way that marriage and motherhood were regarded.[110] Women's work was also devalued in another significant way. According to David Harvey, throughout history skilled labor has been categorized "in gendered terms." A task could be deemed unskilled "simply because women could do it."[111] Even today, the feminization of many branches of labor persists. For example, personal digital assistants are anthropomorphized as female: Siri, Alexa, Cortana.

One of Ibsen's most important economic insights about women's work is the indelible fact that household management plays a crucial role in the social reproduction of class society. As Anna Westerståhl Stenport puts it in her rich and historically grounded reading, *A Doll's House* "clearly seeks to challenge the gendered conventions of production and consumption, and of public and private spheres."[112] Ibsen's insight is particularly impressive given the historical context in which he lived and wrote, a time when, as Nancy Armstrong has shown, political economy was considered the realm of men, and domesticity—that is, the realm of women—was ideologically promoted as "the only haven from the trials of a heartless economic world."[113] *A Doll's House*, by contrast, shows that it is impossible to separate the reproduction of labor power from the overall reproduction of capitalist society.[114] Like any capitalist household, the Helmers' home depends on the accumulation of capital and participates in the consumption of commodities. Nora needs to earn money from her irregular jobs—"sewing, crocheting, embroidery," but also "copying"—in order to keep her financial crime a secret. That crime enabled Torvald to get back into the workforce so that he could continue to accumulate capital, so it is a never-ending cycle. No doubt, Ibsen's economic lesson (that the private household was an integral part of the social reproduction of the entire capitalist society) was enabled and made all the more prominent by the fact that the private and public spheres collide in the theater through the work of the actress. As Tracy Davis has persuasively shown, the nineteenth-century actress embodied the contradiction of performing "an idealized femininity" (whose realm was the home) in public, onstage.[115]

Like Torvald's position in the bank, Nora's secret side jobs are crucial for the management and financial survival of their *hyggeligt* home. And both spouses, not just Nora, commit a crime in order to afford their bourgeois marriage in the first place. Although Nora's forgery often receives the most attention, Torvald's record is not spotless. To marry Nora, Torvald too had to immerse himself in the murky ethical waters of capitalist modernity. Throughout the play, we are given numerous signs of idealist Torvald's supposedly high moral standards but also clues to his failings. As

Nora informs Mrs. Linde early on, "Being a lawyer is an insecure way to make a living, especially if you do not want to deal with businesses that are not fine and beautiful" (8). Presumably this, along with the lack of prospects for a promotion, was why Torvald left the Ministry when he married Nora. Yet the true motive behind Torvald's departure is revealed in the play gradually, with the final piece of the puzzle falling into place during the confrontation over Krogstad's letter, when Nora's offense comes to light. So does Torvald's. "Oh, how I have been punished for turning a blind eye to him," Torvald says to Nora (68).[116] Torvald left the Ministry not too long after he was called to investigate Nora's father, whose unidentified financial activities were hovering in "the grey area."[117] Shortly after that, Torvald leaves his post ("when we were married"), and during that first year, he overworks, tries to make ends meet, and falls ill (10). The rest is history. If Torvald had not saved Nora's father, she would have lost her dowry and reputation. No marriage would have been possible then. These details are all available in the text, but they are scattered because Nora is being framed from the very beginning. In a sense, the play first encourages us to look at Nora's actions through the eyes of men and then puts that same male perspective on trial. For this reason, focusing solely on the character of Nora is insufficient.

Only by taking a step back and studying the *oikos* of the entire household can we begin to see what every agent contributes to its management. Nora gets caught, while Torvald and her father do not, because, as Ibsen explains in "Notes for a Modern Tragedy": "There are two kinds of moral laws, two kinds of conscience, one for men and one, quite different, for women."[118] In 1884, Ibsen supported a petition in favor of separate property rights for married women, emphasizing (in a somewhat patronizing manner) that men should not be consulted about this property bill because "to consult men in such a manner is like asking wolves if they desire better protection for the sheep."[119] Like the foundation of the corporation in *Pillars of the Community* and like the infrastructure of the baths in *An Enemy of the People*, the foundation of the bourgeois marriage in *A Doll's House* is revealed to be corrupt. The management of the marital household is exposed as relying on the exploitation of women's labor.

The issue of women's work also features prominently in the journey of widow Kristine Linde, who relates her trials and tribulations to Nora in the following manner: "Yes, I had to make ends meet through a bit of trade and a bit of teaching and whatever else I could come up with. The last three years have been one long relentless workday for me" (12). Kristine is also the one character that the audience actually witnesses performing work—she mends Nora's tarantella costume. In act 2, Nora asks Kristine to "help her with her costume," but at no point do we see Nora do any work on it (37). Kristine is the one doing all the sewing in real time. When Kristine goes into the other room to continue her work offstage because, as Nora points out, her husband "can't stand the sight of mending lying about," Torvald walks in and asks: "Was that the seamstress . . . ?" Nora responds: "No, it was Kristine; she's helping me with my costume" (37). The next time Kristine reappears onstage is to announce that she has finished fixing Nora's dress. In a metatheatrical manner, this episode exposes the labor being performed offstage during performances of *A Doll's House*. Torvald presumably thinks Nora and he can afford a dressmaker, but his wife, who needs her allowance to repay her debt, knows better. So she asks Kristine to do it for free because, after all, are they not friends? She also asks Kristine to do her hair for the party. In still another metatheatrical twist, Kristine Linde figures as the invisible costume and makeup designer for Nora's performance of the tarantella. Is Nora taking advantage of Kristine? Or is she simply asking a favor in return for putting a good word in for her to Torvald? After all, Kristine getting her post at the bank is directly connected to Krogstad losing his. In turn, Nora's dance also highlights the theatrical labor of the nineteenth-century actor. As Moi persuasively argues, Nora's tarantella is an example of Ibsen's "fully realized" modernism, as he "asks us to consider that even the most theatrical performance may at the very same time be a genuine expression of the human soul."[120]

A Doll's House expresses anxiety about women entering the workforce and competing with men for employment but, in the end, skirts the issue by conveniently reconciling Kristine Linde and Nils Krogstad. On the one hand, with Kristine becoming the primary breadwinner and Nils becoming "the unproductive consumer at home," the play offers, as Stenport points out, "an unexpected reversal" of gender economic roles.[121] On the other hand, Ibsen sexualizes the intrabourgeois conflict (in this instance, between the employed and the unemployed) so that work competition can be (for the time being) resolved through marriage. The question of how well this setup will work in a *hyggeligt* home is left unanswered. It would be up to Strindberg to challenge the capacity of the sexual contract of marriage to resolve the class struggle and other socioeconomic conflicts.

A Doll's House is constantly undoing the concept of a traditional *hyggeligt* home by exposing what lies beneath the supposedly safe haven, free from financial worries, unresolved tensions, and uncomfortable truths. For example, when Kristine asks Nora why she is hiding the truth from Torvald, Nora's first response is that it would be humiliating for Torvald's masculine independence. But on second thought she adds that "it might be good to have something up [her] sleeve" for the time when she has lost her appeal to Torvald, when her "dancing and dressing-up [literally: "disguising herself"] and reciting no longer have any effect on him" (10). The literal translation from the Dano-Norwegian reads, "It might be good to have something in the *backhand* [*i baghånden*]" (10, emphasis added). The labor that Torvald values Nora for is emotional and sexual—her ability to perform "tricks" for him and to continue being physically attractive. The most significant work, however, that Nora has been doing to keep their household financially afloat involves all the secret side jobs outside the home that she took up to repay her loan. Thus, the invisible hand of the market—the debt with interest, which moves the action of the play—turns out to be not just immaterial capital but also Nora's hidden labor—manual, emotional, and sexual.

The "Sexonomics" of *A Doll's House*

There is perhaps a double entendre in the play's title, as *dollhouse* (or *doll home*) is a well-known synonym for a brothel. What on the surface appears to be a cozy home of a respectable bourgeois couple betrays signs of a barter economy of sex, echoing Engels's view of marriage in *The Origin of the Family, Private Property, and the State* (1884). According to Engels, a marriage that is "conditioned by the class position of the parties" is "to that extent a marriage of convenience," and such a "marriage of convenience turns often enough into crassest prostitution—sometimes of both partners, but far more commonly of the woman, who only differs from the ordinary courtesan in that she does not let out her body on piecework as a wage-worker, but sells it once and for all into slavery."[122] This idea will be explored in greater detail in the following chapter. Indeed, the silk stockings with which Nora playfully hits Dr. Rank across the ear do not fit into the economy of *hygge*. "As far as I can see," writes Strindberg in his uncharitable reading of *A Doll's House*, "Nora is offering herself—in return for hard cash."[123] Of course, this is not exactly the case, and Nora can only entertain the possibility of receiving money from Dr. Rank if the erotic exchange is veiled as something else—the generous help of a friend, for example. For this reason, when Dr. Rank finally verbalizes his feelings for Nora and admits that his friendship has always had a romantic undercurrent (of which Nora must have been at least on some level aware), she ultimately decides against asking him for a financial favor. As Shepherd-Barr notes, "[The] sexual force underlying *A Doll's House* is one of its key elements, all the more difficult to sustain and convey because it is not explicit but deeply imbedded in the dialogue and gestures of the characters."[124] In *Hedda Gabler*, Ibsen would make the dubious family friend an even more pervasive part of the financial economy of the Tesmans' household, with Judge Brack "securing the most favorable terms" for George Tesman's loans in exchange for potential access to his wife.[125] In this way, in *Hedda Gabler*, the financial and sexual predator are the same character.

In her reading of *A Doll's House*, Stenport highlights the "spectre of prostitution" that hovers over Nora as she leaves the safe haven of her bourgeois home to walk alone at night in the streets toward an unknowable future. According to Stenport, whatever "individualism and universalism" is celebrated at the end of *A Doll's House*, these are "compromised by a relentlessly conformist sexonomic structure that neither Nora nor Torvald can ever escape."[126] In other words, regardless of any other scenarios that we can imagine for Nora (including one where she is sheltered by Mrs. Linde and then follows her example in searching for a job at a school), the very fact that Nora might be mistaken for a prostitute and arrested for walking alone at night should draw our attention to the possibility of prostitution. In her incisive analysis, Stenport coins the term "sexonomics" to describe the nineteenth century's "complex discursive relationships between money, gender, sex, and economic paradigms."[127] But sexonomics is not new.

In fact, nineteenth-century economic thought had already begun to explore this tangled relationship between sexuality and economics. Charlotte Perkins Gilman's acclaimed *Women and Economics: A Study of the Economic Relation between Men and Women as a Factor in Social Evolution* (1898), which social reformer Florence Kelley called "the first real, substantial contribution made by a woman to the science of economics,"[128] describes women's economic dependence on men as the "sexuo-economic relation."[129] This social relation will be explored in further detail in the next chapter, which discusses erotic capital. For now, suffice it to note that the relationship between sex and money goes beyond discourse. As I will argue, the conflation of the discourse of sex and the discourse of money leads to a pernicious obfuscation of economic exploitation and gender violence. What is called for, then, is an in-depth analysis of what forms of capital money takes in the circulation of sex in the nineteenth century, a circulation that includes the interlinked institutions of courtship, marriage, and prostitution. In the next chapter, I will also show that although the specter of prostitution haunts *A Doll's House*, there is at least one other venue of economic independence available to the likes of Nora that Ibsen's compatriot, Benedictsson, explores in her novel *Money* (*Pengar*, 1885), which was a direct response both to *A Doll's House* and to Flaubert's *Madame Bovary* (1856).

In recent years, contemporary directors have picked up on *A Doll's House*'s sexonomics and critique of *hygge*. Most productions tend to abandon the supposed "realism" of Ibsen's play for a more adventurous and experimental interpretation of the text. In a sense, Ibsen's original text already calls for it. As Moi notes, *A Doll's House* is full of metatheatrical moments and the "pro-theatrical use[s] of theater."[130] To give a few examples, in 2010, German director Herbert Fritsch reimagined Ibsen's classic as a Christmas horror story where, by the end of the show, Nora is tossed around like a sex doll.[131] Yuri Kviatkovsky's 2014 *A Doll's House* for the Saint Petersburg State Drama Theater (Priyut Komedianta), which won the prestigious Golden Mask, stages the whole action of Ibsen's play in a futuristic "smart" house whose intelligent operating system does everything, rendering the housewife obsolete except for her role as a pretty object to look at and as a sexual companion. Nora is just one feature of the iSystem. While still embracing theatrical realism, British playwright Tanika Gupta transports the action of her 2019 adaptation to Calcutta, India, of 1879, where Nora is now a woman of Bengali origin named Niru, "married to Tom—an English colonial administrator who worships and eroticizes her."[132] This backdrop allows Gupta to explore the history and vestiges of British colonialism as well as the intersections between race, class, and gender. Instead of ending the play on the sound of the reverberating slammed door inside the Helmers' home, Gupta has her heroine "emerge out on to the night streets of Calcutta," as the audience "hear[s] the sounds of carts and people talking" (101). Niru's future is uncertain and precarious as she prepares to navigate the colonial sexonomics of the British Empire as an estranged wife and woman of color.

Exploring what happens to Nora after she leaves Torvald, a few writers have her turn to prostitution. In Nobel Prize–winning Austrian author Elfriede Jelinek's debut play, *What Happened after Nora Left Her Husband; or Pillars of Society* (1979), Nora goes from factory worker to a rich man's mistress, then to an S/M sex worker and political radical, before returning to Helmer, now a proto-Nazi businessman. And let us not forget one of the most infamous flops in musical theater's history: the 1982 *A Doll's Life* (lyrics by Betty Comden and Adolph Green and music by Larry Grossman), in which Nora becomes a bed-hopping waitress in Kristiania. As Marvin Carlson points out in his review of Lucas Hnath's *A Doll's House, Part 2* (2017), sequels to *A Doll's House* usually take one of two routes—either Nora "becomes an exploited member of the working class" who "is driven to revolt or accommodation" or she becomes a celebrated "writer of feminist novels."[133]

Focusing on the management of the Helmers' household allows us to imagine how Nora could potentially make a living after she slams the door. Kristine Linde's story serves as an example, as does Nora's own hidden labor. Long before Hnath's acclaimed *A Doll's House, Part 2*, Ibsen's play had had an illustrious history of alternative endings and sequels. In Ibsen's own time, audiences wanted to know what exactly happens to Nora after she leaves. A variety of endings were penned, including one by Ibsen himself, where Nora stays. As Ibsen explained to his German translator and business manager Wilhelm Lange, he feared that a version with an alternative ending by someone else would be published and become more popular with the North German theaters, where actors refused to play a woman who leaves her children. The altered scene unfolded in the following manner: "Nora does not leave the house but is forcibly led by Helmer to the door of the children's bedroom. A short dialogue takes place, Nora sinks down at the door, and the curtain falls."[134] In Ibsen's own words, this was a "barbarous outrage," but at least it portrayed Nora as collapsing physically rather than failing in her will or drastically changing her intention. Ibsen's reasons for caving in were partly financial. There was no literary copyright agreement between Norway and other countries, so in Germany and other countries of Scandinavia, the translators and their publishers reaped all the profits, and Ibsen had no legal way of protecting his authorial property rights. He would have to wait until Norway was accorded the copyright protection of the Berne Convention after the follow-up conference in Paris in 1896.

Women Who Write: Lucas Hnath's *A Doll's House, Part 2* and the Story of Laura Kieler

Hnath is not the first playwright to depict Nora returning as a writer. In Walter Besant's *The Doll's House and After* (1890), Nora returns as a writer of New Woman novels only to discover that her decision to leave her family had turned her husband and sons into alcoholics and pushed her daughter to commit suicide. Bernard Shaw wrote a polemical sequel to Besant's version: *Still after the Doll's House: A Sequel to Mr. Besant's Sequel to Henrik Ibsen's Play*. And Eleanor Marx-Aveling, in collaboration with Israel Zangwill, penned a parody of what Victorian critics would have liked to see onstage in *A Doll's House Repaired* (1891).[135]

In Hnath's version, Nora returns as a successful feminist writer. She tells Anne-Marie that she has "done really well" and has made "a lot" of money.[136] Hnath's play asks intelligent questions about the institution of marriage as it stands today but abandons the question of women's labor that Ibsen's original explores with such care and nuance. Instead, Nora's financial success becomes a capitalist fantasy and a wish fulfillment, not a realistic outcome for most women who choose to pick up the pen—during Nora's time or even our own. In this way, Hnath's sequel does not question the capitalist myth of pulling oneself by one's bootstraps. Nora appears as the self-made woman par excellence.

The women that Ibsen knew, however, had a challenging time making a living by writing. Despite her fame and recognition, the Norwegian feminist Camilla Collet, who was friends with Ibsen and his wife, struggled with monetary problems all her life. Victoria Benedictsson, whose first novel, *Money*, written under the male pseudonym Ernst Ahlgren, gained her recognition and even some fortune, was subsequently almost erased from literary history by her lover Georg Brandes, who was at the time the most powerful and prolific critic in Scandinavia. The novelist Laura Kieler, née Petersen, whose real-life story inspired *A Doll's House*, forged a check to pay back the loan that she took out so she could take her ailing husband abroad. Before this act of desperation, she resorted to rushed hackwork to make money. Kieler had made a name for herself and became friends with Ibsen after writing her novel *Brand's Daughters* (1869), a sequel to Ibsen's play *Brand* (1865), so she hoped that he would share her new manuscript with his publisher. Ibsen not only refused to pass her subpar (in his view) manuscript to his publisher but also arguably made use of her life story for his own art. When Kieler's husband found out about the forged check, he took away their children and sent her to an insane asylum. She had to beg him to take her back. Later in life, Laura Kieler achieved recognition as a writer but would resent Ibsen for having made her famous as the inspiration for his fictional Nora rather than an artist in her own right. In the press, a rumor persisted that the real "Nora" forged the check "to decorate her house or pay her dressmaker."[137] To add insult to injury, in *A Doll's House* Nora is portrayed not as an artist but as a copyist.

At the end of *A Doll's House*, no deus ex machina makes a miraculous appearance to tie up loose ends and drive the play to a tragicomic resolution. What we have instead is a difficult conversation, a closing of accounts—a final settlement (*opgør*), as Nora calls it—where for the first time in their marriage, Nora and Torvald can speak their minds (55). *A Doll's House* thus ends with a radical opening onto possibilities that have not yet been realized, perhaps not even imagined. A play that begins with a question of finance—how to afford a *hyggeligt* home and how to pay off a debt—ends with the question of work, the practical and utopian sides of it. On the practical side, the play ends with Nora leaving the home to provide for herself. From the utopian point of view, the play asks what kind of work both men and women would need to do in order to radically change their social relations and to leave the shackles of alienated intimacy behind so that a real partnership could happen.

Not everyone found Ibsen's portrayal of bourgeois marriage convincing, however. For Strindberg, *A Doll's House* was a caricature of "the cultured man and woman."[138] He particularly found fault with Ibsen's uncharitable characterization of Torvald. In his review of *A Doll's House*, Strindberg asks:

> Why then cannot Helmer blame his bad upbringing? Or is it nothing more than a play, pure and simple, an example of our modern courtship of the ladies? If so it should be put among the plays classed as "Public Entertainments," not be regarded as a matter for serious discussion, still less have the honor of setting the two halves of humanity against each other.[139]

Strindberg was not so much justifying Torvald's behavior toward Nora as criticizing Ibsen for not developing in greater detail the husband's background, psychology, and heredity, instead choosing to present him as a doll in order to build up the character of Nora in the eyes of the audience. To give Strindberg credit, we know far more about Nora's childhood and upbringing than we do about Torvald's formative years. In *Miss Julie*, Strindberg would offer his own version of "setting the two halves of humanity against each other" and explore the drama of courtship in the age of capital, which is the subject of our next chapter.

Chapter 2

The Dowry versus Erotic Capital

The Drama of Courtship in Strindberg, Shaw, and Benedictsson

Strindberg's *Miss Julie* and the Contradiction of the Theory of Erotic Capital

There is a striking moment in August Strindberg's *Miss Julie* (*Fröken Julie*, 1888) that has received little attention—Jean pays, or rather pretends to pay, Julie for sex. Soon after Jean and Julie have consummated their relationship and Jean has proposed that they run away and open a hotel at the Italian lakes, he realizes that he has miscalculated Julie's financial situation. "I do not own anything" are her exact words to him.[1] What was supposed to be the "first branch" (*första grenen*) of his class ascendancy turns out to be an unsuccessful speculation on Jean's part, a mistake that he can put behind him, but one that might cost Julie her life (22). What follows is a confrontation during which the new lovers try to define the meaning of their erotic encounter:

> JULIE: Do you know what a man owes [*skyldig*] to the woman he has shamed?
> JEAN [*Takes out his wallet and throws a silver coin on the table*]: You're welcome! I don't want to owe anything [*vara skyldig något*]!
> JULIE [*Without pretending to notice the insult*]: Do you know what the law demands?
> JEAN: Unfortunately the law does not demand a penalty from a woman who seduces a man!
> JULIE: Do you see any way out but to travel, get married, and get divorced?
> JEAN: And if I refuse to enter this misalliance? (27)

Julie talks about marriage, while Jean, with his gesture of flinging the coin in Julie's direction, essentially calls her a prostitute. Earlier, however, when pitching his hotel idea, Jean invited Julie to be his companion (*kompanjon*). His use of the word "companion" explicitly refers to a business partnership and leaves the romantic side of things conveniently ambiguous (21). Given Jean's drawn-out and tenuous "engagement" to Kristin, perhaps a similarly nebulous promise to wed is on the table for Julie. It is only when Jean learns that Julie has no capital to invest in his hotel scheme that his tune changes—her role in his life immediately changes from partner to prostitute.[2] While many eighteenth- and nineteenth-century works of fiction trace the similarities between marriage and prostitution and chronicle women's movements between the two, nowhere does the switch from potential wife to prostitute happen as quickly as it does in *Miss Julie*. All it takes is a throw of a coin. What determines Julie's societal role is money.

This charged stage moment encapsulates the late nineteenth-century discursive and socioeconomic interconnections between financial speculation, marriage, and prostitution. As Gayle Rogers notes, starting in the eighteenth century the marriage market began to be compared to an "actual stock market."[3] When searching for spouses, men were encouraged to be savvy investors. At the same time, the parents of young women of marriageable age were reproached for speculating on their daughters' personal attributes and achievements in hopes of landing rich husbands.[4] What is striking about Julie and Jean's situation is that in their case it is the man who is speculating on his charm and sex appeal to get ahead, while the woman's future is still constrained by the older system of the dowry. In this way, *Miss Julie* dramatizes both the changing gender dynamics at the turn of the century and the turbulent and uneven transition from the importance of the dowry for wedlock to the modern idea of marrying for love.

This chapter explores the inherent contradiction of courtship and the love marriage in the age of capital through a close examination of August Strindberg's *Miss Julie*, Bernard Shaw's *Mrs. Warren's Profession*, and Victoria Benedictsson's *Money* and *The Enchantment* in their historical context. All three writers critique the socioeconomic situation, in which everyone is free in principle to marry for love, but the outcome is often economic coercion and exploitation. As previously emphasized, while the capitalist mode of production gives rise to the ideals of freedom and equality, it results in myriad forms of exploitation, including but not limited to ableism, gender inequality, racism, wealth inequality, and so on. But the capitalist mode of production also generates the possibility of immanent critique, which makes possible the awareness of the discrepancies between liberal ideals and the dismal realities on the ground. Strindberg, Shaw, and Benedictsson throw this contradiction into stark relief by focusing on alienated forms of intimacy under capitalism.

Although courtship as speculation has been a recurring metaphor in educational treatises and works of fiction since the eighteenth century, *what* is actually being speculated with on the marriage market is not always clear. What exactly determines one's value? Is it economic capital, positive personality traits, social accomplishments, physical attributes, or some combination of these? And how does the importance of each of these factors vary with gender? Such questions percolate precisely because what one finds valuable in a potential spouse becomes a matter of contention under capitalism. In Julie and Jean's postcoital negotiations, there are seemingly two forms of capital at stake. There is the dowry, the economic capital that Jean was counting on Julie to have immediate access to. Then there is the noneconomic power that Jean believes he has thanks to his handsome appearance, chameleonic charm, sexuality, and way with words (a skill he acquired by eavesdropping on the conversations of upper-class people, reading novels, and frequenting the theater). This power is not just something that Jean wields over Julie but also something that he hopes to convert into economic capital through their intimate relationship.

Indeed, the marriage plots of many plays and novels often explore how a subject's attractiveness can be translated into financial gain and/or a rise in social status. For example, in Henry James's *The Wings of the Dove* (1902), Aunt Maud refers to her impoverished but charming niece Kate Croy as one of her "investments" that she has been "saving" and "letting ... appreciate" for "a high bidder."[5] Shaw's Kitty Warren, in turn, admits that, as a poor young woman, she profited financially from her looks and "turn for pleasing men."[6] Mrs. Warren might not have married up, but she expects her daughter to make a good match. Although the subject is usually a young woman, the "young man from the provinces" is a literary and dramatic prototype who also often relies on his appearance and charms to get ahead in the big city.[7] Without explicitly naming this type of capital, these works of fiction capture how agents with limited economic resources (dowerless women and young men from the provinces) attempt to speculate with their would-be noneconomic capital, with varying degrees of success.

Sociologist Catherine Hakim's controversial theory of "erotic capital" can not only give this noneconomic form of capital a name but also throw light on its possibilities and limitations as a tool for socioeconomic advancement. Hakim's neoliberal theory has value not because it compellingly explains how sexual desirability can be converted into economic capital (it does not) but because erotic capital, by Hakim's own logic, turns out to be a volatile, risky, and contradictory "personal asset."[8] On rare occasions, it can help a lucky individual rise in social status. More often than not, it proves to be a ruse by which patriarchy under capitalism disguises coercion and exploitation as personal empowerment. In this way, the promise of erotic capital reveals what Rebecca Munford calls "the dangerous slippage between feminist agency and patriarchal recuperation."[9] As Mary

Wollstonecraft already warned her female readers in 1794, when women are encouraged to rely on beauty and "some corporeal accomplishment," they are being "duped by their lovers, as princes by their ministers, while dreaming that they reign over them."[10]

Reading modern dramas alongside Hakim's theory can show us what Hakim gets wrong about Bourdieu's forms of capital (which she claims to expand) and foreground the internal contradiction of courtship under capitalism that these plays register. Moreover, the lineage of Hakim's neoliberal "economism" (i.e., "the tendency to interpret all phenomena in market terms")[11] can be traced back to the emergence of marginalism in the second half of the nineteenth century, a time when modern drama took both bourgeois individualism and marginalist economics to task.

Hakim defines erotic capital as "a combination of aesthetic, visual, physical, social, and sexual attractiveness to other members of . . . society" and identifies it as her contribution to Bourdieu's system of economic, social, and cultural capital.[12] It bears noting that erotic capital, as Hakim emphasizes, is not just physical attractiveness and can include any other quality that might be desirable to others in their search for a short- or long-term sexual or romantic partner, such as personal charisma or what the French call *je ne sais quoi*. It can also overlap with social and/or cultural capital. Acknowledging that erotic capital is an uncertain and unstable asset, Hakim sees its inherent volatility as an advantage. Since, in her view, no class has an intrinsic monopoly on erotic capital, members of the lower classes can employ it for their socioeconomic advancement. According to Hakim, erotic capital has been neglected because "the elite cannot monopolize it, so it is in their interest to marginalize it."[13] In this respect, Hakim's proposal that women climb the social ladder with the help of their feminine wiles sounds a lot like the wish of many a dowerless heroine encountered in nineteenth-century novels and plays. The crucial difference between Hakim's manifesto—which urges women to use erotic capital as a weapon to fight gender inequality by demanding higher pay for it—and the aforementioned fictional works is that the latter are attuned to the "structures of age, race, class and context that mediate women's desirability," while Hakim's theory is not.[14] As Adam Green points out in his critique of Hakim, erotic capital is not "democratically distributed across women" and can be expensive to acquire and preserve if one does not already have financial resources.[15] For example, in Benedictsson's *The Enchantment*, a young woman spends all of her bank savings buying fashionable dresses and maintaining an expensive apartment in Paris, all to keep the romantic interest of a rakish artist. In fact, Bourdieu links the expansion of the fashion and cosmetic industries to the social reality that "certain women derive occupational profit from their charm(s) and that beauty thus acquires a value on the labor market."[16] This is certainly true of Mrs. Warren and the women she employs in her brothels.

Hakim's contradictory theory of erotic capital stems from a profound misunderstanding of Bourdieu's argument about the forms of noneconomic capital, which was influenced by Marx. According to Hakim, Bourdieu and other social scientists failed to recognize erotic capital because it does not have economic capital at its "root," like social and cultural capital, but is "separate, with its own origins and rules."[17] This description of erotic capital proves to be contradictory by Hakim's own logic. First, even as Hakim maintains that erotic capital is not economic in origin (for example, one can simply be born with it), she also insists that anyone can acquire it with the help of cosmetics and fashion (which require spending money). In other words, erotic capital turns out to have an economic origin after all, except in rare cases when it is present at birth; even then, its power is short-lived, and its maintenance always requires financial resources. Second, Hakim compares erotic capital to human capital in that both can be "developed and learned and people can be trained in it."[18] Marxist scholars have long criticized Gary Becker's definition of "investments in human capital" ("activities that influence monetary and psychic income by increasing resources in people") as confounding labor with capital and suppressing arguments about class conflict and the fight for workers' rights.[19] By giving workers a false sense of empowerment through sheer individual effort, the idea of human capital conceals their economic coercion, exploitation, and collective strategies such as protest, strike, and seizing the means of production. As mentioned earlier, this process of obscuring class conflict is at play in the contradictory nature of erotic capital, which also conceals gender inequality.

Moreover, it is simply not true that Bourdieu "overlooked" erotic capital, as Hakim claims.[20] In *Distinction* (1979), Bourdieu mentions that "the logic of social heredity sometimes endows those least endowed in all other respects with the rarest bodily properties, such as beauty (sometimes, 'fatally' attractive, because it threatens the other hierarchies), and, conversely, sometimes denies the 'high and mighty' the bodily attributes of their position, such as height or beauty."[21] Bourdieu was aware that certain people born with attractive physical characteristics could *sometimes* move up the social ladder with the help of their beauty, but he believed this happened so rarely that it did not merit serious attention as a collective strategy for social transformation. Thus, Hakim's most glaring error in reading Bourdieu is ignoring his theory of the field. Social fields, according to Bourdieu, are "arenas of production, circulation, and appropriation and exchange of goods, services, knowledge, or status, and the competitive positions held by actors in their struggle to accumulate, exchange, and monopolize different kinds of power resources (capitals)."[22] To put it another way, erotic capital is not simply a portable personal asset, as Hakim would have it, but is always "embedded," as Green emphasizes, in "structures of race, class, and age."[23] What counts as attractive varies across historical periods, cultures, classes, and social groups. Hakim's own theory throws light on gender inequality that shapes the sexual field. She notes in passing but cannot explain why men are rewarded higher salaries than women for their erotic capital or why some women, especially in prestigious occupations, might be penalized for it.[24] Although Hakim does acknowledge patriarchy's sexual double standard, she offers no solution for overcoming it.

It is important to note all the ways that Hakim misreads Bourdieu because her theory of erotic capital as a tool for upward social mobility is a tempting idea that seduces many characters in bourgeois novels and plays, just the way that the notion of human capital wins over many workers under neoliberalism. Both erotic and human capital might give one a false sense of freedom and empowerment through individual effort and luck rather than class consciousness and solidarity. While Bourdieu rightly claims that socioeconomic rises of the dispossessed and marginalized, fueled by their good looks, are few and far between, Hakim's belief in the possibility of such a socioeconomic rise is widespread and influential. The social messages that women (and men) receive from an early age about the importance of physical attractiveness, money, and fame prove this point.

In this way, Hakim's manifesto—calling on women to demand higher compensation for their erotic capital—is nothing new but goes back to the rise of bourgeois individualism under capitalism. And Hakim's insight that economics and sexuality are intertwined had already been made at the turn of the twentieth century by American writer and socialist Charlotte Perkins Gilman, who was more attuned to structures of age and class than Hakim is. In her acclaimed *Women and Economics: A Study of the Economic Relation between Men and Women as a Factor in Social Evolution* (1898), Gilman argues that human beings "are the only animal species in which the female depends on the male for food, the only animal species in which the sex-relation is also an economic relation."[25] This state of dependency, according to Gilman, results in a family situation where women have to repay the financial support they receive from their husbands by providing them with domestic and sexual services, or what Gilman calls women's "sex functions."[26] As a remedy, Gilman proposes the professionalization of childcare, the specialization and division of labor in housekeeping, and cooperative kitchens to lighten the domestic burden of women. But she also insists that men, too, must change by engaging in labor at home and welcoming women into the public sphere. Echoing John Stuart Mill's *The Subjection of Women* (1869), Gilman stresses that women's socioeconomic advancement would benefit humanity at large.

As I will address in further detail later in the chapter, once the importance of the dowry subsided (but did not disappear) in the marriage market in the late eighteenth century, other noneconomic assets of the would-be bride came into play. These noneconomic assets, such as positive personality traits, intelligence, kindness, beauty, charm, and so on, are what women would speculate with when they tried to marry up. For this reason, the term "erotic capital" becomes helpful in grouping these noneconomic assets under a catchall phrase that serves as a foil to economic capital (the dowry, in the case of marriageable women) and exposes the internal contradiction of courtship under capitalism. In other words, the value of the term "erotic capital" lies in its very contradiction—it presents itself as a capital when it often is not. What was alleged to be a process by which two free agents got to know one another romantically to decide whether there would be an engagement was, in reality, embedded in gender inequality and class conflict. Courtship was a risky business. As Shaw explains in *Getting Married*:

> It is no doubt necessary under existing circumstances for a woman without property to be sexually attractive, because she must get married to secure a livelihood; and the illusions of sexual attraction will cause the imagination of young men to endow her with every accomplishment and virtue that can make a wife a treasure. The attraction being thus constantly and ruthlessly used as a bait, both by individuals and by society, any discussion tending to strip it of its illusions and get at its real natural history is nervously discouraged. But nothing can well be more unwholesome for everybody than the exaggeration and glorification of an instinctive function which clouds the reason and upsets the judgment more than all the other instincts put together. The process may be pleasant and romantic; but the consequences are not.[27]

According to Shaw, a woman's erotic capital (she needs to be "sexually attractive") is a trap to ensnare the inexperienced and unsuspecting young man. Shaw's social diagnosis implies that a woman's erotic capital is a temporary asset that can make up for her lack of property or money on the marriage market. Although Shaw worried that men might be hoodwinked by their sexual desire and not think clearly when choosing whom to marry, the stakes of courtship for women were even higher.

While men tried not to be swayed by mere sexual attraction and look out for their best economic interests when selecting a spouse, women tried to get the maximum return for their erotic capital (marriage) and not accept any arrangement that would harm their reputation (for example, by becoming a kept woman). However, the less economic capital a woman had to begin with, the weaker her bargaining power was.

This is the case in Henry Becque's *comédie rosse The Scavengers*, which dramatizes how a widow and her three daughters are "scavenged" by her late husband's creditors and business associates. While a melodrama might have ended with the serendipitous marriage of one of the daughters, saving the family from poverty, Becque shows the risks of staking financial survival on a woman's erotic capital in such a desperate situation. Although one of the daughters, Marie, does manage to catch the attention of Teissier, a business associate of her deceased father (who profits significantly from his death), his initial proposal to her is to move in with him and become his mistress. Teissier does not think at first that destitute, dowerless Marie can ask for anything more. After all, her sister Blanche witnesses her own engagement fall through when her dowry is swallowed up by the demands of creditors, even though her sexual relationship with her fiancé has already been consummated. According to Teissier's initial calculations, Marie's erotic capital gets her a room in his house and a small monthly stipend, but no matrimony. What changes Teissier's mind is Marie's rejection of his dishonorable offer and his realization that at sixty, his own bargaining power is limited when it comes to getting someone as young and attractive as Marie. His desire stoked by her refusal of him, Teissier finally asks for her hand in marriage, offering her a generous dower (*un douaire*)—half of his fortune after his death.[28] Although, as in a melodrama, Marie's marriage saves her family and her from destitution, the cynical ending does not resolve any social conflicts, leaving the audience with a sour aftertaste, like a *comédie rosse* often does.[29] At the end of the day, Marie marries the man responsible for rendering her family poor in the first place. Moreover, the marriage itself is described as a successful speculation on Marie's part. As the notary Bourdon puts it to Marie and her mother, "You are speculating, and this speculation should bear all its fruit" (537). By playing hard to get with a man much older than herself, Marie is able to convert her erotic capital into economic prosperity, but her sister Blanche, having lost her virginity to her young fiancé, cannot secure a marriage without a dowry. *The Scavengers* thus underscores how erotic capital is embedded in structures of age and class and subject to patriarchy's sexual double standard. Speculating with erotic capital is an unpredictable affair.

A similar cautionary tale is at the heart of Alexander Ostrovsky's play *Without a Dowry* (*Bespridannitsa*, 1879), which centers on an impoverished widow's ill-fated endeavor to marry off her beautiful and musically talented daughter Larisa. The widow, Harita Ogudalova, organizes musical evenings at her home for the purpose of inviting eligible bachelors to meet her daughter. As in *The Scavengers*, the men keep circling Larisa, waiting for her to "fall" so they can scoop her up without marrying her (which would not be in any of their economic interests). Although the man who proposes to Larisa, Yulii Karandyshev, does not do so out of any direct financial benefit for himself, he hopes to achieve social recognition by getting the girl everyone wants but no one is foolish enough to marry. Ostrovsky's play, too, ends on a bitter note. Karandyshev shoots Larisa after she gives herself to the man she loves, the nobleman Sergei Paratov; she erroneously believed the latter intended to marry her. In her final confrontation with Karandyshev, Larisa tells him that love "doesn't exist on this earth" and that "it's no use looking." And since she could not "find love," she will now "search for gold."[30] The cynical ending of *Without a Dowry* echoes that of *The Scavengers*, in which Bourdon tells Marie that "love does not exist . . . , there are only business arrangements in this world" (538). Both plays critique the new capitalist reality where women are treated like commodities on the marriage market and warn women about the risks of speculating with their erotic capital in a man's world. The pessimistic lesson of *The Scavengers* and *Without a Dowry* is that for a dowerless woman to employ her erotic capital for socioeconomic advancement successfully, she must forget all about love.

Even toward the end of the nineteenth century, the dowry was still the most secure capital to guarantee a marriage, since only by becoming a woman's husband could a man gain legal access to her money. Throughout history, the dowry, as Marion Kaplan notes, was "the most significant factor in a young woman's marriageability," influencing the trajectory of her future and thus exposing "the political, economic, and social determinants which limited women's agency."[31] With the advent of capitalism, however, a woman's erotic capital came to figure prominently in the game of courtship. Just how important those other personal and physical attributes were that were *not* the size of her dowry was a crucial question of the epoch. Could a dowerless woman make a good match with the help of such an unstable and unpredictable variable as erotic capital? Because a successful match depended on both luck and a woman's strategic skills of prediction, courtship was often compared to speculation. After all, what a dowerless woman was essentially trying to do on the marriage market was to speculate with her erotic capital in hopes of a financial return, namely a socioeconomic rise or, at the very least, economic security and stability through marriage. Yet erotic capital could only be called a proper "capital" if the speculation turned out to be a successful investment. Otherwise, it was a toxic asset whose consequences were harsher for women than for men.

The unequal compensation for erotic capital and the asymmetrical distribution of risk across gender lines is evident in Strindberg's perceptive portrayal of Jean's versus Julie's ability to gain power through sexuality. As a man in a patriarchal society, Jean has much to gain and little to lose by trying to seduce Julie, whereas she must face punitive social consequences. She suffers while he moves on largely unscathed, even though his financial scheme collapses. The critique of patriarchy in *Miss Julie*, however, goes beyond merely exposing the sexual double standard. Although Strindberg emphasizes Jean's "masculine strength" in the preface, the play highlights not just the way Jean miscalculates the return for his erotic capital but also the way he misjudges all his noneconomic capitals.[32] He takes them to be portable personal assets convertible to money, but he forgets (if only briefly) about the socioeconomic context of the Count's estate, where he is a mere wage-earning laborer and Julie has no capital of her own. Jean regards himself as a free economic agent with many prospects, but the play proves him wrong. He is not as powerful as he believes. Jean and Julie's discussion of what to do before the Count returns reveals Jean's inflated assessment of his different forms of noneconomic capital:

> JEAN: No, but wisely! One folly has been committed—commit no more. The Count may be here at any moment, and before that, our destinies must be decided. What do you think of my plans for the future? Do you like them?
> JULIE: They seem to me quite plausible, but only one question: such a large company requires large capital [*stort kapital*]; do you have it?
> JEAN [*Chewing his cigar*]: I! Certainly! I have my expertise, my incredible experience, my knowledge of languages! That is sufficient capital [*kapital*], I believe!
> JULIE: But with that you cannot even buy a railway ticket.
> JEAN: That is certainly true; but that's why I'm looking for a backer who can provide the funds!
> JULIE: But where can you find one at a moment's notice?
> JEAN: You will find one, if you wish to be my companion.
> JULIE: I can't—and I do not own anything.
> [*A pause.*]
> JEAN: Then the whole matter drops—
> JULIE: And—
> JEAN: Things will remain the same. (20–21)

When Jean floats his idea of opening "a first-class hotel for first-class patrons," Julie immediately asks him where he plans to acquire economic capital ("large capital"). In response, Jean points out that his embodied forms of cultural and social capital—his "expertise," his "incredible experience," and his "knowledge of languages"—are "sufficient capital" (20). All of Jean's knowledge and skills that supposedly make for a successful hotel owner are tied to his person, as they took time to accumulate. Yet, as Julie rightly notes, Jean's social and cultural capital will not even buy him a train ticket. Nor have his supposed assets paid off so far.

At the end of the day, Jean is still a wage-earning laborer on the Count's estate, not an independent entrepreneur. He still needs a liquid asset—cash. This is where Julie presumably comes in. In his dealings with Julie, Jean relies mainly on his erotic capital. And his interactions with his would-be fiancée Kristin reveal that he believes his erotic capital will take him far in life. Jean reminds Kristin that she would be lucky to have such a nice fellow as himself for a husband and that her stock has risen ever since people started calling him her fiancé (6). In Jean's view, Kristin should be happy just being his backup plan. When, at the end of the play, Kristin suggests they leave the estate and he find a job as a janitor, Jean bitterly admits that he envisioned "higher horizons" (*högre vyer*) for himself (56).

In trying to convert his erotic capital into economic resources, Jean simultaneously takes on the roles of the prostitute and the speculator. Like a gigolo, Jean wants to be paid for sex. And, like a speculator, he sees an opportunity, goes for it, and then waits to see if it will generate profit. Although Jean calls Julie "a whore" (*hora*), he is actually the one who tries to use his charm and sexual allure—that is, to speculate with his erotic capital—in order to earn a financial return (22). Throughout the first half of the play, Jean plays the role of the coquette, acting demure when Julie asks him to dance and pretending to be embarrassed to change his coat in her presence. That Jean may have been thinking about a hotel project for quite some time is hinted at by the alacrity with which he comes up with his plan. He is the one to break silence after sex to say that it is impossible for them to remain on the Count's property. And, conveniently, Jean has a train timetable in his pocket, so he can quickly check the next train they can hop on to run away together. Julie, by contrast, gets lost in the moment and only *afterward* tries to salvage her situation. What is more, Jean's financial scheme involves making a profit from Julie's erotic capital. He envisions her as the "mistress" of his hotel who could satisfy his clients with her "most beautiful smile" (19). Although Jean calls Julie the "mistress of the house; the ornament of the firm" (*Husets härskarinna; firmans prydnad*, 19), his idea of "the firm" shares many characteristics with Kitty Warren's hotel company, which, in Shaw's *Mrs. Warren's Profession*, turns out to be a cover for a brothel ring.

Jean acts not only as a speculator but also as a marginalist economist, carefully weighing the benefits of different types of relationships with Julie. Thus, Jean is constantly calculating how much additional utility a particular relationship with Julie will bring him based on her economic value, which he is trying to assess in real time. A partnership with a Julie with substantive investment capital (for example, by means of a dowry) offers him more utility than a marriage to a penniless Julie. And an ongoing secret sexual relationship with her on the estate quickly becomes a liability because of the risk of pregnancy. As discussed previously in the context of Ibsen's *A Doll's House*, the language of economics bleeds into the everyday speech of characters. They begin to refer to their conduct as an economic game by using terms like "utility," "capital," "interest," and so forth. Marriage becomes just another utility among others. As Shaw, who was a fan of the pioneering marginalist economist William Stanley Jevons, puts it: "At present a middle-class man, when his immediate needs are satisfied, furnishes himself with commodities in a certain order, as, for instance, wife, house, furniture, pianoforte, horse and trap. The satisfaction of each desire leaves the mind free to entertain the next, so that you actually make a man feel the want of a horse by giving him a pianoforte."[33] Yet when dramatic characters try to apply such a narrow economic approach to their own behavior as well as the behavior of others, they find themselves imbricated in networks of social relations, pulled in different directions by desires and forces that they have a difficult time controlling.

The Ending of *Miss Julie*—a Tragic Finale or a Gesture toward Capitalist Reality?

The deflating effect that the Count's return has on Jean's bravura underscores the economic fact that Jean is a mere wage earner with limited resources. Once the Count orders Jean via the speaking tube to bring him his coffee and boots, Jean immediately loses all courage and resolve, confessing to Julie that if the Count came down and commanded him to cut his own throat, he would do it. Never seen onstage, the Count personifies not only the old aristocratic class but also the invisible hand of capital, putting an end to the festivities of the previous night and returning the characters to the labor conditions of the estate. Jean's plans having failed, he is back where he started—working as the Count's servant. Then again, the midsummer episode might prove to be a mere setback. As Strindberg suggests in his preface, Jean, the son of an agricultural laborer, has "already come up in the world" and might "end up as the proprietor of a hotel."[34] Still, within the world of the play, Jean does not succeed despite his alleged personal assets. And although Strindberg has Julie exit intent on killing herself, he does not give us a completely unambiguous ending that shows his heroine's suicide. In a letter to Edvard Brandes, Strindberg mentions that if Julie did not immediately kill herself, she would "become a waitress at Hasselbacken," a fashionable restaurant at an upscale hotel in Stockholm.[35]

Strindberg was thus attuned both to the process of suicidal ideation (that suicidal thoughts need not lead to suicide) and to the conditions of the labor market of his time. Critics have long complained that Julie's suicide rarely works in performance, and some directors have gone so far as to change the ending to one where Julie lives on.[36] But it is important to remember that Strindberg does not use conventional melodramatic or tragic means to signal to the audience that a suicide has happened. It does not take place onstage. No gunshot is heard, and no characters discover the female protagonist's body as they do in Ibsen's *Hedda Gabler*. No doctor or messenger reports back to us on an offstage death. All we are left with is Julie's intention, communicated by the stage direction and the last sentence of the play: "She goes firmly out the door" (71). However, this intention of Julie's is revealed to have originated through a series of vacillating emotions, tricks of hypnosis, and metatheatrical impersonations. Julie orders Jean to perform hypnosis on her, just like a professional hypnotist would on a volunteer audience member at a hypnosis show (69). The literal translation of Julie's instruction reads: "You know what I would will, but do not will, will it, you, and command me do it" (69). She knows that the honor code dictates that an aristocratic woman in her position should want to kill herself—but she herself does not have the will, so she asks Jean to lend her his. More precisely, Julie commands Jean to pretend that he is the Count and that she is him, Jean, and to order her to slit her throat, just as Jean described he would do if the Count commanded him. All this theatrical transference and role-playing, coupled with Julie's wavering will, raises the question of whether a suicide will happen offstage. Like Nora's final exit in Ibsen's *A Doll's House*, Julie's departure opens Strindberg's play to the real world beyond the time and space of theatrical performance.

One reason so many readers and spectators assume Julie commits suicide is that they are expecting a tragic ending. After all, Julie sees herself as a heroine trapped in a tragic script. For this reason, she suggests to Jean that they go abroad together and enjoy themselves for as long as they can before dying. His response to her invitation to *Liebestod* is "It's much better to start a hotel" (46). Jean does not see himself as a tragic character; instead he embraces the comedy of capitalism, where things can be down one day and looking up the next. Another reason for assuming Julie's offstage violent death is the fact that Strindberg might have borrowed the method of suicide for his protagonist (slitting her throat) from a real-life event— the suicide of Swedish writer Victoria Benedictsson (about whom more later). Yet Strindberg drew from many sources for *Miss Julie*, including his experience at Countess Frankenau's manor house.[37] Thus, the expectation of tragic conventions, by which a woman in Julie's aristocratic position kills herself, has made readers and spectators miss Strindberg's innovative departure from previous tragic scripts. It is more accurate to say that, rather than a definitive tragic conclusion, the play ends by hovering on the edge of tragedy. Instead of the finality of the paradigmatic female suicide, which so often punctuates tales of fallen women, *Miss Julie* closes with a question mark. *Will* Julie commit suicide, or will she enter the workaday world? After all, Ibsen's Nora, too, contemplates killing herself by jumping into a freezing black river, but in the end she steps into the world to make something of herself.

Subtitled a "naturalistic tragedy," *Miss Julie* is Strindberg's alchemical creation, mixing tragedy with dramatic naturalism. As Strindberg points out in the preface, the "tragic legacy of romanticism . . . is now being dissipated by naturalism, the only aim of which is happiness."[38] Even as *Miss Julie* plays out as a tragedy, especially through Julie's trajectory, it also displays many elements of the comedy of capital. Although Strindberg notes that the most plausible outcome for a count's daughter who has lost her honor and committed theft is suicide, his protagonist also exists in the new capitalist reality, where the fall of one family "gives another the good fortune to rise."[39] It is this new historical reality that Julie steps into when she walks out the door. Strindberg himself admitted that he did not invent a new dramatic form in *Miss Julie* but instead sought to modernize tragedy. The enigmatic "new wine that has broken the old bottles," which Strindberg refers to in the preface, is capital.

Capitalist modernity, where economic survival is an insistent daily worry, pushes the aristocratic code of honor into the background. For this reason, Strindberg notes in his letter to Edvard Brandes that if Julie kills herself, it is something that she does "immediately" after walking out the door, that is, in the state of active suicidal ideation.[40] If she changes her mind, or something or someone stops her, she will have to adjust to living in the capitalist world. In this alternative scenario, the impoverished Count's daughter makes use of her erotic capital and finds a job as a waitress in an elegant establishment instead of allowing Jean to pimp her out, as he intended in his original plan. In this regard, Shaw's Mrs. Warren would probably argue that the restaurant would be reaping most of the profits from Julie's erotic capital and that she would be wiser to turn to prostitution and pocket all the profits from her good looks herself. Whether this is an accurate assessment of prostitution will be discussed in greater detail in the section devoted to Shaw's *Mrs. Warren's Profession*.

Sexuo-Economic Exchanges and the Woman Question

As *Miss Julie*'s representation of labor and capital makes clear, Strindberg had a deep interest in the pressing economic questions of his time. A self-proclaimed "son of a servant" (his mother, Nora, had been a tavern waitress), he expressed sympathy for many arguments of Marxist socialism and believed that in his time, "all enlightened people" were socialists.[41] In his youth, Strindberg's socialist allegiance was on display in such early works as *The Swedish People* (*Svenska folket*, 1880–82), a history of the Swedish common people, and *Swedish Destinies and Adventures: Tales from All Times* (*Svenska öden och äventyr: Berättelser från alla tidevarv*, 1882–83), two volumes of stories set in the historical past. In *The Red Room* (*Röda rummet*, 1879), the novel that first made Strindberg famous in Sweden, the protagonist Arvid Falk is described, like Strindberg himself, as having a "certain weakness" for "those who were overlooked," for "the oppressed and the downtrodden."⁴² Strindberg's main disagreement with Marxism was its focus on industrialism. Fond of the countryside, Strindberg embraced agrarian socialism and a gendered division of labor based on what he believed to be natural differences between men and women. This interest in agrarian reforms led Strindberg to undertake a serious study of the subject that combined sociology and ethnography: *Among French Peasants: Subjective Travel Notes* (*Bland franska bonder: Subjektiva reseskildringar*, 1889). This was supposed to be an in-depth study of European peasantry, but the lack of government funding forced Strindberg to curb his ambitions. As Richard Swedberg notes, Strindberg not only immersed himself in the social science of his day but also, "in contrast to all the famous sociologists before World War I—Durkheim, Simmel, Weber, Sumner, and so on," went into the field to gather information. What Strindberg enjoyed most about his sociological work was meeting, talking to, and listening to French peasants.⁴³ In his conclusion, Strindberg criticized the burdensome taxes that made it impossible for peasants to make profits, driving them from their villages into cities and turning them into precarious industrial laborers.

As a young man, Strindberg also gained firsthand experience with new financial instruments, learning about probability theory and statistics while working at an insurance company in Stockholm. This short stint only made him realize that statistics flattened particularities and produced misleading results.⁴⁴ Strindberg's distaste for insurance companies comes across in *The Red Room* when Falk is commissioned to compose a "novel of ten pages" that would promote a new liability company by the name of Triton in a way that was "not at all obvious"—an advertisement masquerading as art (44).

In addition to Marx, Strindberg (like Chekhov) admired British historian Henry Thomas Buckle, whose groundbreaking *History of Civilization in England* (1857) was translated into Swedish in 1871.⁴⁵ Buckle's claim that the beginnings of civilization depend on material conditions partly influenced Strindberg's *Small Catechism for the Underclass*, a Socratic dialogue with himself that Strindberg composed between 1884 and 1885 while living in Switzerland but that remained unpublished until 1913. It is here that Strindberg asks the question—"What is economics?"—and answers—"A science invented by the overclass to get at the fruit of the underclass's labor."⁴⁶ The short polemical text posits that the overclass (*överklass*) not only exploits the labor of the underclass (*underclass*) but also disseminates their ideology through art, culture, and education. When Strindberg poses the question "What is morality?," he answers, "A sense of justice that has been regulated by the overclass in order to trick the underclass into a sedate lifestyle."⁴⁷ In "The Reward of Virtue," the short story for which he was charged with blasphemy, Strindberg has his main protagonist realize that "school-books were controlled by the upper classes, and they were one and all written for the express purpose of making the lower classes worship the said upper classes."[48]

Strindberg condemned poverty and was convinced of Malthus's theory of population growth, which postulated that population growth was exponential while food supply growth remained linear. However, Strindberg rejected Malthus's solution of "moral restraint."[49] Even as Strindberg shows in "Reward of Virtue" the pernicious effects of abstinence, he was against the Neo-Malthusian idea of birth control to limit family size. For Strindberg, male virility and paternity were subjects of profound anxiety. Instead, Strindberg placed the blame on food distribution. As the conclusion of his short story "Bread" sums it up, "There must surely be something wrong with the way bread is distributed" (231). Although, judging by the accounts of his sisters, Strindberg had a comfortable bourgeois upbringing, he continued to emphasize that his mother had been a waitress and that he was a member of the "underclass."

In Strindberg's black-and-white view of the economy, there were thus two classes, or at least two main groups of classes—one with socioeconomic and political power and the other without. However, Strindberg's political opinions became more contradictory around the time he was composing *Miss Julie*. The aristocratic Swedish writer Verner von Heidenstam introduced Strindberg to Nietzsche's philosophy, and shortly afterward Georg Brandes recommended Nietzsche's *Beyond Good and Evil* (*Jenseits von Gut und Böse*, 1886) to him, awakening in Strindberg an interest in the idea of an intellectual superman and the concept of slave and master moralities.[50] His earlier embrace of socialism was now complicated by his belief in another division, this time an intellectual one, between supposedly conventional minds and superior ones.

Given Strindberg's interest in economics and social justice, it is surprising, as Stenport has noted, that Strindberg's "relevance for an understanding of economic theory throughout the major European economies in the late nineteenth century has been . . . understudied."[51] Indeed, *Miss Julie* explores some of the most urgent economic questions of its day, including the Woman Question—the intellectual debate about women's changing socioeconomic roles and legal rights that brought the institution of marriage, the nuclear family, and prostitution together into conversation. From the mid-nineteenth century, Scandinavian women steadily gained legal rights and economic independence. In 1845, daughters were given equal rights of inheritance as sons, and in 1873 women were permitted to study for any university degree. In 1888, the year that Strindberg composed *Miss Julie*, a statute on marriage in Scandinavia granted married women the right to handle the money they earned. What propelled lawmakers to push for all these reforms was not necessarily any concrete feminist agenda; rather, it was "the economic situation in Scandinavia."[52] By the midcentury, strong population growth, coupled with a declining marriage rate, had increased "the number of unwed females over fifteen . . . by 50 percent," so "something had to be done to find a place in society for these women."[53] At the turn of the century, the Woman Question was at the forefront of cultural debates in Sweden. According to Evert Sprinchorn, it "was debated even more intensely in Scandinavia in the 1880s than in America in the 1960s and 1970s."[54] What was Strindberg's stance on this rise of women?

A socialist who espoused Nietzschean individualism, and a protofeminist in some radical ways while a fierce misogynist in others, Strindberg embodied many of his era's contradictions. Before continuing, it is crucial to clear the air about misogyny—the play's and Strindberg's own. *Miss Julie* occupies a paradoxical place in the canon of modern drama. Hailed as a masterpiece of naturalism ahead of its time, it is often taught now as an outdated take on class hierarchies and an offensive treatment of the relationship between the sexes. It certainly does not help that in the preface Strindberg calls Julie "a man-hating half-woman" and claims that Jean is "superior to Miss Julie in that he is a man."[55] As several commentators have pointed out, however, the preface, though deemed one of the most influential manifestos of naturalism, should be taken with a heavy grain of salt.[56] Strindberg wrote it in part to impress Zola, who was not enthusiastic about *The Father* (*Fadren*, 1887), Strindberg's earlier dramatic attempt at naturalism. Moreover, Strindberg became interested in Nietzsche and Darwin during this time, and his misogyny became more pronounced. Consequently, Julie is described worse in the preface than how she comes off in the play.

Although Strindberg claimed that the Woman Question was "overrated" because it only affected "the cultured woman, representing perhaps 10% of the population," he nevertheless spent a considerable amount of time and effort in the 1870s and 1880s pondering over it and composing the plays *The Marauders* (*Marodörer*, 1886), *The Father*, *Miss Julie*, and *Creditors* (*Fordringsägare*, 1889), all which, in different ways, treat relations between the sexes in the age of capital.[57] And although Strindberg considered *A Doll's House* to be a caricature of "the cultured man and woman," he became obsessed with Ibsen's play and the furor it had caused in Europe and the United States, composing several responses to Ibsen.[58] One early rejoinder came in the form of his play *Sir Bengt's Wife* (1882), in which Strindberg reverses Ibsen's setup. Here it is the husband who selflessly saves his wife, while the wife is an egoist who must change her ways for the marriage to survive. Another response was the collection of short stories *Getting Married* (*Giftas*, 1884), which depicts a variety of twenty marriages, some miserable, some happy, and the preface to which features Strindberg's theater review of *A Doll's House*, where, among many other things, he accuses Ibsen of not developing Torvald's backstory in order to elevate Nora in the eyes of the audience. "That 'hundreds of thousands of women' have sacrificed themselves for their husbands," writes Strindberg, "is a compliment to the ladies that Ibsen should be too old to pay."[59]

In one of the short stories, pointedly titled "A Doll's House," a seemingly happy marriage almost entirely breaks down when the wife begins to doubt the contentedness of her marriage to a naval captain after reading Ibsen's *A Doll's House*. When her husband is at sea, she sends him a copy of Ibsen's play along with a long, detailed letter informing him that she now finally realizes that theirs was never "a true marriage."[60] The story follows the captain's endeavors to win back his wife. It ends with his triumph when he manages to seduce her back into his "own bachelor bed" with a dose of emotional manipulation and psychopathic jealousy games. Strindberg recycles many points from his preface into the letter written by the captain in response to his wife. "And imagine me of all people sitting down to write a review of a play?" muses the captain, who until this moment in his life has never taken an active interest in theater criticism but is able to offer a nuanced dramaturgical account of all the faults of Ibsen's marital drama, including a prescription of what should and should not be shown onstage. It is Strindberg's own voice as playwright and director that comes through in the lines of his protagonist's letter. Ventriloquized by Strindberg, the captain argues that Nora married Torvald "for economic reasons," while he married her "for love."[61] He picks holes in Ibsen's plot (why would Nora leave her children with a "fellow she despised"?) and suggests that the scene where Torvald wants to sleep with his wife after the costume party should have been left offstage for the sake of decorum. However, he also simultaneously criticizes Ibsen for not being realistic enough at that moment, since, according to Strindberg, it is often the other way around—the wife pesters the husband for sex when he is not in the mood for it.[62]

It is important to remember that Strindberg's contradictory views regarding gender relations were marked by his desire for radical egalitarianism in some respects and profound anxiety over female power in others. In fact, American playwright Paula Vogel once admitted that Strindberg is an "extremely powerful ally" for her precisely "because in his plays there is a fear and a power of woman not approached by any other dramatist."[63] On the one hand, in the manifesto accompanying *Getting Married, Part I*, Strindberg goes further than Ibsen in advocating for women's equal rights in voting, education, employment, management of money, and sexual freedom (the "girl shall have the same freedom to 'run wild' and choose what company she pleases").[64] On the other hand, some of the stories, especially in the second volume, published in 1885, are unmistakably misogynistic, referring to women as mean, lazy, and manipulative. And throughout the entire collection, Strindberg emphasizes that a woman's primary role is being a mother and that "a marriage without children is a sad affair."[65] The change of tone between the two volumes may have had something to do with the fact that Strindberg was convinced that Swedish feminists, under the leadership of Queen Sophia, were out to destroy him. He was not wrong. In addition to the charge of blasphemy, of which he was eventually acquitted, the first volume of *Getting Married* earned Strindberg the wrath of two feminist groups—the Society for Married Women's Property Rights and the Federation, an association that sought to abolish prostitution. Strindberg, an early defender of sex work, argued that prostitutes "could fend for themselves if treated fairly."[66] The anger continues to this day. In 2006, to make a statement about how problematic Strindberg is, the Swedish publisher Rosenlarv published "A Feminist Revision" of the second volume of *Getting Married* as a completely blank book without any text inside.

By the time Strindberg had finished *The Father*, he was still "obsessed by the Woman Question," writing to his publisher Isidor Bonnier: "I don't intend to drop it, because I must get to the bottom of it by studying it and experimenting with it before I can give it up."[67] And experiment he did. In its many reversals, *Miss Julie* flips nineteenth-century courtship on its head, with Jean often playing the feminine role of the coquette, especially in the beginning. The first half of *Miss Julie* plays out as a topsy-turvy courtship dance, while the second half unfolds like a protracted, perverse business negotiation in which money and sex are the decisive, intertwined factors of social mobility.

Like *Getting Married*, *Miss Julie* came out of Strindberg's turbulent marriage to divorced Finnish aristocrat and actress Siri von Essen, who created the role of Miss Julie for the play's premiere at the Students' Association in Copenhagen on March 14, 1889. At the time he wrote and directed the play, Strindberg had already begun what would prove to be a complicated and painful divorce from Siri. Still, he attempted to mount a production of his play with Siri on March 2, 1889, at his newly founded Scandinavian Experimental Theater in Copenhagen, but the police raided the theater during the dress rehearsal. *Miss Julie* would not be performed in Sweden until 1906, and the uncensored and unabridged version of the text would not be published until 1984.

Given Strindberg's conflicting views on women's emancipation and angst about female power, it should come as no surprise that his plays capture his era's anxiety about the socioeconomic rise of women. Strindberg described himself as an artist who "experiments with points of view."[68] In many ways, the dramatic form provided Strindberg with an apt venue for his irreconcilable ideas regarding gender. Paradoxically, while it was not Strindberg's aim to show that gender and gender relations are historically contingent, his fear of the destruction of patriarchy and the rise of matriarchy led him to portray patriarchy as inherently unstable and overcomable. In the preface to the second volume of *Getting Married*, Strindberg cites the words of the French sociologist Paul Lafargue as a warning: "The patriarchal family is consequently a comparatively recent form of society, and its rise was marked by as many crimes as we may perhaps expect in the future, should society attempt to revert to matriarchy." Strindberg then offers advice to his target audience: "Therefore: look out, men!"[69] Most importantly, by displaying how class was a social construct and a role to be played, Strindberg ends up (inadvertently) doing the same for gender, as Jean and Julie keep switching their positions of power and "trying on" the other gender's allegedly natural characteristics. Thus, in its focus on theatricality and role-playing, the text of *Miss Julie* offers a potential for performances of the play to radically challenge patriarchal assumptions about gender. And in its intertwinement of money and sex, *Miss Julie* also provides an opportunity to explore the construction of gender under capitalism.

In many ways, the original text of *Miss Julie* already challenges the prevalent gender hierarchies of its day. For one, the power dynamics between the two protagonists are constantly shifting. Even the space that the two share is unstable. As Freddie Rokem points out, "The way the kitchen is cut off diagonally" renders "it impossible to fix or find a constant focal point in either the fictional world of the play or the subjective consciousness of the characters."[70] Moreover, as mentioned earlier in our discussion of Julie's suicidal intention, the play's use of hypnosis often makes it difficult to tell who is in charge. As Una Chaudhuri observes in her rich and attentive reading, "The way in which the play deploys its figure of hypnosis" destabilizes its "'vertical' hermeneutic apparatus," so that instead of a powerful and opportunistic Jean, Julie emerges as the one who is giving him orders and commanding him through hypnosis during the first half of the play.[71] Strindberg was fascinated by theories of hypnosis and mental suggestion at the time of writing *Miss Julie*.[72]

In Strindberg's dramatic oeuvre, we witness an early conversation between economics and psychology, a foreshadowing of the ways the twentieth century would attempt to fuse the ideas of Marxism and Freudianism, arguably the two most influential systems of thought that emerged in the nineteenth century. In particular, *Miss Julie* highlights Strindberg's ability to interweave "social and psychological motives."[73] Although there is no direct evidence that Strindberg ever read Freud, he avidly followed the work of early psychologists and psychiatrists who went on to influence Freud, so Strindberg's plays actually anticipate many of Freud's own insights.[74] Among the texts that Strindberg was familiar with were Henry Maudsley's *The Pathology of Mind* (1879), Théodule-Armand Ribot's *Diseases of Memory* (*Les maladies de la volonté*, 1883) and *Diseases of Personality* (*Les maladies de la personnalité*, 1885), and Hippolyte Bernheim's *Suggestive Therapeutics: A Treatise on the Nature and Uses of Hypnotism* (*De la suggestion et de ses applications à la thérapeutique*, 1886). Strindberg was also aware of Jean-Martin Charcot's research on hysteria at La Salpêtrière.[75] As we will soon see, the importance of dreams in *Miss Julie* anticipates Freud's observations in *The Interpretations of Dreams* (*Die Traumdeutung*, 1899) and "Creative Writers and Day-Dreaming" ("Der Dichter und das Phantasieren," 1908). Freud gave credit to Strindberg's insights: in a 1917 footnote to *The Psychopathology of Everyday Life* (*Psychopathologie des Alltagslebens*, 1901), Freud mentions that Strindberg understood the concept of parapraxes.[76]

Reading Strindberg's nonfiction along with his plays highlights the extent to which his multilayered drama often transcends his sexist beliefs. Although in his socioeconomic writings, Strindberg champions the underclass and bemoans the loss of male authority in the new historical reality of women's emancipation, in *Miss Julie*, the scales of empathy tip more toward Julie, the woman and the alleged "aristocrat" of the conflict. According to Egil Törnqvist and Barry Jacobs, although one might expect the footman Jean to stand in for Strindberg, the "son of a servant," it is Julie who "is really one of Strindberg's most revealing self-portraits."[77]

Moreover, class lines have long been transgressed and blurred before the start of the play's main events. Strindberg's main story is not that of D. H. Lawrence's *Lady Chatterley's Lover* (1928), to which it is sometimes compared in the Anglo-American context. For one, Julie is the illegitimate daughter of a non-noble woman and a count, echoing the biographical fact that Strindberg himself was the son of a former waitress and an upper-middle-class shipping agent. Julie was born out of wedlock because her feminist mother resisted marriage until the Count forced her into one. Whether Julie's father is the Count or her mother's lower-class lover, to whom she entrusted her dowry, is a question the play leaves open. Anxiety over paternity pervades *Miss Julie*.[78] In other words, Julie might not have any blue blood at all. And the Count's own aristocratic heritage is called into doubt when Jean mentions to Julie that he has read in the peerage book that her earliest known ancestor was a "miller who let the king spend a night with his wife during the Danish war" (27). The Count's ancestors, it seems, have bought their nobility just the way Jean dreams he might be able to buy his someday in Romania. As for Jean's lineage, there is no record of it (except the one kept by the police), so Jean can imagine whatever he wants, even that he comes from "a finer ancestry" than Julie does (27).

What is truly radical about *Miss Julie* is not the mere fact that a woman from a higher social class sleeps with a man of lower birth (even though, in a fit of anger, she compares her act to bestiality) but that the entire class system is shown to be a matter of historical violence. For one, the intermingling of classes was already an unexceptional reality in Strindberg's time. Strindberg himself was a product of such an interclass liaison, and so was his first marriage. To be sure, class barriers in late nineteenth-century Sweden were still an irrefutable fact of modern life, but sweeping changes were already underway. Class hierarchies existed, but who got to occupy what position became a matter of social mobility and luck rather than birth. On Julie's side, the mixing of aristocratic and common blood has always taken place. On Jean's side, there is simply a blank canvas. Because paternity is ultimately uncertain, the domination of one class over another cannot be determined or justified by birth but only traced to the violence of usurpation, or what Marx calls "originary accumulation" (*ursprüngliche Akkumulation*)—the continual seizure of material resources and labor by the class in power.[79] Notice the recurrent motif of thievery in the play. Everyone steals in order to stay financially afloat or to get ahead. Julie purloins money from her father in hopes of running away with Jean. Jean pilfers wine from Julie's father and "oats from the stables." Even pious Kristin "take[s] a percentage on the seasonings and bribes from the butcher" (36). Sex also figures as a way to plunder. For Jean, seduction is not only a way to "steal" Julie's virginity but also, most importantly, a way to access capital.

Money is intimately linked to sexuality in *Miss Julie*: the play simultaneously sheds light on the uncanny fungibility of sex and money and the urgent need to differentiate between the two. Instead of merely dramatizing the class struggle, Strindberg's infamous drama reveals the contradictions of love in the age of capital by underscoring the difficulty of disentangling economic and erotic desires. The main clash of *Miss Julie* is between the mercantile exchange, which influences all social relations in the play, and the ideals of freedom and equality promised but not achieved by capitalism.

Strindberg's battle of the sexes is a fight over interpretation—what each interaction between the characters means, how much it is worth (either in money or in emotional expenditure), who gets to have the last word, and, most importantly, who is indebted to whom. *Miss Julie* is as much a play about debt and guilt as it is about class and sex. The Swedish *skuld*, like the German *Schuld*, means both "debt" and "guilt." Strindberg plays on the dual meaning of the adjective *skyldig* ("guilty" or "in debt to someone") throughout *Miss Julie* and his other plays, like *Creditors*.[80] Jean uses *skyldig* to describe his duty and service to the Count—he is *bound* to clean his boots (14). Julie calls midsummer revelry *oskyldigt* (innocent), and Jean uses the same word to tell Julie to stop playing the "innocent" with him (21). Yet it is in the scene where money appears onstage in the form of a silver coin that Jean throws in Julie's direction that the dual meaning crystallizes. Is Jean saying that he does not want to *owe* anything to Julie or that he does not want to be guilty of anything—in this case, of seduction? But who seduced whom?

During Jean and Julie's back-and-forth about who enticed whom, the coin remains on the table (or wherever it may fall during a live performance). After their verbal exchange, the coin is not acknowledged by either of the characters. And neither does Kristin pick it up when she later reenters the kitchen. There are no more directions concerning its stage life. As readers, we might even forget about its presence, but as spectators, we are more likely to notice that the coin remains onstage for the duration of Strindberg's drama. According to Andrew Sofer, a stage prop is "*a discrete, material, inanimate object that is visibly manipulated by an actor in the course of performance.*"[81] Money is perhaps the strangest prop of them all because it acts as a signifier of material conditions. It gestures not only to the economic world depicted *in* the play but also to the economic world *outside* the theater, which includes the theater (both the space of performance and the institution) and the working actor handling the money onstage.

Like Ibsen's *John Gabriel Borkman*, Strindberg's *Miss Julie* is a world of metal. Almost all the props in *Miss Julie*—the count's riding boots with spurs, the old-fashioned bell, the speaking tube, the meat chopper, the cage (with Julie's canary), Jean's razor—are objects that are either made from metal or have a significant metal component to them. For example, the spurs on the riding boots (usually made from metal) are used for directing the movement of horses and echo the play's theme of hypnosis. And the whole act takes place inside a kitchen that is full of "copper kettles, iron casseroles, and tin pans" (*koppar-, malm-, järn-, och tennkärl,* 5). Strindberg was adamant about using real saucepans for when *Miss Julie* was finally staged at André Antoine's Théâtre Libre in 1893. In the preface, Strindberg urges theater artists to "stop painting shelves and kitchen utensils" on canvas walls. "There are so many other stage conventions in which we are asked to believe," writes Strindberg, "that we might be spared the effort of believing in painted saucepans."[82] For Antoine's production, Strindberg borrowed real saucepans from his wife's aunt's kitchen and placed them on real shelves. Even those critics who deplored his play praised the saucepans.[83]

The crucial difference between the silver coin and the rest of the play's metal objects is that, while all other objects derive their significance from what Marx calls their "use value"—that is, the usefulness of a commodity that is "conditioned by [its] physical properties"—the coin is a signifier of exchange value.[84] Most of the play's props change their use value when they are transferred between characters. The meat chopper that Kristin uses in the kitchen to cook the liver that she serves Jean at the top of the play becomes, in his hands, a murderous tool that he uses to kill Julie's canary. And, most strikingly, the razor, which Jean uses for the aesthetic purpose of self-grooming, becomes a tool of violence that Julie might use to kill herself. In other words, Jean's apparatus of erotic capital proves lethal to Julie. By contrast, unclaimed by any character, the silver coin remains a marker of exchange and a question mark. One of the main questions that *Miss Julie* asks is, What kind of an exchange, broadly defined, is sex?

What, if anything, do the parties owe one another? Strindberg wrote *Miss Julie* at a historical moment of transition, when the institution of marriage in Europe was undergoing a crisis and when the meaning of sex acquired the uncertainty that still haunts the alienated forms of intimacy in the age of capital. There is a reason this supposedly outdated play is produced so often.[85] On the surface, the central story is almost contemporary: two people have sex, and things become complicated. What Strindberg brings to this tale are all the myriad ways that economic and social forces function within an intimate relationship.

Contemporary Productions of *Miss Julie*

Despite its allegedly antiquated content, contemporary directors continue to be drawn to *Miss Julie*, and many theater critics remain admirers of the play. For Ben Brantley, Julie is a particularly awarding role for an actor, "a role that makes the celebrated basket cases Hedda Gabler and Lady Macbeth look like child's play."[86] And according to Hilton Als, who himself once worked on an adaptation of *Miss Julie* set in nineteenth-century Haiti, Strindberg offered "the bones for the kind of drama it was almost impossible to wreck through interpretation, particularly if you stuck to his major themes, which was how class and power intersected with sex."[87]

To contextualize and revise some of the play's unpalatable misogynistic elements, many contemporary versions of *Miss Julie* transpose its action to a historical juncture of changing gender norms and/or disruption of a given country's class system. Patrick Marber's *After Miss Julie* (2003), for instance, transports Strindberg's play to postwar Britain on the night of the election of the Labour Party. Jean's business proposal to Julie is to open a nightclub in New York City. Neil LaBute's version (2013) sets the action in the Roaring Twenties with Julie as a flapper, ignoring the historical fact that flappers originally came from the working class.[88] Two recent productions have managed to successfully situate *Miss Julie* in the here and now: Thomas Ostermeier's 2011 Russian-language production of *Miss Julie*, adapted by Mikhail Durnenkov and staged at the Theater of Nations in Moscow, moves the action of the play to Putin's Russia and changes the Midsummer celebration to a New Year's Eve party, while Yaël Farber's *Mies Julie* (2012) takes place in today's Karoo, South Africa. Ostermeier's version highlights Russia's turbulent transition from Soviet power (Julie is the daughter of a Soviet general) to the unbridled capitalism and chaos of new money (Jean is a New Russian businessman-in-the-making). Farber's adaptation treats the political and economic legacy of apartheid. In Farber's version, Jean is renamed John and reimagined as a young Black man born on the farm owned by Julie's father. Kristin is no longer his fiancé but his mother. Farber also adds a fourth silent character—Ukhokho, a

"Xhosa woman, other-worldly ancestor of indeterminate age."[89] During the performance, she "is always present on the periphery, watching" (10). In *Mies Julie*, it is Julie who suggests to John that they flee her father's house and start a hotel business, while John wants to stay and take back the land of his ancestors by fathering a child with Julie.

Farber's version is perhaps the most successful production to foreground racism as underpinning the conflict between Jean and Julie. Casting an actor of color in the role of Jean (as the National Theatre did when Carrie Cracknell directed an adaptation by Polly Stenham in 2018 with Vanessa Kirby and Eric Kofi Abrefa in the lead roles) has become the preferred choice for directors who attempt to find an equivalent contemporary barrier that could work as class allegedly did in Strindberg's time. The problem is that interracial relationships today do not strike most theater audiences as transgressive, at least not the cosmopolitan audiences of London's National Theatre.[90] In any case, as mentioned earlier, there is a tendency to retrospectively assign more transgressive clout to the interclass dimension of Jean and Julie's relationship in Strindberg's original. Class is crucial in *Miss Julie* not because characters cross class lines to get together (again, this was perhaps not as shocking in Strindberg's time as we tend to think) but because Strindberg deconstructs the whole edifice of class hierarchy and shows how the profit motive seeps into all sexual and romantic relationships under capitalism regardless of what class one belongs to.

Thus, what tends to get lost in most contemporary productions of *Miss Julie* is how an oppressive network of systems (patriarchy, capitalism, institutionalized religion) simultaneously pushes Strindberg's Jean and Julie toward one another and tears them apart. Without the social and the economic, we are left with two internally conflicted individuals. The story then becomes a sadomasochistic psychodrama about a toxic relationship between two people with unresolved childhood issues. Interesting? Maybe. Compelling and scandalous as it was during Strindberg's own time? Hardly. By contrast, Farber's *Mies Julie* triumphs for two main reasons. First, interracial relationships were still forbidden in recent history in South Africa (mixed marriages only became legal in 1985 with the passage of the Immorality and Prohibition of Mixed Marriages Amendment Act), so there is a palpable element of transgression to Jean and Julie's relationship that is absent from most productions. Second, the question of land ownership (Julie's ancestors usurped the land, and now Jean wants to take it back) allows Farber's version to offer a powerful commentary on Marx's "originary accumulation,"[91] which Strindberg's *Miss Julie* foregrounds through its intertwined themes of thievery and guilt.

To appreciate what was radical about *Miss Julie* during Strindberg's time, it is helpful to have an overview of courtship, marriage, and prostitution in the nineteenth century.

Dowry and the Love Marriage in the Age of Capital

Although, by the end of the nineteenth century, marrying for love was standard practice among the bourgeoisie, economic considerations, however veiled, never completely disappeared. More curious still is the preoccupation of late nineteenth-century thinkers, like Friedrich Engels and Georg Simmel, with the dowry. Why is it that at a time when the love marriage becomes the norm that an obsession with the dowry persists both in economic thought and in plays about courtship? Indeed, the friction between mercantile and romantic motives in the game of courtship galvanized many dramas on the modern stage.

Before the eighteenth century, it was considered unwise to choose a spouse based on something as irrational, transitory, and volatile as love (though, of course, it did occur). In medieval Europe, it was not marriage but adultery that was hailed as the ideal form of romantic love.[92] According to Stephanie Coontz, the "radical idea of marrying for love" began to take hold after the American and French Revolutions and was a product of Enlightenment's endorsement of individual rights and "the pursuit of happiness."[93] This narrative, endorsed by many historians, posits that marriage, which had once been a strictly economic institution, enabling the transmission of property, the protection of class interests, and the forging of political alliances, transformed into a voluntary contract that two free individuals now entered because they loved one another. Before this historical change, the dowry—that is, property or money that the bride brought to her husband upon their marriage—played a dominant role in matrimonial negotiations and contracts of propertied classes, so that a potential wife's physical attractiveness or age was deemed less important than the size of her dowry. Eventually, the rise of the state, the bourgeoisie, and economic individualism supposedly led, as Lawrence Stone argues, to the "decline of money and the rise of personal choice" as the most significant determinant in the choice of a spouse. Women began to compete for husbands in an "open market," in which their physical characteristics and personality traits—that is, their erotic capital—began to matter just as much as their dowries: "A straight back was now thought to be as important as a substantial cash portion in the struggle to catch the most eligible husband."[94] Consequently, the priority of kin ties diminished, and the conjugal couple and their children became the fundamental family unit. Ideally, within the bourgeoisie, the question of whom to marry ceased to be a parental decision and became a matter of individual choice.

The novel was one genre of capital that captured this historical transition. As Ian Watt observes in his seminal *The Rise of the Novel*, most novels written after Samuel Richardson's *Pamela* (1740) have focused "their main interest upon a courtship leading to marriage" in order to legitimize the rise of the bourgeoisie.[95] Likewise, studies of the novel have predominantly concentrated on courtship—the liminal period when parties get to know one another to decide whether there will be an engagement.[96] According to Watt's liberal claim, the rise of economic individualism led to the greater freedom that people now had in choosing their spouses.[97] By contrast, according to Nancy Armstrong's influential argument that relies on Foucault's notion of the "discourse on sexuality," the novel not only represented but also actively *contributed* to the rise of the bourgeois class by describing and legitimizing "what made a woman desirable" for marriage, namely, all the physical and personal attributes that were *not* her dowry.[98] In other words, bourgeois sexuality was, first and foremost, a cultural construct disseminated through language and writing.

As Armstrong has persuasively shown, the early nineteenth-century novel legitimized the ascendancy of the bourgeoisie by promulgating a certain ideal of the domestic woman, one who had knowledge of "domestic life, emotions, taste, and morality."[99] According to Armstrong, the sexual contract of bourgeois love required that the woman give up political control to her husband in exchange for her economic dependency on him (but also in exchange for her freedom from grueling physical labor) and for her authority over "the household, leisure time, courtship procedures, and kinship relations."[100] While political economy became a masculine dominion, the novel focused on the feminine sphere of domesticity. Yet even as the novel described "domesticity as the only haven from the trials of a heartless economic world," the feminized household was neither apolitical nor as disconnected from the larger capitalist economy as bourgeois ideology purported it to be.[101] Like Carole Pateman's *The Sexual Contract* (1988), which was published the following year, Armstrong's *Desire and Domestic Fiction* (1987) sheds light on how the subordination of women to men is integral to capitalism, or, more precisely, the kind of capitalism we have witnessed so far in the history of humanity.[102] The chief difference between the two studies is that Armstrong is interested in underscoring the power of bourgeois women, however limited it might be, and the consequential ways that white bourgeois women manage to align themselves with white male privilege with the help of the bourgeois sexual contract, that is, marriage.

As Armstrong notes, the split between the masculine and feminine spheres of influence conveniently led to an ideological setup in the novel where competing class interests could be represented as a "struggle between the sexes that can be completely resolved in terms of the sexual contract" (i.e., marriage).[103] By "transform[ing] all social differences into gender differences and gender differences into qualities of the mind," the novel disseminated bourgeois ideology in two important ways.[104] First, by sexualizing and embedding a social conflict (such as between labor and capital or between employee and employer) into the domestic sphere, the novel suggested that despite the staggering economic inequalities of the time, anyone could find private happiness within one's household. Second, by showing someone from an inferior position (usually a woman) ascend in social status regardless of her "claims to fortune and family name," the novel offered its bourgeois readership "a fable for their own emergence."[105] Because this tale of upward social mobility centered on a female protagonist, however, class conflict could be sexualized and thus concealed even as it was encountered in the novel. Marriage as a plot resolution is, of course, a well-rehearsed trope in the history of Western theater as well, especially in comedy, where the union of lovers not only concludes the plot but also reaffirms the status quo. Yet Shakespeare already disrupts and problematizes marriage as a definitive closure and societal restoration.[106] And, as previously discussed, Becque ends his *The Scavengers* with a marriage that, instead of resolving the class conflict, exposes the way women are subjugated economically by men in their intimate relationships. In this respect, that theater would continue the iconoclastic trend of chipping away at the institution of marriage is, perhaps, not too surprising. After all, it was in the theater that new kinds of romantic and sexual relationships (outside marriage) were becoming more visible. No wonder, in Chekhov's *The Seagull*, Nina's father and stepmother worry about their impressionable young daughter spending time with the "bohemia" of actors and writers who mingle at Sorin's estate.[107]

Although conjugal unions based on love became commonplace, anxiety over the love marriage lingered well into the late nineteenth century. Despite the domestic novel's ideological commitment to representing the triumph of personal qualities over material interests, economic considerations never disappeared in the actual marriage market, which arguably became *more* commercial, not less.[108] With the advent of the market economy, wage labor, and women's entrance into the workforce, a woman no longer needed to rely on her parents for a dowry, and marrying for love became part of the capitalist ideology that contended that it was now possible to carve one's destiny regardless of one's origins. A conjugal couple became (in principle) "a voluntary union of two individuals."[109] The invention of marrying for love was thus contemporaneous with increased possibilities of upward social mobility, including by way of marriage. As sociologist Eva Illouz notes, "The modern choice of a mate progressively included and mixed both emotional and economic aspirations."[110] This spelled trouble. Because marriage was now both a commercial *and* a romantic enterprise, courtship could and did result in many uncertain circumstances. How could a young woman be sure of a potential suitor's real motives? What was the main driving force of courtship—love or money? And if it were a combination of the two wants, which one prevailed?

The drama of courtship was made even more fraught because talking about money was now deemed vulgar, and both parties had to circumvent the topic. As Bourdieu notes, in modernity, the "matrimonial exchange" is "the prime example of a transaction that can only take place insofar as it is not perceived or defined as such by the contracting parties."[111] As I mentioned earlier, courtship was a perilous speculation for a woman because she could be seduced and ruined in the process of getting to know a would-be suitor. And if she could not get married, she risked becoming a prostitute or a kept woman, as in the case of Marie in Becque's *The Scavengers*.[112]

Indeed, the other prevalent narrative that competed in popularity with the marriage plot was the prostitute narrative (*Moll Flanders, Roxana, Fanny Hill*).[113] As Brad Kent points out, the prostitute narrative comes in two varieties: the libertine narrative depicts prostitution as a chance at capital accumulation and class mobility, while the reform narrative shows prostitution to be a social fall, focusing on its dangerous and degrading aspects such as abuse, poverty, and venereal disease.[114] Meanwhile, on the nineteenth-century stage, the "fallen woman" became one of the most popular characters (*Camille, Lady Audley's Secret, The Adventuress, The Second Mrs. Tanqueray*, to name just a few examples), so much so that Henry James complained that "adultery" was the "only theme" of French drama, and Bernard Shaw worried that his compatriots were following suit in believing that "a little adultery would purify and ennoble the British stage."[115] Together, the marriage plot and the prostitute narrative exposed the precarious economic situation of women across class lines and the growing importance of erotic capital for the workplace and class ascendancy.

Melodrama attempted to assuage collective anxiety about conflicting motives in courtship by celebrating the triumph of love and personal freedom. In the first half of the nineteenth century, the novel, as Elsie Michie notes, still told "stories about the triumph of individual choice over crass self-interest."[116] And, as Louis Menand observes, Jane Austen "understands courtship as an attempt to achieve the maximum point of intersection between love and money."[117] This is also the case in early nineteenth-century stage melodrama. Take, for example, the plot of Edward Bulwer-Lytton's 1840 *Money*, which satirizes the increasingly commodified practice of courtship. Two young people in love, Alfred Evelyn and Clara Douglas, part ways because neither of them has any money. Clara rejects Alfred because she does not want the two of them to be as miserable as her penniless parents had once been. Yet when Alfred serendipitously receives an inheritance, he does not immediately propose to Clara, worrying that she is too dignified to marry him now that he is rich. To be sure, *Money* shows how materialistic concerns were becoming more important in a capitalist world, as characters make proto-Wildean remarks like "Men are valued not for what they *are*, but what they *seem* to be" and "If you have no merit or money of your own, you must trade on the merits and money of other people."[118] Yet the virtuous characters are still able to hold onto nonmaterial qualities such as honor, dignity, and pride in their quest for love. In his scathing review of a contemporary revival, Bruce Weber summarizes the play's simplistic message: "Did you know that money, though it makes life more comfortable, is no substitute for love?"[119] In other words, Clara Douglas and Alfred Evelyn are no Kate Croy and Merton Densher, the poor scheming betrothed of Henry James's novel *The Wings of the Dove* (1902), whose plan—to swindle a dying heiress of her money in order to get married—offers readers "an exquisite moral dilemma," as Michael Wood puts it.[120]

In their immanent critique of the bourgeois marriage, many nineteenth-century economists compare marriage to prostitution, as Engels does when he famously states in *The Origin of the Family, Private Property, and the State* that the wife "differs from the ordinary courtesan only in that she does not hire out her body, like a wage-worker, on piecework, but sells it into slavery once and for all."[121] In his reasoning, Engels echoes the prevalent attitude of eighteenth-century writers like Defoe and Wollstonecraft, who claimed that marrying for money instead of love was "legal prostitution."[122] This equation between marriage and prostitution underscored the inherent contradiction of the bourgeois love marriage that revealed itself in the residual importance of the dowry and the presence of economic coercion, especially for women entering a conjugal union (although, as Defoe points out, a man too could be considered a prostitute if his reason for marrying was expediency rather than love).[123] Many thinkers were quick to expose the lingering economic motivations underneath the amorous covers. What, after all, was the purpose of the dowry for a marriage that was now supposed to be a voluntary contract between two free individuals in love? To answer this question, economists and sociologists speculated about the origin of the dowry.

In *The Philosophy of Money* (1900), Simmel suggests that the dowry custom began with the money economy itself, for it was money that "makes possible separate production for the market and for the household economy and this separation initiates a more rigorous division of labor between the sexes."[124] Under the conditions of shifting cultivation, claims Simmel, women worked alongside men and thus had "a more tangible economic value."[125] So did their children. In such primitive societies, the bridegroom had to pay a "brideprice" to compensate the bride's family for the loss of her labor.[126] With the advent of plow agriculture, farming became men's work, and women were consigned to household chores, becoming an economic strain along with their children.[127] To be sure, women and children continued to contribute to the wealth of the man's *oikos*, but patriarchal capitalism devalues household labor, reproduction, and the care for one's dependents. For this reason, Simmel argues, the dowry emerged as compensation for the husband's "having to support the wife."[128] So although the dowry was essentially a woman's startup capital, it was ultimately used as a political tool to control her agency and future.

Thus, the dowry ensured that a woman's foundational capital was directly absorbable by patriarchal capitalism. Even in those instances when the dowry was a financial guarantee of the wife's "upkeep" (that is, she could claim that capital back if her husband died or the marriage was dissolved), the dowry forced her into a fixed societal role (wife) and bound her to the intertwined systems of patriarchy and capitalism. Furthermore, the woman's dowry typically became the property of the husband, who had complete legal authority over it. The dowry, then, was capital that was explicitly reserved for marrying a young woman off. She was not free to take that money and/or property and dispose of those resources as she saw fit. Hence, financially independent women, such as heiresses or New Women who managed to make their own living, had always provoked public anxiety (as we will see later in this chapter). This anxiety only increased by the end of the nineteenth century, when the husband's rule over the financial matters of the nuclear family began to weaken.

Although women were gaining more legal power over their property, Engels warned that women's control over their private property was not an adequate solution to liberating them because private property ultimately still engendered a social relation that subjugated women—monogamy under capitalism. Engels is careful to emphasize that under the intertwined systems of capitalism and patriarchy, monogamy is restricted to women, for men continue to enjoy sexual relations outside marriage with no fear of social reprobation or punishment. Monogamy is thus always "supplemented by adultery and prostitution."[129] And according to Simmel, it is the dowry, a woman's startup capital, that functions as "the distinguishing attribute of the legitimate wife in contrast to the concubine, who had no further claim on the husband so that both compensation for her as well as security measures for her would be out of place."[130] Marriage and prostitution are thus simply two sides of the same coin, and, indeed, it is money that arbitrarily separates women into one category or the other.

In this way, Jean's throw of the coin is a visual dramatization of a historically specific social relation. What distinguishes the wife from the mistress or prostitute is capital, or, more precisely, the dowry. Since Julie does not have any money, which could make her a desirable wife in Jean's view, he performs the gesture of paying her for sex to get rid of any guilt and to establish their relationship as that between client and prostitute. This is how much Jean is willing to pay for Julie's erotic capital while demanding a hefty sum for his own. Most importantly, Jean's throw of the coin mimics the act of "flipping the coin," underscoring the contingent manner by which women are separated into wives and mistresses, Madonnas and whores, or simply good women and bad women. This division is enabled not only by the sexual double standard of patriarchy but also by the economic subjugation of women under capitalism. And monogamy under capitalism is one form of such subjugation.

Monogamy, claims Engels, "was the first form of the family based not on natural but on economic conditions, namely, on the victory of private property over original, naturally developed, common ownership."[131] Monogamy ensured the transmission of private property within a nuclear family in a patrilineal society. Like Simmel, Engels emphasizes that the patriarchal nuclear family is a recent historical phenomenon, which emerged with the invention of the plowshare and women's loss of economic power. In fact, Engels believed that in primitive societies, women had even more power than Simmel assumed they did. Following the argument of Lewis H. Morgan's *Ancient Society* (1877), Engels envisions a primitive matriarchal communism where the "original position of the mother as the sole certain parent of her children assured her, and thus women in general, a higher social status than they have ever enjoyed since."[132] Similarly, the German socialist politician and writer August Bebel, whose *Woman and Socialism* (1879) was one of the most widely read socialist texts of the fin de siècle, argues that "matriarchate implied communism and equality of all," while patriarchy depended on private property and the oppression of women.[133]

Although most of Engels's and Simmel's theories about primitive societies have since been disproven, their ideas about bourgeois marriage constitute a helpful background against which to explore late nineteenth- and early twentieth-century literature and drama. Their speculations about the past can be read as thought experiments about the future because, however erroneous the former might be, they suggest that the situation of women, the institution of marriage, and family structure are historically contingent and shaped by material conditions of production. The economic questions that these thinkers asked were being posed and tested in the social laboratory of the theater. Shaw, for one, also identified the protection of private property as the ruthless motive lying underneath the romantic veneer of the bourgeois marriage. He explicitly associated the institution of marriage with the concept of the *oikos*, claiming that the only way that women would ever manage to truly liberate themselves from patriarchal oppression is by "refusing to enter any building where they are publicly classed with a man's house, his ox, and his ass, as his purchased chattels."[134]

Like Marx's critique of capitalism, Engels's and Simmel's critiques of the bourgeois marriage are immanent, meaning they expose the contradiction of matrimony under capitalism on its own terms. In theory, a bourgeois marriage, based on love and the freedom of choice, was supposed to occur between two individuals who willingly entered a contract. In practice, however, one party—usually the woman—was coerced or forced to agree to disadvantageous conditions, including unacknowledged and uncompensated housekeeping labor, the bearing and rearing of children, and various forms of abuse. And it might be tempting to think that, in a capitalist society, a marriage of two rich persons could be based on freedom; but as Theodor Adorno reminds us, "the privileged are precisely those in whom the pursuit of interests has become second nature—they would not otherwise uphold privilege."[135] It is no wonder, then, that Engels saw the capitalist mode of production ultimately resulting in "the proclamation of a conflict between the sexes," a conflict compellingly dramatized by the battle of the sexes in Strindberg's *Miss Julie*.[136]

The internal contradiction of capitalism that we observe in *Miss Julie* is the discrepancy between the ideals of equality and freedom that the capitalist mode of production made possible and the reality of exploitation that takes on the illusory form of a voluntary sexual contract. According to Strindberg, even when two people marry for love, they cannot escape the economic pressures of the capitalist system. Financial worries related to courtship and marriage were somewhat of an obsessive theme for Strindberg, as he himself struggled to support Siri and their three children. In "Love and the Price of Grain," one of his short stories from the collection *Getting Married*, Strindberg shows how reckless everyday expenses can quickly lead to a disintegration of a marriage. Refreshingly, the culpable spendthrift is not a Bovaresque wife, who in this case is an advocate of prudent saving, but instead a profligate husband with a penchant for luxuries.[137] In "Just to Be Married," love between newlyweds never has a chance to fully blossom because of all the costs associated with entertaining the wife's family. The husband, who plays the viola in the orchestra of the Royal Queen Company, must tutor students just to afford the various lunches and dinners that his wife's relatives request and to regularly provide the entire family with free theater tickets. The marriage breaks down because the husband's work at the theater keeps him away from his wife: "But he could not choose another profession. That was impossible. And theatrical performances could not be held during the daytime, because everyone was at work while it was light. He willingly admitted that his wife could not enjoy being married to a man who only came home at night, as if she'd been a prostitute, (and hardly that)."[138] In contrast to Engels, however, Strindberg believed that it was the husband who was often the abused and coerced party in a marriage. In *Small Catechism for the Underclass*, Strindberg defines marriage as "an economic institution through which a man is forced to work for a woman, whose slave he has become" and argues that "it is just that women's so-called property goes under his charge and that the crumbs she can contribute in dowry pay his bachelor debts, through which he learned a trade to support the family."[139] Hence, Jean calls a potential marriage to Julie a "misalliance"

(27). Strindberg further expresses anxiety over women taking control of household management through the play's background. As Julie recounts to Jean, her mother, who "was not of noble birth," not only brought her up as a boy but also made all the women servants of the estate "do men's work, with the result that the property came near being ruined" (25). Before getting married, her mother tried to keep her money by entrusting it to her lover, a brick manufacturer. Otherwise, her capital would have gone straight under the control of the Count. (In Sweden, until 1920, a husband had all the rights to any capital that a woman brought with her to their marriage.) Julie's mother eventually set the estate on fire in order to have her lover rebuild it. But he ended up pinching her money. This background suggests that no one is entirely free in the fictional world of *Miss Julie*, not even the seemingly powerful, invisible Count. He, too, was at someone else's mercy once—his wife's. As Strindberg was careful to emphasize, however, he was attacking not marriage (in fact, he believed that happy marriages were possible, albeit rare), but "marriage under present conditions," namely capitalism.[140]

What would romantic relationships be like under a different socioeconomic system? Engels believed that under communism the annulment of private property and "the passage of all the means of production into common property" would lead to a full realization of monogamy rather than its transformation into free love or polyamory, as advocated by anarchist thinkers like Émile Armand. For Engels, "individual sex love" was not immune to jealousy or the desire to focus on a single romantic partner. Instead, he imagined, when women would no longer be coerced or forced by economic necessity to enter prostitution or to "tolerate the customary infidelity of the men," men would become monogamous because, like women, they would now be compelled to honor their commitments. No longer could men use tools of oppression or coercion to get their way. If a woman's livelihood and the future of her children no longer depended on the economic support of her life partner, there would be no reason for her to stay in a union where she was disrespected, abused, or otherwise maltreated. And monogamy would not be an obligation or sacrifice on the part of men. Engels suggests that men would also benefit from a socioeconomic reality in which the women they encountered were free, independent agents with minds of their own. Men could then be confident that such women were engaging with them not because of what they could get out of them but out of love. Their voluntary coupling would be an end in itself rather than a means for economic mobility or security. This alone could apparently inspire commitment and care. Although, in Engels's view, "individual sex love" is exclusive, it is not necessarily everlasting. What Engels seems to have in mind are common-law marriage and serial monogamy. Two people are free to form a union and to break up after "a definite cessation of affection, or its displacement by a new passionate love" without the constraints of marriage or "the useless mire of divorce proceedings."[141]

There are, of course, many criticisms that we might level at Engels's theory of love under communism—its unquestioned heteronormativity, gender binary, and focus on monogamy; its neglect of gender violence; and, most important, its failure to see gender as a social construct of the capitalist mode of production. Yet Engels's central claim—that patriarchy is maintained by the economic dominance of men and that a change in economic and material conditions would lead to a transformation of social relations—is worth taking seriously. Although we never witness such a transformation of social relations in *Miss Julie*, we do see the negation of a centuries-old sexual contract by which marriage was supposed to resolve class conflict (as practiced in the early nineteenth-century novel and melodrama).

Jean hints to Julie that their socioeconomic situation makes it nearly impossible for genuine love to develop between them: "You have fallen prey to an intoxication and you want to hide your mistake by imagining that you love me. But you do not—unless perhaps it is my appearance that attracts you—and then your love is no better than mine. But I cannot be satisfied with being a mere animal to you, and your real love I could never awaken" (23–24). And Strindberg agrees with Jean on this point:

> I do not believe there can be any love in a higher sense between two such different dispositions, so I let Miss Julie imagine she loves Jean as a way of protecting or excusing herself, and I let Jean suppose he could fall in love with her if his social circumstances were different. I suspect that love is rather like the hyacinth which has to put its roots down in the darkness *before* it can produce a strong flower. Here it shoots up, blossoms, and goes to seed all at once, and that is why it dies so quickly. (68)

Nevertheless, perhaps we do see something blossom between the two in performance, however briefly: a "utopian performative," as Dolan would call it.[142] And it is this unrealized potential for love that elevates the play above the cynicism of a *comédie rosse* and makes the alienated form of intimacy between the two all the more poignant. Unlike Becque's *The Scavengers* and Ostrovsky's *Without a Dowry*, both of which end with the pessimistic conclusion that love does not exist, *Miss Julie* gives us glimpses of love only to show how it withers away under economic pressures. No longer can the class conflict be transformed into a struggle between the sexes that can then be conveniently resolved through the sexual contract of the bourgeois marriage. Instead, Jean and Julie's battle of the sexes exposes the exploitation that has always been latent in sexual-economic relations under capitalism.

Filthy Lucre, Dirty Mind: Freudian Intercourse between Money and Sex

Not only were the risks of courtship compared to the perils of financial speculation, but financial speculation itself was compared to courtship and seduction, especially the way that financial schemes attempted to attract more stock buyers. The way Jean tries to make Julie a financial backer of his hotel scheme by way of seduction is not an isolated incident on the fin-de-siècle stage. The "stock ticker play"[143] regularly intertwined financial melodrama with the drama of courtship. For instance, as Garrett Eisler observes, *Henrietta* (1887), a popular comedy by American playwright Bronson Howard, blurs the excitement of the stock trade with erotic desire.[144] The "Henrietta" of the title refers to several women and entities in the play, including "the most famous ballet-dancer in New York," as well as the railway company at the center of the play's mania for speculation.[145]

Similarly, Martha Morton, the first financially successful American female playwright, whose plays earned her more than $1 million in the span of her career, wrote a financial melodrama—*A Fool of Fortune* (1896)—in which courtship and speculation are intimately intertwined. Jenny, an enterprising and clever young woman whose family has fallen on hard times because of her father's addiction to speculating on Wall Street, is able to catch a desirable French count for a husband even though she does not have a dowry.[146] She attracts him not only through her erotic capital, namely her feistiness, but also because she shows her European beau how to make money the American way—through speculation. In effect, her insider knowledge of Wall Street becomes her dowry, but the play also underscores that her fiery temperament is what makes her attracted to risk-taking—both in love and on the stock exchange.[147]

Even as Jean attempts to be "sensible" and to dispel "sentimentality" with his dealings with Julie, his business model ironically relies on speculation and the volatility of erotic desire. Renting out villas to "loving couples" is "a business that easily generates large profits," in Jean's view (27). According to his plan, couples would pay upfront for half a year but would inevitably end up quarreling within three weeks and go their separate ways. Those vacated vacation homes could then be released to other couples, repeating the cycle. Even if Jean is speaking with tongue in cheek here, his proposed strategy for running a love hotel highlights how the uncertainty and unpredictability of speculation echo the volatility and impermanence of a whirlwind romance. His entire business model is speculative because it counts potential future profits (the surplus of rent left over after three short weeks of romance) as guaranteed revenue. (Presumably, Jean's hotel would not offer a money-back guarantee.) Jean is not unique in associating speculation with erotic desire. Naturalist works often compare the excitement of finance with erotic energy.[148] As mentioned in the introduction, even as naturalism condemns capitalism, it often represents speculation and the highs and lows of business cycles as natural and necessary occurrences. The capitalist boom-and-bust economy is linked not only to the natural world of seasonal changes and weather disturbances but also to the ebb and flow of erotic desire.

For example, in Zola's novel *Money*, the relentless drive for capital accumulation and the appetite for speculation are explicitly compared to the libidinal drive. Here is how financier Saccard explains the irresistible drive for capital to his mistress, Madame Caroline:

> Yes, speculation. Why does this word frighten you? . . . Why, speculation, it is the lure of life itself, it is the eternal desire that compels us to struggle and to live. . . . For the hundred of children that one fails to engender, one barely begets one. It is the excess that brings about the necessary, is it not? Oh! Madame! There are many unnecessary indecencies, but without them the world would certainly come to an end.[149]

For Saccard, the excess, risk, and even the swindling of speculation are necessary evils that enable production, which he compares to the begetting of children. He condones the many unrealized ventures and utter scams associated with reckless gambling on the stock exchange because speculation supposedly stimulates the market and eventually results in real products and development projects. Following the same logic, though, one could also argue that speculation can happen for the thrill of it and lead to unforeseeable consequences, destabilize the status quo, and wreak havoc in people's lives. Are we still talking about speculation? By the end of Saccard's speech, it is unclear whether he is describing finance or has veered into verbal foreplay. Likewise, the last words of the novel compare the ambivalent but still largely positive power of money to carnal love: "Why then should money carry the blame for all the dirt and crimes it causes? For is love less filthy—that which creates life?" (369). Are we still talking about money?

As David Bennett has shown, the "intercourse between languages of money and sex"—from employing economic metaphors for sexual concepts to Freud's imagining the libido as a psychic economy—took hold with the rise of capitalism.[150] For one, psychoanalysis relies on a monetary exchange: the patient pays the analyst for the latter's time and emotional labor. Yet, as Bennett points out, while psychoanalysis relishes frank discussions of sexuality, it often skirts the topic of money, which becomes, instead of sex, *the* taboo subject. (For example, many patients find it more awkward to talk with their therapists about how much they can afford to pay for their sessions than about sex.) For this reason, according to

Bennett and others, psychoanalysis avoids treating monetary issues by "habitually decod[ing] money-talk as metaphoric sex-talk."[151] But the repressed topic of money returns in the way that psychoanalysis employs mercantile metaphors to explain sexuality. For instance, at one point, Freud compares the ego, which is suppressing "a continual flood of sexual phantasies," to "a speculator whose money has become tied up in his various enterprises."[152] And in *The Interpretation of Dreams* he compares the relationship between daytime thoughts and unconscious wishes to a contract between an entrepreneur who has a business idea and a capitalist who can provide the necessary capital for realizing that idea. Because this analogy echoes Jean's plan of enlisting Julie as the financial backer for his hotel scheme, it is worth quoting here at length:

> To put it in the form of a comparison: the daytime thought might possibly play the part of entrepreneur for the dream; but the entrepreneur who has the idea, as we say, and the will to translate it into action, still cannot do anything without capital; he needs a capitalist to take on the expenses, and the capitalist in this case, who contributes the psychical expenditure for the dream, is always and unfailingly, whatever the daytime thought may be, a wish from the Unconscious. On other occasions the capitalist is himself the entrepreneur; in dreams, indeed, that is the more usual case. An unconscious wish has been aroused by the day's work, and it now creates the dream. All the other situations possible in the economic circumstances I have just suggested as an example also have their parallels in the procedures of the dream; the entrepreneur is in a position to contribute a small amount of capital himself; several entrepreneurs might turn to the same capitalist; several capitalists might club together and provide what the entrepreneurs require. Likewise, there are also dreams that are supported by more than one wish, and there are further variations of a similar kind, which can easily be reviewed, and are of no more interest to us.[153]

By the end of this analogy, Freud describes daytime thoughts and unconscious wishes as critical players in a modern-day financial corporation.

It is easy to brush aside Freud's comparison of psychic structures to financial concepts as a helpful metaphor and nothing more, but the intertwinement of the language of sex and the language of money points to the crucial historical fact that the capitalist economy has shaped our awareness of ourselves as "embodied subjects of desire," to borrow Bennett's turn of phrase.[154] What is at stake here is not simply the question of whether or not the unconscious exists (which is outside the scope of this book) but the fact that economic models and ideas have influenced our understanding of psychology and sexuality. As Bennett reminds us, the notion of the libido as an "economy" and "sexual desire as a quantifiable economic resource" comes down to us from economics. In this way, the intercourse between money and sex complicates the notion that performance, as Peggy Phelan argues, "clogs" the circulation of capital and "resists the balanced circulation of finance" because it can vanish into "the realm of invisibility and the unconscious where it eludes regulation and control."[155] But what if the unconscious (particularly that of a subject born into a capitalist society) is already shaped by the culture of capitalism and financial thinking from the very beginning? This does not mean that the performing arts have no way to resist capitalism, but it does make such resistance more challenging than the mere reliance on performance's ephemerality.[156]

That subjects' economic and erotic desires are intimately intertwined is evident in the world of *Miss Julie*, which anticipates Freud's theories. Consider the importance of dreams in *Miss Julie* and their dual nature as both economic and erotic wishes. The entire action of the play takes place on Midsummer Eve, a night of dancing, revelry, and fortune-telling festivities that are believed to prophesy one's future spouse. For this reason, when Jean hears Julie and Kristin discuss the broth that Kristin has prepared for Julie's pregnant dog, he playfully asks if it is "some troll's dish" that they are "both concocting . . . to pierce the future with and evoke the face of [the] intended" (8). In this moment, he is positioning himself as the object of their desire and the presumed groom that both women, in his view, are hoping to see reflected in the broth. Later, Jean and Julie will share with one another their recurring dreams that simultaneously prefigure and challenge Freud's division of men's and women's dreams into "ambitious" and "erotic" wishes, namely that men fantasize about social accomplishments, and women about romance. Jean dreams that he is climbing the trunk of a tall tree to "plunder the birds' nests up there where the golden eggs lie" (13). The only thing standing in his way is the smoothness of the trunk, but if he can just reach that first branch, he will be on his way up.

By contrast, Julie dreams that she is "seated at the top of a high pillar," from which she cannot get down. But she desperately wants to "come down to earth," and if she ever came down, she "would wish [her]self down in the ground" (12–13). Thus, while Jean wants to rise socially, Julie fantasizes about masochistic self-degradation. At first glance, their wishes align with Freud's division of male and female fantasies.[157] But a closer look reveals the presence of an erotic component to Jean's economic dream. The "smoothness" of the trunk has an unmistakably sensual connotation, and the "first branch" of his plan turns out to be Julie. Similarly, there is an economic component to Julie's erotic dream of self-abasement: she does not want just to fall; she wants to go deep *into* the ground. This desire to go underground could signify a return to the soil, namely the agrarian past, when her presumed feudal ancestors had power, and death—hers and her entire family line—in the age of capital. When Jean suggests to Julie that they "should sleep on nine midsummer flowers tonight and then [their] dreams would come true," he is referring to the Midsummer Eve tradition by which one would dream of one's future husband or wife by placing seven kinds of flowers underneath one's pillow (13). In other words, Jean suggests that they would dream about one another, teasing Julie with the possibility of a romantic union. And in a perverse manner, their dreams do come true. Jean gets a hold of his first rung (Julie), though it does not lead anywhere on the social ladder, and Julie is granted the possibility of fulfilling her death wish.

What came first—sexual metaphors for economic concepts or economic metaphors for sex—is a bit of a chicken-or-egg problem. On the one hand, as previously mentioned, Armstrong argues that a new (bourgeois) sexuality, which developed and disseminated through writing, contributed to the economic rise of the bourgeoisie. On the other hand, Lawrence Birken suggests that it was the other way around—that the development of neoclassical economics in the late nineteenth century inspired the birth of sexology. Because the marginal revolution made consumption, namely "the satisfaction of idiosyncratic desire—the end of all human activity," it required, Birken claims, a science that could explain individualistic desire.[158] Enter sexology. Both Armstrong and Birken rely on Foucault's *History of Sexuality*, which argues that the development of capitalism brought about two significant changes in the public's attitude toward sexuality. First, repression and the confinement of sexuality to the home became "an integral part of the bourgeois order."[159] Second, there was a veritable proliferation of a discourse claiming "to reveal the truth about sex." Moreover, because "labor capacity was being systematically exploited," nonreproductive sex was deemed disruptive to work.[160] Time was not to be spent "in pleasurable pursuits, except in those—reduced to a minimum—that enabled it to reproduce itself."[161] Foucault elaborates:

> If it was truly necessary to make room for illegitimate sexualities, it was reasoned, let them take their infernal mischief elsewhere, to a place where they could be reintegrated, if not in the circuits of production, at least in those of profit. The brothel and the mental hospital would be those places of tolerance: the prostitute, the client, and the pimp, together with the psychiatrist and his hysteric.[162]

The collective anxiety surrounding "illegitimate sexualities" echoes the concern about financial speculation in that both activities were tolerated only in moderation and only if they could still stimulate the capitalist economy. In the case of nonreproductive sexuality, the hope was that if it did not reproduce what Marx calls "the reserve army" of labor, it could at least generate profit through carefully controlled, surveilled, and policed establishments.¹⁶³ Similarly, financial speculation was an acceptable economic activity if it proved to be an investment that eventually resulted in production but was considered fraudulent as soon as it inflated values to the point where it caused financial bubbles and crises. Still, in the late nineteenth century, especially in the Victorian context, the misdeeds of financial speculation were more acceptable to the public than acts of sexual transgression were, precisely because finance was part and parcel of the capitalist world order, whereas "illegitimate sexualities" had the potential to distract the population from work. News of salacious sex scandals captured the public's attention more often than financial crimes—so much so that the first could often act as strategic distractions from the latter. As we will soon see, this phenomenon becomes important in Shaw's drama.

Both sexology and neoclassical economics were fledgling disciplines at the end of the nineteenth century, so it is not surprising that their discourses would become cross-pollinated. Given their shared history, the discourse of sex and the discourse of money tend to slip into one another. It is what makes sexual puns so easy but a serious discussion about money and sex so hard. Comparing sex to money and money to sex produces a maddening tautology, as when Marx cites Timon's description of money as the "common whore of mankind" (Shakespeare, *Timon of Athens*, 4.3)¹⁶⁴ or when he writes that prostitution "is only a *specific* expression of the *general* prostitution of the labourer."¹⁶⁵ What does it mean to compare money to a worker who sells sex for money? And what does it mean to argue simultaneously that prostitution is work and that all work under capitalism is prostitution? We are back in the vicious circle of thinking about money and sex together. If, as Marc Shell argues, language and thought internalize money into "money of the mind,"¹⁶⁶ then filthy lucre also seems to inspire a dirty mind. Yet the conflation of money and sex is a problem because it obfuscates economic coercion and gender violence, ignoring historical context and specific social relations within courtship, marriage, prostitution (broadly defined), and their mutual economic network. This is even true of serious discussions about the relationship between libido and the drive for capital accumulation in Gilles Deleuze and Félix Guattari's *Anti-Oedipus: Capitalism and Schizophrenia* (1972) and Jean-François Lyotard's *Libidinal Economy* (1974). Without an analysis of how the mutually reinforcing relationship between patriarchy and capitalism influences the movement of capital in the circulation of sex, a political critique of the capitalist economy is incomplete.¹⁶⁷ *Miss Julie*'s critique of capitalism depends on its exploration of the bonds between capitalism and patriarchy regardless of what Strindberg's own vacillating and often contradictory views of gender relations might have been.

When Jean flings the coin in Julie's direction, we also see a man throw money at a woman inside a theater, an institution linked to the brothel since the early modern era through cultural metaphors, shared geography, and mutual crowds, and are thus faced with our own complicity as onlookers.[168] During Strindberg's time, members of the audience would have most certainly included prostitutes and their clients. It is no wonder that when Jean plays coy with Julie in the first half of the play, she calls out his affectation: "Where did you learn to speak like that? You've spent a lot of time in the theater, is that it?" (10). Later, Jean will indeed credit his storytelling skills to his reading of novels, eavesdropping on conversations of the wealthy, and frequent trips to the theater (16). On the one hand, as a cultural figure, the actor is a subversive chameleon who is able to transgress class lines through mimicry, if only during the time of performance. On the other hand, actors and especially actresses have long been associated with prostitution. As Julie Cassiday reminds us in reference to the early nineteenth century, actresses made "their living by displaying their bodies publicly for the enjoyment of a largely male audience."[169] Still, a certain distinction, however thin, was necessary for social decorum. When the author of *The Swell's Night Guide* (1841), a popular guidebook with reviews of London nightlife establishments including bars, brothels, and theaters, gives tips to men for approaching actresses, he advises that instead of offering money, they should invite actresses over for "private theatricals."[170]

By the end of the nineteenth century, the stock exchange became associated with the theater and the brothel through geographic proximity and mutual attendees. Zola's novels, for example, document how the same personalities mingle and move between the three spaces. If the theater was like a brothel, it was also a space of speculation, where, with some luck, actors could make a fortune, achieve celebrity, and rise to the highest ranks of society, often with the help of their erotic capital. As Sharon Marcus has shown, the nineteenth century saw the rise of celebrity culture that endowed stars like Sarah Bernhardt with substantial social, cultural, and economic capital.[171] The late nineteenth-century theater was where the demise of the bourgeois sexual contract would be dramatized with force. After all, it was in the theater that audiences first encountered women who had had a taste of economic independence. As Tracy Davis has persuasively argued, actresses, despite their hardships, stigmatization, and uncertain status, became "the symbols of women's self-sufficiency and independence."[172] And it was in the theater that the New Woman, the feminist icon who came into prominence in the late nineteenth century, made her voice heard. This New Woman stood for an educated, independent, feminist woman who boasted financial independence and often even a career. The social reformer and sociologist Beatrice Webb suggested to Shaw that he should write a play about the New Woman, a "real, modern, unromantic, hard-working woman."[173] The result of this endeavor was Shaw's *Mrs. Warren's Profession*, a drama that traces the links between financialization, prostitution, and the emergence of this New Woman and explores the role that erotic capital played in her self-realization.

Shaw's Economic Theories

Shaw was vociferous about his persistent interest in and extensive study of economics. In an address delivered to the Political and Economic Circle of the National Liberal Club, Shaw emphasized his serious commitment to the science of economics: "Now gentlemen, I am really a political economist. I have studied the thing. I understand Ricardo's law of rent; and Jevons' law of value. I can tell you what in its essence sound economy means for any nation."[174] In a 1904 letter to his biographer, Archibald Henderson, Shaw writes: "In all my plays my economic studies have played as important a part as a knowledge of anatomy does in the works of Michael Angelo."[175] Shaw was also immersed in the business side of theater. He paid close attention to the box office, and not only for the sake of profit. "An author should always have these [box office] returns," asserts Shaw, "not only to check the accounts, but to be able to follow the history of his play—whether it is getting more or less popular, whether it is gaining with the gallery and losing with the stalls (so as to shew the class of people it appeals to)."[176]

That Shaw was passionate about economics is evident. *How* economic theories and ideas operate in his plays is a more difficult question. Interpreting Shaw's dramatic works as mere economic tracts is fair neither to Shaw's knowledge of economics nor to his dramatic talent. Shaw's writings on economics are as bounteous as they are diverse. And Shaw often contradicted himself not only on economic issues but also on most topics. Thus, my aim is neither to give an extensive survey of Shaw's socialist beliefs nor to instrumentally illustrate how his plays promote specific economic ideas. For one, Shaw's socialism has already generated a wealth of scholarship.[177] Rather, the question I would like to pursue in what follows is how Shavian drama thinks through economic issues and tests economic models by looking at *Mrs. Warren's Profession* as a drama of financial speculation and courtship. What can Shaw's play *contribute* to our understanding of economic thought that a Fabian tract cannot? How does *Mrs. Warren's Profession* experiment with economic ideas and models onstage in a way that an economic text or a political pamphlet cannot?

Shaw was a socialist who embraced the Fabian notions of gradual reforms, parliamentalism, and the permeation of progressive ideas. Although inspired by Marx's critique of capitalism, Shaw rejected his labor theory of value, dialectical materialism, and call to revolution. Toward the end of his life, however, Shaw became more open to radical action. The two economic theories that arguably influenced him the most were Ricardo's law of rent and Jevons's theory of marginal utility. In his magnum opus, *On the Principles of Political Economy and Taxation* (1817), Ricardo defines rent as "that portion of the produce of the earth which is paid to the landlord for the use of the original and indestructible powers of the soil."[178] For Ricardo, the term "rent" does not mean what it usually does today—the payment for hiring a property such as an apartment or a house. Rather, Ricardian rent is, first and foremost, a surplus. In other words, rent is the economic return that land (or any natural factor of production) accumulates during its use in production. The produce obtainable on the best available rent-free land is known as the margin of production. As David Ricci explains, rent is "that portion of any income which accrued to its recipient without work or sacrifice on his part, without cost to him. Such a portion, such a rent—for example, the interest from inherited bonds—while legally sanctioned in capitalist societies, was thought by many to be ethically unearned."[179] Following Jevons, Shaw thought of capital as "spare money" and viewed capitalism as having been established from the "spare money" gained from differential rent.[180] It is not by accident that Fabian socialism was born in Britain, where the landed gentry continued to hold most of the wealth long into the twentieth century. Shaw's focus on capitalists' "spare money" is reflected in his preoccupation with capitalist characters—rarely do we see any laborers on the Shavian stage, even if his plays do condemn their exploitation.

How do all these ideas function in Shaw's plays? Perhaps the best description of Shaw's drama comes from political historian James Alexander: "A play can attract, amuse or repel. But it cannot suggest a direction. It does not take the elbow of anyone who watches it. . . . In his political writing, Shaw took the elbow of those he addressed."[181] Searching for Fabian messages in Shaw's drama is counterproductive because Shaw's socialism is, as Alexander puts it, "partial, argumentative or dialectical" and "almost deliberately offensive."[182] For one, Shaw attempted to differentiate his ideas from both liberalism and Marxism, picking and choosing from various strands of economic thought. Thus, Shaw could uphold the Fabian Society's belief in the advancement of socialism through gradualist and reformist means while simultaneously defending the inquisitional violence of the state. When Shaw tried to express his eclectic political and socioeconomic ideas in public, they often came across as controversial, contradictory, incoherent, and at times downright disturbing (especially his embrace of eugenics and his later praise of Stalin). No wonder Shaw ultimately chose playwriting over a career in politics. It was in the theater and, specifically in the drama of ideas, that Shaw could finally and most successfully give his ideas form and structure. He redistributed his various incompatible ideas to a panoply of characters from different social and political backgrounds and ages without having to be dogmatic or choose sides.

In this light, Shavian drama can be considered a prime example of what Russian linguist Mikhail Bakhtin calls "dialogical" and "polyglot" art.[183] Although Bakhtin argues that it is the novel that is "dialogical" and "heteroglot"—that is, expressive of multiplicitous points of view that include but are not limited to the author's—Bakhtin's statements can easily be applied to drama. In fact, as Puchner points out, Bakhtin borrows the vocabulary for his study of the novel from drama.[184] (For example, according to Bakhtin, Ancient Greek "tragedy is a polyglot genre.")[185] For Bakhtin, it is through the diversity of voices and speech types that "heteroglossia," namely "the internal stratification of any single national language into social dialects," which each expresses the ideological perspective of a particular class, enters the novel.[186] With his careful attention to accents, dialects, and speech rhythms, Shaw was more than aware of the workings of "heteroglossia." After all, Shaw wrote an entire play exploring what Bakhtin calls the "social and historical voices populating language"[187]— *Pygmalion* (1912). Shavian characters are born into and develop in the social matrix of language. In the last scene of *Mrs. Warren's Profession*, Kitty Warren is so distressed that her daughter Vivie has disowned her that she drops the social mask of proper English. Shaw's directions signal that Vivie is "jarred and antagonized by the echo of the slums in her mother's voice" (284). And it is not only the dramatic characters that make Shavian drama heteroglot; Shaw's own many divergent and strong opinions expressed in the apologies, prefaces, epilogues, and even alternative endings to his plays ensure a multiplicity of voices in his drama.[188]

That the practice of courtship was a significant subject of interest to Shaw is evident not only in the preface to his play *Getting Married* but also in his myriad early plays that shed light on the nexus between capital and marriage, including *Widowers' Houses* (1892), *The Philanderer* (1893), *Man and Superman* (1903), *Major Barbara* (1905), and others. Yet it is in *Mrs. Warren's Profession* (1893) that Shaw explores most vividly the links connecting courtship, marriage, prostitution, and financial speculation by paying close attention to the circulation of erotic capital and the dowry. By focusing on prostitution as financial speculation, Shaw was trying not only to show how salacious topics often distract the public from scandals of greed and corruption but also to make his audience experience the same level of indignation over financial crimes as they would over alleged sexual indecency.

One of the crucial questions that *Mrs. Warren's Profession* asks is, What are the economic options available to women in a capitalist society? Shaw wrote *Mrs. Warren's Profession* during the height of Victorian public debates about prostitution (Josephine Butler's activist campaign had led to the repeal of the Contagious Diseases Acts in 1886) and the rise of the New Woman. Although Shaw considered Vivie the true protagonist of *Mrs. Warren's Profession*,[189] the play arguably focuses on the relationship and fallout between mother and daughter. Ultimately, Shaw ended up writing a play that shows how a woman with few economic options (Kitty Warren) would choose to become a prostitute and then raise a daughter (Vivie) who went on to have more opportunities and respect in society. Whether, in fact, Vivie has more choices is one of the crucial economic questions of *Mrs. Warren's Profession*.

Prostitution as International Commerce in *Mrs. Warren's Profession*

Much has been written about the play's treatment of prostitution. As a symbol, the prostitute has long stood for women's subordination under patriarchy. Since Shaw highlights neither the aphrodisiac nor the ugly side of the sex trade, many have read the play's depiction of prostitution as a general metaphor for the human being's condition in capitalism. Thus, Davis argues that "*Mrs. Warren's Profession* is not about sex or even sexual politics. Prostitution is a metaphor for the Fabian 'law of rent': all capitalist production is like rent in that it produces a differential advantage of one social group over another, and the exercise of this control is at everyone's expense."[190] In a similar vein, Germaine Greer contends that Shaw's play shows that "prostitution is universal in a capitalist society in that all talent, all energy, all power is a commodity with a cash value."[191] It is important to remember, however, that Shaw emphasizes that prostitution in *Mrs. Warren's Profession* is not just a broad metaphor for capitalism and that he is committed to exposing the business side of prostitution, which is not often discussed—namely, that

> prostitution is not only carried on without organization by individual enterprise in the lodgings of solitary women, each her own mistress as well as every customer's mistress, but organized and exploited as a big international commerce for the profit of capitalists like any other commerce, and very lucrative to great city estates, including Church estates, through the rent of the houses in which it is practiced.[192]

Arguing that prostitution is run like a financial corporation is different (even if the difference is not immediately obvious) than arguing that prostitution is a metaphor for the economic condition of *all* capitalist subjects. The latter claim involves circular thinking that confuses sex and money, while the former allows Shaw to explore the movement of capital between the brothel, the marriage market, and the stock exchange.

One of the main reasons Shaw did not draw attention to the ghastly and grisly aspects of Victorian prostitution is that he did not wish to make Mrs. Warren a convenient scapegoat. "Nothing would please our sanctimonious British public more than to throw the whole guilt of Mrs. Warren's profession on Mrs. Warren herself," writes Shaw in the preface to the play, noting that his goal "is to throw that guilt on the British public itself" (200–201). To implicate his audience, Shaw needed a structure that could throw light on the sheer interconnectivity of everyone under capitalism. Financial circulation provided him with such a framework. Instead of showing us the labor conditions of prostitutes, detailed in the reform versions of the prostitute narrative, Shaw portrays prostitution as a resourceful way to accumulate capital more in line with the libertine prostitute narratives of the eighteenth century.[193] The difference is that what is at stake in *Mrs. Warren's Profession* is not simply the social rise of one enterprising woman but the entire system of capitalist accumulation of which prostitution is a significant part and not just a universalizing analogy. For Shaw, the sex trade was, first and foremost, a lucrative corporation that pays dividends. This is how Vivie summarizes her mother's business without being able to utter the name of her profession: "'Paid up capital: not less than £40,000 standing in the name of Sir George Crofts, Baronet, the chief shareholder. Premises in Brussels, Ostend, Vienna and Budapest. Managing director: Mrs. Warren'" (276).

Vivie, with her pragmatic view of the world and her predilection for mathematics and statistics, is more than ready to accept the fact that her mother and aunt turned to prostitution as a means of survival because, at the end of the day, it was their most viable economic option. During a tender scene of reconciliation at the end of act 2, Vivie calls her mother "a wonderful woman" and "stronger than all England" for having made the best of her economic precarity as a young woman (251). And Mrs. Warren justifies her choice to become a prostitute by focusing on the dire circumstances in which she found herself during her youth:

> But where can a woman get the money to save in any other business? . . . Of course, if you're a plain woman and can't earn anything more; or if you have a turn for music, or the stage, or newspaper-writing: that's different. But neither Liz nor I had any turn for such things: all we had was our appearance and our turn for pleasing men. Do you think we were such fools as to let other people trade in our good looks by employing us as shopgirls, or barmaids, or waitresses, when we could trade in them ourselves and get all the profits of starvation wages? Not likely. (249)

Without explicitly using the term "erotic capital," Kitty Warren suggests that it was erotic capital ("our appearance and our turn for pleasing men") that was at her disposal when she was poor and that she would get more financial return for it working as a prostitute than in the service industry, which would only exploit her and extract surplus value from her physical and emotional labor. Or it could have turned out even worse. As Mrs. Warren relates, one of her half-sisters "died of lead poisoning" working "in a whitelead factory twelve hours a day for nine shillings a week," while the other "married a Government laborer" and "kept his room and the three children neat and tidy on eighteen shillings a week—until he took to drink" (247). Even as Shaw hints that there are other economic options available to women besides marriage, prostitution, and dangerous factory work—such as a career in the arts—these options are limited and depend on luck and/or prior economic capital. It could be argued, for example, that Kitty Warren did not have "a turn for music" because, having grown up poor, she was never exposed to musical training or instruments. After all, the New Woman who could pursue a white-collar profession or a career in the arts was usually white and predominantly bourgeois or upper class, someone who could afford a postsecondary education—someone like Vivie herself. The irony of the play is that Mrs. Warren and Crofts's business has paid for Vivie's upbringing and education and will also ensure her dowry. This is something that Vivie has difficulty accepting.

Many of Shaw's early dramatic works follow a similar plot: a young person finds out that the origin of their money is tainted.[194] As Shaw puts it in the preface to *Major Barbara*: "The notion that you can earmark certain coins as tainted is an unpractical individualist superstition. None the less the fact that all of our money is tainted gives a very severe shock to earnest young souls when some dramatic instance of the taint first makes them conscious of it" (22). This is exactly Crofts's point when he reveals to Vivie that her "Crofts scholarship at Newnham" was established by his brother, who "gets his 22 percent out of a factory with 600 girls in it, and not one of them getting wages enough to live on" (265). When, in the last scene, Mrs. Warren accuses Vivie of stealing her college education from her, the implication is not only the sacrifice that Mrs. Warren has had to make to raise her daughter but also the mass exploitation of working-class women and working girls who have made Vivie's (and other middle- and upper-class women's) social respectability and wealth possible.

But Vivie fails to fully understand how she herself benefits from the surplus value extracted from the labor of others. She cannot accept that her mother continues to run her business and earn a financial return. Like a good Fabian socialist, Vivie is disgusted by the surplus that her mother continues to receive from rent by exploiting others. Kitty Warren is no longer the struggling poor woman turning to prostitution for economic survival but a member of the idle proprietary class that benefits from the transformation of surplus income into capital. If *Mrs. Warren's Profession* supports a Fabian message, then Vivie's point of view should be the most persuasive. It is not. For one, *Mrs. Warren's Profession* throws light on Vivie's blind spot—she, too, reaps the benefits from surplus value just like her mother does. The play persistently questions not only the morality of Vivie's life choices but also their feasibility. As Mrs. Warren explains to her daughter, what drives her is not the "profit motive," which Greer sees as the focal interest of Shaw's play, but the sheer excitement of work and investment for its own sake as a lifestyle and pastime:[195]

> Why, the very rooks in the trees would find me out even if I could stand the dullness of it. I must have work and excitement, or I

should go melancholy mad. And what else is there for me to do? The life suits me: I'm fit for it and not for anything else. If I didn't do it somebody else would; so I don't do any real harm by it. (283)

For Kitty Warren, it is not just about making more money. She continues to accumulate capital limitlessly not for the sake of profit (or surplus) but because she desires to desire. Her work is tied to her libido. In this, the desire to accumulate capital is analogous to erotic desire and echoes the Faustian bargain. In Goethe's *Faust*, the rules of the bargain dictate that if Faust is finally satisfied with what Mephistopheles gives him to the point where Faust wants to stay in that moment forever, he will die that very instant. For this reason, Faust continues to desire and delay gratification for as long as he can. It is the same with Mrs. Warren. From her perspective, winding up the brothel business would be akin to a death sentence. "And what else is there for me to do?" This is a genuine question that Kitty Warren asks her daughter, who ends up rejecting her mother for being "a conventional woman at heart" without ever truly understanding her (286). In this respect, Kitty Warren has a more capacious view of the economy than Vivie does. For Vivie, the economy comes down to the narrow statistical science of choosing an appropriate career. For Kitty, it means deciding first and foremost what to do with her time and how to live her life.

Incest versus Interest: The Blind Spots of Fabianism

Although Vivie eventually learns the Shavian lesson that "all money is equally tainted,"[196] she believes that she can extricate herself from the financial circulation of prostitution and the marriage market by severing ties with her mother and by choosing never to wed. But is she successful? As a New Woman, she can certainly support herself as a single woman working at the actuarial office of Honoria Fraser. Yet does she manage to exist outside the circulation of money and sex? Rejecting marriage is the simplest of her tasks. In a reversal of roles reminiscent of *Miss Julie*, *Mrs. Warren's Profession* features a young man (Frank) who attempts to convert his erotic capital to economic prosperity. Frank's idiosyncratic and tongue-in-cheek courtship of Vivie seems to be motivated not only by a genuine affection for her but also by a desire to "turn [his] good looks to account by marrying somebody" with brains and money (228). Even the revelation that Vivie might potentially be his half-sister does not deter Frank. And neither does the possibility of incest prevent Crofts from trying to court Vivie. In fact, in an earlier draft of the play, Crofts admits to Mrs. Warren that the very real possibility of Vivie being his daughter might be "one of the fascinations of the thing."[197] Frank and Vivie shudder not so much at the risk of incest as at the tainted source of the money they would be handling if they were to wed. In a perverse reversal that condemns the Victorian public, Shaw shows that the main cultural taboo operating in the fictional world of his play is not incest but interest—financial interest, that is. What most characters in *Mrs. Warren's Profession* (apart from Kitty Warren and Crofts) find distasteful and unacceptable is not that someone whom they romantically desire might turn out to be their blood relative but that their money might derive from financial speculation, an economic activity by which money circulates so promiscuously and indiscriminately that it is no longer possible to track the origin of one's money, which could come from arms factories, sweatshops, slums, or brothels.

One of the central Victorian anxieties surrounding prostitution—the possibility that a proliferation of illegitimate children could unknowingly result in incest—is associated in *Mrs. Warren's Profession* with the anxiety surrounding finance as an unnatural and perverse form of money production. Fabian socialists condemned the transformation of surplus, which they believed came predominantly from land rent, into interest-bearing capital.[198] It is the creation of money from money, rather than incest, that the characters in *Mrs. Warren's Profession* find the most disturbing. In this respect, *Mrs. Warren's Profession* transcends realism. In real life, people are more outraged by incest than they are by financial interest, and they are often more shocked by sex scandals than by financial crimes. The behavior of Shaw's characters in *Mrs. Warren's Profession* is thus markedly strange.

In a way, Shaw has his dramatic characters do what he wishes his audience would—be more appalled by financial misdemeanors than scandalized by erotic transgressions. What finally makes Frank give Vivie up is not the possibility that she might be his half-sister but the financial source of her dowry: "I really can't bring myself to touch the old woman's money now." Significantly, Frank explains to Praed that "it's not the moral aspect of the case" (that Mrs. Warren was once a prostitute) that forces him to end the courtship: "It's the money" (277). Presumably, Frank has a problem with Mrs. Warren's money laundering: she makes sure that the profit from the brothel corporation appears on the books as though it were revenue from a legitimate hotel business. Shaw's biting irony shows up just a couple of lines later when Frank mentions to Praed that he has made some money the day before "in a highly speculative business" (277). Although Frank turns his nose up at Mrs. Warren's business, he himself participates in the shady world of finance. While it is not clear what this business might be, earlier in the scene, Frank tells Vivie that he has made money from "gambling"—more specifically, from "poker" (269). It might also be the case that Frank is somewhat embarrassed to admit to another man that he was gambling and chooses instead to say "a highly speculative business," although he discloses the truth to Vivie.

The Dowry versus Erotic Capital

Whichever it is, Frank evidently does not see a significant difference between gambling and speculation, and neither does Shaw, who in the preface to *Mrs. Warren's Profession* highlights how sex scandals often distract the public from the crimes of financial speculation, an operation not unlike the vice of gambling:

> The notion that Mrs. Warren must be a fiend is only an example of the violence and passion which the slightest reference to sex rouses in undisciplined minds, and which makes it seem natural to our lawgivers to punish silly and negligible indecencies with a ferocity unknown in dealing with, for example, ruinous financial swindling. Had my play been entitled *Mr. Warren's Profession*, and Mr. Warren been a bookmaker, nobody would have expected me to make him a villain as well. Yet gambling is a vice, and bookmaking an institution, for which there is absolutely nothing to be said. The moral and economic evil done by trying to get other people's money without working for it (and this is the essence of gambling) is not only enormous but uncompensated. (202)

Shaw condemns here the profession of the bookmaker, an accountant that accepts and pays off bets on sporting (especially horse racing) and other events at agreed-upon odds. For Shaw, gambling is akin to profiting from rent, as both activities involve taking "other people's money without working for it." Bookmaking was a highly profitable business in nineteenth-century Britain. Some estimates show that by 1850 there were 150 betting houses in London alone.[199] With Frank's economic activity (poker or speculation), Shaw draws a parallel between gambling and the many financial operations that involve predicting and tampering with the future. The nineteenth century attempted to sever the relationship between gambling and speculation by making the former illegal and the latter a legitimate financial activity known as "investment." The proximity of all three economic activities—gambling, speculation, and investment—will be explored in greater detail in the next chapter, on Anton Chekhov.

To sum up, Frank abandons his courtship of Vivie because her money would come from an overseas brothel ring masquerading as a hotel corporation, even as he himself engages in semilegal gambling and /or speculation. At least brothels were legal in the Continental countries where Crofts and Mrs. Warren operate their business. In contrast, gambling existed in a legally "grey area"[200] in nineteenth-century Britain: it was highly regulated. The Gaming Act of 1845 ruled that a wager (such as the one that took place during poker or bridge) was unenforceable as a legal contract. This provision was meant to dissuade gambling. And while the Betting Act of 1853 made betting houses illegal, they continued nevertheless; some bookmakers either employed "runners" who were faster than the police or took their betting to the streets.[201] So Frank remains entrenched in precisely the kind of crooked business that he scorns. What about Vivie?

Rejecting the institution of marriage, Vivie announces toward the end of the play: "I must be treated as a woman of business, permanently single [*to Frank*] and permanently unromantic [*to Praed*]" (274). She relinquishes both her erotic capital and dowry. By choosing to neither marry nor have children, she can avoid incest. But Vivie's decision to become a partner in the actuarial office of Honoria Fraser ironically embeds her further into the circulation of finance in which her mother participates. As J. Ellen Gainor aptly observes, the play's ending "is darkened by the subtle connections between mother and daughter, Fallen Woman and New Woman" (39).[202] Like her mother, Vivie admits that she "like[s] making money" (284). The connections go further than personality traits and love for money, however. Although it is tempting to read Vivie's job at the actuarial office and her rejection of her mother as a way *out* of financial circulation, she does not recognize that she is moving deeper into the very system she condemns. Davis suggests that Vivie's "profession is Shaw's deliberate choice: actuaries statistically predict calamity, but they do not directly profit from or deal with its occurrence." Thus, for Davis, Vivie "becomes one of the competent administrative middle class Fabians needed for bringing about social change."[203] Such a Fabian reading is justifiable given Shaw's politics at the time. Still, if we were to ask what the play does *differently* from a Fabian tract, I would argue that *Mrs. Warren's Profession* questions the feasibility of gradual reforms in a capitalist system that tends to co-opt progressive ideas for its own profit-making.

By exposing Frank and Vivie's myopia (despite their denouncement of dirty money and finance, they themselves do not want to see how they continue to profit from surplus value), Shaw highlights the contradictory position of most Fabians, who also belonged to the propertied classes. The blade of critique is turned inward. How will Fabians, including Shaw, undertake the transformation of a capitalist society of which they are the direct beneficiaries? This is not to argue that Shaw's play is defeatist or pessimistic—far from it. If anything, *Mrs. Warren's Profession* underscores the difficulty of the political struggle ahead.

There is an undeniable sadness at the end of the play when Vivie abandons her mother, as Shaw hints that Vivie's renunciation might have been in vain. An actuary compiles and analyzes statistics and uses them to predict insurance risks and premiums. This information directly benefits speculators on the stock exchange. And in her work as a forecaster of financial futures, Vivie resembles both a poker player who places a wager on a particular outcome and a bookmaker who profits from others' desire to predict. In fact, Vivie herself admits in the very first scene of the play that her ambitions extend beyond the actuarial office: "I shall set up chambers in the City, and work at actuarial calculations and conveyancing. Under cover of that I shall do some law, with one eye on the Stock Exchange all the time" (217). The potential for love and solidarity that *Mrs. Warren's Profession* briefly gives us a glimpse of is not romantic love (one never gets a sense that Frank and Vivie are meant for each other); rather, it is the reconciliation between daughter and mother, a New Woman and a woman who has made her living as a prostitute. Given the feminist wars of the 1980s and 1990s and the fact that sex work remains a controversial topic among the different factions of feminism, Shaw's move to bring mother and daughter together only to separate them is a prescient representation of the political challenge (created by patriarchy) that women face in recognizing themselves as one class with shared economic interests. Having broken her mother's heart, Vivie has not only failed to distance herself from her mother's tainted money but has moved ever closer to the pulsating heart of the whole system: the stock exchange.

As trenchant as Shaw's critique of patriarchal capitalism might be, it still reinscribes the good woman / bad woman dichotomy: Mrs. Warren is the socially unacceptable brothel owner, while her daughter Vivie is the respectable New Woman who has cut herself off from the economy of sex. (Or so she thinks. As mentioned in our discussion of Ibsen's *A Doll's House*, if Vivie, like Nora, were to walk alone at night, she still could be taken for a prostitute in Victorian England.) In the late nineteenth century, the New Woman, despite her education, financial independence, and feminist principles, could still have her reputation ruined by a sexual transgression.[204] The boundary between the New Woman and the Fallen Woman was porous. Shaw hints at this by making Vivie resemble her mother in certain ways. Yet at the end of the day, Vivie remains a paragon of chastity, and Shaw does not explore further the challenges that the New Woman faced in asserting her independence. Vivie's career success is almost too easy. It is therefore imperative to examine the struggles of the New Woman in her own words. The Swedish writer Victoria Benedictsson offers such a perspective in the context of modern drama. Her work addresses the specific challenges faced by women who wished to become artists and whose forays into the professional world of art were akin to daring and risky financial speculations. On the line was not only their economic survival but also their reputation.

Victoria Benedictsson's *Money*:
A Response to Ibsen's *A Doll's House*

Considered one of Sweden's most important nineteenth-century writers, Benedictsson is primarily known in the Anglo-American world as Georg Brandes's mistress and the woman who allegedly inspired the portrayals of Ibsen's *Hedda Gabler* and Strindberg's *Miss Julie*, arguably the two most famous heroines in modern European drama who stand for women's desire for greater autonomy and independence.[205] Yet Benedictsson was an accomplished author in her own right. Her debut novel *Money* (*Pengar*, 1885), written under the male pseudonym Ernst Ahlgren, caught the attention of Brandes, then the most influential critic of Scandinavia, who included it in his list of works of "the Modern Breakthrough."[206] As the English translator Sarah Death notes, Benedictsson's first novel, which includes substantial portions of dialogue and has a structure "like that of a play," already shows Benedictsson's talent for writing drama.[207] Benedictsson composed her most famous play, *The Enchantment*, in 1888 shortly before dying by suicide at the Leopold, a hotel in Copenhagen frequented by artists and writers, including Strindberg. She slit her throat. It is hard not to speculate that Strindberg might have borrowed this detail for the ending of his *Miss Julie*. Benedictsson was in despair after Brandes, who never reviewed works by female authors, refused to make an exception for her novel *Mistress Marianne* (*Fru Marianne*, 1887) passing it to his younger brother Edvard, who promptly dismissed it as women's literature. Brandes not only rejected Benedictsson as a writer but also ended their relationship. Although Brandes translated John Stuart Mill's *The Subjection of Women* in 1869, he himself was not a fan of Benedictsson's portrayal of a utopian marriage in *Mistress Marianne*, a marriage in which the husband and wife share the workload at home and social responsibilities out in public. Earlier that year, Benedictsson had unsuccessfully tried to end her life at the Leopold when Strindberg was staying there with his family. After taking poison, Benedictsson showed up at Strindberg's seven-year-old daughter's room, frightening the little girl.[208]

Benedictsson's novel *Money* is an astute response to both Flaubert's *Madame Bovary* and Ibsen's *A Doll's House*, exploring the intertwinement of sex and money by investigating the erotic power of money. Though it chronicles the fate of Selma Berg, an aspiring visual artist who gets married at age sixteen under economic pressures, *Money* does not regurgitate the threadbare story of a young woman forced into a loveless marriage against her will. Rather, Benedictsson shows how a young woman without much life experience can be coerced into marriage by the promise of financial security and safety, all the while believing that she is acting of her own free will. Economic coercion is presented in the novel as an erotic seduction of an inexperienced young woman. Before marrying a local squire, Selma dreams of becoming an artist and asks her uncle to help her matriculate at the College of Art and Design in Stockholm. Instead, her uncle arranges her marriage. Before telling Selma about the squire's proposal, her uncle hands her a hundred-kronor banknote as a gift, supposedly without any strings attached. In reality, this offering is meant to give Selma her first taste of money. Her uncle leaves the banknote on the bed next to her and waits for her to reach out and accept it. The entire scene has the disturbing undertone of an incestuous seduction, as the banknote figures as a metonymic substitution for her uncle: "There really was a banknote lying on the cover" (31). Selma's desire to take the money is described as accepting the possibility of sexual intercourse: "She did not turn around, but it was clear that the fortress was about to capitulate" (32). Throughout this unsettling episode, as Selma lies in bed with her back turned to the banknote, she asks her uncle if it is a sin to touch the money. Although he keeps assuring her that she would not be doing anything wrong by accepting his present, she keeps asking herself if she is selling herself.

In this way, Benedictsson's *Money*, like Engels's *The Origin of the Family, Private Property, and State*, draws a parallel between the bourgeois wife and the prostitute. Yet instead of merely comparing romantic relationships under capitalism to the commodity exchange, Benedictsson flips the metaphor on its head: it is money that has a palpable erotic draw. Selma's acceptance of her uncle's gift leads to her eventual resignation to marry. In the process, she tries to renounce her love for her cousin Richard and to relinquish her dream of becoming a painter. Although Selma initially hopes that financial security will allow her to continue to paint, domestic chores and familial responsibilities soon take over, and she loses herself in the marriage. One of Benedictsson's novelistic achievements is her multilayered and nuanced portrayal of Selma. Despite her young age, Selma is no ingénue without knowledge of the world. Even though she is not yet old enough to have legal control over her finances, she understands a great deal about money matters. (In general, while male authors of the time tend to depict their female characters as not understanding enough about money, female authors tend to undo such reductive portrayals.) For example, Selma asks her uncle and aunt if she can use her mother's inheritance or "take out a life insurance policy" (her father is still alive) to study drawing in Stockholm. Although her uncle and aunt laugh at her and dismiss her inquiries, she comes off as an informed young woman who is determined to make something of herself and who already knows quite a bit about the management of money. Moreover, while *Money* briefly flirts with the trope of adultery by exploring the lingering attraction between Selma and Richard when both are already married to other people, it ultimately resists the Bovaresque shopworn scenario of a desperate housewife's boredom and erotic abandonment.

One by one, Benedictsson's novel alludes to and then promptly discards the various clichéd roles into which fiction written by male writers of the era usually cast their female protagonists: the seduced maiden, the doting mother (Selma does not have any children, though Benedictsson herself had one daughter), the wayward wife, the woman with a past. Although Selma does not commit adultery, *Money* includes a frank depiction of female sexuality independent of its heroine's relationship with any man or woman. Benedictsson's erotic description of Selma riding her horse, Prince, was deemed so inappropriate that her editors expunged it:

> Her bosom looked higher and her waist smaller, because she was always tight-laced under her riding habit. The black cloth was moulded around her strong arms and the attractive curve of her shoulders. Her cheeks were patches of vivid red, making her brow and chin seem paler than ever; her nostrils flared with her heavy breathing, and beneath the thin lines of her eyebrows, her light eyes were full of spirit and zest for life. She was hot and sweating, her horse matted and wet, and her skirt spattered with yellow clay. (150)

The suggestiveness of the passage, along with Selma's riding crop and her pulled-down jacket, were unacceptable to the censors. To be sure, Benedictsson is mischievously playing here with a popular and evocative nineteenth-century trope of horseback riding, but she does so to underscore how her protagonist is an unapologetically sexual being, not to camouflage an amorous scene between Selma and a male companion. Selma rejects Richard's sexual advances not because she is a prude but because she envisions more from life than being his mistress. And even as Selma is aware that Richard has seen her from his carriage, the "splendidly theatrical effect" of her riding exercise is part of her exhibitionist pleasure.

In many ways, Benedictsson's *Money* picks up where Ibsen's *A Doll's House* leaves off but offers a distinctly feminist perspective on female independence. "But it's all these *Doll's House* theories," Selma's husband tells her when she announces that she is leaving him (170). The ensuing conversation then addresses the audience's questions concerning Nora's fate. To begin with, Selma decides to leave her husband after vising the National Gallery in Stockholm and remembering the aspirations of her youth. At the museum, Selma sees all the famous works of art she has only seen in reproductions and postcards. She also observes a young artistic couple at work on their paintings: "But when she saw the two of them immersing themselves in their work as earnestly as if their lives or their daily bread depended on it, she felt a gnawing envy and could not bear it. Dreams for her future, buried long ago, rose up and came back to hunt her soul" (156). Thus, the marital crisis begins with Selma's own inner change and epiphany about her desires rather than with an external incident provoked by something that her husband does or does not do. And in contrast to Nora, who admits to Torvald that she does not know anything about the law or religion and must educate herself, Selma is well informed and can defend her position. During her last conversation with the squire, Selma emphasizes that she was only a minor when she was married off to him, meaning that she was legally unable to participate fully in economic life. Any promissory note that she would have written "would have been invalid." "If I wasn't mature enough to manage my money," Selma says to her husband, "then I was certainly less capable still of making decisions about myself. A minor should no more be allowed to pawn her future than her possessions" (164). In response, the squire brings up all the financial difficulties and social reprobation that she will face if she severs ties with him: "And where would you be offered work?" (173). In contrast to Ibsen, who leaves the future of Nora uncertain, Benedictsson imagines in greater detail what might happen to her heroine.

If economic references in *A Doll's House* become more abstract as the play unfolds—tangible money appears onstage when Nora tips the porter, but then it gradually transforms into an immaterial metaphor[209]—then, in Benedictsson's *Money*, economic issues become *more* concrete and specific as the novel progresses. "Or was there any tie that bound her to this man, other than money?" Selma asks herself about her marriage (176). And how will Selma earn her living? Although Benedictsson does not downplay the real dangers facing Selma—"the gaping jaws of poverty and abandonment" (174)—she rejects the prostitute narrative for her female protagonist, showing another way out. Selma writes to Richard, asking him to help her find a place "at some institute of physical education down in Germany" (176). As Sarah Death elaborates, Selma probably has in mind physiotherapy, a profession that had become open to women at the time. Benedictsson met several female physiotherapists when she was undergoing treatment after a riding accident.[210] Thus, Benedictsson shows one possible path available to Selma, even though the separation from her husband was going to be a difficult affair. Benedictsson's focus on economic questions does not make her novel narrow-minded; on the contrary, it allows her to present a complex and nuanced portrayal of a woman trying to carve out a life for herself at the turn of the century.

The Enchantment: The Cost of Free Love

Benedictsson continued her exploration of women artists in the age of capital in her last play, *The Enchantment*, which was finished and published after her death by her friend, writer Axel Lundegård. Because the main protagonist—Louise Strandberg—dies by suicide after a traumatic affair with the womanizing sculptor Gustave Alland, Benedictsson's drama unfortunately has largely been seen through a biographical lens.[211] When the play, adapted by Clare Bayley, had its English premiere at the National Theatre in London in 2007, it was positively reviewed. Yet most theater critics chose to describe the play as anticipating *Miss Julie* and *Hedda Gabler* and focus more on Benedictsson's turbulent relationship with Brandes and her suicide rather than treating *The Enchantment* on its own terms.[212] The North American premiere of Benedictsson's play, directed by Lucy Jane Atkinson and produced by the Ducdame Ensemble at the HERE Arts Center in 2017, received even less attention and praise; critics again fixated on its echoes with *Miss Julie* and *Hedda Gabler*.[213] The consensus was that the production's main achievement was to uncover a curious forgotten play by a nineteenth-century Scandinavian feminist.

Perhaps because the Swedish title of *The Enchantment* (*Den bergtagna*) means "one taken away to or by the mountains," commentators have almost exclusively looked at Benedictsson's last play as a cautionary tale of erotic obsession, neglecting its economic questions, even though the play presents the erotic and the economic as deeply intertwined. Benedictsson brought a crucial feminist perspective to her era's debates about marriage, free love, and the importance of financial independence for women. And her play is a powerful testament to how art transcends biography. For one, Benedictsson was painfully aware of how a relationship with a powerful man could be a liability for a woman in her career as an artist. This conflict between a female artist's public image and her personal life is at the heart of *The Enchantment*, a play that in no way reinscribes the paradigmatic female suicide of the fallen woman.

While critics concentrate on Louise as the heroine of *The Enchantment*, there are arguably two female protagonists. The other is Erna, a painter who once had an affair with Allan but survived the ordeal. Apart from the actress, an accomplished female artist is a rare character in modern drama. Strindberg is an exception—Tekla in *Creditors* is a novelist, even though she is not portrayed in a favorable light. And, of course, there is the well-rehearsed argument that Ibsen's Hedda Gabler is a stifled artist. In *The Scavengers*, Becque hints at the reason for the scarcity of female artists. When the musically talented daughter Judith asks her former music teacher, Merckens, if he thinks it would be a good idea for her to give music lessons, pursue the career of a musician, or go onstage to save her family from poverty, he dissuades her: "You'll never be an artiste. You haven't got what it takes" (527). Then he elaborates on her dire economic situation: "There is nothing a woman can do, or rather, there's only one thing" (528). Insinuating that Judith's only path toward economic survival lies through her erotic capital (by way of marriage or prostitution), Merckens crushes the young woman's self-esteem and artistic aspirations. As he leaves the stage, he pauses at the door and says to himself (and the audience): "There was nothing better to say to her" (528). This aside is a cynical wink from Becque. The audience members need not agree with Merckens's assessment of Judith's situation; they need only recognize the music teacher's own insecurity and fear of competition. According to Merckens, the market for musicians and music teachers is quite saturated.

In *The Enchantment*, Louise's romance takes over her life because she lacks a professional calling, but Erna is grounded in her art. She can channel the pain of her heartbreak and her subsequent hatred of Gustave into artistic practice, earning his respect. "Her paintings are so good that if you didn't know better, you'd swear they were done by a man," says Gustave in a veiled reference to Erna's work (16). And Erna describes her artistic triumph over her former lover thus: "I was so abject, I revered him. There I was, scrabbling about in the dust at his feet. But look at me now! I'm his equal. My work hangs side by side with his. Hatred bred strength, and the desire to succeed. If you can hate, you can survive" (41). Later, when Gustave runs into Erna at Louise's apartment, he is a "little flustered," as Erna ignores him and "leaves with an air of defiance," saying to Louise: "Now there's a woman who knows how to maintain her dignity" (41–42). (It is tempting to read Gustave Alland's newfound respect for Erna as the kind of validation from an equal that Benedictsson wanted from Brandes but never received.) Erna is thus an important foil to Louise. While Louise, like Emma Bovary, spends all her bank savings in order to live in Paris and carry on a sexual relationship with Gustave, Erna is "awarded an artist's bursary" and keeps advising Louise against reckless spending. While Louise embraces Gustave's theories of free love, Erna knows there are more costs for women in those arrangements (in that historical moment), as Louise's story proves—she goes bankrupt trying to afford her Parisian lifestyle. Free love is thus associated with spending beyond one's means, while an artistic career—with prudent investment. This is a marked change from Benedictsson's first novel, *Money*, where pursuing an artistic vocation is compared to a riskier, more speculative endeavor.

By focusing on only one of the female protagonists—the one who kills herself—critics reinscribe the way that women artists, and writers in particular, are erased from history by their male partners and by the patriarchal establishment in general. (In the British context, Tracy Davis and Ellen Donkin have shown the myriad ways that "ideological forces . . . preferred to keep women in the background," so that there has been an amnesia of nineteenth-century women's theatrical work, which their volume addresses and corrects.)[214] With two female protagonists, *The Enchantment* lays out two paths—one is the paradigmatic female suicide, and the other is perseverance through art. *The Enchantment*'s two women might also suggest the kind of wavering that Benedictsson herself was perhaps going through at the time before her suicide. Most importantly, although Benedictsson herself was not able to go on with her life, in her work she left a powerful model for a different ending through the triumph of Erna, the artist.

Like Strindberg's *Miss Julie* and Shaw's *Mrs. Warren's Profession*, Benedictsson's *The Enchantment* shows that what determines a woman's societal position is not only sexuality (her chastity or promiscuity) but also money (its lack or its transformation into capital), or, more precisely, the interplay between the two. What Gilman calls the "sexuo-economic relation"[215] played an essential role in the nineteenth century's turbulent circulation of the dowry and erotic capital. In the fin-de-siècle culture, money not only had erotic power but could also lift a fallen woman who had succumbed to sexual transgression. With her massive capital, Kitty Warren can mingle (to a certain extent) in respectable society and send her daughter off to study at the University of Cambridge, allowing Vivie to achieve the kind of social rise that was unavailable to Kitty herself. Whether Julie can save her reputation depends on her access to capital. And Erna can somewhat circumvent societal reprobation of her bohemian lifestyle and relaxed sexual conduct by being a successful and financially independent artist, but the same cannot be said about profligate Louise. Instead, Louise grows more dependent on Gustave's approval as her bank account dwindles and she sinks deeper into debt and despair. Conversely, just as money can elevate a woman with a past, her sexual history can put a check on her socioeconomic power. This is particularly evident in melodramas where a powerful but mysterious woman's past comes back to haunt her.

Speculating with one's erotic capital was not the only path to socioeconomic advancement that was dramatized on the late nineteenth-century stage. In Chekhov, social mobility figures as a gambling enterprise and the modern economy as a casino. At this casino, it seems that—with the help of luck and with a persistent optimistic outlook—one can win the jackpot. But few writers are as ingenious as Chekhov in defying their readers' and spectators' expectations. In Chekhov's casino, things are not what they appear.

Chapter 3

Casino Capitalism
Anton Chekhov and Gambling

Chekhov's Articles on Rykov's Trial and the Temporality of the Near Hit

On November 24, 1884, twenty-four-year-old Anton Chekhov entered the newly renovated Ekaterininsky Hall at the Kremlin Palace to attend the trial of Ivan Rykov and his banking company. Hired as a correspondent by the prestigious *Petersburg Gazette*, Chekhov covered the most notorious bank fraud in the history of nineteenth-century Russia—the Rykov affair, or, as *The Nation* called it, "the Great Russian Bank Swindle."[1] Although the spectacular collapse of the bank took place in the small provincial town of Skopin in Ryazan Oblast, the bank's director, Ivan Rykov, and his pyramid scheme quickly became the talk of all Russia. The scope of the Skopin swindle, which involved more than twelve million rubles, and the longevity of the con, which lasted almost twenty years, highlighted the porous boundaries between gambling, speculation, and investment, making the Rykov affair an international scandal.

Chekhov's early forays into journalism have received little attention aside from the occasional nod to his latent talent for irony and satire.[2] Consequently, the Rykov reportage has not been translated into English or studied in depth in any language. Yet it deserves a closer look. This journalistic assignment not only provided young Chekhov with needed revenue but also exposed him to the growing importance of financial speculation and his countrymen's obsession with forecasting the future. The resultant series of sixteen short articles, running from November 24 to December 10, 1884, detail the bank's various machinations, explain how it was possible for Rykov and his associates to continue their con for as long as they did, and comment on the theatricality of both the trial and financial speculation. These articles thus reveal Chekhov's burgeoning theatrical imagination and his profound interest in the theatricality of Imperial Russia's nascent capitalism. Various details from Skopin's scandal and Rykov's trial echo throughout Chekhov's oeuvre, revealing his interest in exploring the theater of capital and the pitfalls of prediction. In particular, the radical contingency and the potential-laden temporality of gambling provided a model for Chekhov's attention to the accidental detail and his interest in the dramatic potential of what we might call the *near hit*—an event that comes as close to happening as possible but fails to materialize in the last moment. This is not to argue that Chekhov's modernism merely illustrates the economic world in which he lived.[3] Rather, Chekhov's form and style are, to borrow Terry Eagleton's turn of phrase, "products of a particular history."[4]

Given Russia's short flirtation with capitalism in the late nineteenth century and its much longer experience with socialism, it might seem counterintuitive to study Russian history and literature to understand the interrelationship between modernism and financialization. Yet before the Russian Revolution, capitalist ideas and values circulated alongside the dreams of socialism. The teachings of Adam Smith arrived in Russia even before Smith published *An Inquiry into the Nature and Causes of the Wealth of Nations*, in English, in 1776. With the encouragement of Catherine the Great, two Muscovites, Semyon Desnitsky and Ivan Tretyakov, attended Smith's lectures in Glasgow and introduced the Scottish philosopher's theories at the Moscow University, to which they returned in 1767.[5] The second half of the nineteenth century was witness to a proliferation of debate in Imperial Russia about its future economy.

A lot of recent scholarship has shed light on the interpenetration of modernism and financial speculation, focusing on the fictitious nature of money, the volatility of value, and modernists' experiments with the manipulation of aesthetic and commercial values.[6] Yet while critics have explored Chekhov's representation of the randomness of daily life, his attention to the seemingly insignificant detail, and his predilection for events that are expected but "cannot come to pass," there has been little discussion of how these aleatory elements reflect the instability, unpredictability, and moral relativism of the modern economy.[7] As Laurence Senelick notes, "Chekhov's interest in money is so prominent in his life and works that it is surprising that no one has studied it in more detail."[8] Rejected as a bourgeois writer in the wake of the Russian Revolution, Chekhov was later rehabilitated by Soviet Marxists as a denigrator of capitalism. Since this Marxist-Leninist take on Chekhov's oeuvre was reinforced in the Eastern Bloc for so long, it is not surprising that contemporary critics have generally been reluctant to analyze money matters in Chekhov.[9] In the West, scholars have also been largely silent, taking their cue from Virginia Woolf, who contrasted Chekhov's supposed Slavic "soul" to the materialism of "Mr. Wells, Mr. Bennett, and Mr. Galsworthy."[10]

In fact, Chekhov's aesthetic imagination was shaped by Russia's burgeoning capitalist economy, with its focus on prediction and its myth of the swift social rise, generating a literary and dramatic style that is characterized by random details and potential-laden events that either fail to materialize or take an unexpected turn. In his short stories and plays, Chekhov explores speculation in both its financial and contemplative sense. As Gayle Rogers notes, the broad meaning of the term "speculation," which acquired its financial connotation only in the 1700s, is "a mode of contemplative creativity" and a way to "envision a new future."[11] Speculation can thus "create—and potentially destroy—the future."[12] Writing at the end of the nineteenth century, a time of socioeconomic upheavals in Europe and debates about Russia's future, Chekhov creates characters who speculate both in the financial sense—with their money—and in the contemplative sense—imagining what the future holds for them. According to Georg Simmel, the fluctuating modern economy encourages this embrace of forecasting and even influencing the future (and not necessarily for monetary gain).[13] For example, Freud, who often slips into financial language when analyzing human psychology, explains that the goal of daydreaming is to envision a different, more desirable future.[14] As Simmel points out in *The Philosophy of Money* (1900), in contrast to the agrarian economy's "aversion to the unpredictable, the unstable and the dynamic," the modern economy treats the uncertainty of the future as an opportunity for profitable predictions.[15] While the Ancient Greeks believed that mortals' "presumptuous" attempts at foresight "might provoke the wrath of the gods," the moderns not only welcome the fluctuations of the economic game as a chance for gain but also seek an information advantage in order to tamper with future outcomes.[16]

In Chekhov, speculation often, but not always, leads to an unfortunate turn of events. Sometimes speculation results in a win. Most often this win takes the form of a sudden rise in social status. Thus, Chekhov does not merely critique the modern endeavor to influence the future; rather, he shows how tempting such a desire is precisely because—on rare occasions—it pays off. Throughout his oeuvre, Chekhov experimented with the different outcomes that speculation might produce, finally perfecting the representation of "casino capitalism" in *The Cherry Orchard* (*Vishnyovy sad*, 1904), where the economy appears as a zero-sum game, where someone's win is another one's loss.[17] Although this chapter focuses predominantly on Chekhov's dramatic works, it also features a brief discussion of two short stories to highlight the development of Chekhov's style and to compare the representation of money and capital in his prose with that in his drama. As Vadim Shneyder has shown in his excellent study of Chekhov's narrative form, Chekhov's stories—especially "A Woman's Kingdom" (*Babye tsarstvo*, 1894), "Three Years" (*Tri goda*, 1895), "A Case History" (*Sluchai iz praktiki*, 1898), and "In the Ravine" (*V ovrage*, 1900)—feature characters confronting capitalism as "a huge but indefinite presence," an inexplicable force, and a "monster and a primitive inhuman power."[18] Indeed, while, in his short stories, Chekhov often casts capitalist modernity in a menacing light, drawing a distinction between material and spiritual values, he tends to express a more ambivalent attitude toward capital and capitalism in his dramatic works. As mentioned earlier, theater's dependence on capital, coupled with the inherent contradictions of its mode of production, encourages artists to explore the difficulty of disentangling the so-called vulgar economic questions from the supposedly higher pursuits of art, morality, and spirituality. In Chekhov's drama, the economy is not a separate sphere of human activity but part and parcel of the larger world he creates onstage.

At the time of the trial of Rykov and his accomplices, Chekhov was writing under the somewhat conspicuous pseudonym Antosha Chekhonte for Nikolai Leykin's *Fragments* (*Oskolki*), depicting the corruption of Moscow for the entertainment of his Saint Petersburg readers. Based on this work, the editor of *Petersburg Gazette*, Sergei Khudekov, commissioned Chekhov to report on the courtroom proceedings of Rykov's spectacular trial and the story of his infamous bank.[19]

Bank failures and unscrupulous bankers were a common occurrence in late nineteenth-century Russia as well as the rest of Europe, as we see in Vladimir Makovsky's satirical 1881 painting *The Collapse of a Bank* (*Krakh banka*) (see fig. 2). The 1861 abolition of serfdom, rapid industrialization, and the rise of financialization propelled the Russian Empire into capitalism. Joint-stock companies proliferated to finance industrial projects, most notably railroads, and a larger segment of the Russian population could now partake in investment activities.[20] But the law did not immediately catch up to these new economic realities, spurring a wave of financial scandals. By the turn of the twentieth century, Lenin would argue that Russia was marked by "the domination of finance capital."[21]

In addition to bank frauds, hoaxes and forgeries were rampant at the turn of the twentieth century, and early skeptics even leveled accusations of fraud at modernism as an aesthetic project.[22] However, as Chekhov points out in his reportage, the Rykov affair did not begin as a swindle but instead became one under the economic pressures of capitalism. When the citizens of Skopin first came together to form an association in 1857 with a modest capital of about ten thousand rubles, they planned to allocate a third of their capital to the development of infrastructure in Skopin, a third to charitable works, and another third to the expansion of their original capital by means of investment.[23] Chekhov lists the many tangible benefits that Skopin's bank brought to the town, including a railroad, orphanages, schools, homeless shelters, and a fire department. According to Rykov, fraudulent operations only began in earnest when the initial investments did not pay off because of bad luck.[24] Skopin's case thus illustrates how an enterprise that begins with noble intentions can succumb to corruption after failing to weather economic crises. The line between

Figure 2. Vladimir Makovsky, *The Collapse of a Bank* (*Krakh banka*) (1881), 68.2 × 104.2 cm. Tretyakov Gallery, Moscow. Superstock.

an honest and corrupt business becomes blurred in the rapidly fluctuating modern economy.

This speed emerged with the invention of the telegraph in 1837 and the stock price ticker in 1867, both of which enabled the rapid transmission of financial information across great distances, making the modern economy more volatile and vulnerable to radical contingency. This new financial climate, where a slight change in circumstances could potentially influence prices, made speculations, manias, and panics more rampant.[25] Moreover, the exchange of commodities and information became a time-sensitive affair, as trading was now done *almost* in real time.

This volatility and time sensitivity made it tempting to predict and profit from *near hits*, events that have a great probability of happening but, for whatever reason, do not. A near hit can appear in two different forms: as a *near miss* (an event that has a great potential to cause a calamity but does not result in one) and as a *near win* (an event that has a great potential to bring gain but does not). The temporality of the near miss is particularly important for understanding what was driving the bankers of the Rykov affair. Rykov and his associates attempted not only to predict the future but also to *influence* it so that their speculations would pay off. At its core, banking often involves a desire to shape the future. As Yanis Varoufakis explains, a banker borrows "exchange value from the future" and pulls "it into the present."[26] A banker thus attempts to predict and even influence the future by extending loans to those financial ventures that have, in her assessment, the highest probability of turning a profit. When a banker "fails to bring about the future in which that exchange value exists," she "will have disturbed the timeline."[27]

When Skopin's bank was not as prosperous as its bankers had hoped, they began to engage in fraudulent operations in order to raise capital. Their schemes included manipulating promissory notes, selling fictitious stocks for a nonexistent coal mine, and reselling lottery bonds (about which more later). The initial goal was to fudge the numbers until the wheel of fortune turned in their favor. The bankers' hope was that if they could forestall the crash and avoid being discovered, they could buy time and make their bank solvent again. As Chekhov notes, Rykov and his associates came very close to getting caught on several occasions. The temporality of the near miss, however, also worked against their plan, as a few of the bank's clients turned out to be savvy speculators who attempted to benefit from the pyramid scheme by timing their withdrawals right before the bubble burst so as to accumulate the largest profit.[28]

The gambling term "near win" also plays on expectations, but in a different manner. Gamblers who experience the mixture of hope and frustration of a near win—an almost-winning hand at cards, spin of the roulette wheel, or lottery ticket—continue to play because they believe that they are coming closer to a lucky payback.[29] Each time Rykov and his associates concocted a new scheme, they believed that they were approaching a financial win. The concept of the near win was certainly known to Chekhov, who employs it in two of his short stories—"The Winning Ticket" ("Vyigryshny bilet," 1887) and *The Bet* (*Pari*, 1889).

Gambling is a recurrent motif in Chekhov's oeuvre: it includes the chess game at the beginning of *Platonov* (1878), the lotto game at the end of *The Seagull* (*Chaika*, 1896), Andrei Prozorov's gambling addiction in *Three Sisters* (*Tri sestry*, 1901), and Dashenka's lottery ticket in *The Cherry Orchard*. Although never a gambling addict as Dostoevsky was, Chekhov briefly caught the gambling bug while traveling in the South of France.[30] Writing in 1891 from Monte Carlo, Chekhov describes to his sister, Masha, "how thrilling the game" of roulette is. Even though he lost forty francs, Chekhov quips that if he "had money to spare," he would "spend the whole year gambling and walking about the magnificent halls of the casino."[31] And in a letter to his brother Mikhail, he writes: "Anyway, now I can tell my grandchildren that I have played roulette, and know the feeling which is excited by gambling."[32]

As we will soon see, the near hit, both in the form of a near miss and a near win, provides an aspirational temporal structure to many dramatic events in Chekhov's work, where a tiny arbitrary detail can suddenly change the emotional atmosphere of a scene or where expectations are built up in such a way that we expect an event to happen, but it does not. The endings of Chekhov's one-act joke *The Anniversary* (*Yubilei*, 1891) and his full-length comedy *The Cherry Orchard* have this dramatic structure, which Paperny calls Chekhov's "principle of unconsummated action," and Popkin the "event withheld."[33] Near hits can be considered a subgroup of Chekhov's "uncompleted action[s]."[34] What is important is not simply that near hits do not happen but also that when they *almost* happen, their sheer potentiality transforms the lives of the characters and comments on the aesthetic exchange between the author and the reader (or spectator) of Chekhov's work. Moreover, Chekhov connects these near hits to gambling, an economic activity that explicitly relies on volatility and time sensitivity, which greatly increased in modernity.

Given this new speed and volatility of finance, how were Rykov and his entourage able to keep up their charade for as long as they did? In his reportage, Chekhov chronicles how Rykov's team strategically lured out-of-town customers and bribed the postmaster to intercept potentially compromising letters so that no one could look into the affairs of the bank too closely. In particular, the bank targeted monasteries as a way to acquire new customers.[35] Local papers were paid off to publish glowing reviews of Skopin's bank, and the clergy encouraged the laity to deposit their savings in the bank. The bank had over six thousand clients, most of whom came from Russia's emerging middle class—the clergy, government clerks, the military, and teachers. Besides the postmaster, other prominent citizens who enabled the cover-up included a deacon, who shared with Rykov all the gossip circulating in their town; the telegraph operator (Atlasov); the head of the police department (Karchagin); and numerous judges.[36] To encourage his customers' faith in the prosperity of the bank, Rykov made entries in the accounting books that were fictitious financial operations. One of the key witnesses of the trial was an illiterate old man who could hardly write his own name yet signed a contract for the purchase of several millions' worth of imaginary securities. In his defense, Rykov repeatedly brought up the fact that he built a railroad in Skopin, stimulating economic growth and trade. In his testimony, Doctor Pushkarev described Rykov as an "exceptional" (*neobyknovenny*) man who modernized Skopin's infrastructure.[37]

Rykov was what Marx calls "the principal spokesman for credit," who, like John Law and the Péreire brothers, displayed "the nicely mixed character of swindler and prophet."[38] According to Marx, such a mixed character was a product of the dual nature of the credit system itself, which "develops the motive of capitalist production, enrichment by the exploitation of others' labour, into the purest and most colossal system of gambling and swindling," but could also serve as "transition towards a new mode or production."[39] Indeed, in Chekhov's portrayal, Rykov comes across not as a melodramatic villain but as a complicated figure who both wanted to see Skopin prosper and was looking out for his own interests. In his contradictions, he recalls Bernick from Ibsen's *Pillars of the Community*.

Rykov's rise to power reads like a classic rags-to-riches story. Born into a family of poor *meschanins*, the Ovodovs, Rykov was adopted by his rich uncle, who bequeathed to him, along with his last name, the substantial sum of two hundred thousand rubles. For the sake of comparison, the average annual salary of a factory worker in Moscow in the 1850s was about seventy-five rubles.[40] The term *meschanin* designated a person from the lowest and most numerous social class of the urban population in nineteenth-century Russia, who, unless enrolled at a university, could be responsible for six years of military service and be subjected to corporal punishment. In short, Rykov hit the jackpot thanks to his uncle's inheritance. By the time Rykov turned thirty, however, he had already wasted his entire inheritance and turned his attention to politics, relying on his charm to snag the position of the mayor of Skopin. In 1863, he was offered the directorship of Skopin's bank.[41]

The longevity of Skopin's swindle was in part due to the bank's ability to pull off near misses. The first time the bank almost went under was in 1876, when the Ministry of Finance picked up on the "airiness of the coal mining industry."[42] The bank survived because the Russo-Turkish War (1877–78) energized the economy. Yet the economic benefits generated by the war were short-lived. Even the mayor, Vladimir Ovchinnikov, testified that he suspected that not all was well at the bank, but he knew that the citizens of Skopin would hate him if he revealed the town's secret, so he chose to remain silent.[43] Many citizens knew or suspected that the bankers were engaged in fraudulent activities but chose to turn a blind eye. Few asked how it was possible for the bank to pay 7.5 percent interest when the best institutions in Russia were offering only 3 to 5 percent. Chekhov offers a nuanced tableau, highlighting the collective complicity of Skopin's citizens and suggesting that the corruption of Skopin's bank was due to the systemic failures intrinsic to the advent of capitalism, which made the economy volatile and subject to rapid changes in fortunes. This is not to say that Chekhov does not identify the real victims of the scam, the gullible out-of-town clients who lost their entire savings, but he does not place *all* the blame on Rykov and his immediate associates. Moreover, Chekhov shows how understanding the theatricality of the scam could help illuminate the inherent paradox of financial speculation—in trying to predict the fluctuations of an economy that is fundamentally driven by radical contingency and irrational impulses, speculation ends up disrupting the economy, often to disastrous effects.

From the very first page, Chekhov presents the courtroom as a theatrical space and the law as a "performative institution."[44] Tellingly, the weekly magazine *Fragments* ran a humorous cover that featured blindfolded Justice clipping the nails of Rykov, portrayed as a tiger with a human head behind the bars of a cage (see fig. 3). In his articles, Chekhov compares the defense lawyers to the ancient orators Cicero and Demosthenes, averring

Fig. 3. V. I. Porfiriev, caricature of Ivan Rykov during his trial. From *Oskolki* (1884), reprinted in Yulia Korneva, "A Hundred Years before MMM: How a Banker from Ryazan Built a Financial Pyramid in the 19th Century and Robbed His Clients of 12 Million Rubles," VC.ru, September 25, 2021, https://vc.ru/finance/297253-za-100-let-do-mmm-kak-ryazanskiy-bankir-postroil-finansovuyu-piramidu-v-19-veke-i-obmanul-vkladchikov-na-12-mln-rubley.

that the speeches of his contemporaries would continue to be translated into different languages for thousands of years.[45] Even so, Chekhov does not miss an ironic beat, noting that although five hundred tickets were issued for the first day of Rykov's trial, only three hundred seats were claimed. Equipped with binoculars, women outnumbered men by five to one.[46] Chekhov compares one of the defense lawyers, the lanky and thin Skripitsin, to Sarah Bernhardt, whom Chekhov had seen perform in Moscow in 1881 and whom he did not like.[47] He makes numerous references to Nikolai Gogol's 1836 satirical play *Inspector General* (*Revizor*), at one point comparing Skopin's postmaster (Perov), who claimed to have no idea why every month he would receive fifty rubles from Rykov, to Gogol's guileless postmaster, Shpekin.[48]

Yet Chekhov's attitude toward the theatricality of the trial was markedly different from that of many of his contemporaries, who embraced the antitheatrical prejudice and mistrusted institutions that in any way resembled the theater.[49] The banking and legal systems were relatively new institutions at the time of the trial. The state bank was founded in 1860 and the first commercial bank in 1864.[50] It was only in 1864 that the judicial reform of Alexander II established jury by trial, public hearings, and the profession of the advocate. Many Russians were critical of the "potential similarity between the jury trial, the public square, and certain aspects of carnival."[51] And courtroom oratory, which Chekhov praises in his reportage, remained a controversial topic.[52] By contrast, Chekhov emphasizes the potential of legal performance to expose financial corruption and its subsequent cover-up. The theatricality of speculation points to the blurry line between a real business of substance and a smoke-and-mirrors affair.

Indeed, Rykov's bank had to continuously put on a show of financial success to lure more clients.

The Rise of Financialization in Russia and Chekhov's Style

Several features from the Rykov affair would serve as inspiration for Chekhov's stories and plays. Specifically, the use of lottery tickets and certain fraudulent scenarios seem to have been lifted directly from the bank saga. For example, as Senelick notes, in the first version of *Ivanov* (1887), Lebedev tells Sasha that "[her] generous mother will not use the occasion to pass off on [her] coupons that fall due ten years from now or shares in Skopin's bank."[53] This explicit reference to Skopin's bank was taken out of the final version, but allusions to the bank's debacle continued to appear in Chekhov's works. In his court reportage, Chekhov mentions that the testimony of merchant Ivan Afonasov could serve as a fabula for a novel.[54] Afonasov gave up his inheritance because his father's debt to Skopin's bank was larger than the value of his father's estate. When Rykov and his secretary Evtihiev found out about this, they began to bully Afonasov, who was eventually forced to take on his father's promissory notes and marry Rykov's daughter without a dowry. In a twist of banking chicanery, the father's debt became the dowry of the son's bride, a detail that Chekhov echoes in his 1889 one-act comedy *The Wedding* (*Svadba*), where the bride's promised dowry consists of "two winning lottery tickets."[55] If she does not keep her end of the bargain, Aplombov threatens to make her daughter's life a living hell. *Ivanov* features a discussion about how lottery tickets are an "unprofitable investment in [one's] capital," and the short story "The Winning Ticket" explores a marital crisis spurred by the near win of a lottery ticket.[56] *The Cherry Orchard*, too, makes use of the motif of a lottery ticket to signal the unpredictability and instability of the modern economic world, where family fortunes are a matter of gamble. On the formal level, the prolonged deferral of the collapse of Skopin's bank, thanks to numerous near misses, finds an echo in Chekhov's predilection for events that *almost* happen.

After the Crimean War, the Imperial Russian government regularly issued lottery bonds. These early financial instruments meant to attract investors by adding the incentive of a gambling win: on specific "dates a bond [would behave] as a freely traded lottery ticket."[57] Their popularity underscores the close and problematic relationship between gambling and speculation, which the nineteenth century attempted to sever.[58] Although public lotteries were a popular method of raising capital in early modern Europe, as legal and moral worries grew around gambling, governments sought to regulate lotteries, so as to distinguish between legal investment authorized by the government and various private gambling enterprises.

In Russia, however, the use of lottery bonds "continued well into the nineteenth century."[59]

The act of committing money to an economic operation in hopes of earning a monetary return in the future appeared in the nineteenth century most commonly in three forms—gambling, speculation, and investment. Under different names, the boundaries of these economic activities proved porous, and their structural differences were up for debate. What, after all, is the difference between gambling and speculation? What about speculation and investment? One cynical answer is that "speculation is the name given to a failed investment and . . . investment is the name given to a successful speculation."[60] So only time can tell. As the banker Sir Ernest Cassell once admitted to King Edward VII: "When I was young, people called me a gambler. As the scale of my operations increased I was called a speculator. Now I am called a banker. But I have been doing the same all along."[61] To be sure, gambling seems to entail a shorter time interval between the betting of money and the outcome. Yet even this difference has disappeared today with the rise of high-frequency trading, a form of algorithmic trading that can move in and out of positions in fractions of a second. Marx predicted this erasure of the difference between trading and gambling by pointing out that the exchange of money for money (M-M) is akin to gambling. Although in *The Eighteenth Brumaire of Louis Bonaparte* (1852) Marx lists gamblers with the rest of the *lumpenproletariat*, in *Capital*, he considers how the economic behavior of speculators and traders is similar to that of gamblers.[62] The difference is that the financial games of capitalists are played out in the larger arena of the global market. In a similar vein, citing the Cuban French Marxist Paul Lafargue, Walter Benjamin writes in *The Arcades Project* that "modern economic development as a whole tends more and more to transform capitalist society into a giant international gambling house."[63] Indeed, when financial speculation appears in Chekhov's works—for example, in the form of Professor Serebryakov's desire for interest-bearing securities in *Uncle Vanya* (*Dyadya Vanya*, 1898) or Lopakhin's plan for rental cottages in *The Cherry Orchard*—it figures as the liminal economic practice of speculation, existing between the riskiness of gambling and the would-be soundness of investment. The success of these financial endeavors is not certain.

Chekhov lived and worked during a time when luck and radical contingency were replacing notions of fate and divine will. Accordingly, his works capture the turbulent historical transition from the religious system of understanding chance and risk, namely the belief in God's will, to the secular rise of insurance, banking tools, and financial instruments, which sought to make use of prediction to manage risk and to profit from the uncertainty of the global economy. Monetary worries were a pervasive theme in Chekhov's life. Born into a shopkeeper's family, Chekhov grew up watching his father run a grocery store adjacent to a casino in Taganrog, an important commercial port for the import and export of grain.[64] When his father went bankrupt and had to flee from his creditors to Moscow, Chekhov took on the role of the primary caretaker of their house and its remaining members. The complicated and contradictory character of Lopakhin in *The Cherry Orchard*, who is both a predatory businessman and a well-meaning friend, was in part inspired by a former tenant of the Chekhovs—Gavriil Selivanov. Employed in the civil courts, Selivanov was also a professional gambler. He ended up buying Chekhov's family home in order to save them from more bloodthirsty creditors.[65] When Chekhov achieved fame and financial stability and was finally able to purchase a house of his own in the small settlement of Melikhovo just south of Moscow, he insured his property and everything on it, cows included. He also took the precaution of buying "a stirrup-pump with a bell and a long hose mounted on a cart" in case of an accidental fire.[66] Having witnessed each year how fires would destroy homes in the surrounding area (a disaster that he would dramatize to great effect in *Three Sisters*), Chekhov did not want to leave the security of his house to fickle luck.

As capitalism was beginning to transform every aspect of life and culture in nineteenth-century Russia, its literature and drama expressed anxiety over new economic forces. In contrast to Protestantism, which upholds wealth and prosperity as a sign of God's blessing, the Russian Orthodox Church espouses those parts of the Bible that address the sinfulness of greed and money (at least in theory, if not in practice).[67] Russian folklore is full of proverbs that underscore that spiritual values are more important than material riches, such as "Happiness is not found in money" and "Don't have a hundred rubles; have a hundred friends."[68] Moreover, one of the most popular protagonists in Russian fairy tales is Ivan the Fool, the youngest of three brothers who manages to succeed against all odds despite being poor, lazy, and more simple-minded than his siblings. He is also generally kinder than his brothers and prone to follow his heart. Ivan the Fool overcomes obstacles, defeats villains, and wins the czarevna's heart by sheer luck and with the help of magic. A fairy-tale tradition that imagines upward social mobility to happen because of serendipity or sorcery makes sense in the context of Russia's feudalism, which remained firmly in place until the abolition of serfdom in 1861.

As a result of Russia's late modernization and its ambivalent attitude toward capitalism, gambling held a contradictory place in the public imagination.[69] As Ian Helfant notes, although aristocrats needed money more than ever, it was "supposed to be beneath one's notice."[70] Gambling thus permitted players to simultaneously embrace two conflicting behaviors—to show contempt toward money by wasting instead of saving it and to participate in the new culture of capitalism by taking on risks in hopes of greater rewards. This snobbish attitude toward money also prevailed among members of the intelligentsia. Chekhov, however, did not hold money in contempt. Rather, at least in regard to his own income, his view of money echoed that of Émile Zola, who averred: "Money has freed the writer, money has created the modern letters."[71] Chekhov's turn to literature was partially motivated by financial concerns. While studying medicine, he began to write short humorous sketches to support his family. It was a good time to be in the business of writing. As Beth Holmgren has shown, between 1890 and 1917, the market expanded the book-publishing industry and increased mass circulation.[72] Chekhov profited from these developments. Likewise, the desire to make money motivated his first forays into drama.

The volatile and time-sensitive economy of capitalism offered Chekhov models for formal innovations, giving rise to a style characterized by arbitrary details, attention to the seemingly insignificant, and surprising endings, a style that James Wood aptly calls "beautifully accidental."[73] It is the monetary economy that revealed both the arbitrariness and relativity of values. Drawing on Marx, Simmel argues in *The Philosophy of Money* that money "corresponds to the condition of change in mutual value relations because it offers an exact and flexible equivalent for every change of value."[74] The "value relativity of economic objects" translates in aesthetic terms to Chekhov's relativity of representation—what deserves attention, what is significant, what constitutes an event.[75] To put it another way, Chekhov's system of representation, with its tendency toward aleatory elements, arbitrary details, and seemingly insignificant events, is a product of a specific historical moment, when the capitalist economy exposed how different objects could be made equivalent to one another through exchange. In fact, many early critics of Chekhov were unnerved by what they perceived to be Chekhov's aesthetic equivalence—namely, the way he gives equal weight to disparate details and his supposed lack of discrimination when it comes to distinguishing important events from unimportant ones. As Chekhov's contemporary, the populist critic, Nikolai Mikhailovskii, put it, "To Chekhov it's all the same: a man, or just his shadow, a little bell, or a suicide."[76] Popkin has persuasively argued, however, that choosing what is "eventful and significant when it is ordinarily regarded as unimportant (and vice versa)" was Chekhov's way of overturning "the priorities of a system of values."[77]

Such an aesthetic reversal of values becomes possible in a historical situation where other systems of values, including economic and moral, are in a state of flux. In Chekhov's oeuvre, what was once deemed a significant event for dramatic representation (an auction, a scene of seduction, a suicide) is moved offstage, while events that seemingly lack importance (an ordinary card game, the reading of a newspaper at breakfast, accounting work) are given dramatic significance and time onstage. Life, according to Chekhov, is not made up of one major event after another; rather, it is full of boredom, routine, and the seemingly unimportant and random occurrences of the everyday.

Speculation has influenced yet another characteristic feature of Chekhov's narrative and drama—the way the mere *potentiality* of an event, whether in the form of expectations, desires, or dreams, has a direct influence on the life of the characters and the aesthetic exchange between the author and the reader (or spectator). Drama might be better equipped than narrative to represent this potentiality of speculation. What Moretti describes as a characteristic activity of Ibsen's characters—"looking far into the time to come"—is also a distinctive habit of many Chekhovian characters, who often wonder about their future and the future of humanity in hundreds and thousands of years to come.[78] Think of Tusenbach and Vershinin speculating in *Three Sisters* about the beautiful and just life that perhaps will come in hundreds of years. Chekhov's ironic word for their rumination is "philosophizing."[79] Their speculations, in the contemplative sense of the word, often (but not always) have unlucky consequences, as does financial speculation. When missing the mark, predictions of financial speculation and the optimistic practice of counting future gains as current assets can wreak havoc in the present moment. And although speculation in the financial sense and speculation in the contemplative sense have different aims, both activities have the capacity to "disturb the timeline."[80] Thus, Chekhov's focus is not necessarily on whether or not an event takes place but on its *potential* to affect the present.

"The Winning Ticket"

Chekhov's short story "The Winning Ticket" makes use of a lottery ticket and the gambling experience of the near win to blur the line between fantasy and reality and to show that daydreaming and fiction, just like financial speculation, can arouse new desires, leading to a drastic reevaluation of one's life. Although the story is titled "The Winning Ticket," Chekhov hints that it is a lottery *bond* that is at stake, as the wife mentions that she took out the interest on Tuesday. The story concerns the consequences of Ivan Dmitritch's fantasies about his wife winning the jackpot. Chekhov's description of the temporality of Ivan Dmitritch's daydreaming resembles in several striking ways the one that Freud gives in "Creative Writers and Day-Dreaming," revealing how the "past, present and future are strung together" (439). Both Chekhov's short story and Freud's analysis of daydreaming about a more desirable future explore the yearning for upward social mobility and the experience of time. As Freud notes, the mental work involved in daydreaming "hovers, as it were, between three times" (439). First, there must be "some provoking occasion in the present which has been able to arouse one of the subject's major wishes" (439).

Daydreaming, according to Freud, originates from "unsatisfied wishes" because "a happy person never fantasizes" (439). Then, the daydream "harks back to a memory of an earlier experience (usually an infantile one) in which this wish was fulfilled; and it now creates a situation relating to the future which represents a fulfillment of the wish" (439).

In contrast to Freud's account, it is not some "unsatisfying reality" that inspires Ivan Dmitritch to envision a different future for himself; rather, it is the near win of a lottery ticket (439). At the start of the story, he is described as a man "very content with his fate," supporting his family on an annual salary of twelve hundred rubles.[81] It is by mere chance that Ivan Dmitritch glances at the newspaper and sees that his wife's ticket is from the same series as the winner—9 4 99. The newspaper is both a characteristically Chekhovian accidental detail and historically specific. During the second half of the nineteenth century, the circulation of newspapers expanded dramatically: the number of weekly newspapers went from 98 to 226, and dailies from 7 to 70.[82] Newspapers began to print stock exchange figures as well as investment advice.[83] Most importantly, the newspaper became a platform for celebrity culture and advertisements that would tempt readers to desire commodities, services, and experiences that they did not even know they wanted. The marginal revolution (discussed in detail in the previous chapter) transformed human desire into a prime target for psychological manipulation. Usually Ivan Dmitritch "had no faith in lottery happiness" and would not have bothered to look at lottery results, but because "there was nothing to do" and, as luck would have it, the newspaper "was right in front of his eyes," he takes a peek and discovers the increased probability of his wife's win (107). Instead of immediately checking whether his wife has won, he chooses to speculate about what his life would be like if she won seventy-five thousand rubles, which is "not money, but power and capital!" (108).

The thrill that Ivan Dmitritch, along with the reader, experiences is the near-win effect, which tantalizes the gambler with a promise of a greater reward. Just as in Freud's essay, where the daydream about a better future begins with an infantile memory (439), so, in Chekhov's story, the near win triggers a childhood recollection, as Ivan Dmitritch is described smiling at his wife "like a baby when a bright object is shown it" (108). It is the almost-winning ticket that inspires Ivan Dmitritch to want more from life.

"The Winning Ticket" features not only the daydreamer (Ivan Dmitritch) but also the author (Chekhov). According to Freud, the author "sits inside" his character's "mind, as it were, and looks at the other characters from outside" (441). As Ivan Dmitritch begins to fantasize about his future, Chekhov's lush prose shifts from the past into the present tense, depicting a multisensory experience that goes beyond the mental images of Ivan Dmitritch's imagination to include descriptions of taste ("a salted red pine mushroom or a dill pickle"), smell ("a radish smelling of fresh earth"), and the bodily sensation of relaxation (109).[84] The effect is pleasurably disorienting. The present tense makes it sound like Ivan Dmitritch is really living his best life on an estate purchased with lottery money.

Ivan Dmitritch's fantasy about the future thus merges with the present moment of our reading experience. Like the banker, who "disturb[s] the timeline" by "fail[ing] to bring about the future" values that she predicts, Chekhov's tantalizing prose disturbs the timeline between the present and the future within the narrative.[85] As Ivan Dmitritch projects further into the future and daydreams about traveling abroad, he realizes that his wife, who owns the lottery ticket, would control all of their finances and would ultimately restrict his freedom. Ivan Dmitritch becomes disillusioned with his present life and contemplates suicide. This disillusionment takes place *before* he checks the final numbers of his wife's lottery ticket, which ends up missing the jackpot by one digit. It is not "unsatisfying reality" that begets daydreaming about a more desirable future (as it does in Freud); rather, it is the daydream itself that forces the character to see the drab reality of his present life (439). Compared to the imaginary "society of light, careless women" that Ivan Dmitritch imagines would pay attention to him during his would-be travels, his wife appears to him now in a harsher light as a stingy, elderly woman, "smelling of the kitchen" (110). Although we are not privy to the wife's thoughts, as the story is primarily filtered through Ivan Dmitritch's consciousness, we get a sense that she had "her own joyful dreams, her own plans" (111). In this way, the husband and wife, who know each other so well, who can practically read each other's minds, realize that they have drifted apart, that they no longer share the same dreams, that they no longer love one another.

How does the reader experience Ivan Dmitritch's letdown at the end of the story? According to Freud, the chief difference between the daydreamer and the writer is that while the first is ashamed to share her private fantasies with others, the latter "bribes us" with aesthetic pleasure, namely the "liberation of tensions in our minds," by "enabling us thenceforward to enjoy our own day-dreams without self-reproach or shame" (443). The author's offer is compared to an illicit economic exchange to which the reader agrees. Borrowing once again from the language of finance, Freud calls this aesthetic pleasure "*fore-pleasure*" and an "*incentive bonus*" (443). In the same way that the incentive bonus of the almost-winning lottery ticket tantalizes Ivan Dmitritch and tempts him to want more, so Chekhov teases his reader right from the beginning with a near win. The suspense—will the lottery ticket win or not?—imitates the suspense of gambling and speculation and encourages the reader to read on. The difference is that Chekhov's story might prove to be a safer investment, yielding aesthetic pleasure even when the characters experience disappointment or despair. Thus, in this early short story, aesthetic values are shown to be greater (and safer) than material values.

"The Bet"

The parallel between financial speculation and speculation as "a mode of contemplative creativity," to borrow Rogers's turn of phrase, is at the center of "The Bet," a parable that concerns a wager between a young lawyer and an older wealthy banker.[86] Like "The Winning Ticket," "The Bet" begins with a near win and ends on a note of despair.[87] We meet the banker on the eve of his scheduled payment to the lawyer. Through the banker's retrospection, we learn that fifteen years ago he and the lawyer argued about whether the death penalty or imprisonment for life was the more humane punishment. The banker bet two million rubles that the lawyer would not be able to voluntarily stay in confinement even for five years and offered one of his garden lodges as a makeshift prison cell. The lawyer accepted his challenge and voluntarily increased the length of the imprisonment to fifteen years. Thus, the bet concerns nothing less than the experience of time. The suspense derives from wondering whether or not the lawyer will be able to stay in the lodge for the allotted time. During the following *almost* fifteen years, the lawyer spends his time reading as much as he can and studying history, philosophy, and six new languages. Like an interest-bearing savings account, his knowledge and wisdom accrue throughout the years.

The banker, by contrast, spends fifteen years losing money due to the "gambling game on the Stock Exchange, risky speculations, and the hotheadedness which he could not give up even in old age" (232). "The Bet," however, is not simply a bourgeois parable about the wisdom of safe investment versus the folly of risky speculation. Rather, it is a reflection on the potentials and perils of human imagination. Chekhov's story plays on the reader's expectations of a near hit: as the hour of the lawyer's release approaches and the tension and somber tone of the story grow, the reader might expect some unfortunate event to happen that will make the lawyer lose the bet—either he will lose patience or the banker will sabotage him. At one point, the story even veers into the mode of crime fiction, when the banker considers murdering the lawyer. The twist happens when the banker arrives at the lawyer's lodge and discovers a note from him stating that he plans to leave five hours before the deadline, forfeiting the bet and renouncing the monetary award, because he has become disillusioned with humanity. Having spent the last fifteen years in deep contemplation about the future of humanity, he has become disgusted with humanity's materialism. Here, as in "The Winning Ticket," Chekhov draws a connection between speculation in the financial sense of the word—the banker's "gambling game on the Stock Exchange"—and its broader meaning, the lawyer's contemplation about the future (232). Both "disturb the timeline."[88] The banker fails to make his predicted financial future materialize, while the lawyer has no more future to look forward to because all his thinking has led, as it does in "The Winning Ticket," to disillusionment. In both stories, the real devastation happens *before* the financial loss. The disaster is neither losing the bet nor dying; rather, it is realizing life's meaninglessness, the moment when, as Beckett writes in reference to Proust, "the boredom of living is replaced by the suffering of being."[89] That wisdom can lead to bitterness, cynicism, and despair had been a popular theme in Russian literature ever since Alexander Griboedov's widely acclaimed 1825 comedy-in-verse *Woe from Wit* (*Gore ot uma*). Chekhov's innovation was to show how the potentials and perils of imagination play out in both finance and fiction. Looking into the future and speculating about things that are not yet is risky business. Like financial speculation, fiction involves risks in hopes of future gains. While the author presents the reader with a made-up world and advertises the reading experience as an "incentive bonus," it is up to the reader to decide whether her time was well spent and worth the while.[90] In contrast to these two early short stories, Chekhov's early drama represents Russia's burgeoning capitalism and the workings of capital in a satirical and whimsical manner. In particular, the vaudeville genre allowed Chekhov to shake off the gloom and enjoy a bit of mischief while writing for the stage.

The Anniversary

Perhaps the most explicit dramatization of the Rykov affair is found in Chekhov's 1891 one-act joke *The Anniversary*, which shows how a near miss can defer the collapse of a corrupt bank and cover up its ongoing fraud. The one act opens with the chairman of the board of a mutual credit society, Andrei Shipuchin, about to give a celebratory speech to the shareholders of the bank, titled "Our bank now and in the future."[91] He needs to fool his audience into trusting the bank's prosperity, so that they continue to invest. His bookkeeper, Kuzma Khirin, is in charge of writing the speech and coming up with fictitious financial figures necessary to make everything look legal. Thus, the play begins at the moment of a near win, so that the dramatic tension of the farce comes from waiting to see whether or not Khirin will in fact finish the speech in time for the shareholders' arrival. Tension grows as Khirin keeps getting distracted from his task: first Shipuchin's wife shows up blabbering about her visit to her mother, and then an old woman, Nastasya Merchutkina, comes in asking for money for her ailing husband, not realizing that the bank has nothing to do with his employment.

The cruel irony of a bank not being able to dispense out money was not lost on Chekhov's audience. Chekhov witnessed a version of Merchutkina's story—that of a corrupt bank taking advantage of an elderly person—during Rykov's trial.[92] An elderly, ailing monk named Nikodim came all the way from Sarov monastery to testify against Rykov. When asked why he chose to deposit his money into Skopin's bank, Nikodim mentioned the 7.5 percent interest. When the court dismissed him, Nikodim was shocked to learn that he was called only as a witness and not to get his money back.[93] Chekhov's farce ends with Khirin finally snapping and chasing after Tatyana and Merchutkina, screaming that he will commit violent crimes. The five-man deputation of shareholders walks in on Tatyana on the sofa and Merchutkina in Shipuchin's arms, both moaning. The shareholders are so embarrassed to witness what they believe to be a risqué entanglement of bodies that they immediately approve of the bank's alleged financial success so as not to dally in an uncomfortable setting. Their quick departure inadvertently buys Khirin and Shipuchin more time to sort out their figures and finish the report about their bank's future. As in the short stories, Chekhov begins the action near a probable outcome, building up his audience's expectations, and then subverts them. Given all the random distractions from Shipuchin's wife and Merchutkina, we might expect the two men to fail at their financial charade. Instead, they avoid getting caught by a hair, but not through any skill of deception. Mere accidents—the seemingly inopportune appearance of the women and then the early arrival of the delegation—lead to a surprising and successful (at least for the time being) outcome for the men. In the new financial climate of modernity, reactive to every minuscule change in circumstances, the wheel of fortune turns at a rapid pace, so that what was once deemed bad luck or bad timing might become the very thing that saves the day. *The Anniversary* also highlights the problematic intercourse between sex and money (discussed in the previous chapter): an alleged sex scandal becomes the perfect distraction from financial crimes.

Chekhov's Mature Drama and the Temporality of Mortgage

In contrast to his early short fiction and vaudevilles, where money is often the subject of satire and where aesthetic and spiritual values are elevated above material values, Chekhov's mature drama focuses on the vexing interpenetration of capital and the would-be higher pursuits of art, intellectual work, and spirituality. The first play that Chekhov composed when he no longer had to constantly worry about his economic survival was *The Seagull*—"a comedy in four acts"—that explores art as a calling and vocation. In a letter to the publisher Aleksey Suvorin, Chekhov writes: "For the time being I am comfortable, and can afford to write a play for which I shall get nothing."[94] No longer writing primarily *for* money, Chekhov could finally investigate the nature of money and the fraught entanglements between art and capital. Although borrowing freely from symbolism, especially the dreamlike drama of Maurice Maeterlinck, *The Seagull* was also Chekhov's subtle critique of Russian symbolism, particularly the movement's disdain of money and its hypocritical separation of aesthetic and material values. Chekhov challenges the aesthetic idealism of the poet and critic Dmitry Merezhkovsky, whose 1892 series of lectures "On the Causes of the Decline and on the New Trends in Contemporary Russian Literature" ("O prichinakh upadka i o novykh techeniyakh sovremennoy russkoy literatury") became a manifesto for the fledgling symbolist movement in Russia. Merezhkovsky identifies capitalism and the "system of royalties" as the enemies of Russian art and idealism: "It is terrifying to see that literature, poetry—the most delicate and tender of the creations of the human spirit—more and more gives in to the power of this all-consuming Moloch, contemporary capitalism!"[95] Merezhkovsky goes on to contend that a writer should present his oeuvre to the public as a "gift" (*darom*), asking for nothing in return.[96]

By contrast, for Chekhov the refusal to think about money reveals not only one's lack of economic acumen but also the moral failure to take care of one's dependents. Indeed, the avoidance of the topic of money in Chekhovian scholarship echoes the dramatic texts themselves. Many of Chekhov's characters become embarrassed and sidestep the subject of money, deeming it vulgar and beneath the supposedly higher purposes of art and intellectual work, even as they depend on the labors of others to pursue their artistic and academic endeavors. "I'm not a practical person and I don't understand anything about these sorts of things": so claims Professor Serebryakov in *Uncle Vanya* after proposing to sell the family's house, a decision that would essentially leave all of his dependents, including his own daughter, without a roof above their heads, the same people who have toiled away on his estate so that he could enjoy a comfortable life.[97] Their collective labor was not restricted to the upkeep of the estate but also included intellectual work, as they "would spend nights translating [his] books" and "copying" his writings, as Sonya points out to her father (103). In *The Seagull*, Irina Arkadina tells her son: "I have no money. I'm an actress, not a banker."[98] Yet the audience already knows by that point that Arkadina has seventy thousand rubles stored in a bank in Odesa. She eventually admits to her brother that she has capital but needs it for the material upkeep of her artistic practice: "Yes, I have money, but I'm an actress; the costumes alone have completely ruined me" (36). Chekhov shows that art often depends on that which it criticizes the most—commercial values and material comfort. Or, as Trotsky puts it, "Culture feeds on the sap of economics, and a material surplus is necessary, so that culture may grow, develop, and become subtle."[99] In this way, Chekhov's plays already prefigure the recent focus in modernist studies on the complex interpretation of art and commerce. As Stephen Hutchings succinctly puts it, "There is no writer who better epitomizes

Russia's perennial doubts about the value of art."[100] In light of Chekhov's commercial pursuits, Gary Saul Morson has recently argued that Chekhov embraced "bourgeois values."[101] This is perhaps overstating the case. Although Chekhov certainly took care of his income and took great pride in supporting his dependents, he also examined the destructive power of money. For instance, his story "In the Ravine" ends with a condemnation of filthy lucre. The main protagonist, Grigori Tsybukin, refuses to ever touch money again because he can no longer tell the difference between honorably procured cash and dirty money. Chekhov was an ambivalent if avid participant in the capitalist economy.

In Chekhov's last three plays—*Uncle Vanya*, *Three Sisters*, and *The Cherry Orchard*—gambling and speculation become explicitly tied to mortgage, which stems from the Old French expression meaning a "dead pledge."[102] If the future-oriented lottery ticket provides the dramatic tension and the temporal structure of the near hit in Chekhov's early works, it is the unpaid load and missed mortgage payment that puts pressure on the plot in his mature works, serving as a reminder to characters that they are about to lose or have already lost their last chance at changing the course of their lives. Missed chances, missed encounters, and missed romantic opportunities abound. Instead of starting his last three plays with a near hit, Chekhov situates their main action in the aftermath of a lost bet, when his characters' dreams have already been dashed and when they must learn to live out the remainder of their lives with some dignity and purpose.

As in the short story "The Bet," the wagers in these mature works have already been placed in the past, before the start of the main events. When Voynitsky appears onstage in *Uncle Vanya*, he has long ago wagered on the supposed magnanimity of Professor Serebryakov; in *Three Sisters*, when we meet Olga, Masha, and Irina, they have already pinned their hopes on the academic career of their brother, Andrei; and before the start of the main action in *The Cherry Orchard*, Ranevskaya has taken out a risky loan on her estate. The dramatic tension is centered not on whether their financial transactions will come through but on how the characters will learn to cope as they pick up the broken pieces. Dramatic tension has been transmuted into existential anxiety. This is a world where things are broken beyond repair or are no longer of any use to anyone. Chebutykin breaks the expensive clock that once belonged to the sisters' mother. "Our thermometer is shattered," says Varya to Lopakhin during their last meeting.[103] The map of Africa in Vanya's room is "of no use to anyone" (105). Memory is no solace either. Irina can no longer remember the Italian word for "window." Firs, who himself will be forgotten at the end of *The Cherry Orchard*, reminisces about the recipe for cherry jam that the estate once produced and sold in "carts" to other towns, but that recipe has now been lost forever (206).

In this dead time, when the characters' horizon of expectations has shrunk, what is there to speculate and dream about? Characters still speculate, but they do so about a faraway future that they will never live to see. They wonder if and how they will be remembered by future generations. At the start of *Uncle Vanya*, Astrov wonders whether "the people who'll live one or two hundred years from now, the people [they] are blazing a trail for," will remember them at all (64). At the end of *Three Sisters*, Olga hopes that her sisters' and her own suffering will not have been in vain because "those who live now will be remembered with a kind word and a blessing" (188). This is speculation about future historical memory at a moment of tremendous political and socioeconomic upheaval. The audience is simultaneously made aware of the characters' irretrievable past, their stagnant, slow present, and the faraway unknowable future. In other words, we have an experience of time that is specific to the theater. Matthew Wagner calls this theatrical experience of time "the weighting of the present with the past and the future."[104]

At a time when many estates were going under, mortgage melodramas became increasingly popular on the Russian stage. The two prevailing plots featured either a parvenu taking over a gentry's estate or a nouveau riche (a former peasant, for example) marrying a young aristocratic woman whose family is on the brink of bankruptcy.[105] Rather than portraying the dissolution of feudalism as a tragedy or a comedy (one that ends in a serendipitous marriage), Chekhov exposes the new capitalist economy as a world where luck and radical contingency determine who wins and who loses, at least in appearance. As we will see later, Chekhov shows that nineteenth-century capitalist Russia only *appears* to function as a casino. What lies underneath the illusion of the gambling house is a whole different set of social relations.

Chekhov's *Oikos*

Exploring how money and capital function in Chekhov's plays does not mean simplifying his works to the "economism" that Bourdieu argues haunts economic theory: namely, reducing all exchanges to mercantile relationships.[106] Economic issues in Chekhov are first and foremost questions about what we value and what we prioritize beyond the profit motive of the restrictive straitjacket of capitalism. "All Russia is our orchard. The world is wide and beautiful and there are many wonderful places in it," Trofimov tells Anya (227). In a similar vein, Astrov passionately calls for the protection of the environment: "Forests are fewer and fewer, rivers are drying up, wildlife is wiped out, the climate is spoiled, and every day the earth becomes more impoverished and ugly" (73). Because money in Chekhov is never just a prosaic medium of exchange but is also a symbol for the characters' desires and dreams, tracing its movement throughout Chekhov's oeuvre allows us to notice how he asks fundamental questions about how we take care of our *oikos*, our shared home—whether it's a family estate, Russia, or the planet itself.

By contrast, focusing only on the *mercantile* aspects of Chekhov's *oikos* reduces his vision to the kind of economism that his plays critique. The Russian and Soviet poet Osip Mandelstam reinscribes this economism even as he disapproves of Chekhov's supposed choice to present situations that could easily be fixed with the help of money. In his dismissive remarks, Mandelstam joins many early twentieth-century Russian modernists who saw Chekhov as at best a transitional figure, a bridge between nineteenth-century realism and their own modernism. Yet, as I have already mentioned, Chekhov was aware of the new artistic movements of his time, including symbolism. Mandelstam famously argued that the central issues in *Uncle Vanya* could be solved by sorting out everyone's living arrangements, and the drama of *Three Sisters* by buying everyone train tickets to Moscow:

> A biologist would describe the Chekhovian principle as ecological. For Chekhov, cohabitation is the determining factor. His dramas have no action; they only have cohabitation with all the consequent trouble. Chekhov scoops imaginary samples of human "scum" [as if] with a dip net. People are living together and cannot manage to move away from each other and live separately. End of story. Provide them—the "three sisters," for example—with train tickets and the play will be over.[107]

Even as Mandelstam describes Chekhov's interest in *oikos* in startlingly rich details ("ecological," "cohabitation," "people living together and cannot manage to move away from each other"), he downplays Chekhov's expansive and inclusive system of household management. In other words, Mandelstam fails to see that, for Chekhov, managing our shared "home," which the audience shares with the characters (and the actors playing them) in the space and time of the theater, but also outside theater, includes taking care of dependents (children, the elderly, the ailing), the environment, and one's own person. "Everything about a human being ought to be beautiful," says Astrov in *Uncle Vanya* (83).

With every new play, Chekhov rearranges the characters and details of his *oikos* to experiment with different social relations. In this he resembles Ibsen, whose cycle of realist plays Moretti describes as "a twenty-year-long experiment" that Ibsen ran, "changing a variable here and there, to see what happens to the system."[108] For example, if *A Doll's House* dramatizes the events leading up to a wife leaving her husband, then *Ghosts* shows the consequences of a wife's decision to stay in a toxic marriage.

A similar claim can be made about Chekhov's drama. It is an experiment that explores the *oikos* of the Russian estate at the turn of the twentieth century by testing out different scenarios. In *The Seagull*, a young woman who is disinherited by her father decides to try her luck onstage. In *Uncle Vanya*, we have an analogous backstory—Serebryakov decides to spend his remaining money on his second wife, Elena, rather than providing a dowry for Sonya, the daughter from his first marriage. In contrast to the more adventurous Nina, Sonya stays and works on her father's estate. In *Three Sisters*, instead of a world-renowned scholar, we meet an academic manqué. Chekhov's world is full of examples like these—characters and plot elements are recycled, rearranged, revised. It is as though Chekhov is playing with figures in a puppet theater. In Chekhov's case, however, the system is not "a broad bourgeois fresco," as Moretti calls it, but the failing Russian aristocratic estate and the various personalities from a range of old and new classes that populate it.[109]

Even though many of the characters' problems are, in fact, monetary worries, they cannot be entirely reduced to money or solved by it. For example, much has been written about the fact that "Moscow" in *Three Sisters* does not stand for the actual Russian city but is, rather, a metaphor for the sisters' longing for a different life.[110] What seems to frustrate Mandelstam is that, as a metaphor, "Moscow" is quite prosaic and seemingly within geographic reach. But there lies its power. Because "Moscow" is not the faraway, glamorous "Paris" of *The Cherry Orchard* or the cosmopolitan "Genoa" of Dorn's travels in *The Seagull*, the inability to go there is all the more frustrating. In the very first scene when Irina announces the plan to "sell the house, end everything here and—go to Moscow," we immediately learn of the constraints facing the sisters (120). As Irina mentions, their brother, Andrei, "will probably become a professor, he certainly won't go on living here" (120). With what money are they supposed to start a life in Moscow if not with the help of their brother's hoped-for academic career? How will they support themselves if Andrei is not successful? Marriage is one answer, but that would require meeting someone *from* Moscow. But the only people who now visit their house are military men, who do not have control over where they will be stationed next.

Moreover, marriage is shown to be the way that the horizon of a person's life is diminished further still, as in Masha's case. Even if the three sisters were provided with train tickets, as Mandelstam suggests, Masha could not leave the life that she has built with her schoolteacher husband. This is made abundantly clear, again in the very first scene of the play. When Olga and Irina fantasize about living in Moscow, they never imagine Masha moving there with them. She is the one "holding [them] back." The most that Masha can hope for is to "spend all summer in Moscow, every year" (120). Her life has already taken the rigid shape that makes it too late for her to drastically change it. So just as "Moscow" is "symbolic," it also stands for the realistic hard constraints that adult life imposes on people. After all, the bromide that it is never late to change one's life is an example of capitalist ethos that values perpetual innovation, or what Joseph Schumpeter calls "creative destruction."[111] By contrast, in his late plays, Chekhov, who by then was gravely ill with tuberculosis, sheds light on lives that might not change anymore and on people who are no longer productive in the capitalist sense of the word: like Marina, the old nanny in *Uncle Vanya*; the old nanny Anfisa and deaf Ferapont in *Three Sisters*; and mumbling Firs in the *Cherry Orchard*. "And why you keep that old woman around I simply cannot understand!" Natasha says about Anfisa, adding, "There shouldn't be any useless people in a house" (158–59). From a capitalist point of view, these characters are useless because they no longer work and hence cannot generate surplus value. Yet Chekhov does not discard them onto the garbage heap of history; rather, he shows, with great compassion and love, that the life of every human being holds irreplaceable value. And if the current socioeconomic world will not value them, Chekhov's theater becomes a shelter for them.

Although it is no longer the main structuring element, the temporality of the near hit still shows up in Chekhov's late works and speculation remains a common theme. In *Uncle Vanya*, Professor Serebryakov proposes to sell the family estate, "buy a small cottage in Finland," and invest the remaining surplus in interest-bearing securities that would generate a profit of "4 to 5 percent" (99–100). Serebryakov's scheme never goes through, and everything (seemingly) goes back to how it was. Yet the status quo remains unchanged in appearance only. As Nicholas Ridout points out, *Uncle Vanya* dramatizes the circularity of work (both the labor of the characters and the labor of the actors performing the play). Sonya and Vanya announce that they are going back to work after the departure of the unproductive professor and his wife, but the reality onstage of the actors playing their parts also gestures to the end of their labor (and play) onstage and foreshadows them coming back to perform in the near future. The actors, as Ridout acutely observes, will be back performing the same play all over again. Work thus figures as the "grim but safe antithesis to the risks and excitements of love."[112]

Work also provides a prudent alternative to speculation and gambling with one's life. After all, Serebryakov is not the first character to speculate in *Uncle Vanya*. The initial purchase of the estate depended on a gamble on Vanya's part. The house was bought from Waffles's uncle for ninety-five thousand rubles. Sonya's father could only put down seventy thousand, so there was a mortgage of twenty-five thousand, which Vanya paid by relinquishing his inheritance in favor of his sister and by working for ten years to pay off the remaining debt. The estate, once the dowry of Sonya's mother, is now Sonya's dowry. Serebryakov's plan is not only presumptuous, in that it takes for granted Sonya's agreement to the arrangement, but also cruel and exploitative, as it essentially leaves her without a dowry and lowers her chances of getting married. Vanya had thus made an unwise investment both in the career of the professor and in his own future. Having toiled for over a decade for Serebryakov, he now risks becoming homeless. His loss is emphasized by the two missed shots (near hits) that he fires at Serebryakov. Despite the buildup of expectations, the professor does not end up selling the estate. Yet this near hit still has consequences for the characters' lives—they become more despondent by going through the whole ordeal of the professor's visit.

In *Three Sisters*, Andrei Prozorov's gambling addiction echoes his failed academic career and his gradual loss of control of the family estate. His gambling is not what directly causes the fiasco, but it shows the importance of contingency and luck in the lives of the characters. As Masha puts it: "Look at Andrei, our brother. . . . All hope is lost. Thousands of people were raising a bell, a lot of labor and money was spent, and all of a sudden it fell and smashed. All of sudden, without rhyme or reason. It's the same with Andrei" (177). There is no specific reason for Andrei's failure. Although by tacit understanding the house belongs to all the four siblings, Andrei is legally able to mortgage the estate without consulting his sisters so he can pay off his gambling debt of thirty-five thousand rubles, just because he is a man (252). Asking his sisters for forgiveness, Andrei defends his action by reminding them that the three of them receive their "father's pension," while he does not have "any income, so to speak" (171). And although Andrei promises that his gambling days are over, he asks Olga to give him a little key to an offstage case. In a characteristically Chekhovian move, what is inside that case is only implied. The subtext, the hidden secret, is money.

Prediction is a perilous endeavor in Chekhov, as events rarely go according to plan. Yet the desire to profit from prediction and to control future outcomes does not always result in disaster, as it does in "The Winning Ticket," "The Bet," *Uncle Vanya*, and *Three Sisters*. Sometimes, as in *The Anniversary*, it is a win for the characters. Yet just like Rykov and his associates, Khirin and Shipuchin might only get so many near misses before they are discovered. In *The Cherry Orchard*, Chekhov manages to capture the ups and downs of luck and the very combination of rare miraculous wins and the more common devastating losses that characterize the capitalist economy. Through its exploration of gambling and speculation, Chekhov's last comedy dramatizes what Simmel calls "the restlessness, the feverishness, the unrelenting character of modern life," which is "provided by money with the unremovable wheel that makes the machine of life into a *perpetuum mobile*."[113] It is also a work where financial speculation and speculation as poetic imagination about the future meet in the charged locus of the cherry orchard.

Speculation in *The Cherry Orchard*

Throughout the production history of *The Cherry Orchard*, different versions have often sided either with the gentry or with new middle and lower classes. Although Chekhov subtitled his last play "a comedy," the 1904 premiere, directed by Konstantin Stanislavski at the Moscow Art Theatre, was received as a tragedy about an aristocratic family's loss of the estate. Stanislavski famously refused to play the lead character of Lopakhin (perhaps because he himself came from a wealthy merchant family of peasant origins) and chose the role of Gaev.[114] The part of Ranevskaya went to Chekhov's wife, the gifted Olga Knipper. As a result of this casting, the production's focus shifted to the trials and tribulations of the gentry and became tinged with nostalgia for Russia's past. After the revolution, émigrés in exile continued to perpetuate this melancholy vision, while Soviet critics considered *The Cherry Orchard* an anticapitalist takedown of private property. In American theater, there has been a tradition of transposing the action of *The Cherry Orchard* to the US South during Reconstruction.[115]

In recent years, especially in the wake of the 2008 subprime mortgage crisis, *The Cherry Orchard* has been interpreted as a story about the loss of home due to the machinations of predatory banks. For example, in the late summer of 2019, the New York–based Theater Mitu presented a poignant and thought-provoking adaptation of Anton Chekhov's *The Cherry Orchard* titled *House (or How to Lose an Orchard in 90 Minutes or Less)*. Directed by Rubén Polendo, this timely devised work, which also featured interjections from Nobuhiko Obayashi's 1977 cult horror film *House*, excerpts from company-conducted interviews, and live music, explored how, in "a moment of mass migration and displacement, . . . families across the globe must again and again find ways to redefine the idea of home."[116] *House* draws many striking parallels between Chekhov's turn-of-the-twentieth-century comedy about an aristocratic family losing their estate in provincial Russia and the 2008 subprime mortgage crisis, which resulted in over four million foreclosures in the United States. One of the most striking features of the production was the choice to underscore the connection between a housing market crash and a gambling loss. During the "foreclosure dance," one of the performers is seen dealing cards. In this moment, Theater Mitu not only plays on the popular idea that the banks were gambling with people's money but also sheds light on the blurry boundary between gambling and investment.[117]

Regardless of whose side audiences take, they often tend to agree on the would-be financial plot of the play—that the estate is endangered; that the wealthy merchant, Yermolay Lopakhin, whose father was a serf on the estate, has a sound plan to save it; and that the aristocrats are not financially savvy, pragmatic, or humble enough to go along with it. As Galina

Romanova points out, however, the estate has been forfeited long before the start of play.[118] Moreover, when we look closely at the financial matters of Chekhov's comedy, it becomes clear that spectators of *The Cherry Orchard*, like its overly optimistic characters, have bought into a speculation. Neither a lament for Russia's lost past nor a prescient panegyric of the Revolution, *The Cherry Orchard* captures capitalist modernity in all its contradictions.

In nineteenth-century Russia, the auctioning of an estate took place when an estate could have been sold for a higher price but the latter process would take much longer. Such a sale followed the demand to repay one's debt. Once the estate was sold and the creditor was paid, the debtor received the remainder of the money. Lopakhin buys the estate for ninety thousand above the debt, which means either that Ranevskaya should receive some money from the transaction (she does not) or that the sum she originally took out was close to the value of her estate. Put another way, Ranevskaya had essentially forfeited her estate when she used it as a collateral to take out a risky loan.[119] Ranevskaya was gambling with her future, and, like many a gambler, was unrealistically hopeful about her prospects.

In fact, hope is what all the characters have in common in *The Cherry Orchard*. Simeonov-Pishchik keeps asking everyone for money, holding on to the hope that something will soon turn up—maybe his daughter Dashenka's lottery ticket will win. Similarly, instead of changing their profligate ways and coming up with a concrete plan of action, Ranevskaya and her brother Gaev are hoping for nothing less than a deus ex machina in the form of their rich aunt's money or a prosperous marriage (either Varya's marriage to Lopakhin or Anya's to some wealthy aristocrat). Such a rescue, in the form of a rich relative or advantageous marriage, was a popular device in mortgage melodramas of the time—a time when many aristocratic estates were going under.[120] Chekhov, however, was not interested in staging the wish fulfillments of the Russian gentry. Instead, he makes heartbreaking fun of their naive hopes through the near-win event of Lopakhin's marriage proposal to Varya: Lopakhin comes close to proposing but does not go through with it the very last minute. And when the rich aunt's money does eventually arrive, it resolves nothing. Ranevskaya takes this money to Paris to continue the exact same lifestyle that has resulted in her current predicament. In a sense, the characters of *The Cherry Orchard* embrace what Lauren Berlant calls "cruel optimism"—they desire something that is "actually an obstacle to [their] flourishing."[121] However, Simeonov-Pishchik's optimism has paid off before. When he was sure he was done for, a railway company paid him to build across his land. Thus, even as Chekhov pokes fun at Ranevskaya and Gaev's optimism, he underscores its tempting nature by including characters whose wishes do come true.

At first glance, there seems to be a practical and sensible solution to Ranevskaya's economic situation. Lopakhin proposes a plan that would involve cutting the cherry orchard to make space for summer cottages. However, his proposal is also a speculation that relies on an optimistic prognosis for the future. Just as the potential for a railway increased the value of Simeonov-Pishchik's estate and saved his family, so Ranevskaya's estate, which is close to the railway, could capitalize on its location. Investors would lend their family money to purchase back their estate in return for a large share in the real estate development. In fact, Chekhov's father, Pavel, also erroneously believed that "he could sell his house for more than he owed."[122] As Spencer Golub notes, the appearance of the railway in *The Cherry Orchard* is "far more important than the nonarrival of the *deus ex machina* of a financial windfall."[123] Indeed, the turn of the century was marked by the frantic construction of railways, and train traffic more than doubled in Russia. By the time of the premiere of *The Cherry Orchard*, the Trans-Siberian Railroad was near completion.[124] The Moscow Art Theater itself depended on the capital of railroad financiers like Savva Morozov.[125] Although grounded in economic reality, Lopakhin's vision for the estate is speculative because its future success is uncertain. After all, it depends on finding interested investors in just three months before the auction date. (The play opens in May and the auction date is set for August 22.) Chekhov underscores the contingent nature of Lopakhin's enterprise by juxtaposing it with Dashenka's lottery ticket and Simeonov-Pishchik's fluctuating financial luck. Moreover, before his departure, Lopakhin chooses the clumsy Semyon Yepikhodov, who is prone to accidents, as his property's manager. In this new world of capitalist modernity, nothing is certain.

Lopakhin's speculation is not only financial; it also includes a poetic vision of the estate. During the auction, when the merchant Deriganov bets by fives, Lopakhin goes up by tens. He is not only showing off but also inadvertently revealing that to him the estate is worth much more than its market value. The place holds for him a sentimental and symbolic significance. This was the house "where [his] grandfather and father were slaves, where they weren't even allowed into the kitchen" (240). Yet it is also where Lopakhin first experienced an instance of real human kindness: Lyubov Ranevskaya brought him into the washroom after his father punched him in the face and offered him words of comfort. The reason Lopakhin is able to see the speculative potential of the estate in the first place is precisely because the charged location has always been worth more to him than its monetary value. Moreover, given the aesthetic significance of the cherry orchard, its auction has the quality of an art auction, which Jean Baudrillard compares to a game of poker. Like gambling, an art auction is "both a ritual and a unique event": the "rules are arbitrary and fixed, yet one never knows exactly what will take place, nor afterward exactly what has happened, because it involves a dynamic of personal encounter, an algebra of individuals, as opposed to the economic operation where values are exchanged impersonally, arithmetically."[126]

In a letter to Stanislavski, Chekhov stressed that Lopakhin was not only a merchant but also "a wholly dignified, intelligent individual" and "an artistic character." This is why Varya, "a serious and religious young woman," falls in love with him.[127] For example, Lopakhin's poetic speculation differs from the get-rich-quick scheme of Borkin in *Ivanov*, which entails buying up land on the opposite side of the river just to threaten the people who live down the river with the construction of a dam. Borkin's speculative scheme is entirely fictitious—he has no desire or concrete plan to dam the river. He simply wants to force everyone who does not want a dam to pay him not to build one (10). Lopakhin, by contrast, is no melodramatic buffoon. As Holmgren notes, Chekhov "destigmatized the merchant's connection with material goods and consumption."[128] Like Leopold Bloom in James Joyce's *Ulysses* (1922), Lopakhin has both aesthetic and commercial inclinations.

While the loss of Ranevskaya's estate is a foregone conclusion, the fate of Simeonov-Pishchik takes a surprising turn—he comes into money. Although Dashenka does not win the lottery, another chance event occurs. Just as Ranevskaya and her family depart from their lost estate, Simeonov-Pishchik announces that a group of English investors has discovered white clay on his land and that he is now able to pay back his debts. What were the odds that Simeonov-Pishchik's estate would become an object of investment not once but twice? Although, like a gambler's consecutive win, Simeonov-Pishchik's good luck is surprising, it is also realistic because historically specific. It is not the stereotypical rich aunt, an advantageous marriage, or the red herring of a lottery ticket that saves Simeonov-Pishchik, but the invisible hand of English investors. Under Prime Minister Sergei Witte, the Russian Empire relied on foreign investments to raise capital and offset budgetary deficits.[129] The deus ex machina of English capital is moved to the offstage and rescues only one family. However, there is no rhyme or reason as to why one family is spared and the other one ruined. Both families are financially irresponsible. Simeonov-Pishchik's miraculous financial luck shows how capitalism makes use of "cruel optimism" by allowing an occasional social rise or a rare monetary success to serve as tantalizing models for the rest of the population.[130] This exceptional economic prosperity of a few is not unlike the sporadic big win seen in a casino. The house always wins, but it needs to give players hope, so it allows a tiny number of gamblers to score.

Finally, the detail of discovered white clay (also known as kaolin) is significant. White clay began to be used in the nineteenth century in the manufacturing of paper, making it brighter, smoother, and more receptive to ink. Thus, the materiality of the text of *The Cherry Orchard*—the newly improved paper on which the play was written and published—connects Chekhov's own creative output to the culture of financialization and the question of labor. Financialization is neither abstract nor immaterial in Chekhov's universe but always connected to labor.

Having focused most of his attention on the financial machinations of Skopin's bank and the comportment of Rykov and his associates during the trial, Chekhov concludes his reportage with a discussion of labor. He mentions the hard labor that awaits the condemned (only Rykov was sent to Siberia, while his former colleagues were to toil in the provinces) and ends with a word of gratitude to the jurors for their "two-week, hard, and unusual labor" (219). Already in this early reportage, Chekhov displays a preoccupation with work that would characterize much of his later writing. Even as Chekhov portrays the world of *The Cherry Orchard* as a kind of casino, where someone's win is another one's loss, he also shows that this zero-sum economic game is a *visible* drama that hides labor. After all, while the fates of all the characters remain uncertain at the end, two characters are left in a particularly precarious situation. The former governess Charlotta, who lacks a passport, has no idea where she will be employed. And the former serf Firs is forgotten and left inside the boarded-up house to die.

In Chekhov's vision, the social world, as Bourdieu points out, merely *appears* to be a casino roulette that showcases "the opportunity of winning a lot of money in a short space of time, and therefore of changing one's social status quasi-instantaneously, and in which the winning of the previous spin of the wheel can be staked and lost at every new spin."[131] Yet this "imaginary universe of perfect competition or perfect equality of opportunity" is an illusion because it presumes a "world without inertia, without accumulation, without heredity or acquired properties."[132] Chekhov, whose grandfather was a serf, was particularly attuned to social inequality at birth. Against all odds, his grandfather managed to buy his freedom twenty years before the emancipation thanks to hard work and a bit of luck. Chekhov's family history and the vicissitudes of the economic world around him, including the Rykov affair, enabled him to capture the internal contradictions of capitalism—both the injustices and the rare but tempting chances of upward social mobility. And it is this infernal combination that keeps the wheel turning.

Chapter 4

✦

Labor and Strike

Gerhart Hauptmann's *The Weavers* and Its
Legacy in German Expressionism

Hauptmann's Drama of the Masses: Marxist
Theory and the Representability of Labor

In May 2010, the Department of Theater at Dhaka University of Bangladesh presented Gerhart Hauptmann's *The Weavers* to call attention to the plight of local textile workers.[1] This proved prophetic, as the production took place just three years before the horrific collapse of Rana Plaza, an eight-story garment factory in Savar (a city in the greater Dhaka area), now considered the deadliest textile factory accident in history. Although hailed a masterpiece of German naturalism, Hauptmann's social drama about the 1844 spontaneous uprising of Silesian weavers is rarely staged. As Madame Critic of the *New York Dramatic Mirror* put it in 1915, "For those who had read it the play seemed best qualified for library use only."[2] *The Weavers*, however, was not written as a closet drama. Despite her initial skepticism Madame Critic would wax lyrical about Hauptmann's drama after seeing it performed at New York's Garden Theater that same year. As Hauptmann's precise stage directions reveal, he composed *The Weavers* with the intention of seeing it staged and was dismayed when authorities tried to ban performances. *The Weavers* has always been a difficult work to produce because it strains and stretches the limits of theatrical representation in its use—and display—of human labor. A dark drama about starvation, labor exploitation, and rioting, *The Weavers* paradoxically invokes costly logistics and a cast of over forty speaking roles, plus "*a large crowd of young and old weavers and weaver women.*"[3] In other words, the text of *The Weavers* contains the challenge of its own staging, and the arduous relationship between text and production is central to the play's interrogation of human labor.

So far in our exploration of the theater of capital, signs of labor have often been hidden, invisible, erased. Although labor shapes and moves the bourgeois worlds in the works of Ibsen, Strindberg, Chekhov, and Shaw, it is not yet represented in a direct way that dramatizes the conflict between labor and capital. Instead, we see only traces of labor, whether it is Nora's Christmas tree decorations in *A Doll's House* or glimpses of Kristin's cooking and cleaning in *Miss Julie*. Hauptmann's *The Weavers* was not only one of the first European plays to bring forth a true collectivity onto the stage but also one of the first to attempt to represent labor onstage. Even later expressionist works, written in the wake of Hauptmann's *The Weavers*, could not live up to the play's contribution to the theatrical investigation of labor. While those later works wallow in political cynicism, *The Weavers* has played a significant role in ameliorating labor conditions and calling for a new socioeconomic order.

From its very first performance by the Berlin's Free Stage (Freie Bühne) in 1893, *The Weavers* proved to be difficult to put onstage and keep there. Its riotous energy has a nasty habit of spilling out of the theater. The production history of *The Weavers* includes episodes of socialist and anarchist rallies, bans on performance (as recent as the legal battles surrounding the 2004 free adaptation by Volker Lösch and Stefan Schnabel for the Staatsschauspiel Dresden), and a rebellion of actors who took salary matters into their own hands in the first English-language production for the American stage, in 1915. As Jean Chothia notes, what government officials around the globe seemed to worry the most about was the "recreation, within the theatrical performance, of the social performance of protest" as well as the act of destroying private property in the presence of an audience.[4] The focus of this chapter will be not so much on the riots and revolutionary energy that *The Weavers* generated in the late nineteenth century (documented well by Chothia and others) as on the play's exploration of labor, including theatrical labor.

The originality of *The Weavers* lies not solely in its naturalist elements but also in the study of labor and the problem of its artistic representation. The representation of labor in *The Weavers* is not simply undertaken for the sake of the precise, scientific inventory of gritty and seamy material that attracted German naturalist writers. In any case, it bears noting that although *The Weavers* is often called the pinnacle of German naturalism, it is also a radical exception among the dramatic works of the period, including Hauptmann's own plays. As John Osborne points out, while most naturalist plays of the time "tend to treat social or ethical problems from a bourgeois intellectual standpoint and in a bourgeois setting," *The Weavers* is "a genuine working-class drama."[5] In other words, while most German naturalist plays, particularly those written under the influence of Ibsen, stage a central dramatic conflict between an exceptional individual and the community, Hauptmann's *The Weavers* places the community at the center of the dramatic action. As Marvin Carlson puts it, *The Weavers* "make[s] the masses a true dramatic agent."[6] Hauptmann would return to the more conventional scenario of enlightened hero versus the masses in his later play, *Florian Geyer* (1896).

Similarly, the German expressionist plays that came after Hauptmann's *The Weavers*, such as Georg Kaiser's *The Coral* (*Die Koralle*, 1917) and *Gas I* (1918) and Ernst Toller's *The Machine Wreckers* (*Maschinenstürmer*, 1922), follow the journey of a radicalized individual as he or she attempts to awaken the political consciousness of the working class. In Kaiser's *The Coral* and *Gas I*, the socially conscious son and daughter of an industrial billionaire fight for the rights of their father's factory workers. In Toller's *The Machine Wreckers*, an educated activist who was once a weaver himself returns home to rouse his fellow weavers to action. Even as these later dramas feature a member of the bourgeoisie or the upper class championing the cause of the working class, they also betray an unmistakable distrust and fear of the proletariat—the heroes often end up destroyed by an angry mob of workers.

Limiting the discussion of *The Weavers* to its status as a work of naturalism tends to focus on what Kirk Williams identifies as the play's "anti-theatrical bias," expressed in naturalism's "explicit objective . . . to completely remove the barrier separating theater from life, to create an illusion so powerful that it would render the theatrical medium absolutely transparent."[7] In a similar vein, Chothia calls *The Weavers* a "remarkable forerunner of docudrama."[8] And in many ways it certainly is, as Hauptmann closely followed the historical accounts of the spontaneous weavers' revolt provided by Alfred Zimmermann and Wilhelm Wolff.[9] Yet as we will soon see, far from attempting to render the theatrical medium transparent, Hauptmann's drama often openly acknowledges its reliance on the potentials of the theater (an institution that heavily depends on the management and organization of human labor) to represent labor in its temporal and social aspects.

Looking closely at the relationship between Hauptmann's text and its staging, throughout the play's production history, this chapter argues that *The Weavers* can be read as a dramatic work that examines the problem of representing labor in the theater and reveals the signs of labor that capitalist culture often seeks to hide and erase. When it comes to displaying labor, Hauptmann's stage directions are as abundant as they are meticulous. Hauptmann tells us exactly what each character is doing onstage (whether sitting at the loom, reeling yarn, or ironing) and describes the various signs of labor to be represented onstage, from the ticking of clocks and the buzzing noise of looms to the traces of labor left on the bodies of the weavers. In fact, most characters onstage are described as constantly engaged in some type of work activity. In this way, *The Weavers* not only portrays the weaver's wretched living conditions and their revolutionary struggle but also attempts to lay bare, onstage, modern labor conditions, such as the exploitation of wage labor, the ideology of the work ethic, and the fundamental conflict between labor and capital.

The rich and wide-ranging scholarship devoted to *The Weavers* tends to focus on its naturalist elements and revolutionary ethos. For example, in "Anti-theatricality and the Limits of Naturalism," Kirk Williams discusses the weavers' physical environment as "necessarily overdetermined, cluttered with small and seemingly gratuitous objects," "which is typical of Naturalist drama" and "obviously represents an effort to grasp the contingent, material reality of a situation."[10] It is also possible, however, to look at the same objects—which in the play are often raw materials and working tools—not so much as gratuitous but as carefully staged signs of labor. What often gets overlooked in the otherwise careful readings that treat *The Weavers* primarily as a naturalist drama is the way the play exhibits and *denaturalizes* human labor, particularly in its rapport with capital. This rapport comes to the fore precisely when we examine how the play's stage directions describe and choreograph the bodies onstage. Because the staging of *The Weavers* involves managing and conducting a large cast of actors who are to represent labor onstage, it grapples with what Fredric Jameson calls, in *Brecht and Method*, "the representability of capitalism."[11]

While not metatheatrical in an obvious way, *The Weavers* does display a self-awareness of being a dramatic work that pushes against the limits of theatrical labor. In act 5, just before a crowd of dirty, dusty rioters rushes into the tenant house where Old Hilse lives with his family, ragpicker Horning exclaims: "That's quite a theater as well! That's what you don't see every day" (64). Such metatheatricality highlights the sheer labor and artistry that goes into producing the large swarm scenes in *The Weavers*. Horning, who has just come into the house from the outside, uses a theater metaphor to describe the crowd of weavers that he has seen in the streets. Before the riotous weavers enter, the stage directions indicate that we hear the "Weavers' Song," "*a dull, monotonous wail*," sung by "*hundreds of voices*" nearby (64). Moreover, characters onstage comment on what they see from the windows: "There they come swarming like ants.—Where can so many weavers be from?" (64). Hauptmann's strategy for representing such a multitude of weavers is simple and clever. While the cast list does not specify the number of weavers to be included in the "*large crowd of young and old weavers and weaver women*" (6), the stage directions do suggest how to give an illusion of such a throng. We get a sense of the rebellious crowd not only through sound but also through an ingenious setting, which makes use of the interplay between foreground and background in the theater. The stage directions for act 5 indicate that the main action of the scene takes places in Old Hilse's "*very narrow, low, and flat room*" (56). There is a door in the back wall of this narrow room that opens into a larger space (*Hause*), essentially an entryway to the house, where other tenants live. We are thus supposed to see Old Hilse and his family in the foreground, and part of the entryway in the background. It is from this entryway that Hornig refers to the crowd as theater, and it is in this entryway that the crowd of dirty, dusty rioters stands before dispersing throughout the house. Standing huddled in the distance, these rioters indeed give the illusion of a multitude. Only a few weavers actually enter Old Hilse's living quarters—that is, the foreground. In this way, Hornig's comparison of the riot to theater has a dual metatheatrical meaning. On the one hand, it is not every day that the audience gets to see a show like *The Weavers*, which employs a large reserve army of labor to comment on labor. On the other hand, Hornig's remark reminds the audience of the showdown between labor and capital that happens everyday offstage, outside the theater.

Furthermore, the play's stage directions reveal how *The Weavers* goes beyond naturalism's strategies for representing capitalism, particularly the strategies of the naturalist novel. As Jameson notes in *Brecht and Method*, the movement of money and labor in the capitalist system has always posed a challenge to artistic representation. According to Jameson, the novel often depicts either the lack of money, such as Dickensian poverty, or the "effects" of its "incorporeal value" once it becomes capital.[12] The greenbacks of Theodor Dreiser's *Sister Carrie* (1900), for example, become valuable substances in themselves and cease to be tokens of exchange.[13] Put simply, when there is too little money (poverty) or too much (the hoarding of capital), the moment of capitalist exchange, when money changes into capital and capital changes into money (what Marx famously describes in chapter 4 of *Capital* as M-C-M), becomes difficult to capture. It is equally difficult to render the capitalist network of production, circulation, and consumption. Thus, naturalist novelists, from Émile Zola to Frank Norris to Upton Sinclair, reverted to two kinds of representation: "on the one hand the 'Schicksalsschläge' ('blows of fate') of the very poor, who migrate in family units from one big city to another; on the other, the 'malefactors of great wealth,' whose rise and fall, fortunes and downfall, also register the 'fists of destiny.'"[14] Given the difficulty of representing the capitalist exchange, Hauptmann's *The Weavers* stands out by opening, as it does, with an attempt to represent nothing less than wage labor.

The activity of work, too, poses a challenge to artistic representation. In *Resisting Representation* (1994), Elaine Scarry identifies the major problems involved in the representation of work in the nineteenth-century novel. The first difficulty that Scarry diagnoses is that "work is action rather than a discrete action: it has no identifiable beginning or end"; thus, work is "perpetual, repetitive, habitual."[15] The second issue is that "work is social, hence not easily located within the boundaries of the 'individual,' hence not wholly compatible with the nature of 'character' as it is conceived and developed in the novel."[16] For example, Zola's *Germinal*

(1885), a naturalist novel about a coal miners' strike in the north of France to which *The Weavers* is often compared, solves the first problem—the fact that work is habitual—by subdividing the activity of work into smaller tasks throughout the novel.[17] As a dramatic work, written for the stage, *The Weavers* attempts to solve both issues of representation. The repetitiveness and habitual nature of work are expressed through the nearly continual movements of the actors, who are engaged in manual work in the presence of the audience. And the social aspect of work is rendered through the sheer collective effort that is required to mount a production like *The Weavers*.

The first scene of *The Weavers* opens, not with a dialogue between individual characters, but with a detailed pantomime, during which the weavers take turns exhibiting the finished products of their labor—linen samples—for inspection by their manager, Pfeifer. Hauptmann's directions indicate "*a glass door through which weavers, men, women, and children continuously come and go*" and list a series of gestures that Pfeifer repeats with each weaver (7). The manager inspects and evaluates the pieces of cloth proffered by the workers, after which he tells the cashier the payments to be made. There is a clock onstage, and it points to twelve. Significantly, the first spoken words of the play are numbers denoting earned payments. Cashier Neumann counts out money to a weaver woman and announces, "Comes to sixteen silver groschen and ten pfennings" (8). Here we witness nothing less than an exchange between the laborer and the manager, both employed by the millowner, Dreissiger. As the play progresses, we see what the weavers can buy with their wages (very little) and what the capitalists do with the linen (expand and accumulate their capital by selling those products). We learn that the weavers need their wages to survive and that they do not receive enough to cover all their life expenses, as many of them ask Pfeifer for advance payments. We witness, in other words, a dramatization of labor as Marx describes it in "Wage Labor and Capital" (1849): "He [the laborer] works in order to live. He does not even reckon labor as part of his life; it is rather a sacrifice of his life. It is a commodity, which he has made over to another. Hence, also, the product of his activity is not the object of his activity."[18] Every act of *The Weavers*, except act 4—which takes place in the lavish home of capitalist Dreissiger—opens with a display of signs of labor by means of props, actors' gestures, and sound design. Act 2 is set in Wilhelm Ansorge's house and opens with the characters steady at work. Mother Baumert sits at her spooling wheel, while her two daughters, Emma and Bertha, sit at the looms. August Baumert, her son, is reeling yarn. Ansorge is mending a basket. When the characters speak, they do so while toiling away. When Luise Hilse addresses her husband, Gottlieb, she does so "*from the washtub*" (57). The weavers onstage are constantly engaged in work, so much so that Hauptmann has to indicate when they should stop working. When

Jäger begins to repeat to Ansorge the lyrics of the song "Bloody Justice," which the weavers have been singing under Dreissiger's windows, Ansorge *"without continuing to work, sits slumped in deep emotion"* (28). Even when Hauptmann gives us minute descriptions of the weavers' bodies, such details are not solely signs of malady, malnutrition, or exhaustion but are also traces of hard, grueling labor. Thus, Hauptmann calls the weavers *"creatures of the looms . . . whose knees are bent with much sitting"* (7) and their *"sunken eyes* [are] *reddened and watery from wool dust, smoke, and work by lamplight"* (18). Old Hilse is described as *"worn with age, work, sickness, and strain,"* and as having *"deep-set, sore eyes characteristic of the weavers"* (56). Such meticulous descriptions of the characters' physical appearances, however, pose a certain challenge to staging (making the bodies of actors who perhaps have not suffered years of toil resemble those of the weavers) and suggest, as Jameson argues in relation to film, that "labor . . . is [not] accessible in any unmediated way."[19]

Hauptmann's stage directions also indicate the sound design necessary to convey the weavers' unceasing toil. The background noise during act 2 is described as follows: *"The roar of the looms, the rhythmic thud of the lathe, which shakes the ground and walls, and the click and rattle of the shuttles passing back and forth fill the room. Into all this blends the deep, steady whirr of the spooling wheels, resembling the hum of gigantic bumblebees"* (18). Here, in the use of sound produced by work, Hauptmann anticipates expressionist playwrights, who would also find inspiration in the noises of factories, machines, and clocks. Even as Kaiser and Toller (and, across the Atlantic, Elmer Rice and Sophie Treadwell) denounced the dehumanizing aspects of industrialization and the highly organized management techniques for the sake of efficiency, as advocated by American engineer Frederick Winslow Taylor in his *Principles of Scientific Management* (1911), they themselves embraced an aesthetic Taylorization of the stage through algorithmic dramaturgy, the meticulous choreography of bodies, and the creation of music out of noise produced by factory and office machines. Indeed, Frank Castorf's 1997 production of *The Weavers* for Berlin's Volksbühne made use of an expressionist set where a constantly rattling loom dominated the center of the action.

It is surprising, however, how rarely productions take note of Hauptmann's directions for an almost incessant background of work-related noise. Act 3 takes place in a bar parlor that also resembles a workspace rather than a space for recreation. With all the listed *"barrels and brewing utensils,"* the bar is a setting seen from the eyes of a working bartender rather than a customer at leisure (30). An old grandfather clock is ticking. Hauptmann again makes sure to note the kind of work that each member of the staff performs. The innkeeper, Welzel, is drawing beer into a glass from a barrel behind the counter. Mrs. Welzel is ironing at the stove. Anna Welzel, their daughter, is embroidering. Similarly, the stage directions at the beginning of act 5 describe the household of Old Hilse by enumerating the many work instruments lying around: "*A winding-wheel with bobbins stands between table and loom. Old spinning, weaving, and winding implements are housed on the bronzed deck beams; long hanks of yarn are hanging down. There is much useless lumber everywhere around in the room*" (56). The old, discarded spinning instruments signal the changes taking place in the means of production with the invention of the power loom. Old Hilse's weaving craft is becoming a thing of the past.

In this way, Hauptmann portrays the weavers at a moment of historical transition. Not all weavers yet work in factories with power looms. But those who do not are on the verge of losing their jobs. *The Weavers* thus tells a version of the weavers' story that Marx does in *The Grundrisse*:

> The way in which money transforms itself into capital often shows itself quite tangibly in history; e.g. when the merchant induces a number of weavers and spinners, who until then wove and spun as a rural, secondary occupation, to work for him, making their secondary into their chief occupation; but then has them in his power and has brought them under his command as wage laborers.[20]

When weaving was a secondary occupation that villagers undertook to satisfy their needs and those of their immediate rural community, they created what Marx calls, in *A Contribution to the Critique of Political Economy* (1859), "use-value," the usefulness of a commodity that is inextricably tied to "the physical properties of the commodity" and the human needs it actually fulfills.[21] But as soon as the villagers make weaving their primary occupation and begin to work for wages, they create exchange values. The product of their labor—linen—acquires exchange value, the exchange equivalent by which it can be compared to other objects on the market, including the weavers' own labor, which in turn becomes a commodity. *The Weavers*, however, is not a mere illustration of Marx's theories. As a dramatic work that moves the relationship between text and production to the fore through its necessarily arduous staging, *The Weavers* also probes the relationship between critique and praxis. One simply has to compare Hauptmann's drama to Marx's analysis of the weavers' uprising to see the crucial differences. In "Critical Marginal Notes on the Article 'The King of Prussia and Social Reform,'" Marx argues that the weavers' revolt was not carried out in vain, because "*not one* of the French and English workers' uprisings had such a *theoretical* and *conscious* character as the uprising of the Silesian weavers."[22] Marx identifies the song of the weavers—"Bloody Justice" ("Das Blutgericht"), which also features prominently in Hauptmann's drama—as a significant moment when the weavers proclaim their "opposition to the society of private property" and thus acquire "the consciousness of the nature of the proletariat."[23] To be sure, as many critics have pointed out, Hauptmann treats the class of Silesian weavers, in whose dialect he wrote the play, as the main protagonist of *The Weavers*.[24] But Hauptmann, unlike Marx, refuses to give us a united and homogeneous class of weavers. Nor does the playwright offer us a justification for the human tragedy.

Marx, on the other hand, justifies the uprising by noting the sheer volume of discussion it generated among the German bourgeoisie:

> Finally, it is *untrue, actually untrue*, that the German bourgeoisie totally fails to understand the general significance of the Silesian uprising. In several towns the masters are trying to act jointly with the apprentices. All the liberal German newspapers, the organs of the liberal bourgeoisie, teem with articles about the organization of labor, the reform of society, criticism of monopolies and competition, etc. All this is the result of the movement among the workers.[25]

The practice of Silesian weavers finds in Marx a *theoretical* validation—the revolt engendered discussion among the enlightened bourgeois who were now joining the cause of the workers. Arguably, as Chothia points out, the audiences of Otto Brahm's Freie Bühne and Antoine's Théâtre Libre were the "politically radicalized middle classes," so the play appealed to their political leanings.[26] In contrast to Marx's explanation, Hauptmann's play refuses to give the weavers' violence coherent meaning. Rather, *The Weavers* leaves us with questions pertaining to praxis. What else could the workers *do* beyond wreaking havoc and looting? Could they have done more to organize? The audience has the advantage over the weavers in that they can observe the entire social structure of labor in the weavers' community throughout the different acts. The weavers themselves do not have such a luxury and never gain any true Marxist insight into their labor. Their outbreak is spontaneous, disorganized, reckless. One could argue, of course, as Georg Lukács would in his 1923 *History and Class Consciousness*, that "proletarian thought is practical thought and as such strongly pragmatic."[27] According to Lukács, because the worker who "imagines himself to be the subject of his own life" eventually "finds this to be an illusion that is destroyed by the immediacy of his existence," his self-understanding is "simultaneously the objective understanding of the nature of society."[28] In contrast to the bourgeois intellectual, whose work is concealed "behind the façade of 'mental labor,' of 'responsibility' " and who is thus "reified in the only faculties that might enable him to rebel against reification," the proletarian experiences his labor as "the naked and abstract form of the commodity."[29] And it is this labor situation of the proletariat that allegedly leads to a revolutionary consciousness.

But *The Weavers* resists portraying the proletariat as a unified collective that understands its common struggle, and it does so precisely through the weavers' divergent attitudes toward their work. A few individual characters stand out from the very beginning, such as the bold and rebellious Bäcker and reserve soldier Moritz Jäger, whose military service has rendered him worldlier than his poor folk. These two stir the young weavers to destroy the new power looms and the millowners' houses, "hack[ing] at the beautiful furniture as if they were working for wages" (59). Bäcker and Jäger are no leaders, however, as they do not know where or how to direct the revolt beyond causing more wreckage. Characters that refuse to join the riot, such as Old Hilse, further undermine the idea of the weavers' being a homogeneous community. And the play's ending unveils the ideological grip of the work ethic that, in its turn, reifies the weavers in "*the only faculties that might enable [them] to rebel against reification.*"[30]

The weavers' differences and disorganization become particularly evident toward the end of the play. The tumultuous crowd of rioters arrives at Old Hilse's living quarters and orders all the weavers to come out. Seeing Old Hilse still working at the loom, Bäcker tells him that he no longer needs to work (65). But Old Hilse, a one-armed veteran, tells the rebellious weavers that nothing will change and that they have no chance against the soldiers: "They'll show you where the force lies" (68). More striking than Old Hilse's political resignation is his religious fervor in relation to his own labor and his unrelenting belief in the work ethic. Throughout the scene of commotion, he keeps trying to get back to his work, despite his age and disability. When the sound of the soldiers' gunfire is heard, his family warns him to get away from the window where his loom stands. But he adamantly refuses. His last words, delivered right before he resumes weaving, are: "Not I! Even if you all go completely mad! My heavenly Father has placed me here. . . . Here we'll sit and do our duty, though the snow may burn" (71). The pious old weaver chooses to remain at his loom in the midst of all the unrest and violence. The moment Old Hilse returns to weaving, a stray bullet mortally wounds him. He falls dead over his loom, as we hear the riotous weavers shout "Hurrah!" offstage. His granddaughter, six-year-old Mielchen, runs in to tell the news that the weavers have attacked Dittrich's house and are driving the soldiers out of town. But the directions indicate that the weavers' hurrahs become more and more distant. The play ends with Mother Hilse approaching the body of Old Hilse, slumped over his instrument of labor. "Come now, Father—say a word! You're scaring me!" says Mother Hilse before the curtain falls (71).

Hauptmann's ending is enigmatic, for a few reasons. First, *The Weavers* does not show us the violent suppression of the revolt, well documented in historical sources, but instead gives the weavers the last word, "Hurrah!" Or perhaps the waning sound of the hurrahs hints at the defeat to come. Second, instead of imagining the future, the play looks back: Old Hilse is dead, just as his craft and work instruments have become obsolete with the new means of production. Osborne argues that Old Hilse's reactionary attitude "cannot be fully explained in Marxist terms by environment" but is, rather, an example of "Silesian pietism"—that is, of Hilse's "strong psychological need for religion."[31] Yet, as Chothia notes, Hilse's death is "at least[] ambiguous," for the irresolute ending leaves it to the audience to judge the revolt of the weavers and to decide whether and how to take political action.[32] In this, Hauptmann's *The Weavers* anticipates Brechtian dialectical theater even if Brecht himself dismissed the play for its supposedly fatalistic vision.[33]

Moreover, Hilse's work ethic and religion are intimately connected. In this way *The Weavers* anticipates Weber's treatise *The Protestant Ethic and the Spirit of Capitalism* (1905), which would posit the Protestant work ethic as a significant force in promoting "one's duty in a calling," which became "what is most characteristic of the social ethic of capitalistic culture."[34] Indeed, throughout the play Pastor Kittelhaus promotes the work ethic as having religious value in and of itself. It is not by accident that the first time we meet Pastor Kittelhaus and his wife they are at Dreissiger's house, playing a game of whist, and not among the weavers. Kittelhaus denies any direct interest in money, however. When Jäger insinuates that the church is mainly interested in collecting money from the poor, the pastor immediately retorts: "Money, money. . . . Do you perhaps imagine the vile, wretched money. . . . I'd much prefer you keep your money. Such utter nonsense! Behave, be a Christian! Think of what you praised. Follow God's commandments. Be good and pious. Money, money . . . !" (49). In this scene, the main role of the church lies less in collecting money (although it certainly does that as well) than in encouraging principles that help preserve the status quo (e.g., the work ethic). Institutional religion, along with the work ethic, perpetuates the social inequality in Hauptmann's labor drama. The pastor's promotion of the work ethic in *The Weavers* echoes the operations of the Salvation Army in Bernard Shaw's *Major Barbara*, which, through its charitable intentions, inadvertently buttresses the corporate empire of Andrew Undershaft, the powerful arms industrialist of Europe. As Undershaft notes, sober and honest workers, with "their thoughts on heavenly things" and "indifferent to their own interests," are "an invaluable safeguard against revolution."[35]

To appreciate what made Hauptmann's display of labor innovative in 1892, it is helpful to recall the ambivalent attitude toward work in nineteenth-century capitalist culture. On the one hand, the ideology of the work ethic was promoted and celebrated. As Max Weber argues, neither unscrupulousness nor the pursuit of selfish interests but work itself, "performed as if it were an absolute end in itself, a calling," motivated and bolstered the capitalistic enterprise.[36] On the other hand, another cultural imperative of the nineteenth century was a certain cover-up of the signs of labor, especially of hard manual labor. Such concealment of signs of labor was carried out, paradoxically, for the very purpose of promoting the work ethic. Citing the study of labor historian Daniel Rodgers, Cindy Weinstein explains that the aesthetic phenomenon of "the erasure of labor" resulted from changes in production during rapid industrialization, which created new work conditions—"specialized, repetitious, machine-paced, and, often, deadeningly simple."[37] In short, inhumane work conditions threatened the promotion of the ideology of the work ethic. The new tasks requiring no skill—which became the norm as craft guilds dissolved and the division of labor, characteristic of an industrialized economy, came to the fore—were difficult to promote as anyone's calling and thus had to be hidden if the work ethic were still to be encouraged.

The repression of signs of labor not only facilitates the ideology of the work ethic but also encourages guilt-free consumption, including that of art. According to Jameson's seminal argument in *The Political Unconscious* (1981), modernism is "an ideological expression of capitalism, and in particular, of the latter's reification of daily life" and largely operates through the repression of signs of labor beneath its formalized surface.[38] Thus, the impressionistic strategy of classical modernism is to "derealize the content and make it available for consumption on some purely aesthetic level."[39] The example that Jameson gives of this impressionistic strategy is Joseph Conrad's description of the ship and sea in *Lord Jim* (1900):

> Above the mass of sleepers, a faint and patient sigh at times floated, the exhalation of a troubled dream; and short metallic clangs bursting out suddenly in the depths of the ship, the harsh scrape of a shovel, the violent slam of a furnace-door, exploded brutally, as if the men handling the mysterious things below had their breasts full of fierce anger: while the slim high hull of the steamer went on evenly ahead, without a sway of her bare masts, cleaving continuously the great calm of the waters under the inaccessible serenity of the sky.[40]

The waters might be calm, the sky serene, and the passengers asleep, but "the brief clang from the boiler room . . . mark[s] the presence beneath ideology and appearance of that labor which produces and reproduces the world itself."[41] Jameson identifies this impressionistic strategy as the "dominant one" but not the only one "structurally available to the modernists." The other one that he names, though he does not discuss it, is the "much rarer expressionism."[42] While expressionism may not have played a dominant role in the modernist novel, it significantly permeated early twentieth-century German and American modern drama. It is in this expressionist theater that the boiler room of the ship would be entered and exhibited. In Georg Kaiser's *The Coral*, the first play of the *Gas* trilogy, the Billionaire's Son tells his father about his descent into their ship's engine room. Witnessing the exploitation of stokers inspires the Son to become a stoker on a ship and to join the fight of the proletariat. Eugene O'Neill would later stage a parody of this moment in *The Hairy Ape* (1922), which opens inside the boiler room of a transatlantic ocean liner. Mildred, the spoiled daughter of the owner of Nazareth Steel, descends into the belly of the ship only to faint at the sight of Yank, a brutish-looking stoker. Instead of repressing signs of labor, expressionist plays such as Kaiser's *Gas* trilogy, Toller's *The Machine Wreckers*, O'Neill's *The Hairy Ape*, Rice's *Adding Machine*, and Treadwell's *Machinal* exhibit labor onstage, but not for any good-feeling resolutions. Instead of being, like the impressionistic strategy of modernism, a strategy of displacement or symbolic resolution, the expressionistic strategy exhibits and even flaunts the artist's neuroses, doubts, and a general feeling of malaise. This acknowledgment and display of malaise became a self-justifying tactic for playwrights who were all too painfully aware that they came from higher social strata than the working class that they sought to represent. In the way it betrays a general sense of anxiety and displays labor, Hauptmann's *The Weavers* can be said to employ the expressionistic, rather than the impressionistic, strategy of modernism.

In the preface to *The Weavers*, Hauptmann admits to doubting the power of his creative work. He dedicated *The Weavers* to his father, Robert Hauptmann, whose own father struggled as a Silesian weaver before finding the means to become a waiter. In his dedication, Hauptmann addresses his father and acknowledges that, as an author, he cannot judge whether "the germ" of his drama "possesses vitality or is rotten at the core," revealing the angst that would be familiar to many German expressionist playwrights writing in his wake.[43] They, too, would question the ability of the artist and intellectual to speak to and for the working class from a position of privilege, expressing public anxieties over the utility of mental work and the very term "bourgeois." The tense and ambiguous relationship between an extraordinary individual (the intellectual, the artist, or the Nietzsche-inspired "New Man") and the mass of laborers would become the focus of dramatic conflict in the early plays of Kaiser and Toller. In particular, Toller's *The Machine Wreckers*, inspired by the Luddite Rebellion (1811–13), can be taken as a direct artistic response to *The Weavers*. In this play, instead of a spontaneous revolt spurred on by a few rowdy individuals, a politically radicalized former worker named Jimmy tries to educate a mob of weavers in socialism and lead an uprising against their capitalist exploiters. If Jimmy fails to convert the weavers, it is because they are not yet prepared or patient enough to carry out his socialist program, the details of which remain rather vague and incoherent.

The Impact of the Early Productions of *The Weavers* on Working-Class Audiences

Given that Hauptmann's drama lays bare onstage the ideological constructs inherent to the capitalist mode of production (e.g., commodities, wages, and the work ethic), it should come as no surprise that the play's potential for revolutionary impact, especially on the workers themselves, has been contested ground ever since its first performance. After the play's premiere at Otto Brahm's Freie Bühne, in 1893, which was resurrected specifically for the purpose of staging *The Weavers*, socialist Franz Mehring excoriated reviewer Julius Hart for suggesting that *The Weavers* was not so much "the revolutionary utterance of a party politician" as "simply the manifestation of universal humanitarianism."[44] Mehring, whose book *The Lessing Legend* (1893) is regarded as one of the first attempts at Marxist literary criticism, believed that associating Hauptmann's play with the myth of humanitarianism meant obscuring the "steam and vapor of [its] political partisanship."[45] As proof, Mehring listed the many instances in *The Weavers* where Hauptmann closely follows his sources: the historical accounts of Wilhelm Wolff and Alfred Zimmermann. Wilhelm Wolff was the "bold, true, and noble champion of the proletariat" to whom Marx dedicated volume 1 of *Capital*.[46] According to Mehring, Hauptmann seems to have lifted the destitution of the weavers, their insurgent song, and even Dreissiger's remark that "the weavers could eat grass if they were hungry" (59) straight out of Wolff's *German Citizen Book for 1845* (*Deutsches Bürgerbuch für 1845*). But even Mehring had doubts about the efficacy of the play's revolutionary spirit: he remarked that the "ovation it received from the public at the Freie Bühne proved nothing," because its public came "exclusively from the bourgeoisie," the "press and stock-exchange."[47] Mehring's comment raises a question that is difficult to gauge: Did laborers see the play, and, if so, what was their reaction? Although the weavers, in the play, do not acquire any Marxist insight into the alienation of their labor, could *The Weavers* spur real workers to action, through pedagogy and/or emotional impact? After all, the year 1890 saw the development of the Freie Volksbühne (People's Theater) under the leadership of Bruno Wille, whose goal was to bring theater to a working-class public that, until then, had essentially been barred from commercial theater because of the high cost of tickets. The response of the working class to this mission was significant: by the end of its first year, the Freie Volksbühne boasted a membership of 1,873.[48]

In 1892, a split in the Freie Volksbühne led to the new leadership of Franz Mehring and closer ties to the Social Democratic Party of Germany (SPD). Resisting the dogmas of the SPD, Bruno Wille and his supporters left to found the Neue Freie Volksbühne (New People's Theater).[49] While Mehring's Freie Volksbühne unapologetically promoted the political agenda of the SPD, the predominant aim of Wille's Neue Freie Volksbühne was to educate the proletariat about the art of theater, including the difference between dramatic character and actor. In Wille's opinion, the working class could not teach itself and thus had a conservative taste in theater.[50] A census of members from the 1893–94 season shows that the association was primarily working class and was particularly popular with skilled workmen.[51] Both Mehring and Wille were great admirers of Hauptmann's *The Weavers*. When the play finally had its public performance at the Deutsches Theater on September 25, 1894, the kaiser canceled his box, and authorities continued to try to prevent performances of *The Weavers* until the turn of the century. In the meantime, the play was put on three times by Wille's Neue Freie Volksbühne and seven by Mehring's Freie Volksbühne.[52] While it is difficult to assess how effective Mehring and Wille's programs were at galvanizing the working class, these were two of the earliest attempts at subsidizing tickets and bringing theater art to the masses. Wille claimed that *The Weavers* "made a more powerful impact on the working class than any other social drama" he had ever known.[53] Yet there is also evidence that the play "drew some inappropriate laughter" from the working-class crowds.[54]

Across the Atlantic, *The Weavers* also earned notoriety during the 1890s, when the German-language theaters of the United States attempted to stage it. The play appealed to labor unions as a potential piece of political agitation and to anarchists as an occasion to stir mayhem.[55] The mayor of Newark even issued an edict forbidding the play's performance because the city had a large German laboring population.[56] Hauptmann's drama also resonated with working actors. In 1909, *The Weavers* was performed at the New Deutsches Theater in New York, specifically to raise funds for German actors who needed money for their journey back home, as the company was soon to be dissolved.[57]

Emanuel Reicher's 1915 Production of *The Weavers* and the Revolt of His Actors

The English-language premiere of *The Weavers* in the United States in 1915 inadvertently played a role in the labor movement of actors. In fact, the actors involved in the production quoted lines from *The Weavers* to support their struggle for the recognition of their rights as workers in the theater. This curious chapter in American theater history began in October 1914, when Emanuel Reicher, an eminent German actor and one of the founders of Berlin's Freie Bühne, arrived in the United States with the ambitious goal of regenerating American drama.[58] For this purpose, Reicher attempted to found an independent stage in New York, called the Modern Stage, that would be akin to André Antoine's Théâtre Libre in Paris and Otto Brahm's Freie Bühne in Berlin. After a few misses, the Modern Stage put on Hauptmann's *The Weavers* as its second play of the 1915–16 theatrical season. It would prove to be the Modern Stage's most successful production. It would also be its demise. At first glance, the choice of *The Weavers*, with its expensive logistics and large cast, might seem an odd and risky choice for Reicher, whose company was already facing financial troubles. Yet there were reasons for hoping that *The Weavers* could be a hit. Gerhart Hauptmann had received the Nobel Prize in Literature in 1912, Ludwig Lewisohn had begun publishing the translated and edited volumes of the author's work, and Barrett H. Clark had written glowingly about *The Weavers* in *The Continental Drama of Today*. Most importantly, Reicher himself had played the part of Old Ansorge during the premiere of *The Weavers* at the Freie Bühne in 1893 and thus had extensive experience with the text. He reprised the role in his American production.

The Weavers earned almost unanimous critical acclaim when Reicher directed its English translation, by Mary Morison, on December 14, 1915, at the Garden Theater in New York. It would see eighty-seven performances, not a spectacular number (the original production at the Freie Bühne boasted two hundred performances) but still respectable, given that year's generally abysmal theatrical season.[59] The production also briefly went on tour to Chicago's Princess Theater. Critic Heywood Broun wrote that "no other performance in New York [that] season ha[d] elbowed perfection so closely" and that "possibly December 14, 1915 will be of some significance in the theatrical history of New York."[60] The *New York Dramatic Mirror* stated that the remarkable performance of *The Weavers* was "very likely to give an impetus to the movement which [would] have the same tendency to jar local playgoers out of their complacency regarding the merit of plays and productions that the Theater Antoine had in Paris and the Freie Bühne in Berlin."[61] The *New York Times* praised Reicher's performance as wretched weaver Ansorge as well as his intelligent directing of the large cast.[62] Because Reicher knew that the English translation lost the particularity of the Silesian dialect, he attempted to "solv[e] the problem by permitting every one [of his actors] to use his [or her] favorite lingo—the result being . . . a strange mix of Irish, cockney, low German, and plain Yankee."[63] While praising Reicher's version, the *Evening Mail* expressed doubts about the play's appeal to the broader audience: "Our American public is inclined toward the marshmallow of comedy or the jeweled poison vial of individualistic tragedy. But the taste of *The Weavers* is the taste of hunger, and that America has never liked."[64] As Madame Critic, of the *New York Dramatic Mirror*, pointed out, the audience of the opening night was composed almost entirely of critics or subscribers to the Modern Stage, and it required "a pronounced love for the theater in general, and for Hauptmann in particular" to trek all the way to the Garden Theater on a cold, dreary Tuesday night in December.[65] Despite the critical accolades, the production did not attract more theatergoers or sponsors to the Modern Stage Society. As Charles Collins, of the *Chicago Post*, put it, Hauptmann's "doggerel of despair," no matter how expertly directed, did not "belong to the pleasure-seeking game of the American Stage."[66] In 2007, writing for the *Arts Fuse Review* about the "once-in-a-life-time chance to see" *The Weavers* on the American stage, in a production by the Boston University College of Fine Arts, Bill Marx echoed those early critics, noting that Hauptmann's "poetics of paucity" would not sit well with audiences in the "land of plenty."[67] To put it crudely, a play as grim and unsettling as *The Weavers* might not generate enough box office profits to make it worth staging, as it costs too much money to produce. It should come as no surprise, then, that university programs are more likely to find the necessary supply of theatrical labor than professional companies, which are bound by the laws of Actors' Equity. Yet even the Boston University College of Fine Arts had to make do with just twenty-nine actors for its production. In fact, most contemporary stagings of *The Weavers* opt for a smaller cast than the one indicated by Hauptmann's original text. For example, Michael Thalheimer's 2011 production, at the Deutsches Theater in Berlin, rotated twenty actors for the entire show. Reicher's version, however, employed over forty actors, in addition to the theater staff, and ran into problems of labor and employment.

Events took a turn for the revolutionary when Reicher tried to close *The Weavers*. A lack of funds and the need to move on with the rest of his Modern Stage subscription series motivated his decision. His actors, however, wanted the show to go on, so they rebelled. The *Brooklyn Eagle*, which covered the real-life drama of Reicher's actors, ran a headline that read: "How the Actors in *The Weavers* Put Its Teachings into Practice." Reicher did not fully consider that canceling the show would mean "throwing forty actors and actresses, as well as the theater crew[,] out of employment in the middle of a terrible theatrical season."[68] And since, as *Harper's Bazaar* reported, Reicher had "conscripted even the married men and children to fill Hauptmann's wholesale order for actors," he would be throwing whole families out onto the street.[69]

Like the riot of weavers, the actors' revolt was spontaneous, as they began to quote lines from the play to support their idea for a commonwealth plan. Augustin Duncan, actor and stage director, "suggested they appoint an executive committee to take charge of the management."[70] Duncan was immediately appointed chairman. The following plan was executed: "A minimum equal salary was agreed upon to be paid after the running expenses of the theater and advertising were met, then from all money over the expenses and minimum salaries, the balance was to be divided in proportion to the contract salary of each member of the organization."[71] Duncan reached out to the Industrial Relations Committee in hopes that it would sponsor the New York run of *The Weavers* as well as its tour to spread information about the labor conditions in the United

States. In the end, while the Industrial Relations Committee agreed that Hauptmann's drama was relevant to the situation of American laborers, it was not as generous as Duncan had hoped.[72]

In early February 1916, Duncan invited the Actors' Equity Association (AEA) to finance the failing show. As Sean Holmes relates, "More than a thousand AEA members turned out to see an Equity-sponsored performance of Hauptmann's play" on February 26, 1916.[73] Between the third and fourth acts, the AEA founder Frank Gillmore delivered a speech during which he compared the exploitative practices of theater employers to those of Hauptmann's millowner.[74] Having used the play as a springboard for discussion, the AEA left the sinking production in the wake of a growing anti-German sentiment. In April 1917, the United States entered World War I, and discussions about German drama became unpopular. Reicher briefly presented *The Weavers* again in the fall of 1918 at an old playhouse at the corner of Madison Square Garden, when he was the director of the Jewish Art Theatre, but the production did not generate nearly the same media frenzy as its premiere.[75] This performance took place in the midst of the Spanish flu pandemic and World War I, when New York theaters made the unorthodox decision to stay open in an "effort to keep the public's spirits up."[76]

Hauptmann's play would not be performed again in New York until the revolutionary year 1989, when the newly formed East Village Theater Company chose it for its debut and produced it, at RAPP Arts Center, to lukewarm reviews. In her review for the *Village Voice*, Alisa Solomon found fault with Linda Shirey's "flaccid direction" of her thirty actors and the play's "hokey language and sentimental treatment of the downtrodden." But what struck the critic as the weakest link in the production was the missed opportunity to dramatize the tensions of the local neighborhood where the play was performed—Alphabet City of the late 1980s. As Solomon noted, "The walk to the RAPP Arts Center (at 4th Street between A and B)," where the shabby reality of the homeless coexisted with overpriced amenities, "sets you up for its lessons in living Marxism."[77]

The Dresden Weavers and the Chorus of the Unemployed

While Shirey's 1989 production of *The Weavers* was criticized for not engaging in a more daring fashion with the politics of its day, the 2004 free adaptation by Volker Lösch and Stefan Schnabel, for Staatsschauspiel Dresden, came under fire for contemporizing Hauptmann's play and injecting it with the unemployment issues of the day. Dresden's political version caused a scandal and contrasted starkly with the farcical deconstruction of the play that Frank Castorf staged at the Berlin's Volksbühne in 1997. Instead of trying to stir a passive audience, the Dresden production essentially treated the audience as a coauthor. Director Lösch and playwright Schnabel added "a chorus of the unemployed," comprising thirty-three amateurs who vented frustration and raged in the face of growing unemployment and unpopular welfare reforms (the federal government's Hartz IV). To come up with the text for this chorus, Lösch and Schnabel interviewed the citizens of Dresden about their experiences with work and unemployment. Specifically, what sparked the controversy in the media was one line in which a member of the chorus voiced the desire to shoot the television journalist Sabine Christiansen.[78] The latter vehemently protested the text and the performance. The publishing house Felix Bloch Erben, along with the playwright's granddaughter Anja Hauptmann, sought to stop performances, arguing that the added material amounted to hate speech (which also included neo-Nazi remarks) and contradicted the spirit of Hauptmann's original play. Lösch attempted to justify his creative vision by stressing that the alleged hate speeches were precisely the kinds of things said out loud by people at the end of their rope at unemployment offices. He also noted that the audience did not get upset at these passages but instead applauded. The production had clearly hit a nerve. When the Berlin Regional Court issued a temporary injunction banning the version that included the new text, the Dresden media cast the court's decision as a conspiracy against East Germany. Conspiracy questions aside, the legal case essentially pitted the copyright of the publishing house against the law of artistic freedom of expression. Lösch and Schnabel eventually got around the injunction by creating a new production under the title *The Dresden Weavers: A Tribute to Gerhart Hauptmann (Die Dresden Weber: Eine Hommage an Gerhart Hauptmann)*, which "was completely free of text by Hauptmann, but in the spirit of his work [and that] retained the controversial choral passages."[79] This version went up in February 2005. When the Berlin Higher Regional Court overruled the decision of the lower court in May 2005, the first version was once again put on in Dresden.[80] Evidently productions of *The Weavers* have the power to make actors and spectators alike examine their roles as laborers.

Mental versus Menial Labor in the Expressionist Plays of Kaiser, Toller, and Čapek

While early expressionist plays, inspired by Hauptmann's *The Weavers*, stir up at least some hope of arousing the revolutionary spirit of the proletariat, later works, composed after the horrors of World War I, the German Revolution of 1918–19, and the Weimar hyperinflation of 1921–24, betray political cynicism and a general sense of pessimism through gallows humor, bitter self-parody, and absurdist elements.[81] Shifting attitudes toward the working class can be discerned within the evolving oeuvre of one artist, as in the case of Georg Kaiser (1878–1945). Kaiser begins on an optimistic note: even as his early plays exhibit angst about industrialization, they also exalt the Nietzsche-inspired "New Man" who is to lead the proletariat in the revolution. Yet a change can already be seen in the *Gas* trilogy. If, in *The Coral*, the Billionaire's Son takes on the cause of the oppressed workers of his father's factory, then the final play of the trilogy, the apocalyptic and satirical *Gas II*, imagines the utter destruction of humanity, which has allowed its economic production to rely exclusively on war.

The main contradiction of early twentieth-century German drama lies in its self-appointed role as the mediator between intellectuals and the working class. Although Kaiser and Toller denounced so-called bourgeois values and were committed to promoting socialist ideals, their dramatic works also inadvertently reveal their distrust of the proletariat, fear of mob rule and of the destruction of private property, and even a latent desire to preserve their socioeconomic status. After all, it was these writers' very right to make art that was being challenged at the time. The provisional guidelines of the BRPS (Bund Proletarisch-Revolutionärer Schriftsteller; League of Proletarian Revolutionary Writers) maintained that "the literary, just as much as the economic and political, emancipation of the proletariat can be achieved only by the working class itself," and its official journal, *Linkskurve* (1929–32), regularly featured acerbic takedowns of "petty-bourgeois intellectuals" such as Kaiser, Toller, and eventually the young Brecht.[82] Even Toller, who served as the president of the short-lived Bavarian Soviet Republic (April–May 1919) and was imprisoned for his radical politics, was not immune to the smear of the epithet "bourgeois." Kaiser and Toller fought back and in turn dubbed their literary critics "bourgeois." In the introduction to *Man and the Masses* (*Masse-Mensch*, 1921), a play dedicated "to the workers," Toller calls his detractors "bourgeois" and argues that proletarian art must ultimately focus on "universal human interests, must at its deepest, like life or death, embrace all human themes."[83] In other words, such art must also include the educated classes to which Toller himself belonged. Consequently, in the drama of Kaiser and Toller, we encounter, time and again, an enlightened "New Man" who awakens and leads the laborers in their struggle to seize the means of production. Every new drama tests out a different labor scenario and a different relationship between this special individual and the workers.

In Kaiser's *The Coral* and *Gas I*, the Billionaire's quixotic Son and Daughter decide to help their father's workers, who make poisonous gas that drives the entire economy. After a devastating explosion, the Billionaire's Son attempts to persuade the workers to leave the factory and found an agrarian utopia, while the Head Engineer tries to sway them to stay. The story of an enlightened and compassionate industrialist championing the cause of the proletariat would inspire Fritz Lang's expressionist film

Metropolis (1927), cowritten with his wife, Thea von Harbou. The film's memorable sentimental tagline—"There can be no understanding between the hands and the brain unless the heart acts as mediator"—promulgates the idea that empathy on the part of the capitalists would lead to better conditions for the working class.[84]

Overall, Kaiser espouses exactly the kind of nostalgia for an apocryphal agrarian past that Marx explicitly rejects. The Billionaire's Son's argument rehearses some of the main points that Kaiser makes in his Nietzschean manifesto of 1922, "The Coming Man, or Poetry and Energy" ("Der kommende Mensch oder Dichtung und Energie"), which puts forward an idealistic program where human beings can rise above their machine-age environment by returning to "nature."[85] Yet *Gas I*, written four years before this manifesto, ends with the government arriving onstage like a deus ex machina to take control of production. It is no longer up to the Son or the Engineer to decide the fate of the workers: the drama concludes on a dark note, with the government conserving the capitalist war machinery and exacerbating the laborers' exploitation. The last words of the play, however, still express hope for future generations, as the Billionaire's Daughter announces that she will give birth to a *new* New Man.

A similar fantasy of rebirth and the belief that real systemic changes could only arrive with the next generation inform the ending of Karel Čapek's 1920 sci-fi play *R.U.R.* (*Rossum's Universal Robots*), which coined the word "robot" from the Czech word *robota*, meaning "drudgery" or "serf labor."[86] Prefiguring biogenetic engineering, Čapek's enigmatic play stages a nightmarish situation where robots—mass-produced androids artificially synthesized from organic material—end up revolting against humanity and massacring all human beings except the head engineer. They spare him because he works with his hands, not just his head, and because they believe he has the blueprint for their biomechanical reproduction. Ironically, he no longer has it in his possession because his fellow humans burned the formula right before their annihilation. In the wake of humanity's violent end, *R.U.R.* ends on a mystical and religious note. As two of the robots fall in love, they appear as the new "Adam and Eve" who have finally figured out reproduction.[87]

The most explicit response to Hauptmann's *The Weavers* is Toller's *The Machine Wreckers*, which imagines a politically radicalized individual leading a crowd of weavers in their overthrow of capitalist order. The play's title likely originates from Max Beer's *History of Socialism in England* (*Geschichte des Sozialismus in England*, 1913), which Toller was reading at the time.[88] But instead of choosing an enlightened capitalist, like Kaiser's Billionaire's Son, Toller purposely makes his protagonist a former weaver, who has gone into the world and has now returned to educate his peers about socialism. Jimmy describes himself first and foremost as a manual rather than mental worker: "I am a tramper, a craftsman, looking for work.... I am a worker, a weaver."[89] In contrast to his brother, who is proud of having become an overseer and having earned a commercial title (*kaufmännische Würde*), Jimmy maintains that he remains at heart a common laborer (24). As such, Jimmy hopes to act as an arbiter between the laborers and the capitalists, leading a peaceful revolution. In this light, Jimmy is an upgraded version of Hauptmann's Moritz Jäger. While Jäger, a conceited reserve soldier, merely stirs the mob to destroy the power looms, Jimmy tries to educate the workers. For example, he explains to them that they cannot stop the technological changes in production and advises them to wait for the right time to revolt—when other towns join their cause. Jimmy believes that once all workers seize the means of production, they can make machines work for them, but to violently hack at the machines seems useless to him: "You fight against the machine?... I know that the machine is our inescapable fate" (21).

If Jimmy fails to reason with the weavers, it is because they are not yet ready, not patient enough to wait for the realization of his socialist program, which remains rather nebulous in the play. In fact, Toller slyly shifts his audience's attention from Jimmy's political plan to the manipulability and violence of the crowd. In the end, the bloodthirsty mob, spurred by the villain and double-dealer John Wibley, senselessly break the machines, tear Jimmy to pieces, and pluck his eyes out. Toller's melodrama thus paints the weavers as savage, irrational, and easily impressed by rhetoric. Wibley sways the crowd by two crucial rhetorical moves. First, he ruins Jimmy's reputation as a manual worker by insisting that Jimmy's education has separated him forever from the common weavers. Embracing anti-intellectualism, Wibley tells the workers, "He is a workman no more though he wants to take our part. He can read and write like the masters!" (89) In short, it is the workers' distrust of Jimmy's cultural capital that provokes them to murder the one man who could have led them to liberation.

Second, when describing the machines, Wibley perversely employs the language of Marx, especially when he calls the factory's machinery "Moloch" and "Monster" (*Ungeheuer*) (40). In *Capital*, Marx uses the term "mechanical monster" (*mechanisches Ungeheuer*) for the organized network of machines used to exploit the workers.[90] These metaphors of demons and monsters are used to discredit the notion that industrial machines shorten labor time. Instead, according to Marx, it is precisely because the machine is "the most powerful instrument of shortening labor-time" that it becomes the "most powerful means of lengthening the working day beyond all natural limits."[91] In Toller's drama, however, Wibley uses the same tropes not to explain economic facts but to stir the crowd's emotions. Wibley anthropomorphizes the machine in order to portray it as an enemy that the workers must kill. One of the most salient features of expressionist theater is its dramatization of visions as seen through a subconscious mind.[92] Indeed, in *The Machine Wreckers*, the monster machine arises from the collective unconscious, as we witness the workers fall under the spell of the gigantic engine and John Wibley's inflammatory rhetoric. By representing the workers as easily manipulable and roused to senseless violence, Toller's drama expresses anxiety about the proletariat's ability to recognize their best interests.

What is more, the workers are portrayed as violent from the very beginning of *The Machine Wreckers*. One of the first crowd scenes opens with the weavers hanging strikebreakers—that is, fellow weavers who went back to work at the machines for wages. We find a similarly anxious depiction of the proletariat as irrational and brutal in Toller's earlier drama *Masses and the Man*. Sonia, the leader of a workers' strike, goes to fight with her own government-employed husband. At the center of this conflict, we have the rare chance to see a "New Woman" instead of a "New Man." But here too the masses betray their self-appointed leader: the workers abandon Sonia's pleas for nonviolence. Their rampage results in Sonia's imprisonment and the suppression of their revolt. Likewise, by the end of *The Machine Wreckers*, Jimmy plays the role of a Christ-like figure who could have led the weavers to their freedom had they listened to him. Instead, he becomes the scapegoat of a savage community that looks back in horror at his death and professes to be better and wiser the next time their messiah arrives. With its cautionary tale, *The Machine Wreckers* attempts to valorize intellectual work and to imagine a potentially productive relationship between mental and menial workers, if only in the future. Still, as with many other expressionist plays of the time, Jimmy's political program, as conceived by Toller, remains underdeveloped.

"The Eternal Bourgeois": A Turn to Cynicism and Self-Destruction

In the twilight of the Weimar Republic, expressionist dramas became gloomier still as the playwrights turned the satirical blade toward themselves. Instead of the hope of an enlightened individual leading the workers, we find in these works acerbic self-critique, a dark parody of artistic and intellectual work, and self-hatred spurred by the realization of being the beneficiaries of capitalism. The angst is not so much about the potential violence of the working class as it is about the utility and value of mental work. Ivan Goll's *Methusalem or The Eternal Bourgeois* (*Methusalem oder Der ewige Bürger*, 1922), for example, tells the story of a filthy rich shoe businessman who is killed in a riot by his workers. But, true to the play's title, Methusalem comes back, this time as a devil reborn from the marriage of his daughter and her husband, an incompetent idealist.

Similarly, in *Hoppla, We're Alive!* (*Hoppla, wir leben!*, 1927), Toller stages a parody of a meeting of minds under the title "An evening of discussion of the Union of Intellectual Head Workers" (*Diskussionsabend der Gruppe der geistigen Kopfarbeiter*).[93] Amid the vain intellectual bickering, Lyric Poet Y keeps interrupting to ask, "Where is this in Marx?" until Philosopher X finally asks him to be quiet: "Stop showing off that you've read Marx" (78–79). It is not clear, however, whether the poet has read any Marx at all or is just regurgitating quotations that he has picked up elsewhere, perhaps during another evening at the Union of Intellectual Workers. Toller is no longer indiscriminately valorizing intellectual work; now he is questioning in a self-critical manner where the exposure to Marx has led poets like himself. His play thus expresses skepticism about the possibility of any productive rapport between mental and menial workers, between critique and praxis. No doubt this cynical attitude was at least in part influenced by Toller's six turbulent days as president of the Bavarian Soviet Republic during the German Revolution of 1918–19. *Hoppla, We're Alive!* suggests that it is not so much the supposed irrationality and violent nature of the working class that impedes social change as the eternal bourgeois hiding behind the mask of the artist and intellectual. After all, most of the surviving revolutionaries in Toller's play end up as complacent bureaucrats perpetuating the very system they once fought against when they were young. The one man who wants to stand up to the oppressive regime, Karl Thomas, ends up back where he started—imprisoned and under psychiatric observation.

The last play of Kaiser's *Gas* trilogy disposes of even such an ineffective protagonist. There are barely any recognizable human beings left in Kaiser's apocalyptic *Gas II* (1920). Kaiser takes *Telegrammstil*, the telegram style of clipped and fragmented dialogue pioneered by expressionism, to the extreme in order to stage disturbing and humorous conversations between humanoids at work.[94] The play opens with "Blue Figures" (*Blaufiguren*) performing work onstage and discussing production numbers. Kaiser never explains to us why these characters are called "Figures" (*Figuren*) or who they might be. We do not even know whether they are automata or humans who have become like automata through the division of labor and mechanization of tasks. The opening of Kaiser's drama presents us with the following intriguing dialogue and set of gestures:

SECOND BLUE FIGURE
(In front of a red-glowing disk)
Message of the third battle section: concentration of enemy in the making. Disk faded.
FIRST BLUE FIGURE
(Puts in a red plug)
FIFTH BLUE FIGURE
(In front of a green-glowing disk)
Message of the third workshop: production line below one order.[95]

And so on. These Blue Figures keep on changing the glowing disks and surveying production for the war economy. The play ends with a change in the ruling order, but the only change registered onstage is that the Figures are now all yellow instead of blue. They still move the same disks and utter the same sentences. Whether the figures are human or not seems not to matter because the play cynically suggests that even if we are dealing with humans, they have become powerless and utterly useless in transforming their political reality. The figures eventually decide that the only way out of the maddening system is complete autodestruction. Figure in Yellow ends the play by yelling into a telephone, "Turn your bullets on yourselves—exterminate yourselves—the dead crowd out of their graves—day of judgment—*dies irae—solvet-in favil* . . ." (101). The last image of *Gas II* is a landscape devoid of all human life: "In the distant gray haze sheaves of fireballs rush against each other—distinctly in self-destruction" (104).

Despite its pessimistic conclusion, Kaiser's drama is innovative and fascinating to watch. In its use of abstract figures and color-changing blocks, *Gas II* resembles a moving cubist painting and Fernand Léger's film *Ballet méchanique* (1923–24). In theatrical terms, Kaiser's strange stage tableau imagines the destruction of bourgeois theater, or at least one chapter in its history. The theater plays and performance art that would come later would attack the institution of theater in a much more vehement manner. But even as *Gas II* presents its audience with a vision of the end of humanity, it also spotlights the contribution of human labor to the making of theater.

CODA

As I write this coda in July 2023, it has been almost two years since theaters in New York have reopened after an eighteenth-month shutdown due to the COVID-19 pandemic. Having the necessary space and financial resources, Broadway and New York's larger venues, such as the Park Avenue Armory, St. Ann's Warehouse, and the Shed, were the first to announce in-person productions. During the pandemic, online streaming of theater, audio plays, and ingenious experiments in digital performance not only tided over theater makers and their audiences but also spawned hybrid forms, which are here to stay. Recovery has been slow and precarious, however. Theaters are struggling to entice audiences back and to solve their financial problems. Several regional theaters, such as Southern Repertory Theatre in New Orleans and Triad Stage in Greensboro, North Carolina, have closed permanently. Others have laid off staff, downsized their programs, or, like the Long Wharf Theatre, lost their homes, adopting an itinerant model. New York has not been an exception to this distressing trend. The Public Theater has put its Under the Radar Festival on an indefinite hiatus. Many smaller venues and artistic development opportunities, such as the Lark (a beloved home for many emerging playwrights) and the Directors Lab of Lincoln Center Theater, have closed down.

The uncertainty concerning the future of theater is magnified by the sweeping political and socioeconomic upheavals underway. More than 6.9 million people worldwide have died from COVID-19, including more than 1.1 million in the United States, and the death toll is still rising. Vaccines allow for some protection, especially against hospitalization and death, but new, more contagious variants continue to present challenges. The Black Lives Matter protests, which began on May 25, 2020, in Minneapolis–Saint Paul after the killing of George Floyd by the police and which quickly spread to the rest of the United States, became the largest racial justice protest in American history. In the wake of Floyd's murder, other stories of police killings quickly gained mainstream attention, including the wrongful deaths of Breonna Taylor, Elijah McClain, Tony McDade, and many others. In Europe, the people of Belarus took to the streets by the thousands to protest the disputed presidential victory of Alexander Lukashenko, the country's dictator for the past twenty-six years, showing the rest of the world the kind of collective mobilization required even to begin resisting authoritarianism once an electoral system has become completely corrupt. In Nigeria, demonstrators rose against the Special Anti-Robbery Squad, a unit of the Nigerian federal police force, with innumerable counts of police brutality and violence. On February 24, 2022, Russia launched a full-scale invasion of Ukraine, escalating the Russo-Ukrainian War that began in 2014.

The survival of our global ecosystem is at risk. Deadly fires have devastated Brazil's Amazon rainforest, whole parts of Australia, large swaths of the US Pacific Coast, and Arizona and Colorado. Record hurricanes keep ravaging the most vulnerable segments of the population. Science tells us that to prevent the most extreme scenario of a climate catastrophe, we must act now.

Should our energies and resources not go, then, to the pressing issues of the here and now—police brutality, voter suppression, staggering economic inequality, the persistence of white supremacy, nuclear threat, environmental and public health disasters rather than to art? This anxiety about the value of art is not new. As we have seen in the case of German expressionist playwrights writing during the Spanish flu pandemic and World War I, doubts about the significance of art intensify in times of crisis. If we take an example discussed earlier in this book—Ostermeier's *An Enemy of the People*, and specifically the moment when the production breaks the fourth wall to invite spectators to have a discussion—we confront the paradox of political theater. As Peter Boenisch suggests in his conversation with Ostermeier, many "would argue that by producing theatre"—by "making people engage with and articulate their political energies in [his] 'Enemy of the People' "—Ostermeier may "absorb these energies and prevent them from being invested in realizing such a radical utopia."[1] Ostermeier does not entirely disagree with this line of thinking. He concedes that Julien Coupat, whom some believe to be one of the anonymous writers of *The Coming Insurrection*, the excerpts of which are interwoven into Thomas Stockmann's assembly speech in Ostermeier's version, would agree with the idea that theater, no matter how political, is ultimately a distraction because it tends to "pacify radical energies and channel them into art, away from direct action."[2] Although Ostermeier sympathizes with this claim, he maintains that the "process of developing political consciousness," the ability to say no to the prevalent state of affairs and to raise one's voice inside a theater, enables people to muster the courage to do so "in real life too."[3]

The Brazilian theater director and political activist Augusto Boal concurs that although "perhaps theater is not revolutionary in itself, . . . it is surely a rehearsal for the revolution," as the "liberated spectator, as a whole person, launches into action."[4] To be sure, Boal and Ostermeier approach theater's capacity to rouse the spectator (or, as Boal calls her, "spect-actor") to action from different positions. Boal developed theatrical techniques and exercises to support marginalized communities in their fight for political change and social justice, while Ostermeier admits to fashioning Trojan horses out of theater's "classical canon" for members of the contemporary "bourgeois class" who go see his productions, to make them confront their own historical role in perpetuating the injustices of capitalism. Similarly, writing at the turn of the twentieth century, Emma Goldman believed that modern drama could raise the political consciousness of the beneficiaries of capitalism. (Ostermeier also acknowledges that his endeavor might ultimately be "wishful thinking.")[5] In Marxian terms, Boal engages the proletariat, whereas Ostermeier might be encouraging the bourgeoisie to join the fight of the proletariat. These are two different methods, but there is arguably space and political need for both.

It has been the argument of this book that the bourgeois theater of the fin de siècle, and more specifically the theater of capital—theater invested in exploring the nature of capital—has contributed to the development of spectators' political consciousness by dramatizing the internal contradictions of capitalism and by experimenting with economic ideas at a historical juncture when marginalism was transforming into the narrow science known today as neoclassical economics and when vibrant socialist debate about the various strands of socialism reached a crescendo. In this way, the late nineteenth-century theater of capital became a repository for economic ideas, models, and dreams that neoclassical economics discarded. While the marginal revolution turned its attention to the desires of the individual consumer, the theater of capital engaged in an immanent critique of capitalism and continued to explore collective labor, material conditions, and socialist ideas. It was in the theater that the links between economics and the supernatural, the religious, and the erotic were investigated. And it was in the theater that economic questions were staged not as insular issues but as part and parcel of broader political and moral concerns.

The humanities' lingering hostile attitude toward the world of economics is due to our own historical position of subjects brought up in a world where "economics" usually means an abstract science whose scope is limited to the study of mercantile exchanges. As a consequence, paying attention to economic questions and ideas raised in a given dramatic work might strike us as reductive, trivial, or vulgar. Yet if we remember the ancient, broader meaning of *oikos*—that of household management, including the health and spiritual well-being of the members of the household, a meaning that has been important to the development of dramatic theory from the time of Aristotle's *Poetics*—then the theater of capital still has a wealth of knowledge to share with us, especially about how, on a fundamental level, economic questions concern what values we prioritize and how we organize our political and spiritual lives. When Ibsen,

Strindberg, Chekhov, Shaw, Benedictsson, Hauptmann, and numerous other nineteenth-century playwrights were writing for the stage, the economic imaginary was broader, wilder, and more open to public debate than it has been in our own century. But change is in the air.

When I began this project, Occupy Wall Street, the protest movement against economic inequality, had sprung up in Zuccotti Park in New York and was quickly expanding to other cities in the United States and around the globe. The very term "capitalism" was reentering mainstream conversations. The narrow kind of economic thinking, the capitalist realism that Mark Fisher and others have described as an "invisible barrier constraining thought and action,"[6] has been steadily crumbling, so that alternatives to capitalism have once again galvanized the public's imagination. New generations (millennials and Gen Z) have come of age, influenced more by their lack of substantial property and economic precarity than by the legacy of the Cold War or by a distrust of socialism and communism. Here, in the United States, economic possibilities that for a long time have been neglected by the mainstream media have been steadily gaining the attention and approval of large sections of the population: ideas such as universal basic income, universal health care, the New Green Deal, and even a reevaluation of the profit motive underpinning the drive for capital accumulation. This opening up of the economic imaginary is no doubt due in part to the challenges of our times. We no longer have to "imagine" alternatives to neoliberal capitalism. With climate change happening before our very eyes, dystopian futures have already arrived. But these ecological disasters also give urgency to economic ideas about how to potentially reverse the course and start building a different world. As I have also suggested throughout the book, this more expansive economic imaginary had been sustained and developed in the works of the theater of capital beginning in the nineteenth century.

Ibsen repurposed the shopworn deus ex machina for his dramatic closures, leaving his bourgeois audience with either a bad aftertaste or a radical opening to provoke debate about life under capitalism. He made the invisible hand of the market visible by staging its social implications and exposing the labor behind it. Having conjured up a *hyggeligt* home, seemingly safe from the market, he then proceeded to ask how much that cozy, lovely home really cost, whose labor was sustaining it, and whether it was, in fact, sheltered from the outside economic world.

Strindberg contracted the dramatic form to the two-handler, motivated in part by his intellectual interest in the psychological "battle of the brains" and in "setting the two halves of humanity against each other."[7] Prefiguring what Gilman would call the "sexuo-economic"[8] relation between men and women, Strindberg negated the centuries-old sexual contract by which class conflict had been sexualized and neutralized through the marriage plot in nineteenth-century novels and melodramas. As Strindberg admits, his aim in *Miss Julie* is to dismantle the "bourgeois concept of the immobility of the soul," the very idea of the dramatic character that had been "transferred to the stage, where bourgeois values have always been dominant."[9] Thus, Jean and Julie are, in Strindberg's famous pronouncement, "conglomerates of past and present stages of culture, bits out of books and newspaper, scraps of humanity, torn shreds of once fine clothing now turned to rags, exactly as the human soul is patched together."[10] This commitment to overturning the bourgeois concept of character inadvertently pushed Strindberg's drama to undermine the bourgeois concept of gender. Paradoxically, the notion of gender as fluid, performative, and dependent on the socioeconomic structure of a given historical moment appears in modern drama in the work of an author infamous for his misogyny and anxiety over female power.

In treating the Woman Question, Strindberg, Shaw, and Benedictsson explored the interplay between the dowry and erotic capital in the late nineteenth-century network of courtship, marriage, and prostitution. All of these patriarchal institutions support capitalism and are still supported by it, especially through financial speculation. Although by the turn of the nineteenth century women were gaining more economic autonomy regarding their earning potential and property rights, the importance of the dowry persisted as a form of capital that limited the extent of a woman's power. Through money and property, the dowry controlled the trajectory of a woman's life, ensuring that her starting capital went directly into bolstering patriarchy. As with money, so with sex. Even as erotic capital somewhat diminished the importance of the dowry for the love marriage, patriarchy dictated how a woman could manage her erotic capital. In the theater, however, transgressive exchanges involving erotic capital began to take place. The actress's role in blurring the boundary between the public and private realms and the male actor's reliance on erotic capital (traditionally considered a woman's asset for upward social mobility in the marriage market) profoundly disturbed gender divisions and norms. By addressing economic questions, particularly those raised but not resolved in Ibsen's *A Doll's House*, Benedictsson was able to create female protagonists who attain financial independence and who do not capitulate to the hokey scripts of her more famous male contemporaries, scripts populated by spendthrift, wayward wives, fallen women, and, on occasion, formidable female protagonists, who establish their autonomy only to commit suicide by the end of the play.

The burgeoning capitalist economy of late nineteenth-century Russia, with its porous boundary between gambling, speculation, and investment, and its embrace of radical contingency and luck, offered an aesthetic model for Chekhov. His predilection for the accidental, seemingly insignificant detail, his representation of the randomness of everyday life, and the particular temporality of his drama, fueled by events that almost happen, were all products of the unpredictability, volatility, and moral relativism of the modern economy. Chekhov explored the kind of "cruel optimism" that Berlant has shown to be endemic to capitalist social relations. In his dramatizations of casino capitalism, Chekhov highlights how the spectacle of the occasional, rare win keeps everyone engrossed in the economic game for personal gain and makes solidarity all the more challenging.

With *The Weavers*, Hauptmann brought the question of labor to the fore, revealing the advantages of the stage over the novel in representing labor through theater's reliance on a collective body of actors and stagehands and theater's capacity for repetitive action. Rarely staged today, *The Weavers* continues to pulsate with raw revolutionary energy. The rousing songs, calling for "bloody justice," and the spectacular destruction of private property before the beneficiaries of capitalism, seated in the auditorium, remain as transgressive as they were at the end of the nineteenth century. That Hauptmann pushed the limits of theatrical illusion and the economic imaginary is evident from the ways that German expressionist playwrights, writing in his wake, backtracked on his staging of the revolt of the working class. The violence of the Russian and German Revolutions of the early twentieth century seems to have instilled in them a veritable distrust of the proletariat and a fear of mob rule.

Contemporary playwrights continue to be drawn to the exploration of money and capital, many of them studying the workings of finance in order to educate their audiences, to reflect back to the financiers sitting in the auditorium the unhinged world that they helped create, and to engage in an immanent critique of capitalism. Caryl Churchill captures the hypnotic and enticing language of speculation, what Moretti calls the "*poetry* of capitalist development,"[11] through the rhyming couplets of her satirical *Serious Money* (1987), which dramatizes the crimes of the London International Financial Futures and Options Exchange (LIFFE) and which seems to have been most popular with the stock-jobbers themselves.[12] Lucy Prebble's *Enron* (2009) tells the infamous story of the bankruptcy of the eponymous energy company, which wildly misrepresented its financial performance through intricate financial maneuvers, shady balance sheet modifications, and various accounting loopholes. Inspired by the fact that Enron used to hire Cirque du Soleil for their parties, Prebble embraces magical absurdism, heightened theatricality, epic spectacle, and the use of song and dance. Ingenious theatrical conceits, including actors donning velociraptor heads to signify the debt-laden shell companies that finally caused Enron's collapse, and a dance of business execs who fight one another with light sabers, allows Prebble to make finance exciting and to keep her audience's attention long enough for her to explain financial concepts and to expose the mythmaking and fantasy fabrication at the core of contemporary finance.

Swedish writer Jonas Hassen Khemiri's play ≈ [*Almost Equal To*] (2014) explores how everyone is affected by capitalism and attempts "to give the audience a maximized entertainment value for every dollar invested."[13] This brutal dark comedy, however, is not without hope, showing how economic questions can inspire us to imagine different political futures. Addressing the audience, one of the characters explains,

> No, no, no. Don't believe everything you hear. The history of economics is not boring. It's not soulless. It's not a bunch of dry theories and dull graphs. In fact, it's the opposite. The history of economics is full of scatterbrains and freethinkers, geniuses and madmen. Theorists who were so smothered by the ages they lived in that they felt compelled to use their knowledge to create credible alternative worlds. Worlds that still shimmer and fill those of us who are left behind with hope and courage.[14]

Ayad Akhtar, whose dramatic work and firm grasp of economics have already been mentioned in this study, has clearly learned from Ibsen when he makes the "free market" the deus ex machina in his aptly titled financial thriller *The Invisible Hand*. Akhtar also satirizes the intertwinement of the economic and the erotic that is so prominent in Strindberg's drama and Freudian psychoanalysis. In *Junk*, Akhtar pokes fun at the frustrating tautology that the capitalistic fungibility of money and sex engenders when he has the play's narrator, journalist Judy Chen, reminisce about what it was like to have sex with billionaire Leo Tresler:

> And his body's in good shape—for his age—but he has a trainer and a chef on staff. So that's money, too. It was like everything I could think about him, good or bad, could be traced to his money. But *then* I thought, *he* made that money. Not everybody can do that. So maybe all these things *about* him, maybe they're *why*—I mean *how* he had made a billion dollars. Maybe it's not the money that defines him. Maybe he defines the money. That idea, that thought . . . It was at that point that I started to have an orgasm. It was a powerful orgasm. (72)

Chen's circular thinking (M-Tresler-M) mimics the process of capitalist circulation in Marx. Each time she thinks of this or that feature of Tresler, her imagination immediately transforms it into money until she begins to envision Tresler as somehow defining money itself. But her logical fallacy does not offer her any deeper understanding of either the nature of money or the power dynamics at play. Instead, the short circuit results in an explosion. The drive for capital accumulation targets the libido, turning human beings into "desiring-machines," a term famously coined by Deleuze and Guattari and inspired by Antonin Artaud's "body without organs."[15] This circulation of desire and money distracts Chen from the ways that patriarchy and capitalism mutually reinforce one another.

While the junk bond financiers can do as they please—committing numerous white-collar crimes and getting off scot-free—Chen's one-time indiscretion will cost her her book, a work that was meant to expose corporate misdemeanors and felonies. When Chen is blackmailed into taking the money and abandoning her exposé, Akhtar seems to wink at this audience. After all, *he* is able to take the money and put contemporary finance on trial in front of his paying audience at the Lincoln Center for the Performing Arts, whose corporate sponsors include numerous banks (such as Bank of America and First Republic Bank) and the multinational financial services company Morgan Stanley. But what is the political goal of it all? Akhtar says that he hopes "people can zoom out just a little bit and see that what's been going on in the country has a lot more to do with finance than it does to do with identity politics." According to Akhtar, we "are increasingly ensnared by these various points of view and all the while the country continues to be sold out from us—from under *all* of us."[16] On the one hand, understanding how the corporate elites manipulate the public can be empowering and can encourage us to organize and take action. On the other hand, some of Akhtar's most devoted spectators include members of the financial elite, who might just take the Shakespearean undertones and the epic scope of *Junk* as a celebration of their worldview.

While the face of capitalism has changed since Hauptmann's time, modern and contemporary drama's fascination with people at work and their fight for labor rights has persisted, particularly in plays where, as Bill Naismith puts it, "the entire workplace, and much of the workforce, is reconstructed on stage,"[17] such as Eugene O'Neill's *The Hairy Ape* (1922), Elmer Rice's *The Adding Machine* (1923), Sophie Treadwell's *Machinal* (1928), Lillian Hellman's *Days to Come* (1936), Clifford Odets's *Waiting for Lefty* (1935), Arnold Wesker's *The Kitchen* (1957) and *The Journalists* (1972), Peter Nichols's *The National Health* (1969), David Mamet's *Glengarry Glenn Ross* (1983), Leslye Headland's *Assistance* (2008), Annie Baker's *The Flick* (2013), Elizabeth Irwin's *My Mañana Comes* (2014), Branden Jacobs-Jenkins's *Gloria* (2015), Lynn Nottage's *Sweat* (2015) and *Clyde's* (2021), Dominique Morisseau's *Skeleton Crew* (2016), and many others. The question of whether observing the process of alienation (by which laborers are made to feel foreign to the products of their labor) in the theater can lead to the awakening of the audience's political consciousness or rouse them to political action is a question that remains from the time of Hauptmann's *The Weavers*. Throughout its production history, *The Weavers* has inspired audience members and actors alike to become aware of themselves as laborers and to take action to change their condition.

Today, as we find ourselves returning to in-person shows, many theater leaders and practitioners have taken the opportunity of the prolonged intermission to rethink and reevaluate the possibilities of theater. For some, this has meant focusing their attention on the digital, an epistemological shift that had begun long before the global pandemic. For others, this has meant using their empty theater spaces to stand in solidarity with social movements, as when American theaters joined the Open Your Lobby Initiative by lending support to the Black Lives Matter protesters in the summer of 2020 by providing them with a space to rest and offering them snacks and water bottles.

Still, for many others, this has meant reimagining the future of the theater in economic terms. In early June 2020, the "We See You White American Theatre" alliance published a twenty-nine-page document calling for a complete restructuring of American theater, a dismantling of the white supremacy of the stage, and the inclusion and leadership of Black and Indigenous people and other People of Color (BIPOC). Many of their demands explicitly involve economic questions—namely, new ways of organizing the various institutions of theater. Thus, their demands include but are not limited to making sure that BIPOC constitute "the majority of writers, directors, and designers onstage for the foreseeable future," ending security contracts with police departments, limiting the salary of top-paid staff members to no more than ten times the salary of the lowest-paid workers, and providing on-site counseling for everyone working on productions that deal with "racialized experiences, and most especially racialized trauma."[18]

In the fall of 2021, the Skirball Cultural Center at New York University hosted a symposium titled "Re:Opening?: Rethinking New York City's Performance Infrastructures" to take stock of the return of in-person, live performances and to discuss whether theaters and performing arts organizations have made good on the promises and statements of solidarity put forth during the historic year-and-a-half hiatus. A few speakers, most notably April Matthis (actor from the collective AFROFEMONONOMY), Ximena Garnica (choreographer and organizer of Arts Workers Rally), and Adam Krauthamer (president of Local 802, American Federation of Musicians) addressed the economic challenges that performing artists faced during the shutdown and strategies that they developed to survive. The need for a living wage for artists was brought up time and again. Chris Myers, founder of Anticapitalism for Artists, talked about initiatives to raise the class consciousness of artists. Melanie Joseph (artistic producer of the Foundry Theater) and Eric Klinenberg (director of the Institute of Public Knowledge) discussed the possibility of theaters operating in the model of the public library—a shared public space that is open to everyone and that contributes to the flourishing of its community.[19] All that is needed is a commitment to social infrastructure.

Likewise, when the *New York Times* asked twenty theater figures to offer suggestions about "how to 'revolutionize' their world," many responses addressed changing the financial structure and labor organization of American theater. Writer and dramaturg Lauren Halvorsen recommends abolishing "unpaid internships and low-paying apprenticeships" to make sure that professional opportunities are not restricted to the most privileged of applicants. Director and playwright Jay Stull asks producers and entertainers "who began in the theater and have gone on to 'make a killing' on Broadway or in Hollywood" to "help sustain the community by creating a pooled fund with the excesses of their wealth to provide medical insurance and universal basic income for theater-makers who need it."[20] Others pin their hopes not on individual acts of charity but on robust public funding from the government. Lear deBessonet, artistic director of *Encores!*, envisions a "new Federal Theater Project, a national arts program in all 50 states as ambitious in scope as the original New Deal–era program."[21] This solution, however, would require a larger structural change in how American economics is run.

Without a substantial change in the economic system, reforms—such as individual attempts at redistributing income in the theater world—are not enough to revolutionize contemporary theater, which still maintains an intimate and perverse relationship to capital. Without overcoming the profit motive and the attendant focus on capital accumulation and financial growth in the economy at large, theater is bound to submit to the demands of capital. Not always and not completely, of course. Just as early modern theater developed through a complex relationship to sovereignty (it panegyrized the monarch, but also sought to critique the sovereign's power and to express anxieties about royal favor and terror), so bourgeois theater evolved through a tumultuous, mutually dependent, and conflictual relationship with capital. This is what the playwrights and theater practitioners of the fin de siècle understood well.

As beneficiaries of capitalism, nineteenth-century bourgeois playwrights did not try to hide the fact that they, like their dramatic characters, earned their living off the suffering of others (colonial subjects, the proletariat, women), that they constantly worried about monetary constraints, and that their aesthetics was connected to their economics. They did not, like the Romantic poets before them, claim the moral superiority of making art that allegedly towered above the mire of commerce. Instead, they flaunted the internal contradictions of their historical position and betrayed anxiety about being bourgeois, succumbing to the seductions of capital, not doing enough or, on the contrary, doing too much by presuming to speak for the working class. Their social malaise, coupled with their passionate interest in economic questions, engendered many aesthetic innovations in dramatic writing and theatrical staging, while also contributing to a deeper understanding of fin-de-siècle European economies. If this book has managed to show that we can learn from their work and their struggle, it will have succeeded in its aim.

NOTES

Introduction

1. Lorena Muñoz-Alonso, "How to Best Navigate the Venice Biennale's Political and Moral Contradictions," *artnet*, May 14, 2015, https://news.artnet.com/art-world/venice-biennale-art-renegades-296011.

2. Charlotte Higgins, "*Das Kapital* at the Arsenale: How Okwui Enwezor Invited Marx to the Biennale," *The Guardian*, May 7, 2015, https://www.theguardian.com/artanddesign/2015/may/07/das-kapital-at-venice-biennale-okwui-enwezor-karl-marx.

3. Cristina Ruiz, "Fierce Debate over Christoph Büchel's Venice Biennale Display of Boat That Sank with Hundreds Locked in Hull," *Art Newspaper*, May 14, 2019, https://www.theartnewspaper.com/news/christoph-buechel.

4. Ryan Anthony Hatch, "Hallucinating Networks and Secret Museums: Hito Steyerl on Our Aesthetic Immiseration," *PAJ: A Journal of Performance and Art* 41, no. 2 (2019): 119–24, at 121.

5. Bruce Robbins, *The Beneficiary* (Durham, NC: Duke University Press, 2017).

6. Robbins, *The Beneficiary*, 5.

7. Robbins, *The Beneficiary*, 49.

8. Karl Marx, *Capital: A Critique of Political Economy*, vol. 1 (1867), trans. Ben Fowkes, with introduction by Ernest Mandel (New York: Penguin, 1990), 258–69.

9. Boris Groys, "On Art Activism," *e-flux* 56, June 2014, https://www.e-flux.com/journal/56/60343/on-art-activism/.

10. Okwui Enwezor, introduction to *La Biennale di Venezia*, 2015, https://www.labiennale.org/en/art/2015/intervento-di-okwui-enwezor, accessed June 2, 2019.

11. Louis Blanc, *Organisation du travail*, 9th ed. (Paris: Société de l'industrie fraternelle, 1850), 161.

12. Pierre-Joseph Proudhon, *Les confessions d'un révolutionnaire*, 3rd ed. (Paris: Garnier, 1851), 358.

13. For more on the history of the term "capitalism," see Geoffrey M. Hodgson, *Conceptualizing Capitalism: Institutions, Evolution, Future* (Chicago: University of Chicago Press, 2015), 252. As Hodgson notes, its frequent use in German was spurred by the publication of *Kapitalismus und Sozialismus* by the nonsocialist economist Albert Schäffle in 1870. See also Fernand Braudel, *The Wheels of Commerce: Civilization and Capitalism, 15th–18th Century*, vol. 1 (Berkeley: University of California Press, 1992), 237.

14. This is also true of playwrights who wrote closet dramas, as those, too, can be seen as a response to the conditions of the theater. This hostility to the stage led to some significant achievements in modern drama and theater. See Martin Puchner, *Stage Fright: Modernism, Anti-theatricality, and Drama* (Baltimore: Johns Hopkins University Press, 2002).

15. Marvin Carlson, "Theatrical Performance: Illustration, Translation, Fulfillment, or Supplement?," *Theatre Journal* 37, no. 1 (1985): 5–11, at 11.

16. Carlson, "Theatrical Performance," 11.

17. I thank the first anonymous reader for bringing this to my attention. I mean "cultural capital" in Bourdieu's sense of the word. See Pierre Bourdieu, "The Forms of Capital," in *Handbook of Theory and Research for the Sociology of Education*, ed. J. G. Richardson (New York: Greenwood, 1986), 241–58, at 241.

18. John D. Buenker and Joseph Buenker, eds., *Encyclopedia of the Gilded Age and Progressive Era* (Armonk, NY: Sharpe, 2005), 28.

19. S.v. "capital, n. 2," *Online Etymology Dictionary*, last modified on November 2022, https://www.etymonline.com/word/capital; Adam Smith, *An Inquiry into the Nature and Causes of the Wealth of Nations* (1776), ed. Edwin Cannan, 5th ed., with introduction by Alan B. Krueger (New York: Bantam, 2003), 353.

20. Bernard Shaw, *Widowers' Houses* (1892), in *Plays Unpleasant*, definitive text under the editorial supervision of Dan H. Laurence, with introduction by David Edgar (New York: Penguin, 2001), 29–96.

21. Harvey appeared in Isaac Julien's *KAPITAL* (2013), part of a film installation at SFMOMA Artist Gallery, Venice Biennale, Venice, Italy, 2015; described (with the quotation) at https://fortmason.org/event/playtime, accessed May 12, 2018.

22. Jane Moody, "The Drama of Capital: Risk, Belief, and Liability on the Victorian Stage," in *Victorian Literature and Finance*, ed. Francis O'Gorman (Oxford: Oxford University Press, 2007), 91–110, at 92.

23. August Strindberg, *Fröken Julie*, in *Fröken Julie, Fadren, Ett drömspel* (Milton Keynes, UK: Jiahu Books, 2013), 20. Translations of *Fröken Julie* (*Miss Julie*) are my own unless otherwise noted.

24. Bourdieu, "The Forms of Capital," 241.

25. Catherine Hakim, *Erotic Capital: The Power of Attraction in the Boardroom and the Bedroom* (New York: Basic Books, 2011).

26. Regenia Gagnier, *The Insatiability of Human Wants: Economics and Aesthetics in Market Society* (Chicago: University of Chicago Press, 2000), 5.

27. Bernard Shaw, *The Intelligent Woman's Guide to Socialism, Capitalism, Sovietism and Fascism* (1937), ed. Polly Toynbee (London: Alma Classics, 2012), 169.

28. Marx, *Capital*, 1:248.

29. Marx, *The Grundrisse: Foundations of the Critique of Political Economy (Rough Draft)*, trans. Martin Nicolaus (New York: Penguin, 1993), 706.

30. Marx, *Capital*, 1:253.

31. Martin Hägglund, "What Is Democratic Socialism? Part III: Life after Capitalism," *Los Angeles Review of Books*, July 15, 2020, https://lareviewofbooks.org/article/what-is-democratic-socialism-part-3-life-after-capitalism/.

32. Hägglund, "What Is Democratic Socialism? Part III: Life after Capitalism."
33. Hägglund, "What Is Democratic Socialism? Part III: Life after Capitalism."
34. Marx, *Capital*, 1:129.
35. Hägglund, "What Is Democratic Socialism? Part III: Life after Capitalism."
36. Marx, *Capital*, 1:526.
37. Karl Marx, *Capital*, vol. 3 (1894), prepared by Friedrich Engels, trans. David Fernbach, with introduction by Ernest Mandel (New York: Penguin, 1993), 359.
38. Marx, *Capital*, 1:990.
39. See Tracy C. Davis, *The Economics of the British Stage 1800–1914* (Cambridge: Cambridge University Press, 2000); Michael McKinnie, *Theatre in Market Economies* (Cambridge: Cambridge University Press, 2021); Derek Miller, *Copyright and the Value of Performance, 1770–1911* (Cambridge: Cambridge University Press, 2018); Marlis Schweitzer, *Transatlantic Broadway: The Infrastructural Politics of Global Performance* (New York: Palgrave Macmillan, 2015); and Brandon Woolf, *Institutional Theatrics: Performing Arts Policy in Post-Wall Berlin* (Evanston, IL: Northwestern University Press, 2021).
40. As Michael McKinnie points out, questions regarding the "relationship between capital, labour, and the state" are "not always best seen onstage" but "arise, instead, throughout the entire domain of the performance." McKinnie, *Theatre in Market Economies*, 7. Likewise, the authors of "Marxist Keywords for Performance" note that a "performance may have radical political themes while also continuing to play the same material role for capitalist accumulation." Jaswinder Blackwell-Pal, Michael Shane Boyle, Ash Dilks, Caoimhe Mader McGuinness, Olive Mckeon, Lisa Moravec, Alessandro Simari, Clio Unger, and Martin Young, "Marxist Keywords for Performance," *Journal of Dramatic Theory and Criticism* 36, no. 1 (Fall 2021): 25–53, at 51.
41. Karl Polanyi, *The Great Transformation: The Political and Economic Origins of Our Time* (1944), foreword by Joseph E. Stiglitz, introduction by Fred Block (Boston: Beacon, 2001), 60.
42. Fred Block, introduction to Polanyi, *The Great Transformation*, xviii–xxxviii, at xxiv.
43. Block, introduction to Polanyi, *The Great Transformation*, xxv; Polanyi, *The Great Transformation*, 80.
44. R. H. Tawney, *Religion and the Rise of Capitalism* (1926; repr., New Brunswick, NJ: Transaction, 1998), 100.
45. Sheryl L. Meyering, introduction to *Women and Economics: A Study of the Economic Relation between Men and Women as a Factor in Social Evolution* (1898), by Charlotte Perkins Gilman (Mineola, NY: Dover, 1998), iii–v, at iii.
46. John Ruskin, "Essays on Political Economy," in *Fraser's Magazine: For Town and Country* 65 (January–June 1862), ed. James Anthony Froude and John Tulloch (London: Savill and Edwards, 1862), 784–92, at 784.
47. Cheryl Anne Cox, *Household Interests: Property, Marriage Strategies, and Family Dynamics in Ancient Athens* (Princeton, NJ: Princeton University Press, 1998), 131.
48. D. Brendan Nagle, *The Household as the Foundation of Aristotle's Polis* (New York: Cambridge University Press, 2006), 177.

49. Ruskin, "Essays on Political Economy," 784.
50. Blackwell-Pal et al., "Marxist Keywords for Performance," 30.
51. Ulrich Rippert, "August Bebel and the Political Awakening of the Working Class," *World Socialist*, August 28, 2013, https://www.wsws.org/en/articles/2013/08/28/bebe-a28.html.
52. James M. Brophy, review of *Arbeitskämpfe und Gewerkschaften in Deutschland, England, und Frankreich: Ihre Entwicklung vom 19. zum 20. Jahrhundert* by Friedhelm Boll and Dieter Dowe, *Journal of Modern History* 67, no. 1 (1995): 118–20, at 119.
53. Alfred Marshall, *Principles of Economics* (1890; repr., London: Palgrave Macmillan, 2013), 1.
54. Steven G. Medema and Warren J. Samuels, *The History of Economic Thought: A Reader* (New York: Routledge, 2003), 408.
55. Gagnier, *The Insatiability of Human Wants*, 4.
56. Gary S. Becker, *The Economic Approach to Human Behavior* (Chicago: University of Chicago Press, 1976).
57. Gagnier, *The Insatiability of Human Wants*, 5.
58. Bourdieu, "The Forms of Capital," 252–53.
59. Bourdieu, "The Forms of Capital," 242.
60. Henrik Ibsen to King Oscar II, 20 July 1880, *Henrik Ibsens Skrifter*, https://www.ibsen.uio.no/brev.xhtml, accessed May 20, 2018.
61. Gerhart Hauptmann, *The Dramatic Works of Gerhart Hauptmann*, ed. and introduction by Ludwig Lewisohn (New York: B. W. Huebsch, 1912).
62. Tracy C. Davis, *George Bernard Shaw and the Socialist Theatre* (London: Greenwood, 1994), 7.
63. Rosa Luxemburg, *Reform or Revolution and Other Writings*, with introduction by Paul Buhle (Mineola, NY: Dover, 2006), 8.
64. Luxemburg, *Reform or Revolution*, 8.
65. Luxemburg, *Reform or Revolution*, 36, 35.
66. Luxemburg, *Reform or Revolution*, 36.
67. Luxemburg, *Reform or Revolution*, 5.
68. See Martin Puchner, *The Drama of Ideas: Platonic Provocations in Theater and Philosophy* (New York: Oxford University Press, 2010).
69. T. J. Clark, *Farewell to an Idea: Episodes from a History of Modernism* (New Haven, CT: Yale University Press, 1999), 9.
70. T. J. Clark, *Farewell to an Idea*, 9.
71. Evert Sprinchorn, *Ibsen's Kingdom: The Man and His Works* (New Haven, CT: Yale University Press, 2021), 212.
72. Ibsen to H. L. Braekstad, 18 August 1890, in *Ibsen: Letters and Speeches*, ed. Evert Sprinchorn (Clinton, MA: Colonial Press, 1964), 292.
73. Ivo de Figueiredo, *Henrik Ibsen: The Man and the Mask*, trans. Robert Ferguson (New Haven, CT: Yale University Press, 2019), 297.
74. Martin Hägglund, *This Life: Secular Faith and Spiritual Freedom* (New York: Penguin Random House, 2019), 225. As Hägglund elaborates, "[This] contradiction is immanent because it is intrinsic to the institution or the ideology itself" (225).
75. See Bruno Latour, "Why Has Critique Run Out of Steam? From Matters of Fact to Matters of Concern," *Critical Inquiry* 30 (Winter 2004): 225–48;

Jacques Rancière, *Aesthetics and Its Discontents*, trans. Steven Corcoran (Cambridge: Polity, 2009), and *The Emancipated Spectator*, trans. Gregory Elliott (London: Verso, 2009); Rita Felski, *The Limits of Critique* (Chicago: University of Chicago Press, 2015); Elizabeth S. Anker and Rita Felski, eds., *Critique and Postcritique* (Durham, NC: Duke University Press, 2017).

76. Hal Foster, "Post-critical," *October*, no. 139 (Winter 2012): 3–8, at 6.

77. Felski barely touches on the "distinction between transcendent and immanent critique," noting the latter's importance in Adorno's thought, but not its origins in Hegel and Marx. Felski, *The Limits of Critique*, 125–27.

78. Felski, *The Limits of Critique*, 127.

79. As Maurya Wickstrom notes, "Capitalism and performance have been bound up in one another since the inception of capitalistic economic structures in the early modern period." Maurya Wickstrom, *Performing Consumers: Global Capital and Its Theatrical Seductions* (New York: Routledge, 2006), 6–7.

80. Ginia Bellafante, "'The Lehman Trilogy' Criticizes Capitalism, at $2,000 a Seat," *New York Times*, April 18, 2019, https://www.nytimes.com/2019/04/18/nyregion/lehman-trilogy-theater-ultra-rich.html.

81. James Surowiecki, "How Online Ticket Scalping (Eventually) Helped 'Hamilton,'" *New Yorker*, June 11, 2016, https://www.newyorker.com/business/currency/how-online-ticket-scalping-eventually-helped-hamilton.

82. Chelsea Whitaker, "Exploring an Anti-policing Theatre," *Howlround*, August 6, 2020, https://howlround.com/exploring-anti-policing-theatre.

83. Donatella Galella, "Being in 'The Room Where It Happens': *Hamilton*, Obama, and the Nationalist Neoliberal Multicultural Inclusion," *Theatre Survey* 59, no. 3 (2018): 363–85. See also Elena Machado Sáez, "Blackout on Broadway: Affiliation and Audience in *In the Heights* and *Hamilton*," *Studies in Musical Theatre* 12, no. 2 (2018): 181–97; and Matthew Clinton Sekellick, "Hamilton and Class," *Studies in Musical Theatre* 12, no. 2 (2018): 257–63. "Neoliberalism" can often be a vaporous term. When I use the terms "neoliberal" or "neoliberalism" in this book, I'm referring to David Harvey's definition of neoliberalism—"a theory of political economic practices that proposes that human well-being can best be advanced by liberating individual entrepreneurial freedoms and skills within an institutional framework characterized by strong private property rights, free markets, and free trade" (2). At its core, neoliberalism involves "much 'creative destruction,' not only of prior institutional frameworks and powers (ever challenging traditional forms of state sovereignty) but also of divisions of labour, social relations, welfare provisions, technological mixes, ways of life and thought, reproductive activities, attachments to the land and habits of the heart" (30). David Harvey, *A Brief History of Neoliberalism* (New York: Oxford University Press, 2005).

84. Mark Fisher, *Capitalist Realism: Is There No Alternative?* (Winchester, UK: O Books, 2009), 21.

85. M. Fisher, *Capitalist Realism*, 2.

86. Exceptions to this trend are recent studies that investigate the relationship between theater and its economic context. These include Davis, *The Economics of the British Stage*; James Fisher, ed., *To Have or Have Not: Essays on Commerce and Capital in Modernist Theatre* (Jefferson, NC: McFarland,

2011); Hillary Miller, *Drop Dead: Performance in Crisis, 1970s New York* (Evanston, IL: Northwestern University Press, 2016); Nicholas Ridout, *Stage Fright, Animals, and Other Theatrical Problems* (Cambridge: Cambridge University Press, 2006) and *Passionate Amateurs: Theatre, Communism, and Love* (Ann Arbor: University of Michigan Press, 2013); Patricia A. Ybarra, *Latinx Theater in the Times of Neoliberalism* (Evanston, IL: Northwestern University Press, 2017).

87. Bernard F. Dukore, *Money and Politics in Ibsen, Shaw, and Brecht* (Columbia: University of Missouri Press, 1980), xxii. In a similar vein, some critics have argued that *A Doll's House* is not a feminist work precisely because Ibsen "did not stoop to 'issues.'" Instead, he "was a poet of the truth of the human soul," as if the two intellectual interests were incompatible. See Joan Templeton, *Ibsen's Women* (New York: Cambridge University Press, 1997), 111.

88. Beth Holmgren, *Rewriting Capitalism: Literature and the Market in Late Tsarist Russia and the Kingdom of Poland* (Pittsburgh: University of Pittsburgh Press, 1998), 50.

89. Leon Trotsky, *Literature and Revolution* (1925), ed. William Keach, trans. Rose Strunsky (Chicago: Haymarket, 2005), 120, 44, 29.

90. Davis, *The Economics of the British Stage*, 7.

91. Jill Dolan, *Utopia in Performance: Finding Hope at the Theater* (Ann Arbor: University of Michigan Press, 2005), 5.

92. Dolan, *Utopia in Performance*, 8.

93. Ridout, *Stage Fright*, 4.

94. Ridout, *Passionate Amateurs*, 9, 4.

95. Ridout, *Stage Fright*, 4. As Ridout points out, "You perhaps have to look much harder and with greater ingenuity for your resistance or your challenge than you do in the more explicitly oppositional, self-consciously antibourgeois terrain of performance."

96. Elizabeth Hewitt, "The Vexed Story of Economic Criticism," *American Literary History* 21, no. 3 (2009): 618–32, at 620.

97. Martin Bodenham, "What Makes a Great Financial Thriller?," January 14, 2018, https://www.martinbodenham.com/what-makes-a-great-financial-thriller/.

98. Leigh Claire La Berge, *Scandals and Abstraction: Financial Fiction of the Long 1980s* (New York: Oxford University Press, 2014), 15, 85.

99. Ayad Akhtar, *Junk: A Play* (New York: Back Bay Books, 2017), 148. Subsequent page references are given in the text.

100. Paul Crosthwaite, Peter Knight, and Nicky Marsh, eds., *Show Me the Money: The Image of Finance, 1700 to Present* (Manchester: Manchester University Press, 2014), 7.

101. Nicky Marsh, "The Cosmopolitan Coin: What Modernists Make of Money," *Modernism/modernity* 24, no. 3 (2017): 485–505, at 486.

102. Karl Marx and Friedrich Engels, *The Communist Manifesto* (1848), trans. Martin Milligan (Amherst, NY: Prometheus Books, 1988), 211.

103. Marx and Engels, *The Communist Manifesto*, 215.

104. Nicholas Ridout, *Scenes from Bourgeois Life* (Ann Arbor: University of Michigan Press, 2020), 24.

105. Ridout, *Scenes from Bourgeois Life*, 24.

106. Roy Pascal, *From Naturalism to Expressionism: German Literature and Culture 1880–1918* (London: Weidenfeld and Nicolson, 1973), 36–37. As Pascal notes, "[The] figure of the artist that appears in so many plays and novels of the period implicitly or explicitly refers to some image of the bourgeois and bears as great a variety of meanings as the latter" (35).

107. Harry G. Carlson, introduction to *The Social Significance of Modern Drama* (1914), by Emma Goldman, preface by Erika Munk (Montclair, NJ: Applause Theatre Book Publishers, 1987), v–xii, at xi.

108. Carlson, introduction to Goldman, *The Social Significance of Modern Drama*, vi.

109. Goldman, *The Social Significance of Modern Drama*, 1.

110. Goldman, *The Social Significance of Modern Drama*, 3.

111. Luc Boltanski and Eve Chiapello, *The New Spirit of Capitalism*, trans. Gregory Elliott (New York: Verso, 2005), 4.

112. Boltanski and Chiapello, *The New Spirit of Capitalism*, 4.

113. Boltanski and Chiapello, *The New Spirit of Capitalism*, 8.

114. Boltanski and Chiapello, *The New Spirit of Capitalism*, 7.

115. Boltanski and Chiapello, *The New Spirit of Capitalism*, 35.

116. Joseph Schumpeter, *Capitalism, Socialism, and Democracy* (1942; repr., New York: Harper, 2008), 143.

117. Jürgen Kocka, "Capitalism and Its Critics," in *The Lifework of a Labor Historian: Essays in Honor of Marcel van der Linden*, ed. Ulbe Bosma and Karin Hofmeester (Leiden: Brill, 2018), 71–89, at 88.

118. Kocka, "Capitalism and Its Critics," 88.

119. Kocka, "Capitalism and Its Critics," 88.

120. Augusto Boal, *Theatre of the Oppressed* (1974), trans. Charles A. McBride (New York: Theatre Communications Group, 1993), 45.

121. Marx and Engels, *The Communist Manifesto*, 211.

122. Hägglund, *This Life*, 237.

123. Hägglund, "What Is Democratic Socialism? Part III: Life after Capitalism."

124. Katy Waldman, "Has Self-Awareness Gone Too Far in Fiction?," *New Yorker*, August 19, 2020, https://www.newyorker.com/books/under-review/has-self-awareness-gone-too-far-in-fiction.

125. Waldman, "Has Self-Awareness Gone Too Far in Fiction?"

126. Waldman, "Has Self-Awareness Gone Too Far in Fiction?"

127. Ridout, *Scenes from Bourgeois Life*, 13.

128. Ridout, *Scenes from Bourgeois Life*.

129. Moody, "The Drama of Capital," 92. See also Anna Weterståhl Stenport, "The Sexonomics of *Et dukkehjem*: Money, the Domestic Sphere and Prostitution," *Edda* 106, no. 4 (2006): 339–53, at 341. As Stenport points out, although money "is generic to modern drama," "little drama and performance theory actively engages with the theme, form and function of economics in modern theatre." By contrast, the influence of economics on the novel and on poetry has been well documented. I discuss the novel of capital later in the introduction. For studies on poetry and money, see Jochen Hörisch, *Heads or Tails: The Poetics of Money* (1996), trans. Amy Homing Marschall (Detroit: Wayne State University Press, 2000); and Christopher Nealon, *The Matter of*

Capital: Poetry and Crisis in the American Century (Cambridge, MA: Harvard University Press, 2011).

130. Ridout, *Scenes from Bourgeois Life*, 12. Ridout identifies "the spectator's powerlessness" as "a constituent element of a distinctive spectatorial subjectivity, produced by the defensive self-construction of a colonial bourgeoisie" (12). See also Stanley Cavell, "The Avoidance of Love: A Reading of King Lear," in *Must We Mean What We Say?* (Cambridge: Cambridge University Press, 2002), 267–354.

131. Ridout, *Scenes from Bourgeois Life*, 11.

132. Ridout, *Scenes from Bourgeois Life*, 12.

133. Quoted in Ridout, *Scenes from Bourgeois Life*, 194. See Terry Eagleton, "The Subject of Literature," *Cultural Critique* 2 (1985–86): 95–104, at 96 and 97.

134. Ridout, *Scenes from Bourgeois Life*, 2n54. See also Louis Althusser, "Ideology and Ideological State Apparatuses (Notes towards an Investigation)," in *Lenin and Philosophy and Other Essays*, trans. Ben Brewster (New York: Monthly Review Press, 2001), 85–126.

135. Ridout, *Scenes from Bourgeois Life*, 177.

136. Ridout, *Scenes from Bourgeois Life*, 178.

137. Dukore, *Money and Politics*, 122.

138. Bernard Shaw, *Major Barbara* (1905/1907; repr., New York: Penguin, 2001), 133. Subsequent page references are given in the text.

139. André Gorz, "Reform and Revolution" (1967), trans. Ben Brewster, *Socialist Register* 5 (1968): 111–43, at 125.

140. Michelle M. Dowd and Natasha Korda, eds., introduction to *Working Subjects in Early Modern English Drama* (Burlington, VT: Ashgate, 2011), 1–16, at 7. See also Henry S. Turner, *The Corporate Commonwealth: Pluralism and Political Fictions in England, 1516–1651* (Chicago: University of Chicago Press, 2016).

141. For a general overview and list of works published on the subject, see Douglas Bruster, "On a Certain Tendency in Economic Criticism of Shakespeare," in *Money and the Age of Shakespeare: Essays in New Economic Criticism*, ed. Linda Woodbridge (New York: Palgrave Macmillan, 2003), 67–79.

142. Jean-Christophe Agnew, *Worlds Apart: The Market and the Theater in Anglo-American Thought, 1550–1750* (New York: Cambridge University Press, 1986), 11. When mentioning the "long sixteenth century," Agnew is quoting Immanuel Wallerstein, *The Modern World-System: Capitalist Agriculture and the Origins of the European World-Economy in the Sixteenth Century* (New York: Academic Press, 1974), chap. 2.

143. Kristen Guest, "The Subject of Money: Late-Victorian Melodrama's Crisis of Masculinity," *Victorian Studies* 49, no. 7 (2007): 635–57; and Moody, "The Drama of Capital," 91–110.

144. Guest, "The Subject of Money," 636.

145. Guest, "The Subject of Money."

146. Jean Chothia, *André Antoine* (New York: Cambridge University Press, 1991), 92.

147. Friedrich Engels, *Supplement* to Karl Marx, *Capital*, vol. 3 (1894), prepared by Engels, trans. David Fernbach, with introduction by Ernest Mandel (New York: Penguin, 1993), 1027–47, at 1045.

148. Engels, *Supplement* to Marx, *Capital*, 3:1047.

149. Thorstein Veblen, *The Theory of the Leisure Class* (1899; repr., Mineola, NY: Dover, 1994), 169.

150. "Financial Crises: The Slumps That Shaped Modern Finance," *The Economist*, April 12, 2014, https://www.economist.com/news/essays/21600451-finance-not-merely-prone-crises-it-shaped-them-five-historical-crises-show-how-aspects-today-s-fina.

151. "The true barrier to capitalist production is capital itself." Marx, *Capital*, 3:358.

152. Oscar Wilde, *Lady Windermere's Fan* in *The Plays of Oscar Wilde*, new introduction by John Lahr (New York: Vintage, 1988), 1–82, at 7.

153. Wilde, *An Ideal Husband*, in *The Plays of Oscar Wilde*, 219–343, at 255. Subsequent page references are given in the text.

154. David McCullough, *The Path between the Seas: The Creation of the Panama Canal 1870–1914* (New York: Simon & Schuster, 1977), 227–33.

155. For statistics on theater attendance and ticket prices, see Tracy C. Davis, "The Sociable Playwright and Representative Citizen," in *Women and Playwriting in Nineteenth-Century Britain*, ed. Tracy C. Davis and Ellen Donkin (Cambridge: Cambridge University Press, 1999), 15–34, at 19, and *The Economics of the British Stage*; Michel Autrand, *Le théâtre en France de 1870 à 1914* (Paris: Honoré Champion, 2006), 15–16.

156. Chekhov to Al. P. Chekhov, February 21, 1899, in A. P. Chekhov, *Polnoe sobranie sochinenii i pisem v tridtsati tomah* (*Complete Works and Letters in Thirty Volumes*), vol. 3 (Moscow: Nauka, 1976), 164. Translations from Russian, for this and other works herein, are my own unless otherwise noted.

157. As Davis eloquently puts it, "Being shy of political content the stage was ripe for a maverick infusion of ideological polemics." Davis, *George Bernard Shaw and the Socialist Theatre*, 15.

158. Sarah J. Townsend, *The Unfinished Art of Theater: Avant-Garde Intellectuals in Mexico and Brazil* (Evanston, IL: Northwestern University Press, 2018), 3.

159. Ridout, *Scenes from Bourgeois Life*, 131.

160. Ayad Akhtar, "Greed Is Good Drama," interview by Ruthie Fierberg, *Playbill*, October 2017, 5, *Measure for Measure* at the Public Theater, New York. This can be found online as Ruthie Fierberg, "Why You Won't Be Able to Stop Thinking about Ayad Akhtar's New Broadway Play *Junk*," *Playbill*, October 2, 2017, http://www.playbill.com/article/why-you-wont-be-able-to-stop-thinking-about-ayad-akhtars-new-broadway-play-junk.

161. Ayad Akhtar, "Finance and the Figure of Now," in *The Invisible Hand* (New York: Back Bay Books, 2015), xv. Subsequent page references are given in the text.

162. See Alan Ackerman, *The Portable Theater: American Literature and the Nineteenth-Century Stage* (Baltimore: Johns Hopkins University Press, 1999); and David Kurnick, *Empty Houses: Theatrical Failure and the Novel* (Princeton, NJ: Princeton University Press, 2011).

163. Halina Suwala, *Autour de Zola et du naturalisme* (Paris: Honoré Champion, 1993). See also David A. Zimmerman, *Panic! Markets, Crises, and Crowds in American Fiction* (Chapel Hill: University of North Carolina Press, 2006).

164. Earlier examples also include Balzac's *César Birotteau* (1837) and Charles Dickens's *Little Dorrit* (1857).

165. Peter Brooks, *The Melodramatic Imagination: Balzac, Henry James, Melodrama, and the Mode of Excess* (New Haven, CT: Yale University Press, 1976), 20.

166. Frank Norris, *The Pit: A Story of Chicago* (1903; repr., Cambridge, MA: Seven Treasures, 2008), 138.

167. Marx, *Capital*, 1:251.

168. Franco Moretti, *The Bourgeois: Between History and Literature* (New York: Verso, 2013), 185, italics in the original.

169. Edward Chancellor, *Devil Take the Hindmost: A History of Financial Speculation* (London: Macmillan, 1999), x.

170. Steve Fraser, *Every Man a Speculator: A History of Wall Street in American Life* (New York: HarperCollins, 2005), xvii.

171. Émile Zola, *Nana*, trans. with introduction and notes by Douglas Parmée (New York: Oxford University Press, 1998), 3.

172. Pierre-Cyrille Hautcoeur, Amir Rezaee, and Angelo Riva, "Stock Exchange Industry Regulation: The Paris Bourse, 1893–1898," Economic History Association, http://eh.net/eha/wp-content/uploads/2013/11/Hautcoeurb.pdf, accessed September 1, 2019.

173. Edmond Benjamin and Henry Buguet, *Coulisses de Bourse et de théâtre*, preface by Francisque Sarcey (Paris: Paul Ollendorf, 1882), v.

174. Jonas A. Barish, *The Antitheatrical Prejudice* (Berkeley: University of California Press, 1981).

175. Zimmerman, *Panic!*, 155–56.

176. See Martha Woodmansee and Mark Osteen, eds., *New Economic Criticism* (New York: Routledge, 1999); and Marc Shell, *The Economy of Literature* (Baltimore: Johns Hopkins University Press, 1978).

177. Woodmansee and Osteen, *New Economic Criticism*, 3.

178. Kurt Heinzelman, *The Economics of Imagination* (Amherst: University of Massachusetts, 1980), 11.

179. Quoted in Woodmansee and Osteen, *New Economic Criticism*, 4. See also Martha Woodmansee, "The Genius and the Copyright: Economic and Legal Conditions of the Emergence of the 'Author,'" *Eighteenth-Century Studies* 17 (1984): 425–48; and *The Author, Art, and the Market: Rereading the History of Aesthetics* (New York: Columbia University Press, 1994).

180. See Nancy Armstrong, *Desire and Domestic Fiction: A Political History of the Novel* (New York: Oxford University Press, 1987); David Kaufmann, *The Business of Common Life: Novels and Classical Economics between Revolution and Reform* (Baltimore: Johns Hopkins University Press, 1995); and Seamus O'Driscoll, "Invisible Forces: Capitalism and the Russian Literary Imagination, 1855–1881" (PhD diss., Harvard University, 2005).

181. James Thompson, *Models of Value: Eighteenth-Century Political Economy and the Novel* (Durham, NC: Duke University Press, 1996), 1, quoted in Woodmansee and Osteen, *New Economic Criticism*, 4.

182. Mary Poovey, *Genres of the Credit Economy: Mediating Value in Eighteenth- and Nineteenth-Century Britain* (Chicago: University of Chicago Press, 2008), 1–2. Poovey joins John Guillory in arguing that it is the eighteenth century that witnessed the separation between economic and aesthetic value. See John Guillory, *Cultural Capital: The Problem of Literary Canon Formation* (Chicago: University of Chicago Press, 1993). See also Raymond Williams, *Culture and Society, 1780–1950* (New York: Columbia University Press, 1958); Philip Connell, *Romanticism, Economics, and the Question of 'Culture'* (New York: Oxford University Press, 2001); Donald Winch, *Riches and Poverty: An Intellectual History of Political Economy in Britain, 1750–1834* (New York: Cambridge University Press, 1996).

183. Shell, *The Economy of Literature*, 90–91. Shell discusses Aristotle's writing on Euripides where the former mentions that the latter may be "faulty" in economy (*oikonomia*) (*Poetics*, 1453a22ff). Shell elaborates: "He [the tragedian] must manage a household on stage in such a way as to ensure that it is somewhat familiar to that of his audience (hence eliciting fear) but not too familiar to that of his audience (since that would make pity impossible). The poet-economist, then, must be a master of familiarities and unfamiliarities, of similarities and differences. He must be a master of metaphorization between human families and between the families of words" (91).

184. Hägglund, *This Life*, 313–14.

185. Akhtar, "Finance and the Figure of Now," xv.

186. Michael Shane Boyle is careful to note, however, that to "ask whether theatrical labor has been subsumed to capital requires examining the social relations that give form to value itself." Michael Shane Boyle, "Performance and Value: The Work of Theatre in Karl Marx's *Critique of Political Economy*," *Theatre Survey* 58, no. 1 (2017): 3–23, at 4.

187. Bernard Shaw, preface to *Major Barbara*, *Major Barbara* (1905/1907; repr., New York: Penguin, 2001), 49.

188. Shaw, preface to *Major Barbara*, 26.

189. The Krupp Foundation Minda de Gunzburg Center for European Studies Dissertation Research Fellowship helped fund research for this project.

190. One possible scenario involves dramatic writers who, disappointed with the institution of theater, begin writing closet dramas (plays not intended to be performed). See Puchner, *Stage Fright*, 58–118.

191. Judith Butler, "Performative Agency," *Journal of Cultural Economy* 3, no. 2 (2010): 147–61, at 148.

192. Butler, "Performative Agency," 149.

193. For the British context, see Davis, *The Economics of the British Stage*. For the relationship between capitalism and modernism (including theater), see John Xiros Cooper, *Modernism and the Culture of the Market Society* (Cambridge: Cambridge University Press, 2004). See also J. Fisher, ed., *To Have or Have Not*.

194. Martin Puchner, *Modern Drama*, vol. 1 (New York: Routledge, 2007), 64n104. See also Kirsten E. Shepherd-Barr, *Modern Drama: A Very Short Introduction* (New York: Oxford University Press, 2016).

195. Axel Honneth, *The Idea of Socialism: Towards a Renewal* (Malden, MA: Polity, 2017), 47.

196. Evert Sprinchorn, *Strindberg as Dramatist* (New Haven, CT: Yale University Press, 1982), 6.

197. Terry Eagleton, *Marxism and Literary Criticism* (Berkeley: University of California Press, 1976); and Raymond Williams, *Marxism and Literature*, rev. ed. (New York: Oxford University Press, 1978). See also the special issue of *Theatre Survey* dedicated to theater and Marxism, edited by Nicholas Ridout: *Theatre Survey* 58, no. 1 (2017): 1–138.

198. Cf. "reenchantment" in Martin Harries, *Scare Quotes from Shakespeare: Marx, Keynes, and the Language of Reenchantment* (Stanford, CA: Stanford University Press, 2000).

199. Kirsten E. Shepherd-Barr, *Science on Stage: From Doctor Faustus to Copenhagen* (Princeton, NJ: Princeton University Press, 2006), 39.

200. Alison Shonkwiler and Leigh Claire La Berge, "Introduction: A Theory of Capitalist Realism," in *Reading Capitalist Realism*, ed. Alison Shonkwiler and Leigh Claire La Berge (Iowa City: University of Iowa Press, 2014), 1.

201. Shonkwiler and La Berge, "Introduction: A Theory of Capitalist Realism," 1.

202. W. B. Worthen, *Modern Drama and the Rhetoric of Theater* (Berkeley: University of California Press, 1992), 44.

203. See, for example, Robert Brustein, *The Theatre of Revolt: Studies in Modern Drama from Ibsen to Genet* (1964; repr., Chicago: Elephant Paperbacks, 1991), 229–78; and Fredric Jameson, *Brecht and Method* (New York: Verso, 1998).

204. Ridout, *Scenes from Bourgeois Life*, 168.

205. I am inspired here by Ostermeier's use of "classical literary canon" in Peter M. Boenisch and Thomas Ostermeier, *The Theatre of Thomas Ostermeier* (New York: Routledge, 2016), 236.

206. See Esther Kim Lee, ed., *Modern and Contemporary World Drama: Critical and Primary Sources* (London: Bloomsbury, 2022).

207. Boenisch and Ostermeier, *The Theatre of Thomas Ostermeier*, 234–35.

208. For more on theater as a "repository of cultural memory," see Marvin Carlson, *The Haunted Stage: The Theatre as Memory Machine* (Ann Arbor: University of Michigan Press, 2001), 2.

Chapter 1

1. Thomas Ostermeier, *Iconic Artist Talk*, with Branden Jacobs-Jenkins, Brooklyn Academy of Music, October 12, 2017, Brooklyn, NY.

2. As of March 2018, the production was scheduled for fall of 2018. Rachel Shteir, "Ibsen Wrote *An Enemy of the People* in 1882. Trump Has Made It Popular Again," *New York Times*, March 9, 2018, https://www.nytimes.com/2018/03/09/theater/enemy-of-the-people-ibsen.html. The plans seemed to have been postponed or abandoned, however.

3. Shteir, "Ibsen Wrote *An Enemy of the People* in 1882. Trump Has Made It Popular Again."

4. On the free market as a historical construction and political fiction, see Bernard E. Harcourt, *The Illusion of Free Markets: Punishment and the Myth of Natural Order* (Cambridge, MA: Harvard University Press, 2012). For

more on the rift between literary and economic discourses by the nineteenth century, see Woodmansee and Osteen, *New Economic Criticism*, 4–5; and Kaufmann, *The Business of Common Life*, 169–72. Kaufmann argues that "the rapid growth and institutional consolidation of commercial capitalism in the eighteenth century created a demand for new descriptions of and apologias for the economy, the state, morality, and citizenship, a demand that was taken up by an increasingly rationalized public sphere which included both the field of political economics and the novel" (169).

5. On the importance of home markets for Ibsen's success, see Narve Fulsås and Tore Rem, *Ibsen, Scandinavia and the Making of a World Drama* (Cambridge: Cambridge University Press, 2018), 106–13, 183–85, 201–5.

6. Friedrich Nietzsche, *The Birth of Tragedy: Out of the Spirit of Music* (1872), new ed., ed. Michael Tanner, trans. Shaun Whiteside (New York: Penguin, 2003), 92, 85.

7. Nietzsche, *The Birth of Tragedy*, 85.

8. Andrew Sofer, *Dark Matter: Invisibility in Drama, Theater, and Performance* (Ann Arbor: University of Michigan Press, 2013), 4, italics his.

9. Harvey, *A Brief History of Neoliberalism*, 161.

10. Giovanni Arrighi, *The Long Twentieth Century: Money, Power, and the Origins of Our Times* (New York: Verso, 2010), xi.

11. Alessandro Vercelli, "Financialization in a Long-Run Perspective," *International Journal of Political Economy* 42, no. 4 (2013): 19–46, at 19; David Graeber, *Debt: The First 5000 Years* (Brooklyn: Melville House, 2011), 38, italics in the original.

12. Francis Sejersted, *The Age of Social Democracy: Norway and Sweden in the Twentieth Century*, trans. Richard Daly with editing by Madeleine B. Adams (Princeton, NJ: Princeton University Press, 2011), 22–23, at 23.

13. Henrik Ibsen, *En folkefiende*, a new version by Brad Birch (London: Bloomsbury, 2016), 46.

14. Franco Moretti, "The Grey Area: Ibsen and the Spirit of Capitalism," *New Left Review* 61 (January–February 2010): 117–31, at 124.

15. I thank Martin Puchner for bringing this to my attention.

16. Moretti, "The Grey Area," 118.

17. Moretti, "The Grey Area," 131.

18. Robert Ferguson, *Henrik Ibsen: A New Biography* (London: Richard Cohen Books, 1996), 217.

19. On Peer's colonizing vision, see Elizabeth Oxfeldt, *Nordic Orientalism: Paris and the Cosmopolitan Imagination 1800–1900* (Copenhagen: Museum Tusculanum Press, 2005), 144.

20. Ferguson, *Henrik Ibsen*, 165.

21. Ibsen, *Letters and Speeches*, 309–10.

22. Ibsen, *Letters and Speeches*, 308.

23. Moretti, "The Grey Area," 131.

24. Bjørnstjerne Bjørnson, *En fallit*, 2nd ed. (Copenhagen: Gyldendalske Boghandels Forlag [F. Hegel & Søn], 1878). Subsequent page references are given in the text. Translations from Norwegian, for this and other works herein, are my own unless otherwise noted.

25. P. Brooks, *The Melodramatic Imagination*, 20.

26. "Melodramatic good and evil are highly personalized: they are assigned to, they inhabit persons who indeed have no psychological complexity but who are strongly characterized." P. Brooks, *The Melodramatic Imagination*, 16.

27. S.v. "speculation," *Oxford Dictionaries*, https://www.oed.com/view/Entry/186113, accessed May 15, 2020; s.v. "spectacle," *Oxford Dictionaries*, https://www.oed.com/view/Entry/186057, accessed May 15, 2020; Barish, *The Antitheatrical Prejudice*.

28. See Michael Fried, *Art and Objecthood: Essays and Reviews* (Chicago: University of Chicago Press, 1998), 163. Fried understands "theatre" and "theatricality" as art produced specifically to impress an audience.

29. Eric Ries, *The Lean Startup: How Today's Entrepreneurs Use Continuous Innovation to Create Radically Successful Businesses* (New York: Crown, 2011), 85.

30. Literally: "Treated that way, the entire coast is a bankruptcy."

31. Moretti, "The Grey Area," 131.

32. Tawney, *Religion and the Rise of Capitalism*, 104.

33. Ibsen, *Letters and Speeches*, 170.

34. Henrik Ibsen, *Samfundets støtter* (Copenhagen: Gyldendalske Boghandels Forlag [F. Hegel & Søn], 1877). Subsequent citations are given parenthetically in the text.

35. Robert F. Sharp translates Bernick's phrase as "the hand of Providence," thus echoing Vigeland's, two lines earlier: "There is no denying that it looks as though Providence had just planned the configuration of the country to suit a branch line" (144). Henrik Ibsen, *The Pillars of Society* (1877), in *The Pretenders; Pillars of Society; Rosmersholm*, trans. R. Farquharson Sharp (London: J. M. Dent, 1913), https://ebooks.adelaide.edu.au/i/ibsen/henrik/pillars/, act 1, accessed August 20, 2017. William Archer translates the phrase as "a special guidance" (23). Henrik Ibsen, *The Pillars of Society* (1877), trans. William Archer (Boston: Walter H. Baker, 1890), https://archive.org/stream/pillarsofsociety00ibse#page/23/mode/1up/search/guidance, accessed August 20, 2017.

36. *Styrelse* can acquire a religious connotation in certain expressions when coupled with specific modifiers. Otherwise, it is more generic than *forsynet*, which has a strong religious significance. I thank Leonardo Lisi for helping me with the connotations of these Norwegian terms.

37. Joseph Roach, "Gossip Girls: Lady Teazle, Nora Helmer, and Invisible-Hand Drama," *Modern Drama* 53, no. 3 (2010): 297–310, at 297.

38. Norsk Jernbanemuseum (Norwegian Railway Museum), "Norwegian Railway History," http://jernbanemuseet.no/norsk-jernbanehistorie/, accessed August 20, 2017. *Bradshaw's Shareholder's Guide, Railway Manual and Directory, for 1857: A Hand-Book for Companies and Shareholders* (London: W. J. Adams, 1857), 322, https://babel.hathitrust.org/cgi/pt?id=wu.89097040810;view=1up;seq=13, accessed August 20, 2017.

39. It appears once in Smith's posthumously published essay "History of Astronomy" (in *Essays on Philosophical Subjects* [Dublin, 1798]) as a reference to pagan superstitions about phenomena that have a scientific explanation ("The invisible hand of Jupiter," 34); once in *The Theory of Moral Sentiments*

(1759), ed. Knud Haakonssen (Cambridge: Cambridge University Press, 2002), where Smith argues that feudal lords "are led by an invisible hand" to divide with the poor "the produce of all their improvements" (215); and once in *An Inquiry into the Nature and Causes of the Wealth of Nations* (London: Strahan & Cadell, 1776), where Smith alludes to the caution and the risks that induce some merchants to prefer domestic trade over foreign, thereby unintentionally benefiting their native country's economy (2:572). There is much debate among historians of economics what Smith might have meant by his reference to an invisible hand. For an excellent survey of the myth of "the invisible hand" in economic theory as well as the current debate about what Adam Smith might have meant, see the exchanges between Gavin Kennedy and Daniel Klein: Gavin Kennedy, "Adam Smith and the Invisible Hand: From Metaphor to Myth," *Econ Journal Watch* 6, no. 2 (2009): 239–63; Daniel Klein, "Adam Smith's Invisible Hands: Comment on Gavin Kennedy," *Econ Journal Watch* 6, no. 2 (2009): 264–79; Gavin Kennedy, "A Reply to Daniel Klein on Adam Smith and the Invisible Hand," *Econ Journal Watch* 6, no. 3 (2009): 374–88.

40. Kennedy, "Adam Smith and the Invisible Hand," 242. For a discussion of "Thy Bloody and Invisible Hand" and its pertinence to Smith's "invisible hand," see Harries, *Scare Quotes from Shakespeare*, 14–18; and Richard Halpern, *Eclipse of Action: Tragedy and Political Economy* (Chicago: University of Chicago Press, 2017), 29–74.

41. Kennedy, "Adam Smith and the Invisible Hand," 254.

42. Tawney, *Religion and the Rise of Capitalism*, 192. See also note 8.

43. Peter Harrison, "Adam Smith and the History of the Invisible Hand," *Journal of the History of Ideas* 72, no. 1 (2011): 29–49, at 30–31.

44. Carl Schmitt, *Political Theology: Four Chapters on the Concept of Sovereignty* (1922), trans. (from German) George Schwab (1985; repr., Chicago: University of Chicago Press, 2005), 36.

45. Hans Blumenberg, *The Legitimacy of the Modern Age* (1966), trans. (from German) Robert M. Wallace (Cambridge, MA: MIT Press, 1983). For more on the debate between Schmitt and Blumenberg, see Pini Ifergan, "Cutting to the Chase: Carl Schmitt and Hans Blumenberg on Political Theology and Secularization," *New German Critique* 37, no. 3 (2010): 149–71.

46. Engels, Supplement to *Capital*, 3:1046.

47. Harries, *Scare Quotes from Shakespeare*, 15, 1. My own thinking about Ibsen's drama is indebted to Harries's analysis of Adam Smith's "invisible hand" as a kind of scare quote: "Adam Smith's 'invisible hand' has at once become a powerful scare quote in its own right, and has a possible origin in *Macbeth*. Smith's suggestive figure conjures a supernatural index at the heart of a rationalized economy, pointing the way to, controlling, or grasping the wealth of nations. That the phrase so often appears outside its context is also germane to this study; as slogan, the scare tactic inherent in 'the invisible hand' goes unexamined. It demarcates an area where investigation must necessarily encounter a dead end: the hand promises the faithful that the series of effects called the economy has an organizing force at its core, but at the same time warns that this force will never be seen. In the work of editorialists and speech writers, the 'invisible hand' is then the perfect quotation of the kind

Debord has in mind. The phrase alludes to an authoritative concept, but the phrase figures the concept in such a way that challenging it is impossible. If one illuminates the hand, it is no longer 'invisible,' no longer the object one hoped to investigate. The phantom heart of the economy is unrepresentable" (14–15).

48. According to Dukore, "Ibsen spells out the deficiencies of both his protagonist and his protagonist's society; he has this protagonist see the light, confess his guilt publicly, and take what remedial steps he is capable of taking; and the playwright provides a pithy moral to the tale, that the spirits of truth and freedom should become the real pillars of society." Dukore, *Money and Politics*, 165. By contrast, in his biography of Ibsen, Ferguson reads Bernick's public confession as a cynical "object lesson in opportunism and finely judged business acumen" (219). Ferguson describes Bernick in the following manner: "A hundred years on he would be a television evangelist and make himself a great deal more money out of religion than ever he made out of shipping" (220). This interpretation flattens Bernick's character to a mere villain—precisely the kind of melodramatic type that Ibsen's drama resists.

49. Henrik Ibsen, *John Gabriel Borkman* (Copenhagen: Gyldendalske Boghandels Forlag [F. Hegel & Søn], 1896). Subsequent page references are given in the text.

50. For more on Plato's influence on the major European dramatists of the twentieth century, see Puchner, *The Drama of Ideas*.

51. "For thine is the kingdom, the power, and the glory, for ever and ever" (Matthew 6:13, KJV).

52. Shell, *The Economy of Literature*, 11.

53. Shell, *The Economy of Literature*, 8–10.

54. *Brand* (1865) and *Peer Gynt* (1867) were originally written as closet dramas.

55. Felix Martin, *Money: The Unauthorized Autobiography—from Coinage to Cryptocurrencies* (New York: Knopf, 2014), 12, 14. Martin brings up the example of the economy of Yap, which relied on *fei*—"large, solid, thick stone wheels ranging in diameter from a foot to twelve feet" (13). Martin is not the first to posit the credit theory of money. For example, he cites Henry Dunning Macleod's *The Principles of Political Economy* (1882): "We may therefore lay down our fundamental Conception that Currency and Transferable Debt are convertible terms; whatever represents transferable debt of any sort is Currency; and whatever material that Currency may consist of, it represents Transferable Debt, and nothing else" (28, quoting Macleod, 188). For the meaning of money in Ibsen's *Peer Gynt* see Leonardo F. Lisi, "Aesthetics of Fragmentation in Henrik Ibsen's *Peer Gynt*," in *Marginal Modernity: The Aesthetics of Dependency from Kierkegaard to Joyce* (New York: Fordham University Press, 2012), 87–116. Lisi writes: "What money points to is not the shapes that it assumes in the world but the work that constitutes the precondition for such signification to occur" (104).

56. Michael Meyer, *Ibsen: A Biography* (Garden City, NY: Doubleday, 1971), 286, 410.

57. Robert A. Nisbet, *Social Change and History: Aspects of the Western Theory of Development* (New York: Oxford University Press, 1969), 4.

58. Victor Turner, *Dramas, Fields, and Metaphors: Symbolic Action in Human Society* (Ithaca, NY: Cornell University Press, 1974), 25.
59. P. Brooks, *The Melodramatic Imagination*, 13.
60. P. Brooks, *The Melodramatic Imagination*.
61. P. Brooks, *The Melodramatic Imagination*, 13, 61, 65, 137.
62. George Steiner, *The Death of Tragedy* (1961; repr., New York: Knopf, 1980).
63. Halpern, *Eclipse of Action*, 33.
64. Halpern, *Eclipse of Action*, 31.
65. "The original essence of tragedy consists then in the fact that within such a conflict each of the opposed sides, if taken by itself, has justification; while each can establish the true and positive content of its own aim and character only by denying the equally justified power of the other." G. W. F. Hegel, *Aesthetics: Lectures on Fine Art*, trans. T. M. Knox (Oxford: Clarendon, 1975), 1196.
66. Halpern, *Eclipse of Action*, 37.
67. The full title of Defoe's article is telling: "The anatomy of Exchange-Alley: or, A System of Stock-Jobbing. Proving that Scandalous Trade, as it is now carry'd on, to be Knavish in its Private Practice, and Treason in its Publick: . . . By a Jobber." Quoted in Urs Stäheli, *Spectacular Speculation: Thrills, the Economy, and Popular Discourse*, trans. Eric Savoth (Stanford, CA: Stanford University Press, 2013), 31.
68. Henrik Ibsen, *En folkefiende* (Copenhagen: Gyldendalske Boghandels Forlag [F. Hegel & Søn], 1882). Subsequent page references are given in the text.
69. Figueiredo, *Henrik Ibsen*, 297.
70. Branislav Jakovljević, "Père Gynt: Mendacity for the 21st Century," *TDR: The Drama Review* 64, no. 3 (2020): 8–13, at 11.
71. My discussion of Thomas Ostermeier's production is based on its 2013 performance at the Brooklyn Academy of Music, part of the Next Wave Festival.
72. For more on Ibsen's challenge to idealism see Toril Moi, *Henrik Ibsen and the Birth of Modernism: Art, Theater, Philosophy* (New York: Oxford University Press, 2006), esp. 9, 91–96.
73. Karl Marx, *The Grundrisse*, in *The Marx-Engels Reader*, 2nd ed., trans. and ed. Robert C. Tucker (New York: W. W. Norton, 1978), 221–93, at 283.
74. Quoted in Marvin Carlson, *Theatre Is More Beautiful than War: German Stage Directing in the Late Twentieth Century* (Iowa City: University of Iowa Press, 2009), 166.
75. Socialist realism became the official aesthetic doctrine of the Soviet Union at the First Congress of Soviet Writers in 1934. It was defined by Andrei Zhdanov as "the representation of reality in its revolutionary development." Quoted in Abram Tertz, *"The Trial Begins" and "On Socialist Realism,"* trans. Max Hayward and George Dennis, with introduction by Czesław Miłosz (Berkeley: University of California Press, 1960), 148.
76. M. Fisher, *Capitalist Realism*, 16, 2, italics in the original.
77. M. Fisher, *Capitalist Realism*, 21.

78. Ferguson, *Henrik Ibsen*, 266. Hegel "assured him [Ibsen] that the outrage most certainly had harmed sales of the book, detailing the extent of the damage done with implacable severity" (266).
79. Shaw, preface to *Major Barbara*, 18. See also Harley Granville-Barker, *The Voysey Inheritance*, adapted by David Mamet (New York: Vintage, 2005).
80. Blumenberg, *The Legitimacy of the Modern Age*, 224.
81. Ayad Akhtar, *The Invisible Hand* (New York: Back Bay Books, 2015), 6.
82. Ayad Akhtar, "Q&A: *Prospero*," *The Economist*, September 3, 2015, https://www.economist.com/blogs/prospero/2015/09/american-literature.
83. For more on the drama of ideas, see Puchner, *The Drama of Ideas*.
84. See David Harvey, *Marx, Capital and the Madness of Economic Reason* (New York: Oxford University Press, 2018), 25.
85. Moretti, "The Grey Area," 188.
86. "When Humphrey Gilbert set out on the same quest for the Northwest Passage in 1583, he embarked fully prepared to engage in musical diplomacy. 'For the solace of our people, and the allurement of the Savages,' he noted, 'we were provided of Musicke in Good variety: not omitting the leaste toyes, as Morris dancers, Hobby horse, and Maylike conceits to delight the savage people, whom we intended to win by all Faire meanes possible. And to that end we were indifferently furnished of all petty haberdasherie wares to barter with those simple people." D. B. Quinn, *The Voyages and Colonizing Enterprises of Sir Humphrey Gilbert*, vol. 2 (HS, 2nd. ser., vol. 84; London, 1940), 396. I thank Susannah Romney for bringing this historical information and Quinn's book to my attention.
87. Nicole Cooley, "Dollhouses Weren't Invented for Play," *Salon*, July 22, 2016, https://www.theatlantic.com/technology/archive/2016/07/dollhouses-werent-invented-for-play/492581/. See also Thomas E. Jordan, *Victorian Child Savers and Their Culture: A Thematic Evaluation* (Lewiston, NY: E. Mellen, 1998); and Howard P. Chudacoff, *Children at Play: An American History* (New York: New York University Press, 2007).
88. Susan Stewart, *On Longing: Narratives of the Miniature, the Gigantic, the Souvenir, the Collection* (Durham, NC: Duke University Press, 1993), 59.
89. Henrik Ibsen, *Et dukkenhjem* (Copenhagen: Gyldendalske Boghandels Forlag [F. Hegel & Søn], 1879). Subsequent page references are given in the text.
90. Elizabeth Hardwick, *Seduction and Betrayal: Women and Literature* (New York: Random House, 1974), 38.
91. See, for example, Dukore, *Money and Politics*; and Mike Kase, "The Use and Function of Monetary Images in Henrik Ibsen's Play *A Doll's House*," *Theatre Southwest* (April 1989): 23–26.
92. Templeton, *Ibsen's Women*, 110–45; and Moi, *Henrik Ibsen and the Birth of Modernism*, 225–47.
93. Ronald Florence, *Marx's Daughters: Eleanor Marx, Rosa Luxemburg, Angelica Balabanoff* (New York: Dial, 1975), 41. See also Bernard F. Dukore, "Karl Marx's Youngest Daughter and *A Doll's House*," *Theatre Journal* 42, no. 3 (1990): 308–21.

94. For an excellent reading of the tarantella as an example of theatricality and Ibsen's modernism, see Moi, *Henrik Ibsen and the Birth of Modernism*, 237–42.

95. According to Einar Haugen, *dukkehjem* did exist as a term before Ibsen. It meant "a small, cozy, neat home, but his play gave it the pejorative meaning." Einar Haugen, *Ibsen's Drama: Author to Audience* (Minneapolis: University of Minnesota Press, 1979), 103, quoted in Nicholas Grene, *Home on the Stage: Domestic Spaces in Modern Drama* (New York: Cambridge University Press, 2014), 16.

96. Frode Helland, *Ibsen in Practice: Relational Readings of Performance, Cultural Encounters and Power* (London: Bloomsbury, 2015), 57–58.

97. "'Post-truth' Named 2016 Word of the Year by Oxford Dictionaries," *Washington Post*, November 16, 2016, https://www.washingtonpost.com/news/the-fix/wp/2016/11/16/post-truth-named-2016-word-of-the-year-by-oxford-dictionaries/?noredirect=on. The OED defines *hygge* as a "quality of cosiness and comfortable conviviality that engenders a feeling of contentment or well-being; contentment from simple pleasures, such as warmth, food, friends, etc." S.v. "hygge, n.1," *OED Online*, last modified on March 2022, https://www.oed.com/view/Entry/58767802.

98. Bente D. Knudsen, "Danish Hygge—Even Danes Don't Realize That, Surprisingly, It Is Not about the Candles," *Your Danish Life*, July 2, 2019, https://www.yourdanishlife.dk/the-things-you-need-to-know-about-hygge/.

99. For a recent example of treating *A Doll's House* as an example of realism and naturalism, see Grene, *Home on the Stage*, 18, 31.

100. Marx, *Capital*, 1:164–65.

101. Ibsen, *Letters and Speeches*, 169.

102. Charles Lemert, foreword to Georg Simmel, *The Philosophy of Money* (1900), ed. David Frisby, trans. Tom Bottomore and David Frisby from a first draft by Kaethe Mengelberg (New York: Routledge, 2011), viii–xii, at viii.

103. Marx, *Capital*, 1:188.

104. Lisi, *Marginal Modernity*, 105.

105. Lisi, *Marginal Modernity*, 101.

106. See Margaret Benston, "The Political Economy of Women's Liberation," *Monthly Review* 21, no. 4 (1969), reprinted in *Monthly Review* 7, no. 4 (2019), https://monthlyreview.org/2019/09/01/the-political-economy-of-womens-liberation/; Mariarosa Dalla Costa and Selma James, *The Power of Women and the Subversion of the Community* (Bristol: Falling Wall Press, 1972); Silvia Federici, *Wages against Housework* (Bristol: Power of Women Collective and Falling Wall Press, 1975); Wally Seccombe, "The Housewife and Her Labour under Capitalism," *New Left Review* 1, no. 83 (1974): 3–24.

107. As Templeton notes, "*A Doll House* is the greatest literary argument against the notion of the 'two spheres,' the neat, centuries-old division of the world into his and hers that the nineteenth century made a doctrine for living" (*Ibsen's Women*, 137).

108. Karin Bruzelius Heffermehl, "The Status of Women in Norway," *American Journal of Comparative Law* 20, no. 4 (1972): 630–46, at 630.

109. Pat Hudson and W. R. Lee, eds., *Women's Work and the Family Economy in Historical Perspective* (Manchester: Manchester University Press, 1990), 5. See also Pat Hudson, "Women's Work," *BBC*, March 29, 2011, http://www.bbc.co.uk/history/british/victorians/womens_work_01.shtml; Deborah Simonton, *A History of European Women's Work, 1700 to the Present* (New York: Routledge, 1998), 175.

110. Hudson and Lee, *Women's Work and the Family Economy in Historical Perspective*, 280; and Hudson, "Women's Work."

111. David Harvey, *Seventeen Contradictions and the End of Capitalism* (New York: Oxford University Press, 2015), 114. Harvey continues: "Worse still, women were often allocated these tasks for so-called 'natural' reasons (everything from nimble fingers to a supposedly naturally submissive and patient temperament). For this reason, men in the workshops of Second Empire Paris strongly resisted the employment of women since they knew that this would lead to the reclassification of their work as unskilled and worthy only of a lower rate of remuneration" (114).

112. Stenport, "The Sexonomics of *Et dukkehjem*," 343.

113. Armstrong, *Desire and Domestic Fiction*, 8.

114. For more on the relationship between the reproduction of labor power and the reproduction of capitalist society, see Kirstin Munro, "'Social Reproduction Theory,' Social Reproduction, and Household Production," *Science and Society* 83, no. 4 (2019): 451–68, at 455.

115. Tracy C. Davis, *Actresses as Working Women: Their Social Identity in Victorian Culture* (New York: Routledge, 1991), 105.

116. The original, "jeg så igennem fingre med ham," literally translates as "I looked through fingers with him."

117. Moretti, "The Grey Area," 124.

118. Meyer, *Ibsen*, 446.

119. Ibsen, *Letters and Speeches*, 228.

120. Moi, *Henrik Ibsen and the Birth of Modernism*, 240–41.

121. Stenport, "The Sexonomics of *Et dukkehjem*," 346, 342.

122. Friedrich Engels, *The Origin of the Family, Private Property, and the State*, in *The Marx-Engels Reader*, 734–59, at 742.

123. August Strindberg, preface to *Getting Married*, parts I and II, trans., ed., and with introduction by Mary Sandbach (London: Victor Gollancz, 1972), 29–50, at 34.

124. Kirsten E. Shepherd-Barr, *Ibsen and Early Modernist Theater 1890–1900* (Westport, CT: Greenwood, 1997), 45. Although several critics have criticized Nora for her flirtation with Dr. Rank, as Joan Templeton points out, the fact that Nora refuses Dr. Rank's money after he confesses his feelings for her proves "her essential honorableness" (122).

125. Henrik Ibsen, *Hedda Gabler* (Copenhagen: Gyldendalske Boghandels Forlag [F. Hegel & Søn], 1891), 3.

126. Stenport, "The Sexonomics of *Et dukkehjem*," 349–51. See Moi, *Henrik Ibsen and the Birth of Modernism*, 243.

127. Stenport, "The Sexonomics of *Et dukkehjem*," 340.

128. Quoted in Mary A. Hill, *Charlotte Perkins Gilman: The Making of a Radical Feminist, 1860–1896* (Philadelphia: Temple University Press, 1980), 295.

129. Charlotte Perkins Gilman, *Women and Economics: A Study of the Economic Relation between Men and Women as a Factor in Social Evolution* (1898; repr., Berkeley: University of California Press, 1998), 23.
130. Moi, *Henrik Ibsen and the Birth of Modernism*, 229.
131. For an excellent review of the show, see Marvin Carlson, "Reviewed Work(s): *Nora or A Doll House* (Theater Oberhausen): *The Wild Duck* (Off-off-off-Ibsen Festival)," *Ibsen News and Comment* 31 (2011): 7–10.
132. Tanika Gupta, preface to *A Doll's House* (London: Oberon Books, 2019), unpaginated. Subsequent page references are given in the text.
133. Marvin Carlson, review of *A Doll's House Part 2*, by Lucas Hnath, *Ibsen News and Comment* 36/37 (2016), Ibsen Society of America, 13–17, at 14.
134. Ibsen, *Letters and Speeches*, 183.
135. Dukore, "Karl Marx's Youngest Daughter."
136. Lucas Hnath, *A Doll's House, Part 2* (New York: Dramatists Play Service, 2017), 18–19.
137. Sprinchorn, *Ibsen's Kingdom*, 295.
138. Strindberg, preface to *Getting Married*, part I, 33.
139. Strindberg, preface to *Getting Married*, part I, 38.

Chapter 2

1. August Strindberg, *Fröken Julie*, in *Fröken Julie, Fadren, Ett drömspel*, 5–39, at 21. Translations of *Fröken Julie* (*Miss Julie*) are my own unless otherwise noted. Subsequent page references are given in the text.
2. Instead of the contemporary term "sex worker," I am using the term "prostitute," as it was used in the nineteenth century, to be historically specific.
3. Gayle Rogers, *Speculation: A Cultural History from Aristotle to AI* (New York: Columbia University Press, 2021), 156.
4. Rogers, *Speculation*, 156.
5. Henry James, *The Wings of the Dove* (1902), ed. with introduction and notes by Millicent Bell (New York: Penguin, 2008), 82.
6. Bernard Shaw, *Mrs. Warren's Profession*, in *Plays Unpleasant*, 181–286, at 249.
7. For more on "the young man from the provinces," see Lionel Trilling, "The Princess Casamassima," in *The Liberal Imagination: Essays on Literature and Society* (1950; repr., Garden City, NY: Doubleday, 1957), 55–88; and A. K. Chanda, "The Young Man from the Provinces," *Comparative Literature* 33, no. 4 (1981): 321–41. As Trilling points out, the young man from the provinces does not need to literally hail from the provinces—"his social class may constitute his province" (58).
8. Hakim, *Erotic Capital*, 19.
9. Rebecca Munford, "'Wake Up and Smell the Lipgloss': Gender, Generation and the (A)politics of Girl Power," in *Third Wave Feminism: A Critical Exploration*, ed. S. Gillis, G. Howie, and R. Munford (New York: Palgrave, 2007), 266–79, at 274.
10. Mary Wollstonecraft, *A Vindication of the Rights of Woman* (1792), in *"A Vindication of the Rights of Woman" and "A Vindication of the Rights of Men"* (New York: Oxford University Press, 2008), 63–283, at 88, 90.

11. Gagnier, *The Insatiability of Human Wants*, 5.
12. Hakim, *Erotic Capital*, 15.
13. Hakim, *Erotic Capital*, 17.
14. Adam Isaiah Green, "'Erotic Capital' and the Power of Desirability: Why 'Honey Money' Is a Bad Collective Strategy for Remedying Gender Inequality," *Sexualities* 16, nos. 1/2 (2012): 137–58, at 149.
15. Green, "'Erotic Capital' and the Power of Desirability," 149.
16. Pierre Bourdieu, *Distinction: A Social Critique of the Judgement of Taste*, trans. Richard Nice, with introduction by Tony Bennett (New York: Routledge, 1984), 149.
17. Hakim, *Erotic Capital*, 18.
18. Hakim, *Erotic Capital*, 25.
19. Gary S. Becker, *Human Capital: A Theoretical and Empirical Analysis, with Special Reference to Education* (1964), 3rd ed. (Chicago: University of Chicago Press, 1994), 11. For an example of a Marxist critique of Becker's "human capital," see Samuel Bowles and Herbert Gintis, "The Problem with Human Capital Theory—a Marxian Critique," *American Economic Review* 65, no. 2 (1975): 74–82.
20. Hakim, *Erotic Capital*, 17.
21. Bourdieu, *Distinction*, 191.
22. David L. Swartz, "Bourdieu's Concept of Field," *Oxford Bibliographies*, https://www.oxfordbibliographies.com/view/document/obo-9780199756384/obo-9780199756384-0164.xml, accessed May 15, 2021.
23. Green, "'Erotic Capital' and the Power of Desirability," 151.
24. Green, "'Erotic Capital' and the Power of Desirability," 164–66.
25. Gilman, *Women and Economics*, 5.
26. Gilman, *Women and Economics*, 75.
27. Shaw, *Getting Married* and *Press Cuttings*, definitive text under the editorial supervision of Dan H. Laurence (New York: Penguin, 1986), 57–58.
28. Henry Becque, *Les corbeaux*, in *Théâtre complet*, vol. 1 (Paris: Classiques Garnier, 2019), 401–547, at 537.
29. Chothia, *André Antoine*, 92.
30. Alexander Ostrovsky, *Bespridannitsa* (1878), in *Piesy* (Moscow: Eksmo, 2009), 649–784, at 783.
31. Marion A. Kaplan, ed., *The Marriage Bargain: Women and Dowries in European History* (Philadelphia: Haworth, 1985), 2.
32. August Strindberg, preface to *Miss Julie*, in *Strindberg on Drama and Theatre*, ed. and trans. Egil Törnqvist and Birgitta Steene (Amsterdam: Amsterdam University Press, 2007), 62–72, at 68.
33. Bernard Shaw, "The Jevonian Criticism of Marx (A Comment on the Rev. P. H. Wicksteed's Article," *To-day*, January 1885, 22–27, reprinted in Philip H. Wicksteed, *The Common Sense of Political Economy and Selected Papers and Reviews of Economic Theory*, vol. 2 (1933), ed. and with introduction by Lionel Robbins (Abingdon, UK: Routledge, 2003), 724–30, at 730.
34. Strindberg, preface to *Miss Julie*, 67.
35. Strindberg to Edvard Brandes, ca. September 29, 1888, in *Strindberg on Drama and Theatre*, 74. Strindberg also once said that one of the inspirations for Julie was Emma Rudbeck, a noble daughter of a general, who seduced her

stable boy and then relocated to Stockholm, where she "became a waitress." Lennart Josephson, *Strindbergs drama Fröken Julie* (Stockholm, 1965), 232–35, quoted in Sprinchorn, *Strindberg as Dramatist*, 34–35.

36. Sprinchorn, *Strindberg as Dramatist*, 34.

37. While living at the estate, Strindberg witnessed the bizarre relationship between Countess Frankenau and Ludvig Hansen, her servant and illegitimate half-brother. Sue Prideaux, *Strindberg: A Life* (New Haven, CT: Yale University Press, 2012), 12–14.

38. Strindberg, preface to *Miss Julie*, 66.

39. Strindberg, preface to *Miss Julie*, 63.

40. Strindberg to Edvard Brandes, ca. September 29, 1888, in *Strindberg on Drama and Theatre*, 74.

41. Strindberg, preface to *Getting Married*, part I, 49. See also August Strindberg, *The Son of a Servant: The Servant of the Evolution of a Human Being* (1849–67; repr., Garden City, NY: Anchor Books, 1966).

42. August Strindberg, *The Red Room*, trans. Ellie Schleussner (Les Prairies numériques, 2019), 68.

43. Richard Swedberg, "The Literary Author as a Sociologist? *Among French Peasants* by August Strindberg," *Journal of Classical Sociology* 16, no. 1 (2016): 124–30, at 127. See also Anna Westerståhl Stenport, "Rural Modernism: Ethnography, Photography, and Recollection in *Among French Peasants*," in *Locating August Strindberg's Prose: Modernism, Transnationalism, and Setting* (Toronto: University of Toronto Press, 2010), 55–87.

44. Swedberg, "The Literary Author as a Sociologist?," 129.

45. Carl Albert Helmecke, "Buckle's Influence on Strindberg" (PhD diss., University of Pennsylvania, 1924).

46. August Strindberg, *Small Catechism for the Underclass*, trans. Jeff Kinkle and Janina Pedan (Andperseand, 2012), Kindle location 145 of 336.

47. Strindberg, *Small Catechism for the Underclass*, Kindle location 183 of 336.

48. Strindberg, "The Reward of Virtue," in *Getting Married*, 51–82, at 60.

49. Thomas Malthus, *An Essay on the Principle of Population; or, A View of Its Past and Present Effects on Human Happiness; with an Inquiry into Our Prospects Respecting the Future Removal of Mitigation of the Evils which It Occasions*, vol. 1, 4th ed. (London: T. Bensley, 1807), 19 (Kindle), https://babel.hathitrust.org/cgi/pt?id=njp.32101068776341&view=1up&seq=7, accessed May 11, 2020.

50. Egil Törnqvist and Barry Jacobs, *Strindberg's "Miss Julie": A Play and Its Transpositions* (Norwich, UK: Norvik Press, 1988), 11–14.

51. Anna Westerståhl Stenport, "Money Metaphors and Rhetoric of Resource Depletion: *Creditors* and Late-Nineteenth-Century European Economics," in *The International Strindberg: New Critical Essays*, ed. Stenport (Evanston, IL: Northwestern University Press, 2012), 145–66, at 146.

52. Sprinchorn, *Ibsen's Kingdom*, 272.

53. Sprinchorn, *Ibsen's Kingdom*.

54. Sprinchorn, *Strindberg as Dramatist*, 3–4.

55. Strindberg, preface to *Miss Julie*, 66, 67–68.

56. Törnqvist and Jacobs, *Strindberg's "Miss Julie,"* 39.

57. Strindberg, preface to *Getting Married*, part I, 30–31.
58. Strindberg, preface to *Getting Married*, part I, 33.
59. Strindberg, preface to *Getting Married*, part I, 37.
60. Strindberg, "A Doll's House," in *Getting Married*, 167–84, at 172.
61. Strindberg, "A Doll's House," 174.
62. Strindberg, "A Doll's House," 173–74.
63. Arthur Holmberg, "Through the Eyes of Lolita," interview with Paula Vogel, American Repertory Theater, November 17, 2009, https://americanrepertorytheater.org/media/through-the-eyes-of-lolita/.
64. Strindberg, preface to *Getting Married*, part I, 45.
65. Strindberg, preface to *Getting Married*, part I, 41.
66. Prideaux, *Strindberg*, 124.
67. August Strindberg, B. VI 155, quoted in Mary Sandbach, introduction to *Getting Married*, 20.
68. Strindberg to Meijer, December 11, 1890, in Uno Willers, *Strindberg om sig själv* (Stockholm, 1968), 35–36, quoted in Sprinchorn, *Strindberg as Dramatist*, ix.
69. Strindberg, preface to *Getting Married*, part II, 191–208, at 207.
70. Freddie Rokem, *Theatrical Space in Ibsen, Chekhov, and Strindberg: Public Forms of Privacy* (Ann Arbor, MI: UMI Research Press, 1986), 57.
71. Una Chaudhuri, "Private Parts: Sex, Class, and Stage Space in *Miss Julie*," *Theatre Journal* 45, no. 3 (1993): 317–32, at 327. See also Chaudhuri, *Staging Place: The Geography of Modern Drama* (Ann Arbor: University of Michigan, 1995), 27–44.
72. John Greenway, "Strindberg and Suggestion in *Miss Julie*," *South Atlantic Review* 51 (1986): 21–34.
73. Sprinchorn, *Strindberg as Dramatist*, 37.
74. Magnus Johansson, "Letter from Stockholm," *International Journal of Psychoanalysis* 96 (2015): 257–72, at 257.
75. Michael Robinson, *Strindberg and Autobiography* (London: Norvik Press, 1986), 24. See also August Strindberg, "Battle of the Brains," in *August Strindberg: Selected Essays*, ed. and trans. Michael Robinson (Cambridge: Cambridge University Press, 1996), 25–46, at 25.
76. Johansson, "Letter from Stockholm," 257.
77. Törnqvist and Jacobs, *Strindberg's "Miss Julie*," 25.
78. Ross Shideler, *Questioning the Father: From Darwin to Zola, Ibsen, Strindberg, and Hardy* (Stanford, CA: Stanford University Press, 2000).
79. Marx, *Capital*, 1:873. Ben Fowkes translates the phrase as "primitive accumulation," but Rosalind Morris prefers "originary." See Rosalind C. Morris, "Ursprüngliche Akkumulation: The Secret of an Originary Mistranslation" *boundary 2* 43, no. 3 (2016): 29–77.
80. For the theme of guilt in *Creditors*, see Stenport, "Money Metaphors and Rhetoric of Resource Depletion."
81. Andrew Sofer, *The Stage Life of Props* (Ann Arbor: University of Michigan Press, 2003), 11.
82. Strindberg, preface to *Miss Julie*, 71. Strindberg would change his tune after the 1890s when he moved away from naturalism toward expressionism. In an interview in *Svenska Dagbladet* (January 21, 1899), Strindberg embraces

modernism and painted sets: "All these old-fashioned theatrical rags must go! I want only a painted background representing a room, a forest, or whatever it may be, or perhaps a background could be produced by a shadow picture on glass and projected onto a white sheet." Quoted in Frederick J. Marker and Lise-Lone Marker, "Strindberg in the Theatre," in *The Cambridge Companion to August Strindberg*, ed. Michael Robinson (New York: Cambridge University Press, 2010), 135–48, at 136.

83. Prideaux, *Strindberg*, 161.

84. Marx, *Capital*, 1:126.

85. Andrew Watkins, "Reclaiming *Miss Julie*: On Interpreting Classic Drama," *Howlround*, May 17, 2017, https://howlround.com/reclaiming-miss-julie.

86. Ben Brantley, "Seduction by Class Conflict," *New York Times*, October 22, 2009, https://www.nytimes.com/2009/10/23/theater/reviews/23after.html.

87. Hilton Als, "Yaël Farber's *Mies Julie*," *New Yorker*, November 20, 2012, https://www.newyorker.com/culture/culture-desk/yael-farbers-mies-julie.

88. Brantley, "Seduction by Class Conflict"; and Holly L. Derr, "*Miss Julie* and the Timeless Art of Slut-Shaming," *Ms. Magazine*, August 5, 2013, https://msmagazine.com/2013/05/08/miss-julie-and-the-timeless-art-of-slut-shaming/.

89. Yaël Farber, *Mies Julie, Restitutions of Body and Soil since the Bantu Land Act No. 27 of 1913 and the Immorality Act No. 5 of 1927*, based on August Strindberg's *Miss Julie* (London: Oberon Books, 2012), 9.

90. While the conflict between Jean and Julie in Carrie Cracknell's 2018 version fell flat, the show successfully showed how racism underpinned the relationship between Julie and Kristina, played by Thalissa Teixeira. Kristina is a much more developed character in Polly Stenham's *Julie* than she is in Strindberg's original. By casting an actor of color in the role of Kristina, this production was arguably more about the dynamics between the women than it was between Jean and Julie.

91. Marx, *Capital*, 1:873.

92. Stephanie Coontz, *Marriage, a History: From Obedience to Intimacy, or How Love Conquered Marriage* (New York: Viking, 2005), 16.

93. Coontz, *Marriage, a History*, 15, 150.

94. Lawrence Stone, *The Family, Sex and Marriage in England, 1500–1800* (New York: Harper & Row, 1977), 446–47.

95. Ian Watt, *The Rise of the Novel: Studies in Defoe, Richardson and Fielding* (1957), with an afterword by W. B. Carnochan (Berkeley: University of California Press, 2001), 148–49.

96. For a critique of the novel studies' focus on the marriage plot, see Kelly Hager, *Dickens and the Rise of Divorce: The Failed-Married Plot and the Novel Tradition* (Burlington, VT: Ashgate, 2010).

97. Watt, *The Rise of the Novel*, 62.

98. Armstrong, *Desire and Domestic Fiction*, 5.

99. Armstrong, *Desire and Domestic Fiction*, 41.

100. Armstrong, *Desire and Domestic Fiction*, 3. Throughout *Desire and Domestic Fiction*, Armstrong prefers to use the term "middle-class" instead of "bourgeois." This makes sense given the focus on British literature. As

Ridout points out, the term "middle-class" in English does not suggest, as the term "bourgeois" does in Marx, the "inevitability of class conflict"; rather, it "foster[s] an understanding of social relations in which progress toward social harmony is achieved by the emergence and eventual rise of a 'middle class' capable of mediating or moderating class conflict between the classes it imagines as above it and beneath it" (Ridout, *Scenes from Bourgeois Life*, 27). I will be using "bourgeois," as it appears in the European discourse of the nineteenth century and, in particular, in the way that it functions in Marx and Engels. As Ridout elaborates, "For Marx and Engels, the bourgeoisie is the class that owns the means of production, and the proletariat is the class that does the actual production" (Ridout, *Scenes from Bourgeois Life*, 27).

101. Armstrong, *Desire and Domestic Fiction*, 8.

102. Although patriarchy is older than capitalism and serves as a foundation for both nineteenth-century and present-day capitalism, there is a possibility that capitalism could survive even if patriarchy were overcome. For example, I would argue, that it is possible to conceive a world ruled by capitalist matriarchy. The dismantling of patriarchy alone does not guarantee the automatic overcoming of capitalism even though the two systems mutually reinforce one another in our present-day historical reality.

103. Armstrong, *Desire and Domestic Fiction*, 49.

104. Armstrong, *Desire and Domestic Fiction*, 51.

105. Armstrong, *Desire and Domestic Fiction*, 8, 51. Armstrong echoes Ian Watt's point that "in most novels the courtship leads to a rise in the social status not of the hero but of the heroine" (Watt, *The Rise of the Novel*, 163) and John Cawelti's argument that a "chaste and marriageable young woman . . . symbolized the cultural and social aspirations of the mobile middle classes." See John G. Cawelti, *Adventure, Mystery and Romance: Formula Stories as Art and Popular Culture* (Chicago: University of Chicago Press, 1976), 101–2. This leads Armstrong to make her famous claim that "the modern individual was first and foremost a woman" (*Desire and Domestic Fiction*, 8). However, Armstrong suggests that already by the mid-nineteenth century, when the middle class has ascended and won, female power begins to appear in a negative light. Thus, we see a lot of anxiety about women representing "an emergent form of power" at the end of *Jane Eyre* and *Vanity Fair*, for example (56).

106. See Lisa Hopkins, *The Shakespearean Marriage: Merry Wives and Heavy Husbands* (New York: Palgrave Macmillan, 1998), 17–18.

107. Anton Chekhov, *Chaika*, in *Polnoe sobranie sochinenii i pisem v tridtsati tomah*, vol. 13 (Moscow: Nauka, 1978), 3–60, at 10.

108. Citing the importance of the dowry, which newspapers began to aggressively advertise, Watt notes that "marriage became a much more commercial matter in the eighteenth century" (*The Rise of the Novel*, 142). And Moretti describes the marriage market as "a mechanism that crystallized in the course of the eighteenth century, which demands of human beings (and especially of women) a new mobility." See Franco Moretti, *Atlas of the European Novel, 1800–1900* (New York: Verso, 1998), 15.

109. Watt, *The Rise of the Novel*, 139.

110. Eva Illouz, *Why Love Hurts: A Sociological Explanation* (Malden, MA: Polity, 2012), 10.

111. Bourdieu, "The Forms of Capital," 255n2.

112. It bears noting that the meaning of the word "prostitute" was quite loose in the nineteenth century. It referred not only to a person we would today call a sex worker but also to a woman who chose to live with a man or have children outside marriage. It could also paradoxically refer to someone who had sex not for any economic reason but solely for pleasure. See Judith Flanders, "Prostitution," British Library, May 15, 2014, https://www.bl.uk/romantics-and-victorians/articles/prostitution. See also Judith Flanders, *The Victorian City: Everyday Life in Dickens' London* (London: Atlantic Books, 2012), 393–424.

113. For more on the different types of prostitute narratives see Brad Kent, "Eighteenth-Century Literary Precursors of *Mrs. Warren's Profession*," *University of Toronto Quarterly* 81, no. 2 (2012): 187–207.

114. Kent, "Eighteenth-Century Literary Precursors of *Mrs. Warren's Profession*," 191.

115. "The Parisian Stage," *The Nation* 16 (January 9, 1873), reprinted in Henry James, *Henry James: Essays on Art and Drama*, ed. Peter Rawlings (Aldershot, UK: Scholar Press, 1996), 41–42; letter to the editor, *Dramatic Review*, June 27, 1885, reprinted in Bernard F. Dukore, ed., *The Drama Observed: 1880–1895* (University Park: Pennsylvania State University Press, 1993), 33–34, quoted in Sos Eltis, "The Fallen Woman on Stage: Maidens, Magdalens, and the Emancipated Female," in *The Cambridge Companion to Victorian and Edwardian Theatre*, ed. Kerry Powell (Cambridge: Cambridge University Press, 2004), 222–36, at 222. For more onstage representations on "fallen womanhood" (2), see Sos Eltis, *Acts of Desire: Women and Sex on Stage 1800–1930* (New York: Oxford University Press, 2013).

116. Elsie B. Michie, *The Vulgar Question of Money: Heiresses, Materialism, and the Novel of Manners from Jane Austen to Henry James* (Baltimore: Johns Hopkins University Press, 2011), 9.

117. Louis Menand, "How to Misread Jane Austen," *New Yorker*, September 28, 2020, https://www.newyorker.com/magazine/2020/10/05/how-to-misread-jane-austen. See also Trisha Urmi Banerjee, "Austen Equilibrium," *Representations* 143, no. 1 (2018): 63–90.

118. Edward Bulwer-Lytton, *Money* (London, 1840), ProQuest, https://www.proquest.com/docview/2138574743/Z000060889/AFE651A6D40F4545PQ/1?accountid=12768, accessed April 10, 2020, 4.

119. Bruce Weber, "Revelations about Greed, as Seen through 160 Years of Dust," *New York Times*, October 17, 2000, https://www.nytimes.com/2000/10/17/theater/theater-review-revelations-about-greed-as-seen-through-160-years-of-dust.html.

120. Michael Wood, "What Henry Knew," *London Review of Books* 25, no. 24, December 18, 2003, https://www.lrb.co.uk/the-paper/v25/n24/michael-wood/what-henry-knew.

121. Engels, *The Origin of the Family*, 742.

122. Wollstonecraft, *A Vindication of the Rights of Woman*, 229. In 1727, Daniel Defoe writes: "He or She who, with that slight and superficial Affection, Ventures into the Matrimonial Vow, are to me little more than legal Prostitutes." Daniel Defoe, *Conjugal Lewdness: or, Matrimonial Whoredom* (Gainesville: Scholars' Facsimiles and Reprints, 1967), 102.

123. Defoe, *Conjugal Lewdness*, 102.
124. Simmel, *The Philosophy of Money*, 405–6.
125. Simmel, *The Philosophy of Money*, 405.
126. Jack Goody, *Production and Reproduction: A Comparative Study of the Domestic Domain* (Cambridge: Cambridge University Press, 1976), 8.
127. Simmel, *The Philosophy of Money*, 406.
128. Simmel, *The Philosophy of Money*, 406.
129. Engels, *The Origin of the Family*, 745.
130. Simmel, *The Philosophy of Money*, 407.
131. Engels, *The Origin of the Family*, 739.
132. Friedrich Engels, preface to the 4th ed. (1891), in *The Origin of the Family, Private Property, and the State*, with an introduction by Evelyn Reed (New York: Pathfinder, 2000), 31–44, at 35.
133. August Bebel, *Woman and Socialism* (1879; repr., New York: Socialist Literature, 1910), 33, quoted in Gagnier, *The Insatiability of Human Wants*, 68.
134. Shaw, *Getting Married*, 17.
135. Theodor Adorno, *Minima Moralia: Reflections on a Damaged Life* (1951), trans. E. F. N. Jephcott (New York: Verso, 2005), 31.
136. Engels, *The Origin of the Family*, 739.
137. Strindberg, "Love and the Price of Grain," in *Getting Married*, 83–94.
138. Strindberg, "Just to Be Married," in *Getting Married*, 95–102, at 102.
139. Strindberg, *Small Catechism for the Underclass*, Kindle locations 198, 230.
140. Strindberg, preface to *Getting Married*, part I, 50.
141. Engels, *The Origin of the Family*, 750–51.
142. Dolan, *Utopia in Performance*, 5.
143. The expression "stock ticker play" appears in a review of *A Fool of Fortune* in the *New York Times*, March 26, 1893.
144. Garrett Eisler, "'I Am a Mere Business Machine': The Commodification of the Heart in Bronson Howard's *The Henrietta*," *Journal of American Drama and Theatre* 19, no. 2 (2007): 37–60, at 48. "The more profound joke, however, is how easily everyone in the play conflates stock speculation and sexual desire."
145. Bronson C. Howard, *Henrietta*, ed. Allan G. Halline (London, 1901), https://archive.org/details/henriettacomedyi00howa, accessed April 12, 2020, 1–118, at 32.
146. For more on Martha Morton, see Rosemary Gipson, "Martha Morton: America's First Professional Woman Playwright," *Theatre Survey* 23 (1982): 213–22.
147. To highlight the parallels between courtship and speculation, *A Fool of Fortune* features a scene in which the Count asks Jenny's father for "a pointer," meaning a tip about the market, but the father mistakenly believes that the young man is asking him information about his oldest daughter's feelings. The double entendres take off because the French word for stock—*action*—is feminine. See Martha Morton, *A Fool for Fortune* (1896), typescript, Billy Rose Theatre Division, New York Public Library for the Performing Arts, 25.

148. See Hannah Freed-Thall, "Speculative Modernism: Proust and the Stock Market," *Modernist Cultures* 12, no. 2 (2017): 153–72, at 159, 164, 167.

149. Émile Zola, *L'Argent* (*Les Rougon-Macquart*), vol. 18 (Uzès, France: Tite Fée, 2017), 122. Translations from the French are my own unless otherwise noted. Subsequent page references are given in the text.

150. David Bennett, *The Currency of Desire: Libidinal Economy, Psychoanalysis and Sexual Revolution* (London: Lawrence & Wishart, 2016), 1–43, at 3.

151. Bennett, *The Currency of Desire*, 1, 2n1. See also David W. Krueger, ed., *The Last Taboo: Money as Symbol and Reality in Psychotherapy and Psychoanalysis* (New York: Brunner and Mazel, 1986); Richard Trachtman, "The Money Taboo: Its Effects in Everyday Life and in the Practice of Psychotherapy," *Clinical Social Work Journal* 27 (1999): 275–88; Del Loewenthal, "Editorial: Sex, Shit, Money and Marxism—the Continued Demise of the 'Third Way,'" *European Journal of Psychotherapy and Counseling* 11, no. 4 (2009): 349–53; and David Bennett, ed., *Loaded Subjects: Psychoanalysis, Money and the Global Financial Crisis* (London: Lawrence & Wishart, 2012), 7–33.

152. Sigmund Freud, *Inhibitions, Symptoms and Anxiety*, 3rd ed., trans. Alix Strachey, rev. and ed. James Strachey, with a biographical introduction by Peter Gay (New York: W. W. Norton, 1989), 7.

153. Sigmund Freud, *The Interpretation of Dreams*, trans. Joyce Crick, with introduction and notes by Ritchie Robertson (New York: Oxford University Press, 1999), 365–66.

154. Bennett, *The Currency of Desire*, 2.

155. Peggy Phelan, *Unmarked: The Politics of Performance* (New York: Routledge, 1993), 148.

156. One of the most expensive contemporary artists today, Tino Seghal (a one-time student of political economy), is also one of world's most ephemeral, specializing in "constructed situations" and refusing to produce any more objects in a world where there is already "too much stuff." Nevertheless, Seghal's focus on the impermanence of performance and the alleged immateriality of social interaction (while continuing to earn astronomical figures in the art world) perversely echoes the way that financialization creates values out of thin air. See Lauren Collins, "The Question Artist," *New Yorker*, July 30, 2012, https://www.newyorker.com/magazine/2012/08/06/the-question-artist.

157. Sigmund Freud, "Creative Writers and Day-Dreaming," in *The Freud Reader*, ed. Peter Gay (New York: W. W. Norton, 1989), 436–43, at 439.

158. Lawrence Birken, *Consuming Desire: Sexual Science and the Emergence of a Culture of Abundance 1871–1914* (Ithaca, NY: Cornell University Press, 1988), 32.

159. Michel Foucault, *History of Sexuality*, vol. 1: *An Introduction*, trans. Robert Hurley (New York: Vintage, 1990), 5.

160. Foucault, *History of Sexuality*, 8.
161. Foucault, *History of Sexuality*, 6.
162. Foucault, *History of Sexuality*, 4.
163. Marx, *Capital*, 1:781.

164. Karl Marx, *Economic and Philosophic Manuscripts of 1844*, in *The Marx-Engels Reader*, 66–125, at 103.
165. Marx, *Economic and Philosophic Manuscripts of 1844*, 7n82.
166. Shell, *The Economy of Literature*, 11.
167. Edward Thornton, "Deleuze and Guattari's Absent Analysis of Patriarchy," *Hypatia: A Journal of Feminist Philosophy* 34, no. 2 (2019): 348–68. For examples of feminist critiques of the interpenetration of patriarchy and capitalism, see Carole Pateman, *The Sexual Contract* (Stanford, CA: Stanford University Press, 1988); and Silvia Federici, *Caliban and the Witch: Women, the Body and Primitive Accumulation* (New York: Autonomedia, 2004).
168. Joseph Lenz, "Base Trade: Theater as Prostitution," *ELH* 60, no. 4 (1993): 833–55, at 836.
169. Julie A. Cassiday, "The Rise of the Actress in Early Nineteenth-Century Russia," in *Women in Nineteenth-Century Russia: Lives and Culture*, ed. Wendy Rosslyn and Alessandra Tosi (Cambridge, MA: Open Book, 2012), 137–59, at 139. See also Worthen, *Modern Drama and the Rhetoric of Theater*, 40. Worthen too describes acting in the nineteenth century as "a profession" where "an oppressed female class" performed for "the entertainment and stimulation of male patrons" (40).
170. *The New Swell's Night Guide* (London, 1847). See Flanders, "Prostitution."
171. Sharon Marcus, *The Drama of Celebrity* (Princeton, NJ: Princeton University Press, 2019), 9–18.
172. Davis, *Actresses as Working Women*, 69.
173. Quoted in Sonja Lorich, *The Unwomanly Woman in Bernard Shaw's Drama and Her Social and Political Background* (Uppsala: Uppsala Universitet, 1973), 53.
174. G. Bernard Shaw, "The Case for Equality," 11, address delivered on May 1, 1913, published by National Liberal Club Political and Economic Circle (London) in *Transactions* (1913), 85, reprinted in *The Socialism of Shaw*, ed. with introduction by James Fuchs (New York: Vanguard, 1926), 85, quoted in George J. Stigler, "Bernard Shaw, Sidney Webb, and the Theory of Fabian Socialism," *Proceedings of the American Philosophical Society* 103, no. 3 (1959): 469–75, at 469.
175. Quoted in E. E. Stokes Jr., "Bernard Shaw and Economics," *Southwestern Social Science Quarterly* 39, no. 3 (1958): 242–48, at 242.
176. Bernard F. Dukore, *Shaw's Theater* (Gainesville: University Press of Florida, 2000), 131.
177. James Alexander, *Shaw's Controversial Socialism* (Gainesville: University Press of Florida, 2009); Charles A. Carpenter, *Bernard Shaw as Artist-Fabian* (Gainesville: University Press of Florida, 2009); Davis, *George Bernard Shaw and the Socialist Theatre*; Judith Evans, *The Politics and Plays of Bernard Shaw* (Jefferson, NC: McFarland, 2003); Harry Morrison, *The Socialism of Bernard Shaw* (Jefferson, NC: McFarland, 1989); Nelson O'Ceallaigh Ritschel, *Shaw, Synge, Connolly, and Socialist Provocation* (Gainesville: University Press of Florida, 2011). See also "Shaw and Money," ed. Audrey Mcnamara and Nelson O'Ceallaigh Ritschel, special issue, *Shaw: The Journal of Bernard Shaw Studies* 36, no. 1 (2016): 1–185.

178. David Ricardo, *On the Principles of Political Economy and Taxation* (1817; repr., New York: Prometheus Books, 1996), 45.

179. David Ricci, "Fabian Socialism: A Theory of Rent as Exploitation," *Journal of British Studies* 9, no. 1 (1969): 105–21, at 106.

180. Shaw writes: "Spare money is capital; capital is spare money and nothing else. And, accordingly, you see your landed class becomes not only a landed class, but a capitalist class." Bernard Shaw, "Bernard Shaw on Capital and Labor," *New York American*, December 20, 1914, in "Six Fabian Lectures on Redistribution of Income," *Shaw: The Journal of Bernard Shaw Studies* 36, no. 1 (2016): 10–52, at 38.

181. Alexander, *Shaw's Controversial Socialism*, 220.

182. Alexander, *Shaw's Controversial Socialism*, 6, 7.

183. Mikhail Bakhtin, *The Dialogic Imagination: Four Essays*, ed. Michael Holquist, trans. Caryl Emerson and Michael Holquist (Austin: University of Texas Press, 1981), 12, 45–50.

184. Puchner, *The Drama of Ideas*, 124.

185. Bakhtin, *The Dialogic Imagination*, 12.

186. Bakhtin, *The Dialogic Imagination*, 262.

187. Bakhtin, *The Dialogic Imagination*, 300.

188. Shaw's *The Millionairess* (1936), for example, has two endings: one written for "capitalist countries" and another one—for Soviet Russia and "countries with Communist sympathies." In the first version, Epifania marries an Egyptian doctor, who at the beginning of the play thought he could resist her tainted money. In the "Communist" version, Epifania announces her travel plans to Russia, asserting that before the end of the year she will end up high up "in the Politbureau" and "in a thousand years from now holy Russia shall again have a patron saint, and her name shall be Saint Epifania" (319–20). Bernard Shaw, *The Millionairess*, in *Plays Extravagant* (New York: Penguin, 1981), 213–320.

189. Lorich, *The Unwomanly Woman*, 53.

190. Davis, *George Bernard Shaw and the Socialist Theatre*, 49.

191. Germaine Greer, "A Whore in Every Home," in *Fabian Feminist: Bernard Shaw and Woman*, ed. Rodelle Weintraub (University Park: Pennsylvania State University Press, 1977), 163–66, at 166.

192. Bernard Shaw, preface to *Mrs. Warren's Profession*, in *Plays Unpleasant*, 181–212, at 181.

193. On the differences between the libertine and the reform narratives of the prostitute, see Kent, "Eighteenth-Century Literary Precursors of *Mrs. Warren's Profession*," 191.

194. In his early work, Shaw sought to "present a vision of capitalist society in which all money was tainted, in which all hands that touched money received its taint, in which the pernicious alternatives were to receive the taint or perish." Martin Meisel, *Shaw and the Nineteenth-Century Theater* (Princeton, NJ: Princeton University Press, 1963), 162.

195. Greer, "A Whore in Every Home," 166.

196. Shaw, preface to *Major Barbara*, 22.

197. Brian F. Tyson, "Shaw among the Actors: Theatrical Additions to *Plays Unpleasant*," *Modern Drama* 14 (1971–72): 264–75, at 274.

198. This criticism of interest-bearing capital and the comparison of it to incest goes back at least to Aristotle, who in his *Politics* condemns the practice of usury: "The trade of the petty usurer is hated with most reason: it makes a profit from currency itself, instead of making it from the process which currency was meant to serve. Currency came into existence merely as a means of exchange; usury tries to make it increase. This is the reason why it got its name; for as the offspring resembles its parent, so the interest (*tokos*) bred by money is like the principal which breeds it, and it many be called 'currency the son of currency.' Hence we can understand why, of all modes of acquisition, usury is the most unnatural." According to Aristotle, money should remain barren and used only in exchange, because when it produces "offspring" it becomes a narcissistic and incestuous process. Aristotle's metaphor also anticipates the process of cloning. See Aristotle, *Politics*, trans. Ernest Barker, rev. and with introduction and notes R. F. Stalley (New York: Oxford University Press, 1995), 30. The "Greek word for 'interest,' *tokos*, has the primary meaning of 'breed' or 'offspring' " (328, f. 1258b).

199. Roger Munting, *An Economic and Social History of Gambling in Britain and the USA* (Manchester: Manchester University Press, 1996), 91.

200. Moretti, "The Grey Area," 124.

201. Munting, *An Economic and Social History of Gambling*, 92.

202. J. Ellen Gainor, *Shaw's Daughters: Dramatic and Narrative Constructions of Gender* (Ann Arbor: University of Michigan Press, 1991), 39.

203. Davis, *George Bernard Shaw and the Socialist Theatre*, 47.

204. Kristina Brooks, "New Woman, Fallen Woman: The Crisis of Reputation in Turn-of-the-Century Novels by Pauline Hopkins and Edith Wharton," *Legacy* 13, no. 2 (1996): 91–112.

205. Scandinavian scholarship on Victoria Benedictsson is extensive. One of the most important studies is Jette Lundbo Levy, *Dobbeltblikket: Om at beskrive kvinder. Ideologi og aestetik I Victoria Benedictssons forfatterskab* (Copenhagen: Tiderne skifter, 1980). For the most recent biography, see Birgitta Holm, *Victoria Benedictsson* (Stockholm: Natur och Kultur, 2007).

206. Victoria Benedictsson, *Money*, trans. and with afterword by Sarah Death (Norwich, UK: Norvik Press, 1999). Page references are given in the text.

207. Sarah Death, Translator's Afterword to Benedictsson, *Money*, 179–86, at 183.

208. Prideaux, *Strindberg*, 5.

209. Stenport, "The Sexonomics of *Et dukkehjem*," 351: "The many mentions of actual money in Act I give way by the end of Act III to vague and abstract references. Money is no longer a straight-forward referent. Instead it becomes an all-pervasive social force."

210. Death, Translator's Afterword to Benedictsson, *Money*, 181.

211. Victoria Benedictsson, *The Enchantment*, in a new version by Clare Bayley from a literal translation by Ben Anderman (London: Nick Hern Books, 2007). Page references are given in the text.

212. Even as Michael Billington describes Benedictsson's play "extraordinary" and Clare Bayley's version "a major act of reclamation," he still describes *The Enchantment* as "anticipat[ing] Strindberg's *Miss Julie* and Ibsen's *Hedda Gabler*" and chronicling "Benedictsson's tragic affair with the

Danish critic Georg Brandes." Michael Billington, review of *The Enchantment*, *The Guardian*, August 2, 2007, https://www.theguardian.com/stage/2007/aug/02/theatre1. Similarly, Sarah Hemming calls the play "a thinly disguised account of the treatment she received at the hands of Danish critic Georg Brandes." Sarah Hemming, review of *The Enchantment*, *Financial Times*, August 2, 2007, https://www.ft.com/content/28206dc6-4114-11dc-8f37-0000779fd2ac.

213. In her review, Helen Shaw writes: "The playwright allegedly inspired both Ibsen's *Hedda Gabler* and Strindberg's *Miss Julie*, which reads today almost as fetish drama. Benedictsson may have written it because she lived it, but male playwrights wanted to write about her, too." Helen Shaw, "A Disappointingly Muted Mounting of Victoria Benedictsson's *The Enchantment*," *Village Voice*, July 12, 2017, https://www.villagevoice.com/2017/07/12/a-disappointingly-muted-mounting-of-victoria-benedictssons-the-enchantment/. Ran Xia notes that "the different stereotyped gender roles of men and women are constantly repeated and reinforced in the play, however not in a way that serves as commentary." Ran Xia, "*The Enchantment*," *Theatre Is Easy*, July 8, 2017, http://www.theasy.com/Reviews/2017/E/enchantment.php. Darryl Reilly describes *The Enchantment* as a "'lost' play by the relatively obscure Swedish author Victoria Benedictsson" and argues that the production's "absence of depth and tension gives it the sense of a pseudo-Chekhov work nicely performed at an acting conservatory's auditorium." Darryl Reilly, "*The Enchantment*," *Theater Scene*, July 8, 2017, http://www.theaterscene.net/plays/offbway-plays/the-enchantment/darryl-reilly/.

214. Tracy C. Davis and Ellen Donkin, eds., *Women and Playwriting in Nineteenth-Century Britain* (Cambridge: Cambridge University Press, 1999), 3.

215. Gilman, *Women and Economics*, 23.

Chapter 3

1. "The Great Russian Bank Swindle," *The Nation*, April 30, 1885, 357–58, at 357.

2. A recent exception to this is Michael C. Finke, *Freedom from Violence and Lies: Anton Chekhov's Life and Writings* (London: Reaktion Books, 2021), esp. 11–16. Finke discusses all the ways that Chekhov's early prose is already sophisticated.

3. The beginnings of Russian modernism have often been traced to the symbolist movement. As a consequence, Chekhov, whose stories are generally written in the realist mode and whose plays evoke the influence of Belgian symbolist writer Maurice Maeterlinck, is often considered an intermediary between realism and modernism. Yet Chekhov anticipates several recent trends in today's modernist studies: his oeuvre already explores market culture and challenges the autonomy of art. If, as Toril Moi has shown in her seminal study of Henrik Ibsen, "the true aesthetic antithesis of modernism is not realism, but idealism," then Chekhov, whose works critique idealism in general and the myth of artistic autonomy in particular, should, along with Ibsen, be rethought as a key figure in modernism. See Moi, *Henrik Ibsen and the Birth of Modernism*, 5. For more on the taxonomy of Russian modernism,

see Jonathan Stone, *The Institutions of Russian Modernism: Conceptualizing, Publishing, and Reading Symbolism* (Evanston, IL: Northwestern University Press, 2017); and Harsha Ram, "Russia," in *The Cambridge Companion to European Modernism*, ed. Pericles Lewis (New York: Cambridge University Press, 2011), 113–35.

4. Terry Eagleton, *Marxism and Literary Criticism* (1976), with a new preface by the author (New York: Routledge, 2002), 3.

5. Séamus Stiofan O'Driscoll, "Invisible Forces: Capitalism and the Russian Literary Imagination (1855–1881)" (PhD diss., Harvard University, 2005), 76.

6. Hannah Freed-Thall, "'Prestige of a Momentary Diamond': Economies of Distinction in Proust," *New Literary History* 43, no. 1 (2012): 159–78, and "Speculative Modernism: Proust and the Stock Market," *Modernist Cultures* 12, no. 2 (2017): 153–72; Christopher Kempf, "'Addicted to the Lubric a Little': Spectacle, Speculation, and the Language of Flow in *Ulysses*," *Modernism/modernity* 24, no. 1 (2017): 23–43; Marsh, "The Cosmopolitan Coin"; Carey James Mickalites, *Modernism and Market Fantasy: British Fictions of Capital, 1910–1939* (New York: Palgrave Macmillan, 2012); Jennifer Wicke, "Appreciation, Depreciation: Modernism's Speculative Bubble," *Modernism/modernity* 8, no. 3 (September 2001): 389–403, and *Advertising Fictions: Literature, Advertisement, and Social Reading* (New York: Columbia University Press, 1988).

7. For events that "cannot come to pass," see Zinovy Paperny, "'Vopreki vsem pravilam . . . ,'" in *Pyesy i vodevili Chekhova* (Moscow: Iskusstvo, 1982), 236–46, quoted in Paperny, "Vaudevilles," in *Anton Chekhov's Selected Plays*, trans. and ed. Laurence Senelick (New York: W. W. Norton, 2005), 516–24, at 522. For Chekhov's attention to the accidental and the insignificant, see Cathy Popkin, "Anton Chekhov: Reinventing Events," in *The Pragmatics of Insignificance: Chekhov, Zoshchenko, Gogol* (Stanford, CA: Stanford University Press, 1993), 17–51.

8. Laurence Senelick, "Money in Chekhov's Plays," *Studies in Theater and Performance* 29, no. 3 (2009): 327–37, at 327. Senelick offers an excellent overview of Chekhov's interest in the subject of money from his early playwriting to his mature dramatic works. In recent years, a few scholars have looked at Chekhov's oeuvre in the context of Russia's nascent capitalism. See Holmgren, *Rewriting Capitalism*, 42–53; Gary Saul Morson, "Chekhov's Enlightenment," *New Criterion*, November 2012, 20–27; Ridout, *Passionate Amateurs*, 33–57; Vadim Shneyder, "Chekhov and the Naturalization of Capitalism," in *Russia's Capitalist Realism: Tolstoy, Dostoevsky, and Chekhov* (Evanston, IL: Northwestern University Press, 2020), 145–72. However, little attention has been paid to how Chekhov represents money and capital or how the capitalist economy helped shape his temporal aesthetics and dramatic style.

9. Laurence Senelick, General Introduction to *Anton Chekhov's Selected Plays*, xxvii–xl, at xxxiv.

10. Virginia Woolf, "Modern Fiction," in *The Essays of Virginia Woolf*, vol. 4, *1925–28*, ed. Andrew McNeille (London: Hogarth, 1984), 157–65, 163, 158.

11. Rogers, *Speculation*, 1–2, 7. Rogers elaborates: "Speculation provides the language and conceptualization by which we produce contingent

knowledge, ideas, abstractions, risks, and even money and material gains, all of which radically shape our individual and collective futures" (3).

12. Rogers, *Speculation*, 2–3.

13. Simmel, *The Philosophy of Money*, 252.

14. Sigmund Freud, "Creative Writers and Day-Dreaming," in *The Freud Reader*, ed. Peter Gay (New York: W. W. Norton, 1989), 436–43, at 439. Subsequent page references are given in the text. For more on Freud's use of economic language, see Bennett, *The Currency of Desire*, 1–43, esp. 23–30.

15. Simmel, *The Philosophy of Money*, 252.

16. Simmel, *The Philosophy of Money*, 252. For more on the role of prediction in modernism, see Lisi Schoenbach, *Pragmatic Modernism* (New York: Oxford University Press, 2011), 84–86.

17. For more on casino capitalism, see Susan Strange, *Casino Capitalism* (1986), with a new introduction by Matthew Watson (Manchester: Manchester University Press, 2016). Strange writes: "As in a casino, the world of high finance today offers the players a choice of games. Instead of roulette, blackjack, or poker, there is dealing to be done—the foreign exchange market and all its variations; or in bonds, government securities or shares. In all these markets you may place bets on the future by dealing forward and by buying or selling options and all sorts of other recondite financial inventions" (1).

18. Shneyder, *Russia's Capitalist Realism*, 156, 165, 163.

19. Donald Rayfield, *Anton Chekhov: A Life* (Evanston, IL: Northwestern University Press, 2000), 111.

20. Pavel V. Lizunov, "Russian Society and the Stock Exchange in the Late Nineteenth and Early Twentieth Centuries," *Russian Studies in History* 54, no. 2 (2015): 106–42.

21. Vladimir Lenin, *Imperialism: The Highest Stage of Capitalism, a Popular Outline* (New York: International Publishers, 1977), 46.

22. For more on the importance of the discourse of fraud to modernism, see Leonard Diepeveen, *Modernist Fraud: Hoax, Parody, Deception* (New York: Oxford University Press, 2019), esp. v–x; and Freed-Thall, "'Prestige of a Momentary Diamond,'" 160.

23. Anton Chekhov, "Delo Rykova i komp. (ot nashego korrespondenta)" ("Trial of Rykov and His Company [from our correspondent]") (1884), in *Polnoe sobranie sochinenii i pisem v tridtsati tomah*, vol. 16 (Moscow: Nauka, 1979), 179–219, at 182. Translations from Russian, for this and other works herein, are my own unless otherwise noted.

24. Chekhov, "Trial of Rykov," 187.

25. For historical examples, see Charles P. Kindleberger and Robert Z. Aliber, *Manias, Panics, and Crashes: A History of Financial Crises*, 6th ed. (New York: Palgrave Macmillan, 2011).

26. Yanis Varoufakis, *Talking to My Daughter about the Economy: or, How Capitalism Works—and How It Fails*, trans. Jacob Moe and Yanis Varoufakis (New York: Farrar, Straus and Giroux, 2013), 67.

27. Varoufakis, *Talking to My Daughter*, 67.

28. For more on this strategy of speculators, see Chancellor, *Devil Take the Hindmost*, 136.

29. R. L. Reid, "The Psychology of the Near Miss," *Journal of Gambling Behavior* 2 (1986): 32–39.

30. For more on the role of gambling in Dostoevsky, see Ian M. Helfant, *The High Stakes of Identity: Gambling in the Life and Literature of Nineteenth-Century Russia* (Evanston, IL: Northwestern University Press, 2002), 115–29.

31. Anton Chekhov, *Letters of Anton Chekhov to His Family and Friends: With Biographical Sketch*, trans. Constance Garnett (New York: Macmillan, 1920), 248.

32. Chekhov, *Letters of Anton Chekhov*, 249. By contrast, when investigating the prison conditions on the island of Sakhalin, Russia's most remote and notorious penal colony, Chekhov emphasized the nefarious aspects of gambling, comparing it to an "epidemic" that "has already taken control of all the prisons." Anton Chekhov, *Sakhalin Island* (1895), trans. Brian Reeve (Richmond, UK: Alma Classics, 2015), 284.

33. Paperny, "Vaudevilles," 522; Popkin, *The Pragmatics of Insignificance*, 40.

34. Paperny, "Vaudevilles," 524.

35. Ekaterina Meledina, "Genialny Rykov," *Sovershenno Sekretno*, October 1, 2006, https://www.sovsekretno.ru/articles/id/1650/.

36. Chekhov, "Trial of Rykov," 189.

37. Chekhov, "Trial of Rykov."

38. Marx, *Capital*, 3:573.

39. Marx, *Capital*, 3:572.

40. Boris N. Mironov, "Wages and Prices in Imperial Russia, 1703–1913," *Russian Review* 69 (January 2010): 47–72, at 69.

41. Meledina, "Genialny Rykov."

42. Chekhov, "Trial of Rykov," 200.

43. Chekhov, "Trial of Rykov," 188.

44. For more on the relationship between the law and performance, see Julie Stone Peters, "Legal Performance Good and Bad," *Law, Culture and the Humanities* 4 (2008): 179–200, at 181.

45. Chekhov, "Trial of Rykov," 179.

46. Chekhov, "Trial of Rykov," 180.

47. Chekhov, "Trial of Rykov," 211.

48. Chekhov, "Trial of Rykov," 183.

49. For more on the antitheatrical prejudice, see Barish, *The Antitheatrical Prejudice*.

50. Herbert J. Ellison, "Economic Modernization in Imperial Russia: Purposes and Achievements," *Journal of Economic History* 25, no. 4 (December 1965): 523–40, at 537.

51. Harriet Murav, *Russia's Legal Fictions* (Ann Arbor: University of Michigan Press, 1998), 60.

52. Murav, *Russia's Legal Fictions*, 77.

53. Quoted in Senelick, "Money in Chekhov's Plays," 332. Senelick notes that the 1884 spectacular failure of Skopin's bank "was a topic of conversation for years."

54. Chekhov, "Trial of Rykov," 185.

55. Anton Chekhov, *Svadba* (1889), in *Polnoe sobranie sochinenii i pisem v tridtsati tomah*, vol. 12 (Moscow: Nauka, 1978), 107–23, at 109.
56. Anton Chekhov, *Ivanov* (1887), in *Polnoe sobranie sochinenii i pisem v tridtsati tomah*, 12:5–76, at 24.
57. Andrey D. Ukhov, "Preferences toward Risk and Asset Prices: Evidence from Russian Lottery Bonds" (2005), Cornell University, SHA School site, http://scholarship.sha.cornell.edu/workingpapers/7, accessed May 15, 2019.
58. Stäheli, *Spectacular Speculation*, 3.
59. François R. Velde, "Lottery Loans in the Eighteenth Century" (working paper), Federal Reserve Bank of Chicago, May 12, 2018, https://doi.org/10.21033/wp-2018-07, 1–38, at 3.
60. Chancellor, *Devil Take the Hindmost*, xi.
61. Chancellor, *Devil Take the Hindmost*, ix.
62. Karl Marx, *The Eighteenth Brumaire of Louis Bonaparte* (1852), trans. Daniel de Leon (New York: International Publishers, 1994), 48. See Marx, *Capital*, 1:251n4.
63. Walter Benjamin citing Paul Lafargue, *Die Neue Zeit* 24, no. 1 (Stuttgart, 1906), 512, quoted in James F. Cosgrave, introduction to *The Sociology of Risk and Gambling Reader*, ed. Cosgrave (New York: Routledge, 2006), 1.
64. Alexander Chudakov, "Dr. Chekhov: A Biographical Essay (29 January 1860–15 July 1904)," in *The Cambridge Companion to Chekhov*, ed. Vera Gottlieb and Paul Allain (Cambridge: Cambridge University Press, 2000), 3–16, at 3.
65. Rayfield, *Anton Chekhov*, 20–21, 42, at 46.
66. Rayfield, *Anton Chekhov*, 407–8.
67. Galina Romanova, *Motiv deneg v russkoy literature xix veka* (Moscow: Flinta, 2006), 23.
68. Romanova, *Motiv deneg*, 24.
69. Helfant, *The High Stakes of Identity*, xv.
70. Helfant, *The High Stakes of Identity*.
71. "L'argent a émancipé l'écrivain, l'argent a créé les lettres modernes." Émile Zola, "L'argent dans la littérature," *Le messager de L'Europe*, March 1880, quoted in Pascal Bruckner, *The Wisdom of Money*, trans. Steven Rendall (Cambridge, MA: Harvard University Press, 2017), 12.
72. Holmgren, *Rewriting Capitalism*, xi.
73. James Wood, "What Chekhov Meant by Life," in *Serious Noticing: Selected Essays* (New York: Vintage, 2019), 34–48.
74. Simmel, *The Philosophy of Money*, 133–34.
75. Simmel, *The Philosophy of Money*, 138.
76. Mikhailovskii, "Ob otsakh i detiakh," 598, quoted in Popkin, *The Pragmatics of Insignificance*, 20.
77. Popkin, *The Pragmatics of Insignificance*, 50–51.
78. Moretti, "The Grey Area," 129.
79. Anton Chekhov, *Tri sestry* (1901), in *Polnoe sobranie sochinenii i pisem v tridtsati tomah*, 12:117–88, at 131–32. Subsequent page references are given in the text.
80. Varoufakis, *Talking to My Daughter*, 67.

81. Anton Chekhov, "Vyigryshny Bilet" (1887), in *Polnoe sobranie sochinenii i pisem v tridtsati tomah*, vol. 6 (Moscow: Nauka, 1976), 107–11, at 107. Subsequent page references are given in the text.

82. P. S. Karasev, "Obshchii obzor gazetnoy periodiki," in *Ocherki po istorii russkoy zhurnalistiki i kritiki: Vtoraia polovina XIX veka*, 2 vols. (Leningrad: Leningradsky gosudarstvenny universitet, 1965), 2:449.

83. Lizunov, "Russian Society and the Stock Exchange," 114–22.

84. "s solyonym ryzhikom ili s ukropnym ogurchikom"; "redku ot kotoroy pakhnet svezhey zemlyoy."

85. Varoufakis, *Talking to My Daughter*, 67.

86. Rogers, *Speculation*, 1.

87. Anton Chekhov, "Pari" (1889), in *Polnoe sobranie sochinenii i pisem v tridtsati tomah*, vol. 7 (Moscow: Nauka, 1977), 229–35. Subsequent page references are given in the text.

88. Varoufakis, *Talking to My Daughter*, 67.

89. Samuel Beckett, *Proust* (1930; repr., New York: Grove, 1970), 8.

90. Freud, "Creative Writers and Day-Dreaming," 443.

91. Anton Chekhov, *Yubilei* (1891), in *Polnoe sobranie sochinenii i pisem v tridtsati tomah*, 12:203–20, at 205.

92. A prototype of Merchutkina's character appears in an earlier short story by Chekhov titled "Defenseless Creature" (1887). See Vera Gottlieb, *Chekhov and the Vaudeville: A Study of Chekhov's One-Act Plays* (Cambridge: Cambridge University Press, 1982), 86.

93. Chekhov, "Trial of Rykov," 184.

94. Senelick, *Anton Chekhov's Selected Plays*, 411.

95. Dmitry Merezhkovsky, *O prichinakh upadka i o novykh techeniyakh sovremennoy russkoy literatury* (Saint Petersburg: Tipo-litografiia B. M. Vol'fa, 1893), 17, e-book, https://iiif.lib.harvard.edu/manifests/view/drs:46603171$1i, accessed May 15, 2019.

96. Merezhkovsky, *O prichinakh upadka*.

97. Chekhov, *Dyadya Vanya*, in *Polnoe sobranie sochinenii i pisem v tridtsati tomah*, 13:61–116, at 101. Subsequent page references are given in the text.

98. Anton Chekhov, *Chaika*, in *Polnoe sobranie sochinenii i pisem v tridtsati tomah*, 13:3–60, at 37. Subsequent page references are given in the text.

99. Trotsky, *Literature and Revolution*, 29.

100. Stephen C. Hutchings, *Russian Modernism: The Transfiguration of the Everyday* (Cambridge: Cambridge University Press, 1997), 83.

101. Gary Saul Morson, "Chekhov's Art of the Prosaic: Great Ideas and Dramatic Events," in *Approaches to Teaching Works of Anton Chekhov*, ed. Michael C. Finke and Michael Holquist (New York: Modern Language Association of America, 2016), 187–97. See also Morson, "Chekhov's Enlightenment."

102. S.v. "mortgage," *Oxford English Dictionary Online*, https://www.oed.com/dictionary/mortgage_n, accessed September 24, 2020.

103. Anton Chekhov, *Vishnyovy sad* (1904), in *Polnoe sobranie sochinenii i pisem v tridtsati tomah*, 13:195–254, at 251. Subsequent page references are given in the text.

104. Matthew Wagner, *Shakespeare, Theatre, and Time* (New York: Routledge, 2012), 13. See also John H. Muse, *Microdramas: Crucibles for Theater and Time* (Ann Arbor: University of Michigan Press, 2017), 8–11.

105. Senelick, *Anton Chekhov's Selected Plays*, 316. Senelick lists Pyotr Nevezhin's *Second Youth* (1883) as an example of the first scenario and Nikolai Solovyov's *Liquidation* (1883) as an example of the second. These were popular melodramas that Chekhov had seen.

106. Bourdieu, "The Forms of Capital," 252–53.

107. Osip Mandelstam, "O p'iese A. Chekhova 'Diadia Vania,'" *Sobranie sochinenii v chetyrekh tomakh* (Moscow: Terra-Terra, 1991), 4.521–22.

108. Moretti, "The Grey Area," 118.

109. Moretti, "The Grey Area," 117.

110. Anne Lounsbery, *Life Is Elsewhere: Symbolic Geography in the Russian Provinces, 1800–1917* (Ithaca, NY: Cornell University Press, 2019), 208.

111. Schumpeter, *Capitalism, Socialism, and Democracy*, 81–86.

112. Ridout, *Passionate Amateurs*, 34.

113. Georg Simmel, "Money in Modern Culture," in *Simmel on Culture: Selected Writings*, ed. David Frisby and Mike Featherstone (London: Sage, 1997), 243–55, at 252.

114. Laurence Senelick, introduction to *The Cherry Orchard*, in *Anton Chekhov's Selected Plays*, 315.

115. See, for example, Steve Dykes, "*Strange Fruit*, Chekhov's *The Cherry Orchard* in the Deep South," *Stanislavski Studies* 4, no. 2 (2016): 185–203.

116. For more on Theater Mitu's *House (or How to Lose an Orchard in 90 Minutes or Less)*, see https://theatermitu.org/works/house/, accessed April 9, 2020.

117. For more on the discourse about banks "gambling" with people's money, see Peter S. Goodman, "The Financial Crisis and America's Casino Culture," *New York Times*, September 19, 2009, https://www.nytimes.com/2009/09/20/weekinreview/20goodman.html; Charles K. Wilber, "The Casino Economy: How Wall Street Is Gambling with America's Financial Future," *America Magazine*, May 2, 2011, https://www.americamagazine.org/issue/775/article/casino-economy.

118. Romanova, *Motiv deneg*, 153.

119. Romanova, *Motiv deneg*.

120. Senelick, *Anton Chekhov's Selected Plays*, 316.

121. Lauren Berlant, *Cruel Optimism* (Durham, NC: Duke University Press, 2011), 1.

122. Rayfield, *Anton Chekhov*, 44.

123. Spencer Golub, *The Recurrence of Fate: Theatre and Memory in Twentieth-Century Russia* (Iowa City: University of Iowa Press, 1994), 28.

124. Golub, *The Recurrence of Fate*, 28.

125. Golub, *The Recurrence of Fate*, 27.

126. Jean Baudrillard, *For a Critique of the Political Economy of the Sign*, trans. and introduction by Charles Levin (Candor, NY: Telos, 1981), 116.

127. Anton Chekhov to Konstantin Alexeyev (Stanislavski), October 30, 1903, in *Anton Chekhov: A Life in Letters*, ed. Rosamund Bartlett, trans. Rosamund Bartlett and Anthony Phillips (New York: Penguin, 2004), 519–20.

128. Holmgren, *Rewriting Capitalism*, 49.
129. Hans Roger, *Russia in the Age of Modernisation and Revolution, 1881–1917* (London: Longman, 1983), 103.
130. Berlant, *Cruel Optimism*, 1.
131. Bourdieu, "The Forms of Capital," 241.
132. Bourdieu, "The Forms of Capital."

Chapter 4

1. Jamil Mahmud, "Back against the Wall," review of *The Weavers*, by Gerhart Hauptmann, trans. into Bangla by Isail Mohammad, dir. Ahmedul Kabir, *Daily Star* (Dhaka), May 28, 2010, http://archive.thedailystar.net/newDesign/news-details.php?nid=140296.
2. "Madame Critic," *New York Dramatic Mirror*, December 25, 1915 (clipping), Billy Rose Theater Division, New York Public Library for the Performing Arts.
3. Gerhart Hauptmann, *Die Weber* (1892), ed. Hans Schwab-Felisch (Berlin: Ullstein-Taschenbuch-Verlag, 2012), 6. Unless otherwise noted, translations from the original German are my own. Subsequent page references are given in the text.
4. Jean Chothia, "'The Triumph of the Supers': Hauptmann's *The Weavers* as Theatrical Event," *Nineteenth Century Theatre and Film* 34, no. 1 (2007): 45–68, at 46, 47.
5. John Osborne, *Gerhart Hauptmann and the Naturalist Drama*, 2nd ed. (Amsterdam: Harwood, 1998), 137.
6. Marvin Carlson, *The German Stage in the Nineteenth Century* (Metuchen, NJ: Scarecrow, 1972), 215.
7. Kirk Williams, "Anti-theatricality and the Limits of Naturalism," *Modern Drama* 4, no. 3 (2001): 284–99, at 293, 285.
8. Chothia, "'The Triumph of the Supers,'" 50.
9. Osborne, *Gerhart Hauptmann and the Naturalist Drama*, 139, 137.
10. Williams, "Anti-theatricality and the Limits of Naturalism," 292.
11. Jameson, *Brecht and Method*, 149.
12. Jameson, *Brecht and Method*, 150.
13. Jameson, *Brecht and Method*.
14. Jameson, *Brecht and Method*.
15. Elaine Scarry, *Resisting Representation* (New York: Oxford University Press, 1994), 65.
16. Scarry, *Resisting Representation*, 24n87.
17. Scarry, *Resisting Representation*, 65.
18. Karl Marx, "Wage Labor and Capital," in *The Marx-Engels Reader*, 203–17, at 204–5.
19. Jameson, *Brecht and Method*, 17n163.
20. Marx, "The Grundrisse," in *The Marx-Engels Reader*, 221–93, at 273.
21. Marx, *A Contribution to the Critique of Political Economy* (1859), trans. Maurice Dobb (New York: International, 1979), 27–28.
22. Marx, "Critical Marginal Notes on the Article 'The King of Prussia and Social Reform,'" in *The Marx-Engels Reader*, 125–32, at 128.
23. Marx, "Critical Marginal Notes," 129.

24. See Barrett H. Clark, "The Weavers," in *The Continental Drama of Today* (New York: Holt, 1914), 89–93; and Gerhard Schildberg-Schroth, *Gerhart Hauptmann: Die Weber (Gerhart Hauptmann: The Weavers)* (Frankfurt am Main: Moritz Diesterweg, 1992).
25. Marx, "Critical Marginal Notes," 128.
26. Chothia, "'The Triumph of the Supers,'" 49.
27. Georg Lukács, *History and Class Consciousness: Studies in Marxist Dialectics*, trans. Rodney Livingstone (1971; repr., Cambridge, MA: MIT Press, 1999), 198.
28. Lukács, *History and Class Consciousness*, 149.
29. Lukács, *History and Class Consciousness*, 172.
30. Lukács, *History and Class Consciousness*.
31. Osborne, *Gerhart Hauptmann and the Naturalist Drama*, 144.
32. Chothia, "'The Triumph of the Supers,'" 54.
33. Warren R. Maurer, *Understanding Gerhart Hauptmann* (Columbia: University of South Carolina Press, 1992), 49.
34. Max Weber, *The Protestant Ethic and the Spirit of Capitalism* (1930), trans. Talcott Parsons, with introduction by Anthony Giddens (New York: Routledge, 1992), 19.
35. Bernard Shaw, *Major Barbara* (1905), in *John Bull's Other Island and Major Barbara* (New York: Brentano's, 1907), 157–311, at 253.
36. Weber, *The Protestant Ethic and the Spirit of Capitalism*, 25.
37. Daniel T. Rodgers, *The Work Ethic in Industrial America, 1850–1920* (Chicago: University of Chicago Press, 1978), 14, quoted in Cindy Weinstein, *The Literature of Labor and the Labors of Literature: Allegory in Nineteenth-Century American Literature* (Cambridge: University of Cambridge Press, 1995), 20.
38. Fredric Jameson, *The Political Unconscious: Narrative as a Socially Symbolic Act* (1981; repr., London: Routledge, 2002), 225.
39. Jameson, *The Political Unconscious*, 202.
40. Quoted in Jameson, *The Political Unconscious*, 202; Joseph Conrad, *Lord Jim: A Romance* (Garden City, NY: Doubleday, 1920), 16.
41. Jameson, *The Political Unconscious*, 202.
42. Jameson, *The Political Unconscious*, 213–14.
43. Hauptmann, *Die Weber*, 5.
44. Franz Mehring, "On Hauptmann's *The Weavers*," trans. Edward Braun, *New Theatre Quarterly* 11, no. 42 (1995): 184–210, at 184.
45. Mehring, "On Hauptmann's *The Weavers*," 185.
46. Mehring, "On Hauptmann's *The Weaver*."
47. Mehring, "On Hauptmann's *The Weavers*," 188.
48. Osborne, *Gerhart Hauptmann and the Naturalist Drama*, 66.
49. Osborne, *Gerhart Hauptmann and the Naturalist Drama*, 72.
50. Cecil W. Davies, *Theatre for the People: The Story of the Volksbühne* (Manchester: Manchester University Press, 1977), 50.
51. Davies, *Theatre for the People*, 45.
52. Osborne, *Gerhart Hauptmann and the Naturalist Drama*, 136.
53. Osborne, *Gerhart Hauptmann and the Naturalist Drama*.
54. Davies, *Theatre for the People*, 50.

55. John C. Blankenagel, "Early Reception of *Die Weber* in the United States," *Modern Language Notes* 68, no. 5 (May 1953): 334–40, at 335.

56. Blankenagel, "Early Reception of *Die Weber* in the United States," 337; Christine Heiss, "Gerhart Hauptmanns *Weber* auf deutschen Bühnen der USA im neunzehnten Jahrhundert" (Gerhart Hauptmann's *The Weavers* on the German Stages of the United States in the Nineteenth Century), *German Quarterly* 59, no. 3 (1986): 361–74, at 368.

57. "Hauptmann's Grim Starvation Play," review of *The Weavers*, by Gerhart Hauptmann, New Deutsches Theatre, New York, *New York Times*, March 31, 1909, http://query.nytimes.com/mem/archive-free/pdf?res=9B06E EDC1131E733A25752C3A9659C946897D6CF.

58. Edward H. Smith, "A Free Theatre to Regenerate the American Drama," *New York World*, January 24, 1915, clipping, Emanuel Reicher Envelope 1864, Robinson Locke Collection of Scrapbooks, Billy Rose Theatre Division, New York Public Library for the Performing Arts.

59. Peter Bauland, *The Hooded Eagle: Modern German Drama on the New York Stage* (Syracuse, NY: Syracuse University Press, 1968), 21.

60. Heywood Broun, "Art at Its Best in *The Weavers*," unidentified clipping, December 15, 1915, Arvid Paulson Scrapbook, Billy Rose Theatre Division, New York Public Library for the Performing Arts.

61. Review of *The Weavers*, by Gerhart Hauptmann, trans. Mary Morison, dir. Emanuel Reicher, Modern Stage Society, Garden Theatre, New York, *New York Dramatic Mirror*, December 25, 1915, clipping, Arvid Paulson Scrapbook, Billy Rose Theatre Division, New York Public Library for the Performing Arts.

62. "Reicher Presents a Hauptmann Play: Elaborate and Deeply Impressive Production of 'The Weavers' for the Modern Stage,'" *New York Times*, December 15, 1915.

63. "*The Weavers* Is a Gripping Drama," review of *The Weavers*, by Gerhart Hauptmann, trans. Mary Morison, dir. Emanuel Reicher, Modern Stage Society, Garden Theatre, New York, *New York Press*, n.d., clipping, Arvid Paulson Scrapbook, Billy Rose Theatre Division, New York Public Library for the Performing Arts.

64. Review of *The Weavers*, by Gerhart Hauptmann, trans. Mary Morison, dir. Emanuel Reicher, Modern Stage Society, Garden Theatre, New York, *Evening* Mail, December 16, 2015, clipping, Arvid Paulson Scrapbook, Billy Rose Theatre Division, New York Public Library for the Performing Arts.

65. "Madame Critic."

66. Charles Collins, "Harsh Tragedy of *The Weavers*," review of *The Weavers*, by Gerhart Hauptmann, trans. Mary Morison, dir. Emanuel Reicher, Modern Stage Society, Chicago Princess Theatre, Chicago, *Chicago Post*, April 4, 1916, Billy Rose Theatre Division, New York Public Library for the Performing Arts.

67. Bill Marx, "*The Weavers* and the Art of Starvation," review of *The Weavers*, by Gerhart Hauptmann, Calderwood Pavilion at the Boston Center for the Arts, Boston University College of Fine Arts, *Art Fuse Review* (Boston), December 15, 2007, http://artsfuse.org/390/stage-review-the-art-of-starvation/.

68. "How the Actors in *The Weavers* Put Its Teachings into Practice," *Brooklyn Eagle*, March 5, 1916, Emanuel Reicher Envelope, 1864, Billy Rose Theatre Division, New York Public Library for the Performing Arts.
69. "Glooming but Thrilling," review of *The Weavers*, by Gerhart Hauptmann, trans. Mary Morison, dir. Emanuel Reicher, Modern Stage Society, Garden Theatre, New York, *Harper's Bazaar*, February 19, 1916, Billy Rose Theatre Division, New York Public Library for the Performing Arts.
70. "How the Actors."
71. "How the Actors."
72. "*The Weavers* Used to Arouse Public Interest," *Christian Science Monitor*, n.d., clipping, Emanuel Reicher Envelope, 1864, Billy Rose Theatre Division, New York Public Library for the Performing Arts.
73. Sean P. Holmes, *Weavers of Dreams, Unite! Actors' Unionism in Early Twentieth-Century America* (Urbana: University of Illinois Press, 2013), 44.
74. Holmes, *Weavers of Dreams*, 44.
75. Alexander Woollcott, "The Play: Hauptmann in Madison Square," *New York Times*, October 17, 1919, https://www.nytimes.com/1919/10/17/archives/the-play-hauptmann-in-madison-square.html.
76. Laura Collins-Hughes, "'Gotham Refuses to Get Scared': In 1918, Theaters Stayed Open," *New York Times*, July 14, 2020, https://www.nytimes.com/2020/07/14/theater/spanish-flu-1918-new-york-theater.html.
77. Alisa Solomon, "Loose Weave," review of *The Weavers*, by Gerhart Hauptmann, dir. Linda Shirey, East Village Theatre Company, RAPP Arts Center, New York, *Village Voice*, July 11, 1989, 99, clipping, Billy Rose Theatre Division, New York Public Library for the Performing Arts.
78. For the German media coverage of the scandal surrounding the Dresden 2004 production of *The Weavers*, see Henryk M. Broder, "*Weber*—Skandal in Dresden: Geisterbahn Ost" ("*The Weavers*—Scandal in Dresden: East Germany's Tunnel of Horror"), *Spiegel*, November 26, 2004, http://www.spiegel.de/kultur/gesellschaft/weber-skandal-indresden-geisterbahn-ost-a-329820.html; Christine Dössel, "Volker Lösch," May 10, 2013, http://www.goethe.de/kue/the/reg/reg/hl/loe/enindex.htm; "Theaterstreit: *Dresdner Weber* bleiben verboten" ("Theater Dispute: *The Dresden Weavers* Remain Banned"), *Spiegel*, November 1, 2005, http://www.spiegel.de/kultur/gesellschaft/theaterstreit-dresdner-weber-bleiben-verboten-a-336365.html; Gerda-Marie Schönfeld, "*Die Weber*: Subversiv oder Volksverhetzend?" ("*The Weavers*: Subversive or Incited by People's Hate?"), *Stern*, November 29, 2004, http://www.stern.de/kultur/buecher/die-weber-subversiv-oder-volksverhetzend-532909.html.
79. Dössel, "Volker Lösch."
80. Dössel, "Volker Lösch."
81. For more on expressionism in the theater of Ernst Toller and Georg Kaiser, see Renate Benson, *German Expressionist Drama: Ernst Toller and Georg Kaiser* (New York: Grove, 1984).
82. Rob Burns, "Theory and Organization of Revolutionary Working-Class Literature in the Weimar Republic," in *Culture and Society in the Weimar Republic*, ed. Keith Bullivant (Manchester: Manchester University Press, 1977), 135.
83. Ernst Toller, introduction to *Masses and Man, Seven Plays*, trans. with Mary Baker Eddy (New York: Howard Fertig, 1991), 112.

84. Fritz Lang, dir., *Metropolis* (1927; Postdam-Babelsberg, Germany: UFA, Blu-Ray, 2010), DVD.

85. First published as Georg Kaiser, "Der kommende Mensch," *Hannoverscher Anzeiger*, April 9, 1922.

86. Karel Čapek would later acknowledge that it was his brother, Joseph Čapek, another respected Czech writer, who had actually suggested the term to him. Čapek first toyed with the idea of naming his machines "Labori."

87. Karel Čapek, *R.U.R.* (*Rossum's Universal Robots*) (1920), trans. David Short, with foreword by Arthur Miller (London: Modern Voices, 1990).

88. Cecil W. Davies, *The Plays of Ernst Toller: A Revaluation* (Amsterdam: Harwood Academic, 1996), 162. Apparently, Toller at one time considered *Die Ludditen* as a title. The Luddites were skilled textile workers in Nottinghamshire, Yorkshire, and Lancashire, whose livelihood was destroyed by the introduction of machines and other innovations during the Industrial Revolution.

89. Ernst Toller, *Die Machinenstürmer: Ein Drama aus der Zeit der Ludditenbewegung in England, in fünf Akten und einem Vorspiel* (Leipzig: E. P. Tal, 1922), 25.

90. "An organized system of machines, to which motion is communicated by the transmitting mechanism from an automatic centre is the most developed form of production by machinery. Here we have, in the place of the isolated machine, a mechanical monster whose body fills whole factories, and whose demon power, at first hidden by the slow and measured motions of its gigantic members, finally bursts forth in the fast and feverish whirl of its countless working organs." Marx, *Capital*, 1:503.

91. Marx, *Capital*, 1:503.

92. J. L. Styan, *Expressionism and Epic Theatre* in *Modern Drama in Theory and Practice*, vol. 3 (Cambridge: Cambridge University Press, 1981), 54–55.

93. Ernst Toller, *Hoppla, wir leben! Ein Vorspiel und fünf Akte* (1927; repr., Ditzingen: Reclam, 1996), 78.

94. *Telegrammstil* in the theater was influenced by the poetics of expressionist poet August Stamm.

95. Georg Kaiser, *Werke* (Frankfurt: Propyläen Verlag, 1971–72), 68.

Coda

1. Boenisch and Ostermeier, *The Theatre of Thomas Ostermeier*, 236.
2. Boenisch and Ostermeier, *The Theatre of Thomas Ostermeier*.
3. Boenisch and Ostermeier, *The Theatre of Thomas Ostermeier*, 237.
4. Boal, *Theatre of the Oppressed*, 122.
5. Boenisch and Ostermeier, *The Theatre of Thomas Ostermeier*, 237.
6. M. Fisher, *Capitalist Realism*, 16.
7. Strindberg, "Battle of the Brains," 25–46; Strindberg, preface to *Getting Married*, part I, 38.
8. Gilman, *Women and Economics*, 23.
9. Strindberg, preface to *Miss Julie*, 65.
10. Strindberg, preface to *Miss Julie*.
11. Moretti, *The Bourgeois*, 185.

12. Linda Kintz, "Performing Capital in Caryl Churchill's *Serious Money*," *Theatre Journal* 51, no. 3 (1999): 251–65, at 260.

13. Jonas Hassen Khemiri, ≈ [*Almost Equal To*] (2014), http://www.khemiri.se/en/plays/≈-almost-equal-to/.

14. Jonas Hassen Khemiri, ≈ [*Almost Equal To*] (2014), trans. Rachel Willson-Broyles, typescript, provided by author, 5.

15. Gilles Deleuze and Félix Guattari, *Anti-Oedipus: Capitalism and Schizophrenia*, trans. Robert Hurley, Mark Seem, and Helen R. Lane (New York: Viking Penguin, 1977), 32. The "body without organs" appears in Antonin Artaud's radio play *To Have Done with the Judgment of God* (1947). Antonin Artaud, "To Have Done with the Judgment of God," in *Selected Writings*, ed. Susan Sontag (Berkeley: University of California Press, 1976), 571.

16. Ruthie Fierberg, "Why Ayad Akhtar Changed His Tony-Nominated Play *Junk* after Broadway," *Playbill*, April 3, 2019, https://www.playbill.com/article/why-ayad-akhtar-changed-his-tony-nominated-play-junk-after-broadway.

17. Bill Naismith, *Commentary*, in *Serious Money* by Caryl Churchill (1987; repr., London: Methuen, 2002), ix–xxxii, at xiii.

18. We See You W. A. T., https://www.weseeyouwat.com. See also Michael Paulson, "Theater Artists of Color Enumerate Demands for Change," *New York Times*, July 10, 2020, https://www.nytimes.com/2020/07/10/theater/we-see-you-theater-demands.html.

19. "Re:Opening? Rethinking New York City's Performance Infrastructures" (symposium), Skirball Cultural Center, New York University, October 1, 2021.

20. Jennifer Schuessler and Scott Heller, "20 Theater Figures on How to 'Revolutionize' Their World," *New York Times*, September 11, 2020, https://www.nytimes.com/2020/09/11/theater/how-to-revolutionize-theater.html.

21. Schuessler and Heller, "20 Theater Figures on How to 'Revolutionize' Their World."

BIBLIOGRAPHY

Ackerman, Alan. *The Portable Theater: American Literature and the Nineteenth-Century Stage.* Baltimore: Johns Hopkins University Press, 1999.
Adorno, Theodor. *Minima Moralia: Reflections on a Damaged Life* (1951). Translated by E. F. N. Jephcott. New York: Verso, 2005.
Agnew, Jean-Christophe. *Worlds Apart: The Market and the Theater in Anglo-American Thought, 1550–1750.* New York: Cambridge University Press, 1986.
Akhtar, Ayad. "Greed Is Good Drama." Interview by Ruthie Fierberg. *Playbill*, October 2017, 5, *Measure for Measure* at the Public Theater, New York.
———. *The Invisible Hand.* New York: Back Bay Books, 2015.
———. *Junk: A Play.* New York: Back Bay Books, 2017.
———. "Q&A: Prospero." *The Economist*, September 3, 2015. https://www.economist.com/blogs/prospero/2015/09/american-literature.
Alexander, James. *Shaw's Controversial Socialism.* Gainesville: University Press of Florida, 2009.
Als, Hilton. "Yaël Farber's *Mies Julie*." *New Yorker*, November 20, 2012. https://www.newyorker.com/culture/culture-desk/yael-farbers-mies-julie.
Althusser, Louis. "Ideology and Ideological State Apparatuses (Notes towards an Investigation)." In *Lenin and Philosophy and Other Essays*, translated by Ben Brewster, 85–126. New York: Monthly Review Press, 2001.
Anker, Elizabeth S., and Rita Felski, eds. *Critique and Postcritique.* Durham, NC: Duke University Press, 2017.
Aristotle. *Poetics.* Translated by S. H. Butcher, with an introduction by Francis Fergusson. New York: Hill and Wang, 1961.
———. *Politics.* Translated by Ernest Barker, revised and with an introduction and notes by R. F. Stalley. New York: Oxford University Press, 1995.
Armstrong, Nancy. *Desire and Domestic Fiction: A Political History of the Novel.* New York: Oxford University Press, 1987.
Arrighi, Giovanni. *The Long Twentieth Century: Money, Power, and the Origins of Our Times.* New York: Verso, 2010.
Artaud, Antonin. *Selected Writings.* Edited by Susan Sontag. Berkeley: University of California Press, 1976.
Autrand, Michel. *Le théâtre en France de 1870 à 1914.* Paris: Honoré Champion, 2006.
Bakhtin, Mikhail. *The Dialogic Imagination: Four Essays.* Edited by Michael Holquist. Translated by Caryl Emerson and Michael Holquist. Austin: University of Texas Press, 1981.
Banerjee, Trisha Urmi. "Austen Equilibrium." *Representations* 143, no. 1 (2018): 63–90.

Barish, Jonas A. *The Antitheatrical Prejudice*. Berkeley: University of California Press, 1981.
Baudrillard, Jean. *For a Critique of the Political Economy of the Sign*. Translated and with an introduction by Charles Levin. Candor, NY: Telos, 1981.
Bauland, Peter. *The Hooded Eagle: Modern German Drama on the New York Stage*. Syracuse, NY: Syracuse University Press, 1968.
Bebel, August. *Woman and Socialism*. 1879. Reprint, New York: Socialist Literature, 1910.
Becker, Gary S. *The Economic Approach to Human Behavior*. Chicago: University of Chicago Press, 1976.
———. *Human Capital: A Theoretical and Empirical Analysis, with Special Reference to Education* (1964). 3rd ed. Chicago: University of Chicago Press, 1994.
Beckett, Samuel. *Proust*. 1930. Reprint, New York: Grove, 1970.
Becque, Henry. *Les corbeaux*. Vol. 1 of *Théâtre complet*. Paris: Classiques Garnier, 2019.
Benedictsson, Victoria. *The Enchantment*. In a new version by Clare Bayley from a literal translation by Ben Anderman. London: Nick Hern Books, 2007.
———. *Money*. Translated with an afterword by Sarah Death. Norwich, UK: Norvik Press, 1999.
Benjamin, Edmond, and Henry Buguet. *Coulisses de Bourse et de théâtre*. Preface by Francisque Sarcey. Paris: Paul Ollendorf, 1882.
Bennett, David. *The Currency of Desire: Libidinal Economy, Psychoanalysis and Sexual Revolution*. London: Lawrence & Wishart, 2016.
———, ed. *Loaded Subjects: Psychoanalysis, Money and the Global Financial Crisis*. London: Lawrence & Wishart, 2012.
Benson, Renate. *German Expressionist Drama: Ernst Toller and Georg Kaiser*. New York: Grove, 1984.
Benston, Margaret. "The Political Economy of Women's Liberation." *Monthly Review* 21, no. 4 (1969). Reprinted in *Monthly Review* 7, no. 4 (2019).
Berlant, Lauren. *Cruel Optimism*. Durham, NC: Duke University Press, 2011.
Billington, Michael. Review of *The Enchantment*. *The Guardian*, August 2, 2007. https://www.theguardian.com/stage/2007/aug/02/theatre1.
Birken, Lawrence. *Consuming Desire: Sexual Science and the Emergence of a Culture of Abundance 1871–1914*. Ithaca, NY: Cornell University Press, 1988.
Bjørnson, Bjørnstjerne. *En fallit*. 2nd ed. Copenhagen: Gyldendalske Boghandels Forlag (F. Hegel & Søn), 1878.
Blackwell-Pal, Jaswinder, Michael Shane Boyle, Ash Dilks, Caoimhe Mader McGuinness, Olive Mckeon, Lisa Moravec, Alessandro Simari, Clio Unger, and Martin Young. "Marxist Keywords for Performance." *Journal of Dramatic Theory and Criticism* 36, no. 1 (Fall 2021): 25–53.
Blanc, Louis. *Organisation du travail*. 9th ed. Paris: Société de l'industrie fraternelle, 1850.
Blankenagel, John C. "Early Reception of *Die Weber* in the United States." *Modern Language Notes* 68, no. 5 (May 1953): 334–40.

Blumenberg, Hans. *The Legitimacy of the Modern Age* (1966). Translated by Robert M. Wallace. Cambridge, MA: MIT Press, 1983.
Boal, Augusto. *Theatre of the Oppressed* (1974). Translated by Charles A. McBride. New York: Theatre Communications Group, 1993.
Bodenham, Martin. "What Makes a Great Financial Thriller?" January 14, 2018. https://www.martinbodenham.com/what-makes-a-great-financial-thriller/.
Boenisch, Peter M., and Thomas Ostermeier. *The Theatre of Thomas Ostermeier*. New York: Routledge, 2016.
Boltanski, Luc, and Eve Chiapello. *The New Spirit of Capitalism*. Translated by Gregory Elliott. New York: Verso, 2005.
Bourdieu, Pierre. *Distinction: A Social Critique of the Judgement of Taste*. Translated by Richard Nice, with a new introduction by Tony Bennett. New York: Routledge, 1984.
———. "The Forms of Capital." In *Handbook of Theory and Research for the Sociology of Education*, edited by J. G. Richardson, 241–58. New York: Greenwood, 1986.
Bowles, Samuel, and Herbert Gintis. "The Problem with Human Capital Theory—a Marxian Critique." *American Economic Review* 65, no. 2 (1975): 74–82.
Boyle, Michael Shane. "Performance and Value: The Work of Theatre in Karl Marx's *Critique of Political Economy*." *Theatre Survey* 58, no. 1 (2017): 3–23.
Bradshaw's Shareholder's Guide, Railway Manual and Directory, for 1857: A Hand-Book for Companies and Shareholders, 322. London, W. J. Adams, 1857. https://babel.hathitrust.org/cgi/pt?id=wu.89097040810;view=1up;seq=13. Accessed August 20, 2017.
Braudel, Fernand. *The Wheels of Commerce: Civilization and Capitalism, 15th–18th Century*. Vol. 1. Berkeley: University of California Press, 1992.
Brecht, Bertolt. *Brecht on Theatre: The Development of an Aesthetic* (1992). Edited and translated by John Willett. New York: Hill and Wang, 1957.
Brooks, Kristina. "New Woman, Fallen Woman: The Crisis of Reputation in Turn-of-the-Century Novels by Pauline Hopkins and Edith Wharton." *Legacy* 13, no. 2 (1996): 91–112.
Brooks, Peter. *The Melodramatic Imagination: Balzac, Henry James, Melodrama, and the Mode of Excess*. New Haven, CT: Yale University Press, 1976.
Brophy, James M. Review of *Arbeitskämpfe und Gewerkschaften in Deutschland, England, und Frankreich: Ihre Entwicklung vom 19. zum 20. Jahrhundert* by Friedhelm Boll and Dieter Dowe. *Journal of Modern History* 67, no. 1 (1995): 118–20.
Bruckner, Pascal. *The Wisdom of Money*. Translated by Steven Rendall. Cambridge, MA: Harvard University Press, 2017.
Brustein, Robert. *The Theatre of Revolt: Studies in Modern Drama from Ibsen to Genet*. 1964. Reprint, Chicago: Elephant Paperbacks, 1991.
Bruster, Douglas. "On a Certain Tendency in Economic Criticism of Shakespeare." In *Money and the Age of Shakespeare: Essays in New Economic

Criticism, edited by Linda Woodbridge, 67–79. New York: Palgrave Macmillan, 2003.

Buenker, John D., and Joseph Buenker, eds. *Encyclopedia of the Gilded Age and Progressive Era*. Armonk, NY: Sharpe, 2005.

Bulwer-Lytton, Edward. *Money*. London, 1840. ProQuest, https://www.proquest.com/docview/2138574743/Z000060889/AFE651A6D40F4545PQ/1?accountid=12768. Accessed April 10, 2020.

Burns, Rob. "Theory and Organization of Revolutionary Working-Class Literature in the Weimar Republic." In *Culture and Society in the Weimar Republic*, edited by Keith Bullivant, 122–49. Manchester: Manchester University Press, 1977.

Butler, Judith. "Performative Agency." *Journal of Cultural Economy* 3, no. 2 (2010): 147–61.

Čapek, Karel. *R.U.R. (Rossum's Universal Robots)* (1920). Translated by David Short, with a foreword by Arthur Miller. London: Modern Voices, 1990.

Carlson, Marvin. *The German Stage in the Nineteenth Century*. Metuchen, NJ: Scarecrow, 1972.

———. *The Haunted Stage: The Theatre as Memory Machine*. Ann Arbor: University of Michigan Press, 2001.

———. "Reviewed Work(s): *Nora or A Doll House* (Theater Oberhausen): *The Wild Duck* (Off-off-off-Ibsen Festival)." *Ibsen News and Comment* 31 (2011): 7–10.

———. Review of *A Doll's House Part 2*, by Lucas Hnath. *Ibsen News and Comment* 36/37 (2016): 13–17.

———. *Theatre Is More Beautiful than War: German Stage Directing in the Late Twentieth Century*. Iowa City: University of Iowa Press, 2009.

———. "Theatrical Performance: Illustration, Translation, Fulfillment, or Supplement?" *Theatre Journal* 37, no. 1 (1985): 5–11.

Carpenter, Charles A. *Bernard Shaw as Artist-Fabian*. Gainesville: University Press of Florida, 2009.

Cassiday, Julie A. "The Rise of the Actress in Early Nineteenth-Century Russia." In *Women in Nineteenth-Century Russia: Lives and Culture*, edited by Wendy Rosslyn and Alessandra Tosi, 137–59. Cambridge, MA: Open Book, 2012.

Cavell, Stanley. *Must We Mean What We Say?* Cambridge: Cambridge University Press, 2002.

Cawelti, John G. *Adventure, Mystery and Romance: Formula Stories as Art and Popular Culture*. Chicago: University of Chicago Press, 1976.

Chancellor, Edward. *Devil Take the Hindmost: A History of Financial Speculation*. London: Macmillan, 1999.

Chanda, A. K. "The Young Man from the Provinces." *Comparative Literature* 33, no. 4 (1981): 321–41.

Chaudhuri, Una. "Private Parts: Sex, Class, and Stage Space in *Miss Julie*." *Theatre Journal* 45, no. 3 (1993): 317–32.

———. *Staging Place: The Geography of Modern Drama*. Ann Arbor: University of Michigan, 1995.

Chekhov, Anton. *Anton Chekhov: A Life in Letters*. Edited by Rosamund Bartlett, translated by Rosamund Bartlett and Anthony Phillips. New York: Penguin, 2004.

———. *Letters of Anton Chekhov to His Family and Friends: With Biographical Sketch*. Translated by Constance Garnett. New York: Macmillan, 1920.

———. *Polnoe sobranie sochinenii i pisem v tridtsati tomah* (*Complete Works and Letters in Thirty Volumes*). Moscow: Nauka, 1976–83.

———. *Sakhalin Island* (1895). Translated by Brian Reeve. Richmond, UK: Alma Classics, 2015.

Chothia, Jean. *André Antoine*. New York: Cambridge University Press, 1991.

———. "'The Triumph of the Supers': Hauptmann's *The Weavers* as Theatrical Event." *Nineteenth Century Theatre and Film* 34, no. 1 (2007): 45–68.

Chudacoff, Howard P. *Children at Play: An American History*. New York: New York University Press, 2007.

Chudakov, Alexander. "Dr. Chekhov: A Biographical Essay (29 January 1860–15 July 1904)." In *The Cambridge Companion to Chekhov*, edited by Vera Gottlieb and Paul Allain, 3–16. Cambridge: Cambridge University Press, 2000.

Churchill, Caryl. *Serious Money* (1987). Commentary and notes by Bill Naismith. London: Methuen, 2002.

Clark, Barrett H. "*The Weavers*." In *The Continental Drama of Today*, 89–93. New York: Holt, 1914.

Clark, T. J. *Farewell to an Idea: Episodes from a History of Modernism*. New Haven, CT: Yale University Press, 1999.

Collins, Lauren. "The Question Artist." *New Yorker*, July 30, 2012. https://www.newyorker.com/magazine/2012/08/06/the-question-artist.

Connell, Philip. *Romanticism, Economics, and the Question of 'Culture.'* New York: Oxford University Press, 2001.

Conrad, Joseph. *Lord Jim: A Romance*. Garden City, NY: Doubleday, 1920.

Cooley, Nicole. "Dollhouses Weren't Invented for Play." *Salon*, July 22, 2016. https://www.theatlantic.com/technology/archive/2016/07/dollhouses-werent-invented-for-play/492581/.

Coontz, Stephanie. *Marriage, a History: From Obedience to Intimacy, or How Love Conquered Marriage*. New York: Viking, 2005.

Cooper, John Xiros. *Modernism and the Culture of the Market Society*. Cambridge: Cambridge University Press, 2004.

Cosgrave, James F., ed. *The Sociology of Risk and Gambling Reader*. New York: Routledge, 2006.

Cox, Cheryl Anne. *Household Interests: Property, Marriage Strategies, and Family Dynamics in Ancient Athens*. Princeton, NJ: Princeton University Press, 1998.

Crosthwaite, Paul, Peter Knight, and Nicky Marsh, eds. *Show Me the Money: The Image of Finance, 1700 to Present*. Manchester: Manchester University Press, 2014.

Dalla Costa, Mariarosa, and Selma James. *The Power of Women and the Subversion of the Community*. Bristol: Falling Wall Press, 1972.

Davies, Cecil W. *The Plays of Ernst Toller: A Revaluation*. Amsterdam: Harwood Academic, 1996.

———. *Theatre for the People: The Story of the Volksbühne*. Manchester: Manchester University Press, 1977.

Davis, Tracy C. *Actresses as Working Women: Their Social Identity in Victorian Culture*. New York: Routledge, 1991.

———. *The Economics of the British Stage 1800–1914*. Cambridge: Cambridge University Press, 2000.

———. *George Bernard Shaw and the Socialist Theatre*. London: Greenwood, 1994.

Davis, Tracy C., and Ellen Donkin, eds. *Women and Playwriting in Nineteenth-Century Britain*. Cambridge: Cambridge University Press, 1999.

Death, Sarah. Translator's Afterword to Victoria Benedictsson, *Money*, 179–86. Norwich, UK: Norvik Press, 1999.

Defoe, Daniel. *Conjugal Lewdness: or, Matrimonial Whoredom*. Gainesville: Scholars' Facsimiles and Reprints, 1967.

Deleuze, Gilles, and Félix Guattari. *Anti-Oedipus: Capitalism and Schizophrenia*. Translated by Robert Hurley, Mark Seem, and Helen R. Lane. New York: Viking Penguin, 1977.

Denis, Andy. "The Invisible Hand of God in Adam Smith." *Research in the History of Economic Thought and Methodology: A Research Annual 23A* (2005): 1–32.

Derr, Holly L. "*Miss Julie* and the Timeless Art of Slut-Shaming." *Ms. Magazine*, August 5, 2013. https://msmagazine.com/2013/05/08/miss-julie-and-the-timeless-art-of-slut-shaming/.

Diepeveen, Leonard. *Modernist Fraud: Hoax, Parody, Deception*. New York: Oxford University Press, 2019.

Dolan, Jill. *Utopia in Performance: Finding Hope at the Theater*. Ann Arbor: University of Michigan Press, 2005.

Dowd, Michelle M., and Natasha Korda, eds. Introduction to *Working Subjects in Early Modern English Drama*. Burlington, VT: Ashgate, 2011.

Dukore, Bernard F., ed. *The Drama Observed: 1880–1895*. University Park: Pennsylvania State University Press, 1993.

———. "Karl Marx's Youngest Daughter and *A Doll's House*." *Theatre Journal* 42, no. 3 (1990): 308–21.

———. *Money and Politics in Ibsen, Shaw, and Brecht*. Columbia: University of Missouri Press, 1980.

———. *Shaw's Theater*. Gainesville: University Press of Florida, 2000.

Dykes, Steve. "*Strange Fruit*, Chekhov's *The Cherry Orchard* in the Deep South." *Stanislavski Studies* 4, no. 2 (2016): 185–203.

Eagleton, Terry. *Marxism and Literary Criticism*. Berkeley: University of California Press, 1976. Reprint, New York: Routledge, 2002.

———. "The Subject of Literature." *Cultural Critique* 2 (1985–86): 95–104.

Eisler, Garrett. "'I Am a Mere Business Machine': The Commodification of the Heart in Bronson Howard's *The Henrietta*." *Journal of American Drama and Theatre* 19, no. 2 (2007): 37–60.

Ellison, Herbert J. "Economic Modernization in Imperial Russia: Purposes and Achievements." *Journal of Economic History* 25, no. 4 (December 1965): 523–40.

Eltis, Sos. *Acts of Desire: Women and Sex on Stage 1800–1930*. New York: Oxford University Press, 2013.

———. "The Fallen Woman on Stage: Maidens, Magdalens, and the Emancipated Female." In *The Cambridge Companion to Victorian and Edwardian Theatre*, edited by Kerry Powell, 222–36. Cambridge: Cambridge University Press, 2004.

Engels, Friedrich. *The Origin of the Family, Private Property, and the State*. In *The Marx-Engels Reader*, 2nd ed., edited and translated by Robert C. Tucker, 734–59. New York: W. W. Norton, 1978.

———. Preface to the Fourth Edition (1891). In *The Origin of the Family, Private Property, and the State*, with an introduction by Evelyn Reed, 31–44. New York: Pathfinder, 2000.

———. *Supplement* to Karl Marx, *Capital*, vol. 3 (1894). Prepared by Engels, translated by David Fernbach, with an introduction by Ernest Mandel, 1027–47. New York: Penguin, 1993.

Enwezor, Okwui. Introduction. *La Biennale di Venezia*, 2015. https://www.labiennale.org/en/art/2015/intervento-di-okwui-enwezor. Accessed June 2, 2019.

Evans, Judith. *The Politics and Plays of Bernard Shaw*. Jefferson, NC: McFarland, 2003.

Evensky, Jerry. "Ethics and the Invisible Hand." *Journal of Economic Perspectives* 7, no. 2 (1993): 197–205.

Farber, Yaël. *Mies Julie, Restitutions of Body and Soil since the Bantu Land Act No. 27 of 1913 and the Immorality Act No. 5 of 1927*. Based on August Strindberg's *Miss Julie*. London: Oberon Books, 2012.

Federici, Silvia. *Caliban and the Witch: Women, the Body and Primitive Accumulation*. New York: Autonomedia, 2004.

———. *Wages against Housework*. Bristol: Power of Women Collective and Falling Wall Press, 1975.

Felski, Rita. *The Limits of Critique*. Chicago: University of Chicago Press, 2015.

Ferguson, Robert. *Henrik Ibsen: A New Biography*. London: Richard Cohen Books, 1996.

Fierberg, Ruthie. "Why Ayad Akhtar Changed His Tony-Nominated Play *Junk* after Broadway." *Playbill*, April 3, 2019. https://www.playbill.com/article/why-ayad-akhtar-changed-his-tony-nominated-play-junk-after-broadway.

———. "Why You Won't Be Able to Stop Thinking about Ayad Akhtar's New Broadway Play *Junk*." *Playbill*, October 2, 2017. http://www.playbill.com/article/why-you-wont-be-able-to-stop-thinking-about-ayad-akhtars-new-broadway-play-junk.

Figueiredo, Ivo de. *Henrik Ibsen: The Man and the Mask*. Translated by Robert Ferguson. New Haven, CT: Yale University Press, 2019.

"Financial Crises: The Slumps That Shaped Modern Finance." *The Economist*, April 12, 2014. https://www.economist.com/news/essays/21600451-finance-not-merely-prone-crises-it-shaped-them-five-historical-crises-show-how-aspects-today-s-fina.

Finke, Michael C. *Freedom from Violence and Lies: Anton Chekhov's Life and Writings*. London: Reaktion Books, 2021.

Fisher, James, ed. *To Have or Have Not: Essays on Commerce and Capital in Modernist Theatre*. Jefferson, NC: McFarland, 2011.
Fisher, Mark. *Capitalist Realism: Is There No Alternative?* Winchester, UK: O Books, 2009.
Flanders, Judith. *The Victorian City: Everyday Life in Dickens' London*. London: Atlantic Books, 2012.
Florence, Ronald. *Marx's Daughters: Eleanor Marx, Rosa Luxemburg, Angelica Balabanoff*. New York: Dial, 1975.
Foster, Hal. "Post-critical." *October*, no. 139 (Winter 2012): 3–8.
Foucault, Michel. *History of Sexuality*, vol. 1: *An Introduction*. Translated by Robert Hurley. New York: Vintage, 1990.
Fraser, Steve. *Every Man a Speculator: A History of Wall Street in American Life*. New York: HarperCollins, 2005.
Freed-Thall, Hannah. "'Prestige of a Momentary Diamond': Economies of Distinction in Proust." *New Literary History* 43, no. 1 (2012): 159–78.
———. "Speculative Modernism: Proust and the Stock Market." *Modernist Cultures* 12, no. 2 (2017): 153–72.
Freud, Sigmund. "Creative Writers and Day-Dreaming." In *The Freud Reader*, edited by Peter Gay, 436–43. New York: W. W. Norton, 1989.
———. *Inhibitions, Symptoms and Anxiety*. 3rd ed. Translated by Alix Strachey. Revised and edited by James Strachey, with a biographical introduction by Peter Gay. New York: W. W. Norton, 1989.
———. *The Interpretation of Dreams*. Translated by Joyce Crick, with an introduction and notes by Ritchie Robertson. New York: Oxford University Press, 1999.
Fried, Michael. *Art and Objecthood: Essays and Reviews*. Chicago: University of Chicago Press, 1998.
Fulsås, Narve, and Tore Rem. *Ibsen, Scandinavia, and the Making of World Drama*. Cambridge: Cambridge University Press, 2018.
Gagnier, Regenia. *The Insatiability of Human Wants: Economics and Aesthetics in Market Society*. Chicago: University of Chicago Press, 2000.
Gainor, Ellen J. *Shaw's Daughters: Dramatic and Narrative Constructions of Gender*. Ann Arbor: University of Michigan Press, 1991.
Galella, Donatella. "Being in 'The Room Where It Happens': *Hamilton*, Obama, and the Nationalist Neoliberal Multicultural Inclusion." *Theatre Survey* 59, no. 3 (2018): 363–85.
Gilman, Charlotte Perkins. *Women and Economics: A Study of the Economic Relation between Men and Women as a Factor in Social Evolution*. 1898. Reprint, Berkeley: University of California Press, 1998.
Gipson, Rosemary. "Martha Morton: America's First Professional Woman Playwright." *Theatre Survey* 23 (1982): 213–22.
"Glooming but Thrilling." Review of *The Weavers*, by Gerhart Hauptmann, translated by Mary Morison, directed by Emanuel Reicher, Modern Stage Society, Garden Theatre, New York. *Harper's Bazaar*, February 19, 1916.
Goldman, Emma. *The Social Significance of Modern Drama*. Introduction by Harry G. Carlson. Preface by Erika Munk. 1914. Reprint, Montclair, NJ: Applause Theatre Book Publishers, 1987.

Golovin, K. J. *Russkii roman i russkoe obshchestvo*. Ann Arbor: University of Michigan Library, 1909.
Golub, Spencer. *The Recurrence of Fate: Theatre and Memory in Twentieth-Century Russia*. Iowa City: University of Iowa Press, 1994.
Goody, Jack. *Production and Reproduction: A Comparative Study of the Domestic Domain*. Cambridge: Cambridge University Press, 1976.
Gorz, André. "Reform and Revolution" (1967). Translated by Ben Brewster. *Socialist Register* 5 (1968): 111–43.
Gottlieb, Vera. *Chekhov and the Vaudeville: A Study of Chekhov's One-Act Plays*. Cambridge: Cambridge University Press, 1982.
Graeber, David. *Debt: The First 5000 Years*. Brooklyn: Melville House, 2011.
Granville-Barker, Harley. *The Voysey Inheritance*. Adapted by David Mamet. New York: Vintage, 2005.
Green, Adam Isaiah. "'Erotic Capital' and the Power of Desirability: Why 'Honey Money' Is a Bad Collective Strategy for Remedying Gender Inequality." *Sexualities* 16, nos. 1/2 (2012): 137–58.
Greenway, John. "Strindberg and Suggestion in *Miss Julie*." *South Atlantic Review* 51 (1986): 21–34.
Greer, Germaine. "A Whore in Every Home." In *Fabian Feminist: Bernard Shaw and Woman*, edited by Rodelle Weintraub, 163–66. University Park: Pennsylvania State University Press, 1977.
Grene, Nicholas. *Home on the Stage: Domestic Spaces in Modern Drama*. New York: Cambridge University Press, 2014.
Groys, Boris. "On Art Activism." *e-flux* 56, June 2014. https://www.e-flux.com/journal/56/60343/on-art-activism/.
Guest, Kristen. "The Subject of Money: Late-Victorian Melodrama's Crisis of Masculinity." *Victorian Studies* 49, no. 7 (2007): 635–57.
Guillory, John. *Cultural Capital: The Problem of Literary Canon Formation*. Chicago: University of Chicago Press, 1993.
Hager, Kelly. *Dickens and the Rise of Divorce: The Failed-Married Plot and the Novel Tradition* Burlington, VT: Ashgate, 2010.
Hägglund, Martin. *This Life: Secular Faith and Spiritual Freedom*. New York: Penguin Random House, 2019.
———. "What Is Democratic Socialism? Part III: Life after Capitalism." *Los Angeles Review of Books*, July 15, 2020. https://lareviewofbooks.org/article/what-is-democratic-socialism-part-3-life-after-capitalism/.
Hakim, Catherine. *Erotic Capital: The Power of Attraction in the Boardroom and the Bedroom*. New York: Basic Books, 2011.
Halpern, Richard. *Eclipse of Action: Tragedy and Political Economy*. Chicago: University of Chicago Press, 2017.
Harcourt, Bernard E. *The Illusion of Free Markets: Punishment and the Myth of Natural Order*. Cambridge, MA: Harvard University Press, 2012.
Hardwick, Elizabeth. *Seduction and Betrayal: Women and Literature*. New York: Random House, 1974.
Harries, Martin. *Scare Quotes from Shakespeare: Marx, Keynes, and the Language of Reenchantment*. Stanford, CA: Stanford University Press, 2000.
Harrison, Peter. "Adam Smith and the History of the Invisible Hand." *Journal of the History of Ideas* 72, no. 1 (2011): 29–49.

Harvey, David. *A Brief History of Neoliberalism*. New York: Oxford University Press, 2005.
———. *Marx, Capital and the Madness of Economic Reason*. New York: Oxford University Press, 2018.
———. *Seventeen Contradictions and the End of Capitalism*. New York: Oxford University Press, 2015.
Hatch, Ryan Anthony. "Hallucinating Networks and Secret Museums: Hito Steyerl on Our Aesthetic Immiseration." *PAJ: A Journal of Performance and Art* 41, no. 2 (2019): 119–24.
Haugen, Einar. *Ibsen's Drama: Author to Audience*. Minneapolis: University of Minnesota Press, 1979.
Hauptmann, Gerhart. *The Dramatic Works of Gerhart Hauptmann*. Edited and introduction by Ludwig Lewisohn. New York: B. W. Huebsch, 1912.
———. *Die Weber* (1892). Edited by Hans Schwab-Felisch. Berlin: Ullstein-Taschenbuch-Verlag, 2012.
Hautcoeur, Pierre-Cyrille, Amir Rezaee, and Angelo Riva. "Stock Exchange Industry Regulation: The Paris Bourse, 1893–1898." Economic History Association, http://eh.net/eha/wp-content/uploads/2013/11/Hautcoeurb.pdf. Accessed September 1, 2019.
Heffermehl, Karin Bruzelius. "The Status of Women in Norway." *American Journal of Comparative Law* 20, no. 4 (1972): 630–46.
Hegel, G. W. F. *Aesthetics: Lectures on Fine Art*. Translated by T. M. Knox. Oxford: Clarendon, 1988–98.
Heinzelman, Kurt. *The Economics of Imagination*. Amherst: University of Massachusetts Press, 1980.
Heiss, Christine. "Gerhart Hauptmanns *Weber* auf deutschen Bühnen der USA im neunzehnten Jahrhundert" (Gerhart Hauptmann's *The Weavers* on the German Stages of the United States in the Nineteenth Century). *German Quarterly* 59, no. 3 (1986): 361–74.
Helfant, Ian M. *The High Stakes of Identity: Gambling in the Life and Literature of Nineteenth-Century Russia*. Evanston, IL: Northwestern University Press, 2002.
Helland, Frode. *Ibsen in Practice: Relational Readings of Performance, Cultural Encounters and Power*. London: Bloomsbury, 2015.
Helmecke, Carl Albert. "Buckle's Influence on Strindberg." PhD diss., University of Pennsylvania, 1924.
Hewitt, Elizabeth. "The Vexed Story of Economic Criticism." *American Literary History* 21, no. 3 (2009): 618–32.
Hill, Mary A. *Charlotte Perkins Gilman: The Making of a Radical Feminist, 1860–1896*. Philadelphia: Temple University Press, 1980.
Hnath, Lucas. *A Doll's House, Part 2*. New York: Dramatists Play Service, 2017.
Hodgson, Geoffrey M. *Conceptualizing Capitalism: Institutions, Evolution, Future*. Chicago: University of Chicago Press, 2015.
Holledge, Julie, Jonathan Bollen, Frode Helland, and Joanne Tompkins. *A Global Doll's House: Ibsen and Distant Visions*. London: Palgrave Macmillan, 2016.
Holm, Birgitta. *Victoria Benedictsson*. Stockholm: Natur och Kultur, 2007.

Holmberg, Arthur. "Through the Eyes of Lolita." Interview with Paula Vogel. American Repertory Theater, November 17, 2009. https://americanrepertorytheater.org/media/through-the-eyes-of-lolita/.

Holmes, Sean P. *Weavers of Dreams, Unite! Actors' Unionism in Early Twentieth-Century America.* Urbana: University of Illinois Press, 2013.

Holmgren, Beth. *Rewriting Capitalism: Literature and the Market in Late Tsarist Russia and the Kingdom of Poland.* Pittsburgh: University of Pittsburgh Press, 1998.

Honneth, Axel. *The Idea of Socialism: Towards a Renewal.* Malden, MA: Polity, 2017.

Hopkins, Lisa. *The Shakespearean Marriage: Merry Wives and Heavy Husbands.* New York: Palgrave Macmillan, 1998.

Hörisch, Jochen. *Heads or Tails: The Poetics of Money* (1996). Translated by Amy Homing Marschall. Detroit: Wayne State University Press, 2000.

Howard, Bronson C. *Henrietta.* Edited by Allan G. Halline. London, 1901. https://archive.org/details/henriettacomedyi00howa. Accessed April 12, 2020.

Hudson, Pat, and W. R. Lee, eds. *Women's Work and the Family Economy in Historical Perspective.* Manchester: Manchester University Press, 1990.

Hutchings, Stephen C. *Russian Modernism: The Transfiguration of the Everyday.* Cambridge: Cambridge University Press, 1997.

Ibsen, Henrik. *Et dukkenhjem.* Copenhagen: Gyldendalske Boghandels Forlag (F. Hegel & Søn), 1879.

———. *En folkefiende.* Copenhagen: Gyldendalske Boghandels Forlag (F. Hegel & Søn), 1882.

———. *En folkefiende.* A new version by Brad Birch. London: Bloomsbury, 2016.

———. *Hedda Gabler.* Copenhagen: Gyldendalske Boghandels Forlag (F. Hegel & Søn), 1891.

———. *Henrik Ibsens Skrifter.* https://www.ibsen.uio.no/brev.xhtml. Accessed May 20, 2018.

———. *Ibsen: Letters and Speeches.* Edited by Evert Sprinchorn. Clinton, MA: Colonial Press, 1964.

———. *John Gabriel Borkman.* Copenhagen: Gyldendalske Boghandels Forlag (F. Hegel & Søn), 1896.

———. *The Pillars of Society.* Translated by William Archer. Boston: Walter H. Baker, 1890. https://archive.org/stream/pillarsofsociety00ibse#page/23/mode/1up/search/guidance.

———. *The Pretenders; Pillars of Society; Rosmersholm.* Translated by R. Farquharson Sharp. London: J. M. Dent, 1913. https://ebooks.adelaide.edu.au/i/ibsen/henrik/pillars/.

———. *Samfundets støtter.* Copenhagen: Gyldendalske Boghandels Forlag (F. Hegel & Søn), 1877.

Ifergan, Pini. "Cutting to the Chase: Carl Schmitt and Hans Blumenberg on Political Theology and Secularization." *New German Critique* 37, no. 3 (2010): 149–71.

Illouz, Eva. *Why Love Hurts: A Sociological Explanation.* Malden, MA: Polity, 2012.

Jakovljević, Branislav. "Père Gynt: Mendacity for the 21st Century." *TDR: The Drama Review* 64, no. 3 (2020): 8–13.
James, Henry. *Henry James: Essays on Art and Drama*. Edited by Peter Rawlings. Aldershot, UK: Scholar Press, 1996.
———. *The Wings of the Dove* (1902). Edited with an introduction and notes by Millicent Bell. New York: Penguin, 2008.
Jameson, Fredric. *Brecht and Method*. New York: Verso, 1998.
———. *The Political Unconscious: Narrative as a Socially Symbolic Act*. 1981. Reprint, London: Routledge, 2002.
Johansson, Magnus. "Letter from Stockholm." *International Journal of Psychoanalysis* 96 (2015): 257–72.
Jordan, Thomas E. *Victorian Child Savers and Their Culture: A Thematic Evaluation*. Lewiston, NY: E. Mellen, 1998.
Julien, Isaac. *DAS KAPITAL Oratorio*. 2015. https://fortmason.org/event/playtime. Accessed May 12, 2018.
Kaiser, Georg. *Werke*. Frankfurt: Propyläen Verlag, 1971–72.
Kaplan, Marion, ed. *The Marriage Bargain: Women and Dowries in European History*. Philadelphia: Haworth, 1985.
Karasev, P. S. "Obshchii obzor gazetnoy periodiki." In *Ocherki po istorii russkoy zhurnalistiki i kritiki: Vtoraia polovina XIX veka*. 2 vols. Leningrad: Leningradsky gosudarstvenny universitet, 1965.
Kase, Mike. "The Use and Function of Monetary Images in Henrik Ibsen's Play *A Doll's House*." *Theatre Southwest* (April 1989): 23–26.
Kataev, V. B. *Literaturnye sviazi Chekhova*. Moscow: Izdatel'stvo Moskovskogo Universiteta, 1989.
Kaufmann, David. *The Business of Common Life: Novels and Classical Economics between Revolution and Reform*. Baltimore: Johns Hopkins University Press, 1995.
Kempf, Christopher. "'Addicted to the Lubric a Little': Spectacle, Speculation, and the Language of Flow in *Ulysses*." *Modernism/modernity* 24, no. 1 (2017): 23–43.
Kennedy, Gavin. "Adam Smith and the Invisible Hand: From Metaphor to Myth." *Econ Journal Watch* 6, no. 2 (2009): 239–63.
———. "A Reply to Daniel Klein on Adam Smith and the Invisible Hand." *Econ Journal Watch* 6, no. 3 (2009): 374–88.
Kent, Brad. "Eighteenth-Century Literary Precursors of *Mrs. Warren's Profession*." *University of Toronto Quarterly* 81, no. 2 (2012): 187–207.
Khemiri, Jonas Hassen. ≈ *[Almost Equal To]*. Translated by Rachel Willson-Broyles. Typescript, provided by author.
Kindleberger, Charles P., and Robert Z. Aliber. *Manias, Panics and Crashes: A History of Financial Crises*. 6th ed. New York: Palgrave Macmillan, 2011.
Kintz, Linda. "Performing Capital in Caryl Churchill's *Serious Money*." *Theatre Journal* 51, no. 3 (1999): 251–65.
Klein, Daniel. "Adam Smith's Invisible Hands: Comment on Gavin Kennedy." *Econ Journal Watch* 6, no. 2 (2009): 264–79.

Knudsen, Bente D. "Danish Hygge—Even Danes Don't Realize That, Surprisingly, It Is Not about the Candles." *Your Danish Life*, July 2, 2019. https://www.yourdanishlife.dk/the-things-you-need-to-know-about-hygge/.
Kocka, Jürgen. "Capitalism and Its Critics." In *The Lifework of a Labor Historian: Essays in Honor of Marcel van der Linden*, edited by Ulbe Bosma and Karin Hofmeester, 71–89. Leiden: Brill, 2018.
Krueger, David W., ed. *The Last Taboo: Money as Symbol and Reality in Psychotherapy and Psychoanalysis*. New York: Brunner and Mazel, 1986.
Kurnick, David. *Empty Houses: Theatrical Failure and the Novel*. Princeton, NJ: Princeton University Press, 2011.
La Berge, Leigh Claire. *Scandals and Abstraction: Financial Fiction of the Long 1980s*. New York: Oxford University Press, 2014.
Lang, Fritz, dir. *Metropolis*. 1927; Postdam-Babelsberg, Germany. UFA, 2010. Blu-Ray DVD.
Latour, Bruno. "Why Has Critique Run Out of Steam? From Matters of Fact to Matters of Concern." *Critical Inquiry* 30 (Winter 2004): 225–48.
Lee, Esther Kim, ed. *Modern and Contemporary World Drama: Critical and Primary Sources*. London: Bloomsbury, 2022.
Lenin, Vladimir. *Imperialism: The Highest Stage of Capitalism, a Popular Outline*. New York: International Publishers, 1977.
Lenz, Joseph. "Base Trade: Theater as Prostitution." *ELH* 60, no. 4 (1993): 833–55.
Lisi, Leonardo F. *Marginal Modernity: The Aesthetics of Dependency from Kierkegaard to Joyce*. New York: Fordham University Press, 2012.
Lizunov, Pavel V. "Russian Society and the Stock Exchange in the Late Nineteenth and Early Twentieth Centuries." *Russian Studies in History* 54, no. 2 (2015): 106–42.
Loewenthal, Del. "Editorial: Sex, Shit, Money and Marxism—the Continued Demise of the 'Third Way.' " *European Journal of Psychotherapy and Counseling* 11, no. 4 (2009): 349–53.
Lorich, Sonja. *The Unwomanly Woman in Bernard Shaw's Drama and Her Social and Political Background*. Uppsala: Uppsala Universitet, 1973.
Lounsbery, Anne. *Life Is Elsewhere: Symbolic Geography in the Russian Provinces, 1800–1917*. Ithaca, NY: Cornell University Press, 2019.
Lukács, Georg. *History and Class Consciousness: Studies in Marxist Dialectics* (1971). Translated by Rodney Livingstone. Cambridge, MA: MIT Press, 1999.
Lundbo Levy, Jette. *Dobbeltblikket: Om at beskrive kvinder. Ideologi og aestetik i Victoria Benedictssons forfatterskab*. Copenhagen: Tiderne skifter, 1980.
Luxemburg, Rosa. *Reform or Revolution and Other Writings*. Introduction by Paul Buhle. Mineola, NY: Dover, 2006.
Machado Sáez, Elena. "Blackout on Broadway: Affiliation and Audience in *In the Heights* and *Hamilton*." *Studies in Musical Theatre* 12, no. 2 (2018): 181–97.
Malthus, Thomas. *An Essay on the Principle of Population; or, A View of Its Past and Present Effects on Human Happiness; with an Inquiry into Our Prospects Respecting the Future Removal of Mitigation of the Evils which It*

Occasions. Vol. 1. 4th ed. London: T. Bensley, 1807. https://babel.hathitrust.org/cgi/pt?id=njp.32101068776341&view=1up&seq=7. Accessed May 11, 2020.

Mandelstam, Osip. "O p'iese A. Chekhova 'Diadia Vania." In *Sobranie sochinenii v chetyrekh tomakh*, 4:521–22. Moscow: Terra-Terra, 1991.

Marcus, Sharon. *The Drama of Celebrity*. Princeton, NJ: Princeton University Press, 2019.

Marker, Frederick J., and Lise-Lone Marker. "Strindberg in the Theatre." In *The Cambridge Companion to August Strindberg*, edited by Michael Robinson, 135–48. New York: Cambridge University Press, 2010.

Marsh, Nicky. "The Cosmopolitan Coin: What Modernists Make of Money." *Modernism/modernity* 24, no. 3 (2017): 485–505.

Marshall, Alfred. *Principles of Economics*. 1890. Reprint, London: Palgrave Macmillan, 2013.

Martin, Felix. *Money: The Unauthorized Autobiography—from Coinage to Cryptocurrencies*. New York: Knopf, 2014.

Marx, Bill. "*The Weavers* and the Art of Starvation." Review of *The Weavers*, by Gerhart Hauptmann, Calderwood Pavilion at the Boston Center for the Arts, Boston University College of Fine Arts. *Art Fuse Review* (Boston), December 15, 2007. http://artsfuse.org/390/stage-review-the-art-of-starvation/.

Marx, Karl. *Capital: A Critique of Political Economy*. Vol. 1 (1867). Translated by Ben Fowkes, with an introduction by Ernest Mandel. New York: Penguin, 1990.

———. *Capital: The Process of Capitalist Production as a Whole*. Vol. 3 (1894). Prepared by Friedrich Engels, translated by David Fernbach, with an introduction by Ernest Mandel. New York: Penguin, 1993.

———. *A Contribution to the Critique of Political Economy* (1859). Translated by Maurice Dobb. New York: International, 1979.

———. *The Eighteenth Brumaire of Louis Bonaparte* (1852). Translated by Daniel de Leon. New York: International Publishers, 1994.

———. *The Grundrisse: Foundations of the Critique of Political Economy (Rough Draft)*. Translated by Martin Nicolaus. New York: Penguin, 1993.

———. *The Marx-Engels Reader*. 2nd ed., translated and edited by Robert C. Tucker, 66–125. New York: W. W. Norton, 1978.

Marx, Karl, and Friedrich Engels. *The Communist Manifesto* (1848). Translated by Martin Milligan. Amherst, NY: Prometheus Books, 1988.

Maurer, Warren R. *Understanding Gerhart Hauptman*. Columbia: University of South Carolina Press, 1992.

McCullough, David. *The Path between the Seas: The Creation of the Panama Canal 1870–1914*. New York: Simon & Schuster, 1977.

McKinnie, Michael. *Theatre in Market Economies*. Cambridge: Cambridge University Press, 2021.

McNamara, Audrey, and Nelson O'Ceallaigh Ritschel, eds. "Shaw and Money." Special issue, *Shaw: The Journal of Bernard Shaw Studies* 36, no. 1 (2016): 1–185.

Medema, Steven G., and Warren J. Samuels. *The History of Economic Thought: A Reader*. New York: Routledge, 2003.

Mehring, Franz. "On Hauptmann's *The Weavers*." Translated by Edward Braun. *New Theatre Quarterly* 11, no. 42 (1995): 184–210.
Meisel, Martin. *Shaw and the Nineteenth-Century Theater*. Princeton, NJ: Princeton University Press, 1963.
Meledina, Ekaterina. "Genialny Rykov." *Sovershenno Sekretno*, October 1, 2006. https://www.sovsekretno.ru/articles/id/1650/.
Menand, Louis. "How to Misread Jane Austen." *New Yorker*, September 28, 2020. https://www.newyorker.com/magazine/2020/10/05/how-to-misread-jane-austen.
Merezhkovsky, Dmitry. *O prichinakh upadka i o novykh techeniyakh sovremennoy russkoy literatury*. Saint Petersburg: Tipo-litografiia B. M. Vol'fa, 1893. https://iiif.lib.harvard.edu/manifests/view/drs:46603171$1i. Accessed May 15, 2019.
Meyer, Michael. *Ibsen: A Biography*. Garden City, NY: Doubleday, 1971.
Meyering, Sheryl L. Introduction to *Women and Economics: A Study of the Economic Relation between Men and Women as a Factor in Social Evolution* (1898), by Charlotte Perkins Gilman, iii–v. Mineola, NY: Dover, 1998.
Michie, Elsie B. *The Vulgar Question of Money: Heiresses, Materialism, and the Novel of Manners from Jane Austen to Henry James*. Baltimore: Johns Hopkins University Press, 2011.
Mickalites, Carey James. *Modernism and Market Fantasy: British Fictions of Capital, 1910–1939*. New York: Palgrave Macmillan, 2012.
Miller, Derek. *Copyright and the Value of Performance, 1770–1911*. Cambridge: Cambridge University Press, 2018.
Miller, Hillary. *Drop Dead: Performance in Crisis, 1970s New York*. Evanston, IL: Northwestern University Press, 2016.
Mironov, Boris N. "Wages and Prices in Imperial Russia, 1703–1913." *Russian Review* 69 (January 2010): 47–72.
Moi, Toril. *Henrik Ibsen and the Birth of Modernism: Art, Theater, Philosophy*. New York: Oxford University Press, 2006.
Moody, Jane. "The Drama of Capital: Risk, Belief, and Liability on the Victorian Stage." In *Victorian Literature and Finance*, edited by Francis O'Gorman, 91–110. Oxford: Oxford University Press, 2007.
Moretti, Franco. *Atlas of the European Novel, 1800–1900*. New York: Verso, 1998.
———. *The Bourgeois: Between History and Literature*. New York: Verso, 2013.
———. "The Grey Area: Ibsen and the Spirit of Capitalism." *New Left Review* 61 (January–February 2010): 117–31.
Morris, Rosalind C. "Ursprüngliche Akkumulation: The Secret of an Originary Mistranslation." *boundary 2* 43, no. 3 (2016): 29–77.
Morrison, Harry. *The Socialism of Bernard Shaw*. Jefferson, NC: McFarland, 1989.
Morson, Gary Saul. "Chekhov's Art of the Prosaic: Great Ideas and Dramatic Events." In *Approaches to Teaching Works of Anton Chekhov*, edited by Michael C. Finke and Michael Holquist, 187–97. New York: Modern Language Association of America, 2016.
———. "Chekhov's Enlightenment." *New Criterion*, November 2012, 20–27.

Munford, Rebecca. "'Wake Up and Smell the Lipgloss': Gender, Generation and the (A)politics of Girl Power." In *Third Wave Feminism: A Critical Exploration*, edited by S. Gillis, G. Howie, and R. Munford, 266–79. New York: Palgrave, 2007.

Muñoz-Alonso, Lorena. "How to Best Navigate the Venice Biennale's Political and Moral Contradictions." *artnet*, May 14, 2015. https://news.artnet.com/art-world/venice-biennale-art-renegades-296011.

Munro, Kirstin. "'Social Reproduction Theory,' Social Reproduction, and Household Production." *Science and Society* 83, no. 4 (2019): 451–68.

Munting, Roger. *An Economic and Social History of Gambling in Britain and the USA*. Manchester: Manchester University Press, 1996.

Murav, Harriet. *Russia's Legal Fictions*. Ann Arbor: University of Michigan Press, 1998.

Muse, John H. *Microdramas: Crucibles for Theater and Time*. Ann Arbor: University of Michigan Press, 2017.

Nagle, D. Brendan. *The Household as the Foundation of Aristotle's Polis*. Cambridge: Cambridge University Press, 2006.

The Nation. "The Great Russian Bank Swindle." *The Nation*, April 30, 1885, 357–58.

Nealon, Christopher. *The Matter of Capital: Poetry and Crisis in the American Century*. Cambridge, MA: Harvard University Press, 2011.

The New Swell's Night Guide. London, 1847.

Nietzsche, Friedrich. *The Birth of Tragedy: Out of the Spirit of Music* (1872). New ed., edited by Michael Tanner. Translated by Shaun Whiteside. New York: Penguin, 2003.

Nisbet, Robert A. *Social Change and History: Aspects of the Western Theory of Development*. New York: Oxford University Press, 1969.

Norris, Frank. *The Pit: A Story of Chicago*. 1903. Reprint, Cambridge, MA: Seven Treasures, 2008.

Norsk Jernbanemuseum (Norwegian Railway Museum). "Norwegian Railway History." http://jernbanemuseet.no/norsk-jernbanehistorie/. Accessed August 20, 2017.

O'Driscoll, Séamus Stiofan. "Invisible Forces: Capitalism and the Russian Literary Imagination, 1855–1881." PhD diss., Harvard University, 2005.

O'Gorman, Francis., ed. *Victorian Literature and Finance*. Oxford: Oxford University Press, 2007.

Osborne, John. *Gerhart Hauptmann and the Naturalist Drama*. 2nd ed. Amsterdam: Harwood, 1998.

Ostermeier, Thomas. *Iconic Artist Talk*, with Branden Jacobs-Jenkins. Brooklyn Academy of Music, October 12, 2017, Brooklyn, NY.

Ostrovsky, Alexander. *Bespridannitsa* (1878). In *Piesy*, 649–784. Moscow: Eksmo, 2009.

Oxfeldt, Elizabeth. *Nordic Orientalism: Paris and the Cosmopolitan Imagination 1800–1900*. Copenhagen: Museum Tusculanum Press, 2005.

Paperny, Zinovy. "Vaudevilles." In *Anton Chekhov's Selected Plays*, translated and edited Laurence Senelick, 516–24. New York: W. W. Norton, 2005.

Pascal, Roy. *From Naturalism to Expressionism: German Literature and Culture 1880–1918*. London: Weidenfeld and Nicolson, 1973.

Pateman, Carole. *The Sexual Contract*. Stanford, CA: Stanford University Press, 1988.
Phelan, Peggy. *Unmarked: The Politics of Performance*. New York: Routledge, 1993.
Polanyi, Karl. *The Great Transformation: The Political and Economic Origins of Our Time* (1944). Foreword by Joseph E. Stiglitz, introduction by Fred Block. Boston: Beacon, 2001.
Poovey, Mary. *Genres of the Credit Economy: Mediating Value in Eighteenth- and Nineteenth-Century Britain*. Chicago: University of Chicago Press, 2008.
Popkin, Cathy. "Anton Chekhov: Reinventing Events." In *The Pragmatics of Insignificance: Chekhov, Zoshchenko, Gogol*, 17–51. Stanford, CA: Stanford University Press, 1993.
Prideaux, Sue. *Strindberg: A Life*. New Haven, CT: Yale University Press, 2012.
Proudhon, Pierre-Joseph. *Les confessions d'un révolutionnaire*. 3rd ed. Paris: Garnier, 1851.
Puchner, Martin. *The Drama of Ideas: Platonic Provocations in Theater and Philosophy*. New York: Oxford University Press, 2010.
———. *Modern Drama*. New York: Routledge, 2007.
———. *Stage Fright: Modernism, Anti-theatricality, and Drama*. Baltimore: Johns Hopkins University Press, 2002.
Quinn, D. B. *The Voyages and Colonizing Enterprises of Sir Humphrey Gilbert*. Vol. 2. HS, 2nd ser., vol. 84. London, 1940.
Ram, Harsha. "Russia." In *The Cambridge Companion to European Modernism*, edited by Pericles Lewis, 113–35. New York: Cambridge University Press, 2011.
Rancière, Jacques. *Aesthetics and Its Discontents*. Translated by Steven Corcoran. Cambridge: Polity, 2009.
———. *The Emancipated Spectator*. Translated by Gregory Elliott. London: Verso, 2009.
Rayfield, Donald. *Anton Chekhov: A Life*. Evanston, IL: Northwestern University Press, 2000.
Reid, R. L. "The Psychology of the Near Miss." *Journal of Gambling Behavior* 2 (1986): 32–39.
Reilly, Darryl. "*The Enchantment*." *Theater Scene*, July 8, 2017. http://www.theaterscene.net/plays/offbway-plays/the-enchantment/darryl-reilly/.
Ricardo, David. *On the Principles of Political Economy and Taxation*. 1817. Reprint, New York: Prometheus Books, 1996.
Ricci, David. "Fabian Socialism: A Theory of Rent as Exploitation." *Journal of British Studies* 9, no. 1 (1969): 105–21.
Ridout, Nicholas. "From the Editor." *Theatre Survey* 58, no. 1 (2017): 1–2.
———. *Passionate Amateurs: Theatre, Communism, and Love*. Ann Arbor: University of Michigan Press, 2013.
———. *Scenes from Bourgeois Life*. Ann Arbor: University of Michigan Press, 2020.
———. *Stage Fright, Animals, and Other Theatrical Problems*. Cambridge: Cambridge University Press, 2006.

Ries, Eric. *The Lean Startup: How Today's Entrepreneurs Use Continuous Innovation to Create Radically Successful Businesses.* New York: Crown, 2011.

Rippert, Ulrich. "August Bebel and the Political Awakening of the Working Class." *World Socialist*, August 28, 2013. https://www.wsws.org/en/articles/2013/08/28/bebe-a28.html.

Ritschel, Nelson O'Ceallaigh. *Shaw, Synge, Connolly, and Socialist Provocation.* Gainesville: University Press of Florida, 2011.

Roach, Joseph. "Gossip Girls: Lady Teazle, Nora Helmer, and Invisible-Hand Drama." *Modern Drama* 53, no. 3 (2010): 297–310.

Robbins, Bruce. *The Beneficiary.* Durham, NC: Duke University Press, 2017.

Robinson, Michael. *Strindberg and Autobiography.* London: Norvik Press, 1986.

Rodgers, Daniel T. *The Work Ethic in Industrial America, 1850–1920.* Chicago: University of Chicago Press, 1978.

Roger, Hans. *Russia in the Age of Modernisation and Revolution, 1881–1917.* London: Longman, 1983.

Rogers, Gayle. *Speculation: A Cultural History from Aristotle to AI.* New York: Columbia University Press, 2021.

Rokem, Freddie. *Strindberg's Secret Codes.* London: Norvik Press, 2006.

———. *Theatrical Space in Ibsen, Chekhov, and Strindberg: Public Forms of Privacy.* Ann Arbor: UMI Research Press, 1986.

Romanova, Galina. *Motiv deneg v russkoy literature xix veka.* Moscow: Flinta, 2006.

Ruiz, Cristina. "Fierce Debate over Christoph Büchel's Venice Biennale Display of Boat That Sank with Hundreds Locked in Hull." *Art Newspaper*, May 14, 2019. https://www.theartnewspaper.com/news/christoph-buechel.

Ruskin, John. "Essays on Political Economy." In *Fraser's Magazine: For Town and Country* 65 (January–June 1862), edited by James Anthony Froude and John Tulloch, 784–92. London: Savill and Edwards, 1862.

Scarry, Elaine. *Resisting Representation.* Oxford: Oxford University Press, 1994.

Schildberg-Schroth, Gerhard. *Gerhart Hauptmann: Die Weber (Gerhart Hauptmann: The Weavers).* Frankfurt am Main: Moritz Diesterweg, 1992.

Schmitt, Carl. *Political Theology: Four Chapters on the Concept of Sovereignty* (1922). Translated by George Schwab. 1985. Reprint, Chicago: University of Chicago Press, 2005.

Schoenbach, Lisi. *Pragmatic Modernism.* New York: Oxford University Press, 2011.

Schumpeter, Joseph. *Capitalism, Socialism, and Democracy.* 1942. Reprint, New York: Harper, 2008.

Schweitzer, Marlis. *Transatlantic Broadway: The Infrastructural Politics of Global Performance.* New York: Palgrave Macmillan, 2015.

Seccombe, Wally. "The Housewife and Her Labour under Capitalism." *New Left Review* 1, no. 83 (1974): 3–24.

Sejersted, Francis. *The Age of Social Democracy: Norway and Sweden in the Twentieth Century*. Translated by Richard Daly with editing by Madeleine B. Adams. Princeton, NJ: Princeton University Press, 2011.

Sekellick, Matthew Clinton. "Hamilton and Class." *Studies in Musical Theatre* 12, no. 2 (2018): 257–63.

Senelick, Laurence, ed. and trans. *Anton Chekhov's Selected Plays*. New York: W. W. Norton, 2005.

———. "Money in Chekhov's Plays." *Studies in Theatre and Performance* 29, no. 3 (2009): 327–37.

Shakespeare, William. *Timon of Athens*. Edited by Barbara A. Mowat and Paul Werstine. Folger Shakespeare Library. New York: Simon & Schuster, 2020.

Shaw, G. Bernard. "Bernard Shaw on Capital and Labor." *New York American*, December 20, 1914. In "Six Fabian Lectures on Redistribution of Income," special issue, *Shaw: The Journal of Bernard Shaw Studies* 36, no. 1 (2016): 10–52.

———. *Getting Married* and *Press Cuttings*. Definitive text under the editorial supervision of Dan H. Laurence. New York: Penguin, 1986.

———. *The Intelligent Woman's Guide to Socialism, Capitalism, Sovietism and Fascism* (1937). Edited by Polly Toynbee. London: Alma Classics, 2012.

———. "The Jevonian Criticism of Marx (A Comment on the Rev P. H. Wicksteed's Article." *To-day*, January 1885, 22–27. Reprinted in Philip H. Wicksteed, *The Common Sense of Political Economy and Selected Papers and Reviews of Economic Theory*, vol. 2 (1933), edited and with an introduction by Lionel Robbins, 724–30. Abingdon, UK: Routledge, 2003.

———. *Major Barbara* (1905). In *John Bull's Other Island and Major Barbara*, 157–311. New York: Brentano's, 1907.

———. *Major Barbara*. 1905/1907. Reprint, New York: Penguin, 2001.

———. *Plays Extravagant*. New York: Penguin, 1981.

———. *Plays Unpleasant*. Definitive text under the editorial supervision of Dan H. Laurence, with an introduction by David Edgar. New York: Penguin, 2001.

———. *The Socialism of Shaw*. Edited and with an introduction by James Fuchs. New York: Vanguard, 1926.

Shaw, Helen. "A Disappointingly Muted Mounting of Victoria Benedictsson's *The Enchantment*." *Village Voice*, July 12, 2017. https://www.villagevoice.com/2017/07/12/a-disappointingly-muted-mounting-of-victoria-benedictssons-the-enchantment/.

Shell, Marc. *The Economy of Literature*. Baltimore: Johns Hopkins University Press, 1978.

Shepherd-Barr, Kirsten E. *Ibsen and Early Modernist Theater 1890–1900*. Westport, CT: Greenwood, 1997.

———. *Modern Drama: A Very Short Introduction*. New York: Oxford University Press, 2016.

———. *Science on Stage: From Doctor Faustus to Copenhagen*. Princeton, NJ: Princeton University Press, 2006.

Shideler, Ross. *Questioning the Father: From Darwin to Zola, Ibsen, Strindberg, and Hardy*. Stanford, CA: Stanford University Press, 2000.

Shneyder, Vadim. *Russia's Capitalist Realism: Tolstoy, Dostoevsky, and Chekhov*. Evanston, IL: Northwestern University Press, 2020.
Shonkwiler, Alison, and Leigh Claire La Berge, eds. *Reading Capitalist Realism*. Iowa City: University of Iowa Press, 2014.
Simmel, Georg. "Money in Modern Culture." In *Simmel on Culture: Selected Writings*, edited by David Frisby and Mike Featherstone, 243–55. London: Sage, 1997.
———. *The Philosophy of Money* (1900). Edited by David Frisby, translated by Tom Bottomore and David Frisby from a first draft by Kaethe Mengelberg. New York: Routledge, 2011.
Simonton, Deborah. *A History of European Women's Work, 1700 to the Present*. New York: Routledge, 1998.
Smith, Adam. *The Essential Adam Smith*. Edited and with an introduction by Robert L. Heilbroner with the assistance of Laurence J. Malone. New York: W. W. Norton, 1986.
———. *An Inquiry into the Nature and Causes of the Wealth of Nations* (1776). Edited by Edwin Cannan (1904), 5th ed., with an introduction by Alan B. Krueger. New York: Random House, 2003.
———. *The Theory of Moral Sentiments* (1759). Edited by Knud Haakonssen. Cambridge: Cambridge University Press, 2002.
Sofer, Andrew. *Dark Matter: Invisibility in Drama, Theater, and Performance*. Ann Arbor: University of Michigan Press, 2013.
———. *The Stage Life of Props*. Ann Arbor: University of Michigan Press, 2003.
Sprinchorn, Evert. *Ibsen's Kingdom: The Man and His Works*. New Haven, CT: Yale University Press, 2021.
———. "Shaw and Strindberg." In "Shaw and Other Playwrights," special issue, *Shaw* 13, no. 1 (1993): 9–24.
———. *Strindberg as Dramatist*. New Haven, CT: Yale University Press, 1982.
Stäheli, Urs. *Spectacular Speculation: Thrills, the Economy, and Popular Discourse*. Translated by Eric Savoth. Stanford, CA: Stanford University Press, 2013.
Steiner, George. *The Death of Tragedy*. 1961. Reprint, New York: Knopf, 1980.
Stenport, Anna Westerståhl. *Locating August Strindberg's Prose: Modernism, Transnationalism, and Setting*. Toronto: University of Toronto Press, 2010.
———. "Money Metaphors and Rhetoric of Resource Depletion: *Creditors* and Late-Nineteenth-Century European Economics." In *The International Strindberg: New Critical Essays*, edited by Anna Westerståhl Stenport, 145–66. Evanston, IL: Northwestern University Press, 2012.
———. "The Sexonomics of *Et dukkehjem*: Money, the Domestic Sphere and Prostitution." *Edda* 106, no. 4 (2006): 339–53.
Stewart, Susan. *On Longing: Narratives of the Miniature, the Gigantic, the Souvenir, the Collection*. Durham, NC: Duke University Press, 1993.
Stigler, George J. "Bernard Shaw, Sidney Webb, and the Theory of Fabian Socialism." *Proceedings of the American Philosophical Society* 103, no. 3 (1959): 469–75.

Stokes, E. E., Jr. "Bernard Shaw and Economics." *Southwestern Social Science Quarterly* 39, no. 3 (1958): 242–48.
Stone, Jonathan. *The Institutions of Russian Modernism: Conceptualizing, Publishing, and Reading Symbolism.* Evanston, IL: Northwestern University Press, 2017.
Stone, Lawrence. *The Family, Sex and Marriage in England, 1500–1800.* New York: Harper & Row, 1977.
Stone Peters, Julie. "Legal Performance Good and Bad." *Law, Culture and the Humanities* 4 (2008): 179–200.
Strange, Susan. *Casino Capitalism* (1986). With a new introduction by Matthew Watson. Manchester: Manchester University Press, 2016.
Strindberg, August. *August Strindberg: Selected Essays.* Edited and translated by Michael Robinson. Cambridge: Cambridge University Press, 1996.
———. *Fröken Julie, Fadren, Ett drömspel.* Milton Keynes, UK: Jiahu Books, 2013.
———. *Getting Married.* Parts I and II. Translated, edited, and with an introduction by Mary Sandbach. London: Victor Gollancz, 1972.
———. *The Red Room.* Translated by Ellie Schleussner. Les Prairies numériques, 2019.
———. *Small Catechism for the Underclass.* Translated by Jeff Kinkle and Janina Pedan. Andperseand, 2012. Kindle.
———. *The Son of a Servant: The Servant of the Evolution of a Human Being.* 1849–67. Reprint, Garden City, NY: Anchor Books, 1966.
———. *Strindberg on Drama and Theatre.* Edited and translated by Egil Törnqvist and Birgitta Steene. Amsterdam: Amsterdam University Press, 2007.
Styan, J. L. *Expressionism and Epic Theatre.* In *Modern Drama in Theory and Practice*, vol. 3. Cambridge: Cambridge University Press, 1981.
Surowiecki, James. "How Online Ticket Scalping (Eventually) Helped 'Hamilton.'" *New Yorker*, June 11, 2016. https://www.newyorker.com/business/currency/how-online-ticket-scalping-eventually-helped-hamilton.
Suwala, Halina. *Autour de Zola et du naturalisme.* Paris: Honoré Champion, 1993.
Swartz, David L. "Bourdieu's Concept of Field." *Oxford Bibliographies.* https://www.oxfordbibliographies.com/view/document/obo-9780199756384/obo-9780199756384-0164.xml. Accessed May 15, 2021.
Swedberg, Richard. "The Literary Author as a Sociologist? *Among French Peasants* by August Strindberg." *Journal of Classical Sociology* 16, no. 1 (2016): 124–30.
Tawney, R. H. *Religion and the Rise of Capitalism.* 1926. Reprint, New Brunswick, NJ: Transaction, 1998.
Templeton, Joan. *Ibsen's Women.* New York: Cambridge University Press, 1997.
Tertz, Abram. *"The Trial Begins"* and *"On Socialist Realism."* Translated by Max Hayward and George Dennis, with an introduction by Czesław Miłosz. Berkeley: University of California Press, 1960.
Thompson, James. *Models of Value: Eighteenth-Century Political Economy and the Novel.* Durham, NC: Duke University Press, 1996.

Thornton, Edward. "Deleuze and Guattari's Absent Analysis of Patriarchy." *Hypatia: A Journal of Feminist Philosophy* 34, no. 2 (2019): 348–68.
Toller, Ernst. *Hoppla, wir leben! Ein Vorspiel und fünf Akte*. 1927. Reprint, Ditzingen: Reclam, 1996.
———. Introduction to *Masses and Man: Seven Plays*. Translated with Mary Baker Eddy. New York: Howard Fertig, 1991.
———. *Die Maschinenstürmer: Ein Drama aus der Zeit der Ludditenbewegung in England, in fünf Akten und einem Vorspiel*. Leipzig: E. P. Tal, 1922.
Törnqvist, Egil, and Barry Jacobs. *Strindberg's "Miss Julie": A Play and Its Transpositions*. Norwich, UK: Norvik Press, 1988.
Townsend, Sarah J. *The Unfinished Art of Theater: Avant-Garde Intellectuals in Mexico and Brazil*. Evanston, IL: Northwestern University Press, 2018.
Trachtman, Richard. "The Money Taboo: Its Effects in Everyday Life and in the Practice of Psychotherapy." *Clinical Social Work Journal* 27 (1999): 275–88.
Trilling, Lionel. *The Liberal Imagination: Essays on Literature and Society*. 1950. Reprint, Garden City, NY: Doubleday, 1957.
Trotsky, Leon. *Literature and Revolution* (1925). Edited by William Keach, translated by Rose Strunsky. Chicago: Haymarket, 2005.
Turner, Henry S. *The Corporate Commonwealth: Pluralism and Political Fictions in England, 1516–1651*. Chicago: University of Chicago Press, 2016.
Turner, Victor. *Dramas, Fields, and Metaphors: Symbolic Action in Human Society*. Ithaca, NY: Cornell University Press, 1974.
Tyson, Brian F. "Shaw among the Actors: Theatrical Additions to *Plays Unpleasant*." *Modern Drama* 14 (1971–72): 264–75.
Ukhov, Andrei D. "Preferences toward Risk and Asset Prices: Evidence from Russian Lottery Bonds" (2005). Cornell University, SHA School. http://scholarship.sha.cornell.edu/workingpapers/7. Accessed May 15, 2019.
Varoufakis, Yanis. *Talking to My Daughter about the Economy: or, How Capitalism Works—and How It Fails*. Translated by Jacob Moe and Yanis Varoufakis. New York: Farrar, Straus and Giroux, 2013.
Veblen, Thorstein. *The Theory of the Leisure Class*. 1899. Reprint, Mineola, NY: Dover, 1994.
Velde, François R. "Lottery Loans in the Eighteenth Century." Working paper, Federal Reserve Bank of Chicago, May 12, 2018. https://doi.org/10.21033/wp-2018-07.
Vercelli, Alessandro. "Financialization in a Long-Run Perspective." *International Journal of Political Economy* 42, no. 4 (2013): 19–46.
Wagner, Matthew. *Shakespeare, Theatre, and Time*. New York: Routledge, 2012.
Waldman, Katy. "Has Self-Awareness Gone Too Far in Fiction?" *New Yorker*, August 19, 2020. https://www.newyorker.com/books/under-review/has-self-awareness-gone-too-far-in-fiction.
Wallerstein, Immanuel. *The Modern World-System: Capitalist Agriculture and the Origins of the European World-Economy in the Sixteenth Century*. New York: Academic Press, 1974.

Watkins, Andrew. "Reclaiming *Miss Julie*: On Interpreting Classic Drama." *Howlround*, May 17, 2017. https://howlround.com/reclaiming-miss-julie.
Watt, Ian. *The Rise of the Novel: Studies in Defoe, Richardson and Fielding* (1957). With an afterword by W. B. Carnochan. Berkeley: University of California Press, 2001.
Weber, Max. *The Protestant Ethic and the Spirit of Capitalism* (1930). Translated by Talcott Parsons, with an introduction by Anthony Giddens. New York: Routledge, 1992.
Weinstein, Cindy. *The Literature of Labor and the Labors of Literature: Allegory in Nineteenth-Century American Literature*. Cambridge: University of Cambridge Press, 1995.
Wells, H. G. *Tono-Bungay*. 1909. Reprint, New York: Penguin, 2005.
Werhane, Patricia H. *Adam Smith and His Legacy for Modern Capitalism*. Oxford: Oxford University Press, 1991.
Whitaker, Chelsea. "Exploring an Anti-policing Theatre." *Howlround*, August 6, 2020, https://howlround.com/exploring-anti-policing-theatre.
Wicke, Jennifer. *Advertising Fictions: Literature, Advertisement, and Social Reading*. New York: Columbia University Press, 1988.
———. "Appreciation, Depreciation: Modernism's Speculative Bubble." *Modernism/modernity* 8, no. 3 (September 2001): 389–403.
Wickstrom, Maurya. *Performing Consumers: Global Capital and Its Theatrical Seductions*. New York: Routledge, 2006.
Wilde, Oscar. *The Plays of Oscar Wilde*. With a new introduction by John Lahr. New York: Vintage, 1988.
Willers, Uno. *Strindberg om sig själv*. Stockholm: Bonnier, 1968.
Williams, Kirk. "Anti-theatricality and the Limits of Naturalism." *Modern Drama* 44, no. 3 (2001): 284–99.
Williams, Raymond. *Culture and Society, 1780–1950*. New York: Columbia University Press, 1958.
———. *Marxism and Literature*. Rev. ed. New York: Oxford University Press, 1978.
Winch, Donald. *Riches and Poverty: An Intellectual History of Political Economy in Britain, 1750–1834*. New York: Cambridge University Press, 1996.
Wollstonecraft, Mary. *A Vindication of the Rights of Woman*. In *"A Vindication of the Rights of Woman" and "A Vindication of the Rights of Men,"* 63–283. Oxford: Oxford University Press, 2008.
Wood, James. "What Chekhov Meant by Life." In *Serious Noticing: Selected Essays*, 34–48. New York: Vintage, 2019.
Wood, Michael. "What Henry Knew." *London Review of Books* 25, no. 24, December 18, 2003. https://www.lrb.co.uk/the-paper/v25/n24/michael-wood/what-henry-knew.
Woodbridge, Linda, ed. *Money and the Age of Shakespeare: Essays in New Economic Criticism*. New York: Palgrave Macmillan, 2003.
Woodmansee, Martha. *The Author, Art, and the Market: Rereading the History of Aesthetics*. New York: Columbia University Press, 1994.
———. "The Genius and the Copyright: Economic and Legal Conditions of the Emergence of the 'Author.'" *Eighteenth-Century Studies* 17 (1984): 425–48.

Woodmansee, Martha, and Mark Osteen, eds. *New Economic Criticism*. New York: Routledge, 1999.
Woolf, Brandon. *Institutional Theatrics: Performing Arts Policy in Post-Wall Berlin*. Evanston, IL: Northwestern University Press, 2021.
Woolf, Virginia. "Modern Fiction." In *The Essays of Virginia Woolf*, vol. 4, *1925–1928*, edited by Andrew McNeille, 157–65. London: Hogarth, 1984.
Worthen, W. B. *Modern Drama and the Rhetoric of Theater*. Berkeley: University of California Press, 1992.
Xia, Ran. "*The Enchantment*." *Theatre Is Easy*, July 8, 2017. http://www.theasy.com/Reviews/2017/E/enchantment.php.
Cooper, John Xiros. *Modernism and the Culture of the Market Society*. Cambridge: Cambridge University Press, 2004.
Ybarra, Patricia A. *Latinx Theater in the Times of Neoliberalism*. Evanston, IL: Northwestern University Press, 2017.
Zimmerman, David A. *Panic! Markets, Crises, and Crowds in American Fiction*. Chapel Hill: University of North Carolina Press, 2006.
Ziter, Edward. *The Orient on the Victorian Stage*. New York: Cambridge University Press, 2003.
Zola, Émile. *L'Argent (Les Rougon-Macquart)*. Vol. 18. Uzès, France: Tite Fée, 2017.
———. *Nana*. Translated and with an introduction and notes by Douglas Parmée. New York: Oxford University Press, 1998.

INDEX

Page locators in italic indicate figures.

Actors' Equity Association (AEA), 191–92
Adorno, Theodor, 115
adultery, 108, 111, 113, 137
Afonasov, Ivan, 152
AFROFEMONONOMY, 209
Agnew, Jean-Christophe, 26
agrarian economy, 97, 121–22, 145, 194–95
Ahlgren, Ernst. *See* Benedictsson, Victoria
Akhtar, Ayad, 17, 19, 31, 35–36, 38; *The Invisible Hand*, 30, 66–67, 207; *Junk*, 19, 30, 207–8
Alexander, James, 126
Alexander II (czar), 151
Als, Hilton, 106
Althusser, Louis, 24
American Federation of Musicians, 209
American Revolution, 108
anarchism, 11, 16, 21, 43, 63, 67, 116, 176, 189
Andersen, Hans Christian, *The Snow Queen*, 60
Anticapitalism for Artists, 209
antitheatrical prejudice, 34, 48–50, 151, 177–78
Antoine, André, 105, 183, 189
apartheid, 106–7
Archer, William, 51
Aristotle, 11, 35, 40, 203, 244n198
Armand, Émile, 116
Armstrong, Nancy, 73, 109–10, 122
Arrighi, Giovanni, 45
Artaud, Antonin, 208
Arts Workers Rally, 209
Atkinson, Lucy Jane, 140
Augier, Émile, 27

Augustine, Saint, 52
Austen, Jane, 111
Aveling, Edward, 69

Bacon, Francis, 11
Bajevic, Maja, 3
Baker, Annie, 208
Bakhtin, Mikhail, 126–27
Bakunin, Mikhail, 11
Balzac, Honoré de, 26; *César Birotteau*, 50, 222n164
bank fraud. *See* financial crimes/scandals; Rykov, Ivan
Bank of America, 208
Barish, Jonas, 34, 48
Bastiat, Frédéric, 14
Baudrillard, Jean, 171–72
Bavarian Soviet Republic, 11, 194, 198
Bayley, Clare, 139
Bebel, August, 114
Becker, Gary, 13, 87
Beckett, Samuel, 160
Becque, Henry, *The Scavengers*, 27, 89–91, 110–11, 117, 140
Beer, Max, 195
Bellafante, Ginia, 17
Benedictsson, Victoria: canon and, 40, 205; *The Enchantment*, 38, 84, 86, 136, 139–42; *Fru Marianne*, 136; life and travails of, 79, 95, 135–36, 139, 141; *Money*, 31, 38, 77, 79, 84, 136–39
beneficiaries of capitalism: conceptualized, 4; playwrights as, 20, 30, 40, 186–87, 194, 210–11; self-awareness of, 22–25, 36, 40, 134, 186–87, 197–98; spectators as, 23–25, 29–30, 43, 190–91, 202–3, 206; theater as, 5–6, 10

283

Benjamin, Edmond, 33
Benjamin, Walter, 153
Bennett, Arnold, 144
Bennett, David, 119–21
Benston, Margaret, 72
Berlant, Lauren, 170, 206
Berne Convention, 79
Bernhardt, Sarah, 124, 151
Bernheim, Hippolyte, 102
Bernstein, Eduard, 14–15, 22
Besant, Walter, *The Doll's House and After*, 79
Billington, Michael, 244n212
Birch, Brad, 43, 46
Birken, Lawrence, 122
Bjørnson, Bjørnstjerne, *A Bankruptcy*, 47–51, 54, 56, 59
Black Lives Matter, 201, 209
Blanc, Louis, 5
Blumenberg, Hans, 53, 65
Boal, Augusto, 22, 202–3
Boccardo, Gerolamo, 14
Bodenham, Martin, 19
Boenisch, Peter, 202
Boltanski, Luc, 21
bonds, 33, 47, 56, 126, 208, 247n17; lottery, 148, 152–53, 156
Bonnier, Isidor, 101
Borchmeyer, Florian, 63–64
Boston University College of Fine Arts, 191
Boucicault, Dion, 26
Bourdieu, Pierre, 7, 13, 86–88, 111, 164, 173, 214n17
bourgeoisie: artists as, 20, 40, 163, 187, 194, 197–98; cultural construct of, 38, 48–50, 69–70, 109–10; distrust/fear of proletariat, 23, 39, 177, 194, 196–97, 206; historical usage of term, 20, 187, 194; immanent critique and, 22–24, 113–15; invisible labor and, 72–76, 78, 183; vs. middle class, 237n100, 238n105; revolution and, 20–22, 177, 183, 194, 203; sexual contract of, 108–10, 112–17, 122, 124, 204–5; Strindberg's "overclass" and, 97–98; subjectivity of, 23–25, 63, 87–88; theater audiences, 23–25, 29, 188, 190–93, 203, 208; as transitional class, 22, 46, 110. *See also hygge*; proletariat
Boyle, Michael Shane, 36
Brahm, Otto, 183, 188–89
Brandes, Edvard, 94, 96, 136
Brandes, Georg, 79, 98, 135–36, 139, 141
Brantley, Ben, 106
Braudel, Fernand, 45
Brecht, Bertolt, 6, 18, 20–21, 24, 37, 40, 185, 194
British labor movement, 11–12, 21
Broadway, 17, 43, 201, 210
Brooklyn Academy of Music, 43, 229n71
Brooks, Peter, 31, 48
brothel: dollhouse as, 76; illegitimate sexualities and, 122; in *Mrs. Warren's Profession*, 93, 127–32, 135; stock exchange and, 124, 128; theater's resemblance to, 5, 123–24. *See also* prostitution
Broun, Heywood, 190
Büchel, Christoph, 3–4
Buckle, Henry Thomas, 97
Buguet, Henry, 33
Bulwer-Lytton, Edward, *Money*, 26, 111–12
Butler, Josephine, 127
Butler, Judith, 36

Čapek, Joseph, 256n86
Čapek, Karel, 25; *R.U.R. (Rossum's Universal Robots)*, 37, 195
capital: attractiveness/charm as, 85–86, 89, 92–93; conceptualized, 4–9; cultural, 6–7, 86, 92, 124, 196; vs. currency, 228n55, 244n198; human, 87–88; irresistible drive for, 118–19, 123, 130–31; vs. labor, 87, 176, 178–80; movement of, 45–46, 128–34; social, 7, 86, 92, 124; subsuming force of, 58–60; surplus value and, 8, 125–26, 129–30, 132, 134, 167. *See also* dowry; erotic capital; inheritance; invisible hand; Marx, Karl
capitalism: alienated intimacy under, 84–85, 105–6, 117; bootstraps myth of, 17, 79, 87–88, 110; casino,

Index

39, 142, 145, 153–54, 164, 172–73, 206; complicity in, 34, 43–44, 149–51; consumption, 13, 68, 73, 122, 186; contradictions of, 3–4, 8, 61, 114–16, 173, 203; critique's relationship to, 21–22, 24, 37; cruel optimism of, 170, 172, 206; culture of, 17–18, 119–21, 130–31, 154–55, 185–86; earliest beginnings of, 26–28, 45–46, 58, 112–14, 146–47, 154; as enslavement/exploitation, 9–10, 36–37, 129–30, 149, 177, 192, 195; vs. feudalism, 20, 25, 121, 154, 164, 226n39; historical usage of term, 4–6; household as integral to, 70–74; immanent critique of, 5, 14–17, 203, 206; megalomania of, 47–49, 55–56, 63, 130–31, 134–35; modern secular values of, 53–54, 58, 153–55; money and sex under, 119–23, 128–29, 136, 141–42, 207–8; novel vs. theater of, 30–35, 37; originary accumulation under, 104, 107, 130; oscillating fortunes of, 59, 96, 119, 145, 150, 152, 168, 172–73; performatively produced, 36, 54, 241n56; profit motive of, 8–9, 61, 63, 107, 130, 164, 204, 210; socioeconomic advancement under, 92–94, 103–4, 109–10, 141–42, 145, 150, 172; truth destabilized by, 46, 60–62; unproductive lives and, 122–23, 167; as villainy, 48–51, 54; volatility of economy in, 146–49, 155, 157; war and, 66–67, 150, 152, 194–95, 198–99. *See also* beneficiaries of capitalism; commodities; money; patriarchy

capitalist realism (ideology), 17, 62, 64–65, 204. *See also* realism

Carlson, Marvin, 5–6, 78, 176

Carlyle, Thomas, 11

Carnegie, Andrew, 37

Cassell, Ernest, 153

Cassiday, Julie, 124

Castorf, Frank, 181, 192

Castro, Alfredo, 69

Catherine the Great (empress), 144

Cavell, Stanley, 24

Cawelti, John, 238n105

celebrity culture, 52, 124, 157

Charcot, Jean-Martin, 102–3

Chaudhuri, Una, 102

Chekhov, Anton: Benedictsson and, 245n213; capitalist modernity examined by, 20, 35–36, 144–46, 164, 205–6; expansive *oikos* of, 164–68; financial rewards of writing, 29, 155, 161, 163; gambling motif in, 148–49, 152, 154, 156–58, 168, 170; journalism work by, 14, 28, 39, 143–44, 146–52, 160–61, 173; material vs. spiritual/aesthetic in, 146, 158, 161–64, 167, 171–72; near hit in works of, 39, 144, 148–49, 152, 157–59, 163, 167–68, 170; personal life of, 97, 153–55, 167, 171, 173; reader's experience of, 157–60; relativity of representation in, 155–56; socioeconomic themes in, 18, 37, 133, 142, 160–61, 248n32; speculation in works of, 144–46, 153–54, 156–57, 159–60, 167–68; stories vs. drama of, 31, 145–46, 163

Chekhov, Anton, works of: *The Anniversary*, 149, 160–61, 168; "The Bet," 148, 159–60, 163, 168; "A Case History," 145; "Defenseless Creature," 250n92; "In the Ravine," 145, 163; *Ivanov*, 152, 172; *Platonov*, 148; *The Seagull*, 110, 148, 161–62, 166; "Three Years," 145; *The Wedding*, 152; "The Winning Ticket," 148, 152, 156–60, 168; "A Woman's Kingdom," 145. *See also Cherry Orchard, The*; *Three Sisters*; *Uncle Vanya*

Chekhov, Mikhail, 148

Chekhov, Pavel, 171

Chekhova, Masha, 148

Cherry Orchard, The (Chekhov): capitalist modernity in, 168, 170–73; casino capitalism in, 39, 145, 153–54; English investors in, 6, 172; environment in, 164; gambling/speculation/mortgage in, 148–49, 152, 163, 168–71; "Paris" in, 166; "useless" people in, 163, 167

Chevalier, Michel, 14

Chiapello, Eve, 21
Chicago Board of Trade, 27, 45
Chothia, Jean, 176–77, 183, 185
Christiansen, Sabine, 193
Churchill, Caryl, 35–36; *Serious Money*, 26, 206
Cicero, 11, 150
Cirque du Soleil, 206
Clark, Barrett H., 190
Clark, T. J., 15
climate crisis, 202, 204
closet dramas, 26, 175, 214n14, 223n190, 228n54
Collet, Camilla, 79
Collins, Charles, 191
colonialism/colonization, 23–24, 27, 40, 46, 67–68, 78
Comden, Betty, *A Doll's Life*, 78
comédie rosse, 27, 89–91, 117
comedy: of capital, 58–60, 95–96; Chekhov's, 169; cynical/bitter, 27, 89–91, 117, 193; dark (tragicomedy), 58–60, 95–96, 207; marriage in, 110, 164; *oikos* and, 35; US taste for, 190; Victorian, 26
commodities: fetishism/consumption of, 69–71, 73; labor as, 72, 180, 182–83; love as, 56; Marx on, 7–9, 70–71, 180; prostitution as, 128–29; theater as, 36–37; use value of, 105, 155, 182; women treated as, 85, 91, 93–94, 136–37, 205
communism, 11, 18, 37, 114, 116–17, 243n188
Compagnie Universelle du Canal Interocéanique de Panama, 28–29
Conrad, Joseph, 31; *Lord Jim*, 186
contemporary art, 3–4, 241n156
contemporary theater: money/capital explored by, 66–67, 206–8; upheavals in, 201–2, 204, 209–10. *See also* Akhtar, Ayad
Coontz, Stephanie, 108
copyright law, 79, 193
Coulisse, 32–33
Coupat, Julien, 202
courtship: bourgeoisie legitimated by, 108–10; capital and, 38–39, 77, 89–91; contradictions of under capitalism, 88–89, 111–12, 114–16; economic coercion and, 136; erotic desire and, 118–19; love marriage and, 84–85, 90–91, 108, 110–12, 114–15; in melodrama, 111–12, 117–18; vs. prostitution, 83–84, 113–14; as speculation, 83–86, 88–93, 111, 118–19. *See also* dowry; marriage; prostitution
COVID-19 pandemic, 201, 209
Cox, Cheryl Anne, 11
Cracknell, Carrie, 107
Crimean War, 152
critique. *See* immanent critique

Dalla Costa, Mariarosa, 72
dark matter, 45
Darwin, Charles, 14, 99
Davis, Tracy, 18, 73, 124, 128, 134, 141, 221n157
Death, Sarah, 136, 139
deBessonet, Lear, 210
debt: as dowry, 152; free love and, 141–42; guilt and, 104; mortgage and, 163–64, 167–70; promissory notes, 56–57, 138–39, 148, 152
Defoe, Daniel, 60, 111–12
Deleuze, Gilles, 123, 208
Deller, Jeremy, 3
Demosthenes, 150
Desnitsky, Semyon, 144
deus ex machina: in Akhtar, 207; in Chekhov, 170–72; in Ibsen, 44–45, 53, 58–60, 62–63, 65, 80, 204; in Kaiser, 195
Deutsches Theater, 189, 191
Dhaka University, 175
Dickens, Charles, 222n164
Dolan, Jill, 18–19, 117
Doll's House, A (Ibsen): Benedictsson's *Money* and, 31, 136, 138–39, 205; feminism of, 68, 72–73, 78, 165, 218n87; finance's workings in, 44, 56–57, 71, 73–74, 93; gossip in, 52; hidden/erased labor in, 38, 45, 67–69, 71–76, 78, 176; *hygge* in, 69–71, 73, 75–77, 80, 204; money appearing in, 36, 56, 71, 139;

Nora's final exit in, 63, 95, 138–39; productions/adaptations of, 69, 77–79; prostitution and, 76–78, 135; real-life inspiration for, 79–80; Strindberg on, 75–76, 80–81, 99–100; tarantella in, 69, 74–75
Donkin, Ellen, 141
Dostoevsky, Fyodor, 148
dowry: changing significance of, 84, 88–91, 108–10, 142, 205; debt as, 152; insider knowledge as, 118; lack of, 74, 83–86, 91; origins of, 112–15; relinquished, 134; shielded by woman, 103, 116; stolen, 166–68; "tainted" money and, 130, 132–33. *See also* inheritance
Dreiser, Theodore, 31; *Sister Carrie*, 179
Ducdame Ensemble, 140
Dukore, Bernard, 18, 25, 228n48
Dumas, Alexandre, 27, 111
Duncan, Augustin, 191–92
Durkheim, Émile, 5, 97
Durnenkov, Mikhail, 106

Eagleton, Terry, 24, 144
East Village Theater Company, 192
economic crashes, 16, 26, 28, 169, 193
economics: culture's reliance on, 162–63; emergence/growth of discourse of, 5, 10–14, 26–27, 44, 58; gendering of labor in, 71–75, 127; humanities bias against, 17–19, 34–35, 203, 219n129; marginalism, 7, 12–14, 86, 93, 122, 157, 203; "market," 10, 65–68, 110; neoclassical, 5, 7, 12–14, 19, 38–39, 112–13, 203; sexuality and, 7, 38–39, 76–78, 85–89, 104–6, 120–23; Strindberg's theory of, 97–98, 103; supply and demand, 12, 14, 19, 39, 44, 59; theater as testing grounds for, 36–37, 39, 101–2, 125, 144, 165–66, 182–84, 194. *See also* capitalism; financialization; *oikos*; political economy
economism, 7, 13, 55, 86, 164–66
Edward VII (king), 153
Eisler, Garrett, 118
Eliot, George, 4

Ellams, Inua, 40
Encores!, 210
Enemy of the People, An (Ibsen): destabilization of truth in, 43, 60–62, 67; financial capital's workings in, 28, 34, 44–46, 71; immanent critique in, 65–66; productions/adaptations of, 43, 46, 63–65, 202; radical individualism in, 62–63, 65
Engels, Friedrich: on bourgeoisie, 20–22, 38, 237n100; estate of, 14–15; on love under communism, 116–17; on marriage/dowry, 38, 76, 108, 112–15, 137; Paris Commune and, 11; on stock exchange, 27, 53
Enron, 206
Enwezor, Okwui, 3–4
erotic capital: conceptualized, 7, 77, 85–89; dangers of speculating with, 89–91; growing importance of, 108–9, 111, 118, 124, 140, 205; in *Miss Julie*, 7, 38, 91–94, 96, 104–5, 113, 141–42; in *Mrs. Warren's Profession*, 7, 38, 96, 127, 129, 131, 134, 141–42. *See also* capital
Essen, Siri von, 101, 115
Euripides, 45, 223n183
exchange value, 105, 147–48, 182
expressionism, 176–77, 181, 186–87, 193–99, 202, 206, 236n82

Fabian socialists, 7, 14–15, 25–26, 125–26, 128, 130, 132, 134
factory: conditions in, 129–30, 180–81; garment factory collapse, 175; industrialization of, 181–82, 186–87, 194, 196–97; noise of, 181, 186–87; rights of workers in, 177, 194; "tainted money" and, 129–30, 132; theater's resemblance to, 5; wages of, 150
fake news, 43, 60–62
Farber, Yaël, 40; *Mies Julie*, 106–7
Federal Theater Project, 210
Federici, Silvia, 72
Felix Bloch Erben, 193
Felski, Rita, 16
Ferguson, Robert, 46, 228n48
Figueiredo, Ivo de, 63

financial crimes/scandals: bank failures, 146–47, *147*; collective complicity in, 149–51; Enron, 206; forgeries, 71, 73–74, 79–80, 146, 172; lax laws and, 44; novels about, 31; Panama Canal and, 28–29; predatory banks, 16, 169; pyramid schemes, 143, 148, *151*; vs. sex scandals, 122–23, 127, 131–35, 161, 208; theatricality of, 143–44, 150–52, *151*, 160–61, 206–7. *See also* Rykov, Ivan

financial crises, 16, 26, 28, 169, 193

financialization: actuaries and, 97, 131, 134–35; changing moral landscape of, 51–53, 56, 58, 60–62, 74; circulation of money, 45–46, 128–34; conceptualized, 44–46; erotic energy of, 118–22, 130–31, 207–8; of fin de siècle, 27–29, 31; labor and, 172–73; legal "grey areas" and, 46, 51–52, 74, 133–34, 152–53; legal reforms and, 27, 44–46, 79, 98, 146, 151; railroads and, 32, 36, 44–47, 52, 146, 149; telegraph and, 28, 147. *See also* speculation

Finke, Michael C., 245n2

First Republic Bank, 208

Fisher, Mark, 17, 64, 204

Flaubert, Gustave, *Madame Bovary*, 77, 136–37, 141

Flint water crisis, 43

Floyd, George, 201

Foster, Hal, 16

Foucault, Michel, 109, 122

Foundry Theater, 210

Fowkes, Ben, 236n79

Frankenau, Anna Louisa, 95

Fraser, Steve, 32

free love, 116, 140–42

Freie Bühne, 176, 183, 188–90

Freie Volksbühne, 188–89

French Revolution, 108

French stock exchange, 32–33, *33*

Freud, Sigmund, 102–3, 119–22, 145, 156–58

Fried, Michael, 226n28

Fritsch, Herbert, 77

future(s): casino capitalism and, 247n17; of contemporary theater, 201–2, 209–10; daydreams/imaginings and, 145, 156–60, 164, 168, 171, 207; financial trading, 26–27, 32–33, 46, 50, 206; influencing of, 145, 147–48, 150; predicting of, 121–22, 133–34, 145, 147–48, 150, 153, 168; socialist rebirth and, 195; speculation and, 118, 143–45; "truth" and, 46, 64

Gagnier, Regenia, 13

Gainor, J. Ellen, 134

Galella, Donatella, 17

Galsworthy, John, 65, 144

gambling: art auction and, 171–72; bookmaking, 133–34; casino capitalism and, 39, 142, 145, 153–54, 164, 172–73, 206; as legal "grey area," 133–34, 152–53; lost bet and, 163–64; lottery bonds/tickets, 148, 152–53, 156–58, 163, 170–72; poker, 132–34, 171, 247n17; potential-laden temporality of, 144, 156–58; reckless, 119, 168, 170; roulette, 148; vs. speculation/investment, 5, 39, 132–34, 143, 152–55, 169; swindling and, 149. *See also* investment; luck; near hit; speculation

Garden Theater, 190

Garnica, Ximena, 209

German expressionism. *See* expressionism

German labor movement, 12, 175, 177, 182–83, 192–93

German naturalism, 176

German Revolution, 193, 198, 206

German Social Democratic Party (SPD), 15

Gilbert, Humphrey, 230n86

Gillmore, Frank, 192

Gilman, Charlotte Perkins, 77, 88, 141–42, 204

Goethe, Johann Wolfgang von, *Faust*, 26, 32, 72, 131

Gogol, Nikolai, *Inspector General*, 151

Goldman, Emma, 21, 203

Goll, Ivan, *Methusalem*, 197

Golub, Spencer, 171

Gorz, André, 25–26

Index

Graeber, David, 45
Granville-Barker, Harley, 35–36, 65
Green, Adam, 86–87
Green, Adolph, *A Doll's Life*, 78
Greer, Germaine, 128, 130
Griboedov, Alexander, *Woe from Wit*, 160
Grossman, Larry, *A Doll's Life*, 78
Groys, Boris, 4
Guattari, Félix, 123, 208
Guest, Kristen, 26–27
Guillory, John, 223n182
guilt, 104, 107, 113, 128, 186, 228n48
Gupta, Tanika, 78
Guthrie Theater, 43

Hägglund, Martin, 8, 22, 35, 216n74
Hakim, Catherine, 7, 38, 85–88
Halpern, Richard, 59–60
Halvorsen, Lauren, 210
Hansen, Ludvig, 235n37
Harbou, Thea von, 195
Hardwick, Elizabeth, 68
Harries, Martin, 54
Harrison, Peter, 53
Hart, Julius, 188
Harvey, David, 3, 7, 73, 217n83
Hatch, Ryan, 4
Haugen, Einar, 231n95
Hauptmann, Anja, 193
Hauptmann, Gerhart: capitalism and, 14, 25, 190–91; *Florian Geyer*, 177; life of, 187, 190; naturalism of, 176–77. *See also Weavers, The*
Hauptmann, Robert, 187
Haymarket Affair, 11
Headland, Leslye, 208
Hegel, Frederik, 47, 65
Hegel, Georg Wilhelm Friedrich, 16, 59
Heidenstam, Verner von, 98
Heinzelman, Kurt, 34
Helfant, Ian, 154
Hellman, Lillian, 208
Hemming, Sarah, 244n212
Henderson, Archibald, 125
heteroglossia, 126–27
Hewitt, Elizabeth, 19
Hnath, Lucas, *A Doll's House, Part 2*, 78–79
Hodgson, Geoffrey M., 213n13

Holmes, Sean, 192
Holmgren, Beth, 18, 155, 172
Homer, *Iliad*, 52
Honneth, Axel, 37
Howard, Bronson, *Henrietta*, 118
Howells, William Dean, *The Rise of Silas Lapham*, 31–32
Hudson, Pat, 73
humanities' hostility toward economics, 17–19, 34–35, 203, 219n129
Hutchings, Stephen, 162–63
hygge, 69–71, 73, 75–77, 80, 204

Ibsen, Henrik: capitalist modernity examined by, 20, 31, 35–38, 44–46, 53, 65–67, 73, 204, 207; deus ex machina of capital in, 44–45, 53, 58–60, 62, 65, 204; finances of, 44, 57, 65, 71, 79; modernism of, 75, 245n3; naturalism and, 176; socialist leanings of, 14–16, 34, 38, 46–47, 72; socioeconomic themes in, 18, 31–32, 40, 43–44, 49; theater management by, 5, 44; theme of future in, 156; theories of money in, 56–57, 71
Ibsen, Henrik, works of: *Brand*, 44, 80, 228n54; *Catiline*, 47; *Ghosts*, 44, 53, 65, 165; *Hedda Gabler*, 44, 70, 76, 94, 106, 136, 139–40; *Little Eyolf*, 47; *The Master Builder*, 26, 47; "Notes for a Modern Tragedy," 74; *Peer Gynt*, 26, 46, 63, 72, 228n54; *The Wild Duck*, 44. *See also Doll's House, A*; *Enemy of the People, An*; *John Gabriel Borkman*
Ibsen, Sigurd, 14
Ibsen, Suzannah, 47, 57
idealism, 162, 197, 245n3
Illouz, Eva, 110
immanent critique: bourgeoisie and, 22–24, 113–15; of capitalism, 5, 14–17, 203, 206; conceptualized, 16, 21–22, 37; courtship/love marriage and, 84–86, 112–15; of Fabianism, 134; modern drama as site of, 15–16, 19–21, 25–26, 114–15, 203, 210–11; realism and, 39–40; theater as site of, 24–25, 36–37, 65–66

incentive bonus, 158, 160
incest, 131–32, 134, 136–37
individualism: erotic capital and, 87–88; Ibsen and, 16, 63; love under communism and, 116–17; marginal revolution and, 13, 122; vs. market, 26–27, 58; marriage and, 108–11; "tainted" money and, 130
Industrial Relations Committee, 191–92
Industrial Revolution, 68, 256n88
inheritance, 62, 65, 98, 111, 137, 150, 152, 166–67. *See also* dowry
insider trading, 51, 66
Institute of Public Knowledge, 210
insurance, 53, 97, 134, 137, 153, 210
intellectual superman, 16, 98, 187, 194–97
investment: vs. gambling, 143, 152–53, 169; infrastructure development and, 146–49; as legitimate financial activity, 133, 152. *See also* gambling; speculation; stock exchange
Invisible Committee, *The Coming Insurrection*, 43, 202
invisible hand: Akhtar's play of this name, 30, 66–67, 207; of capital/market, 6, 38–39, 44–45, 52–54, 57–58, 65–67, 94, 204; conceptualized, 52–53; of foreign investors, 172–73; as "icy, iron," 55–60; of labor, 67, 76, 173; of Providence, 38, 44, 51–53, 57, 59; rumor/gossip as, 52; as "scare quote," 227n47
Irwin, Elizabeth, 208
Ivan the Fool, 154

Jacobs, Barry, 103
Jacobs-Jenkins, Branden, 43, 208
Jakovljević, Branislav, 63
James, Henry, 111; *The Wings of a Dove*, 85, 112
Jameson, Fredric, 178–79, 181, 186
Jelinek, Elfriede, *What Happened after Nora Left Her Husband*, 78
Jevons, William Stanley, 13, 34, 93, 125–26
John Gabriel Borkman (Ibsen): comedy of capital in, 58–60, 65; finance's workings in, 26, 44–45, 71; "icy, iron hand" in, 55–60, 105; immanent critique in, 36
Joseph, Melanie, 209–10
journalism. *See* Rykov, Ivan
Joyce, James, 172
Julien, Isaac, 3, 7

Kaiser, Georg, 20, 25, 181, 194–95; "The Coming Man," 195; *Gas* trilogy (*The Coral, Gas I* and *II*), 177, 187, 194–95, 198–99
Kane, Sarah, 43
Kaplan, Marion, 91
Kaufmann, David, 224n4
Kelley, Florence, 77
Kennedy, Gavin, 52, 57
Kent, Brad, 111
Khemiri, Jonas Hassen, ≈ [*Almost Equal To*], 207
Khudekov, Sergei, 146
Kieler, Laura (née Petersen), 79–80
Kirby, Vanessa, 107
Klinenberg, Eric, 210
Knipper, Olga, 169
Kocka, Jürgen, 21–22
Kofi Abrefa, Eric, 107
Krauthamer, Adam, 209
Krupp Foundation, 36
Kviatkovsky, Yuri, 77–78

La Berge, Leigh Claire, 19
labor: artistic representations of, 3, 175–81, 208; commodified, 72, 180, 182–83; erasure under capitalism, 175–77, 185–86; exploitation of, 129–30, 149, 177, 181, 192, 194–96; industrialization of, 181–82, 186–87, 195–99; mental, 183, 195–98; Protestant work ethic and, 21, 58, 154, 178, 183–86, 188; Silesian weaver revolt, 175, 177, 182–84, 187; strikes by, 11–12, 39, 180, 182–84, 191; theatrical, 75, 167, 176, 178–79, 189, 191, 199, 209–10. *See also* proletariat; *Weavers, The* (Hauptmann)
LaBute, Neil, 106
Lafargue, Paul, 101–2, 153
Lampedusa migrant shipwreck, 3–4

Index

Lampkin, Agnes, 69
Lang, Fritz, *Metropolis*, 194–95
Lange, Wilhelm, 78
Latour, Bruno, 16
Law, John, 149
Lawrence, D. H., 103
League of Proletarian Revolutionary Writers (BRPS), 194
Leechman, William, 52
Léger, Fernand, *Ballet méchanique*, 199
Lehman brothers, 16–17
Lenin, Vladimir, 11, 144, 146
Lesseps, Ferdinand de, 28–29
Lewes, George Henry, 26
Lewisohn, Ludwig, 190
Leykin, Nikolai, *Fragments*, 146, 150
Lillo, George, *The London Merchant*, 6, 26
Lincoln Center, 201, 208
Lindberg, August, 47
Lisi, Leonardo F., 72, 228n55
London Dock Strike, 12
London International Financial Futures and Options Exchange, 26, 206
Lösch, Volker, 176, 192–93; *The Dresden Weavers*, 193
luck: in capitalist modernity, 142, 164, 168, 170–73, 205; class hierarchies and, 104, 124; vs. divine order, 52, 153–54; in gambling, 148, 168; speculation and, 27–28, 66, 144–48, 156, 161; women's options and, 91, 130
Luddites, 187, 256n88
Lukács, Georg, 183
Lukashenko, Alexander, 201
Lundegård, Axel, 139
Luther, Martin, 50
Luxemburg, Rosa, 15, 22
Lyotard, Jean-François, 123

Macleod, Henry Dunning, 228n55
Maeterlinck, Maurice, 162, 245n3
Makovsky, Vladimir, *The Collapse of a Bank*, 146, 147
Malthus, Thomas, 98
Mamet, David, 35–36, 208
Mandelstam, Osip, 165–66

Marber, Patrick, *After Miss Julie*, 106
Marcus, Sharon, 124
marginal revolution, 7, 12–14, 86, 122, 157, 203
marginal utility (Jevons's theory), 125–26
market economy, 10, 65–68, 110. See also economics; political economy
marriage: as bourgeois sexual contract, 108–10, 112–17, 122, 124, 204–5; capital and, 38–39, 71–77, 80; as economic utility, 93–94, 112–13; historical transition in, 108–10; interracial, 106–7; as limiting horizons, 166–67; monogamy and, 113–14, 116; vs. prostitution, 38, 76, 112–13, 115–16, 136–37, 140; as slavery, 114–16; women's rights in, 98. See also courtship; prostitution
marriage market, 84–86, 88–92, 108, 110, 128, 131
Marsh, Nicky, 20
Marshall, Alfred, 12–13
Martin, Felix, 228n55
Marx, Bill, 191
Marx, Karl: on bourgeoisie, 20–22, 237n100; capital defined by, 7–9, 87; on capitalist production/capitalism, 5, 27–28, 54, 64, 104, 107, 149, 195; on commodities, 7–9, 70–71, 180; critique of political economy by, 4, 11, 16, 114; family of, 68–69; formula of capital, 7–8, 32, 153, 179, 207; on labor, 39, 67, 71–72, 122–23, 180; legacy of, 3–4, 14–15, 22, 125–26, 198; on machines, 196; Paris Commune and, 11, 15; on proletariat, 182–83, 188; on use value, 105, 155, 182; on weavers' revolt, 39, 182–83
Marx-Aveling, Eleanor, 68–69; *A Doll's House Repaired*, 79
Marxism, 38, 72, 96–97, 102, 125–26, 144; *The Weavers* and, 182–85, 188, 192
Massini, Stefano, *Lehman Trilogy*, 16–17
matriarchy, 101–2, 114, 238n102

Matthis, April, 209
Maudsley, Henry, 102
McClain, Elijah, 201
McCulloch, John Ramsay, 14
McDade, Tony, 201
McKinnie, Michael, 215n40
Mehring, Franz, 188–89
Meisel, Martin, 243n194
melodrama: capitalism represented in, 9, 26–27, 34, 47–51, 54, 89–90; conceptualized, 31, 48; courtship/marriage/sex in, 111–12, 117–18, 142, 204–5; expressionist, 195–97; financial, 34, 47–51, 118; mortgage, 164, 170; suicide in, 94
Menand, Louis, 111
Menger, Carl, 13
Merezhkovsky, Dmitry, 162
metaphor: casino/economy, 142; Chekhov's Moscow as, 166–67; coin flip as, 113; conceptualized, 39, 56–57; dollhouse as, 67–68, 76; machines/monsters, 196–97; prostitution/capitalism, 128; prostitution/marriage, 38, 136–37; sex/money, 120–23, 128; speculation/moral relativism, 28, 32; theater/brothel, 123–24; theater/riot, 178–79; usury/incest, 136–37, 244n198. See also invisible hand; money
metatheatrical devices, 36, 48–49, 58–59, 75, 77, 95, 178–79
Meyering, Sheryl, 11
Michelangelo, 125
Michie, Elsie, 111
middle class. See bourgeoisie
Mikhailovskii, Nikolai, 155
Mill, John Stuart, 11, 88, 136
Miller, Arthur, 54
Miranda, Lin-Manuel, *Hamilton*, 17
misogyny, 71, 99–100, 106, 205
Miss Julie (Strindberg): Benedictsson and, 136, 139–40; courtship/love marriage in, 83–85, 101, 115–17; economic/erotic desire in, 118–22; ending of, 94–96, 102, 136; erotic capital in, 7, 38, 91–94, 96, 104–5, 113, 141–42; gender/class hierarchies in, 102–4, 106–7, 115–16, 131, 176; halves of humanity in, 81, 204–5; money appearing in, 36, 83–85, 104–6, 113–14, 123–24; postcoital negotiations in, 83–85, 104–5, 113–14; productions/adaptations of, 40, 101–2, 104–7, 123–24; Woman Question in, 98–99, 103

modern drama: bourgeois subjectivity and, 23, 203; courtship/love marriage plot in, 84–86, 108, 110; economic experimentation in, 36–37, 39, 101–2, 125, 144, 165–66, 182–84, 194; erotic capital in, 86, 88, 141–42; female tropes in, 140; immanent critique rooted in, 15–16, 19–21, 25–26, 114–15, 203, 210–11; its canon and erasures, 40; materiality of, 5–6, 10, 31, 172–73, 193; nineteenth-century novel and, 30–32; political economy studied by dramatists of, 13–14, 19–20; speculation's energy dramatized in, 32, 130–31
modernism (theater): as "fraud," 146; Ibsen's, 75; impressionist strategy of, 186–87; painted sets and, 236n82; Russian, 144, 165
modernity: capitalist, 4, 35–36, 54, 96, 168, 170–73, 204–6; childhood/play in, 67–68; erasure of labor/money in, 67–68, 72, 110–11; religion/secularization and, 53, 65, 67, 153–54; volatility/time-sensitivity in, 146–49, 155, 157, 161. See also Protestant work ethic
Modern Stage (New York), 189–91
Moi, Toril, 68, 75, 77, 245n3
money: changes in value and, 155; credit theory of, 56–57, 71, 149; erotic power of, 136–37, 141–42, 207–8; labor theory of, 67, 70–71, 73, 76; as medium of exchange, 56–57, 71, 105–6, 119, 153, 164, 179, 244n198; ontology of, 20, 123; paper, 26, 71–72, 136–37; plays about, 26–27, 68; sexuality and, 104, 119–23, 128, 136, 141–42, 207–8; "spare," 7, 126; staged instances of, 36, 50, 56, 83–84,

104–6, 113–14, 123–24, 136–37; as symbol for desires/dreams, 30, 164–66; "tainted," 36, 65, 129–35, 163; tangible vs. intangible, 56–57; as vulgar/taboo topic, 110–11, 119–20, 124, 131–32, 146, 154–55, 162, 168, 172, 185
Moody, Jane, 7, 23
Morell, Purni, *Public Enemy: Flint*, 43
Moreno, Mireya, 69
Moretti, Franco, 32, 46, 49, 67, 156, 165–66, 206, 238n108
Morgan, Lewis H., 114
Morgan Stanley, 208
Morison, Mary, 190
Morisseau, Dominique, 208
Morozov, Savva, 171
Morris, May, 69
Morris, Rosalind, 236n79
Morris, William, 3, 25, 69
Morson, Gary Saul, 163
mortgage: melodrama of, 164, 170; speculation and, 163–64, 167–70; subprime crisis, 16, 169
Morton, Martha, *A Fool of Fortune*, 118
Moscow Art Theater, 18, 169, 171
Mrs. Warren's Profession (Shaw): brothel/prostitution in, 93, 127–32, 135; courtship in, 84–85, 125, 127, 131; erotic capital in, 7, 38, 96, 127, 129, 131, 134, 141–42; financial capital in, 128–29, 128–34; incest in, 131–32, 134; New Woman in, 124, 131, 134–35; in novels, 88, 119; spare/tainted money in, 7, 65, 129–35
Munford, Rebecca, 85
Muñoz-Alonso, Lorena, 3
musical diplomacy, 67–68
Myers, Chris, 209

Naismith, Bill, 208
National Theatre (London), 107, 139
naturalism: as antitheatrical, 177–78; capitalism represented in, 31–32, 118–19, 178–80; *Miss Julie* and, 95–96, 99, 105; *The Weavers* and, 175–78

near hit, 144, 147–48, 163, 167–68; near miss, 147–48, 150, 152, 160, 168; near win, 39, 147–48, 157–60, 170
Nederlander Organization, 17
neoclassical economics. *See* economics
neoliberalism, 45, 85–88, 217n83
Neue Freie Volksbühne, 188–89
Nevezhin, Pyotr, 251n105
New Deutsches Theater, 189
New Man. *See* intellectual superman
New Woman. *See* Woman Question
Nichols, Peter, 208
Nietzsche, Friedrich, 16, 45, 98–99, 187, 194–95
Nisbet, Robert, 57
Noguera, Amparo, 69
Norris, Frank, 179; *The Pit*, 31–32
Norway's modernization, 38, 44–47, 51–52, 61, 72
Nottage, Lynn, 208
novel: of capital, 23, 30–35, 179, 224n4; erotic capital/desire in, 88, 119; female tropes in, 137–39; heteroglossia of, 126–27; marriage plots in, 85, 108–11, 117, 204–5; prostitute narrative in, 111, 139; vs. theater, 23–24, 29–32, 34, 126–27, 179–80, 186; work represented in, 179–80

Obayashi, Nobuhiko, 169
Occupy Wall Street, 204
Odets, Clifford, 208
oikos: Chekhov's expansive view of, 164–68; conceptualized, 11–12, 203; contemporary economic imaginary and, 203–4; natural environment as, 164–65; Nora's home viewed as, 68, 72–74; patriarchal capitalism and, 112–16; in shared home of theater, 35, 38, 40, 165, 209–10
O'Neill, Eugene, *The Hairy Ape*, 187, 208
Open Your Lobby Initiative, 209
Orwell, George, 4
Osborne, John, 176, 185
Oscar II (king), 14
Oslo Børs, 46
Osteen, Mark, 35

Ostermeier, Thomas, 17, 38, 40, 43, 202–3; *An Enemy of the People* production, 43, 63–65, 202; *Miss Julie* adaptation, 106; *Nora*, 69
Ostrovsky, Alexander, *Without a Dowry*, 90–91, 117
Ovchinnikov, Vladimir, 150
Ovid, *Metamorphoses*, 52

Panama Canal, 28–29
Paperny, Zinovy, 149
Paris Bourse, 32–33, *33*
Paris Commune, 11, 15
Park Avenue Armory, 16, 201
Pascal, Roy, 20
Pateman, Carole, 109
patriarchy: challenged, 101–2, 116–17; disguised workings of, 85, 107, 123, 135, 208; sexual double standard of, 88, 90–91, 113–14; women disempowered/devalued by, 109, 112–14, 128, 140–41, 168, 205. *See also* capitalism
Péreire brothers, 149
Phelan, Peggy, 121
Pillars of the Community (Ibsen): capitalist modernity in, 53–55, 66, 149; financial capital's workings in, 44–46, 71; Ibsen's own investment activities and, 46–47; invisible hand in, 51–53
Pinochet, Augusto, 69
Plato, 11, 55
Polanyi, Karl, 10
Polendo, Rubén, *House*, 169
political economy: conceptualized, 6, 12, 224n4; dramatists' exposure to thought of, 13–14, 19–20; gendered, 73–76, 109–10, 127; vs. Greek *oikos*, 11–12; invisible force in, 53–54, 65; Jevons's theory of marginal utility, 125–26; "natural laws" of, 16, 39; neoliberalism, 45, 85–88, 217n83; Ricardo's law of rent, 125–26, 128, 132. *See also* capitalism; economics; financialization; *oikos*
Poovey, Mary, 35
Popkin, Cathy, 149, 155
Porfiriev, V. I., *151*
Prebble, Lucy, 35–36; *Enron*, 206

proletariat: birth of, 20, 22; defined, 237n100; distrust/fear of, 23, 39, 177, 194, 196–97, 206; as dramatic agent, 176, 183–84; exploitation of, 129–30, 149, 177; gamblers in, 153; revolutionary consciousness of, 182–85, 187, 193–94, 202–3; Strindberg's "underclass," 97–98, 103; theater/art of, 188–89, 194. *See also* bourgeoisie; labor
prostitution: actors' association with, 123–24; capitalist enterprise of, 38–39, 76–78, 122, 128–31, 133; capitalist work as, 123, 128; contemporary views on, 135; vs. courtship, 83–84, 113–14; Engels on, 38, 76; incest fears and, 131–32, 134, 136–37; vs. marriage, 38, 76, 112–13, 115–16, 136–37, 140; New Woman and, 124, 134–35; popular narrative of, 111, 128–29, 139; speculation and, 93, 96, 127; Strindberg on, 101; terminology for, 233n2, 239n112; Victorian views on, 127–28, 131–33, 135. *See also* brothel; courtship; marriage
Protestant work ethic, 21, 58, 154, 178, 183–86, 188
Proudhon, Pierre-Joseph, 5
Proust, Marcel, 160
Providence, 38, 44, 51–53, 56–57, 59
psychoanalysis, 119–22, 207
public/private spheres, 72–75, 88, 109–10, 112–13, 121–24, 205
Puchner, Martin, 36–37, 126–27
Putin, Vladimir, 106

Quinn, D. B., 67–68

racism, 17, 24, 106–7, 201, 209
railroads: financialization and, 32, 36, 44–47, 52, 146, 149; Norway's boom in, 44, 46, 51–52; speculation and, 118, 170–71
Rancière, Jacques, 16
Ravenhill, Mark, 43
"Re:Opening?" (symposium), 209–10
realism (theatrical): capitalism and, 39–40, 46, 64–66; Chekhov and, 165, 245n3; in financial melodrama,

Index

49–50; vs. Ibsen, 70, 77–78; vs. Shaw, 132. *See also* capitalist realism
reflexivity trap, 22–23
Reicher, Emanuel, 6, 189–92
Reilly, Darryl, 245n213
revolution: American/French, 108; bourgeoisie and, 20–23, 177, 183, 194; consciousness of, 11, 182–85, 187, 193–94, 202–3; German, 193, 198, 206; Industrial, 68, 256n88; labor/proletariat and, 11, 176–79; vs. reform, 14–15, 22, 25–26, 37, 125–26, 209–10; Russian, 12, 144, 169, 206; theater as rehearsal for, 202–3; as violent destruction, 184–85, 195–97, 199. *See also* marginal revolution
Ribot, Théodule-Armand, 102
Ricardo, David, 125–26
Rice, Elmer, 181; *The Adding Machine*, 65, 187, 208
Richardson, Samuel, 108
Ridout, Nicholas, 18–20, 23–24, 29–30, 167, 237n100
Roach, Joseph, 52
Robbins, Bruce, 4
robot/*robota*, 37, 195
Rodgers, Daniel, 186
Rogers, Gayle, 84, 145, 159
Rokem, Freddie, 102
Romanova, Galina, 169–70
Romanticism, 29, 34, 95–96, 210
Rooney, Sally, 23, 25
Roosevelt, Theodore, 29
Rosenlarv, 101
Rudbeck, Emma, 234n35
Ruskin, John, 11
Russia: capitalism in, 143–47, 151, 154–55, 163–64, 171–72; class system in, 12, 150, 166; failing aristocratic estate in, 164–66, 169–70; newspaper circulation in, 157; railroads in, 146, 149, 170–71; religion/folklore of, 154; serfdom in, 146, 173. *See also* Soviet Union
Russian modernism, 144, 165
Russian Revolution, 12, 144, 169, 206
Russian symbolism, 162
Russo-Turkish War, 150
Russo-Ukrainian War, 202

Rykov, Ivan: Chekhov's journalism on, 14, 28, 39, 143, 146–52, *151*, 160–61, 173; Chekhov's later allusions to, 39, 144, 152, 160, 168

Saint-Simon, Claude Henri, 14
Sakhalin Island, 248n32
Sarcey, Francisque, 33
Scarry, Elaine, 179
Schäffle, Albert, 213n13
Schaubühne, 43, 63, 69
Schmitt, Carl, 53
Schnabel, Stefan, 176, 192–93; *The Dresden Weavers*, 193
Schumpeter, Joseph, 21, 167
Seccombe, Wally, 72
Second International, 11
securities, 55–56, 149, 153, 167
Seghal, Tino, 241n156
Selivanov, Gavriil, 154
Senelick, Laurence, 144, 152, 251n105
sexology, 122–23
sexonomics, 76–78, 141–42
sexuality, 122–23, 137–38. *See also* erotic capital
Shadwell, Thomas, *The Volunteers, or The Stockjobbers*, 26
Shakespeare, William, 110; *King Lear*, 24; *Macbeth*, 52, 106, 227n47; *Timon of Athens*, 26, 123
Sharp, R. Farquharson, 51
Shaw, G. Bernard: acting by, 69; box office receipts and, 5, 125; capitalist modernity examined by, 20, 35–36, 65, 205; heteroglossia in plays of, 126–27; socialist/economic views of, 7, 14–15, 21, 25–26, 125–26; socioeconomic themes in, 18, 123, 126–27, 130, 176; on women/marriage/erotic capital, 89, 111, 114, 123. *See also* Fabian socialists
Shaw, G. Bernard, works of: *Getting Married*, 89, 127; *Major Barbara*, 6, 25–26, 36–37, 65, 127, 130, 185; *Man and Superman*, 127; *The Millionairess*, 243n188; *The Philanderer*, 127; *Pygmalion*, 127; *Still after the Doll's House*, 79; *Widowers' Houses*, 6, 65, 127
Shaw, Helen, 245n213

Shell, Marc, 35, 56, 123
Shepherd-Barr, Kirsten, 39, 76
Sheridan, Richard, 52
Shirey, Linda, 192
Shneyder, Vadim, 145
Silesian weaver revolt, 175, 177, 182–84, 187. *See also Weavers, The* (Hauptmann)
Simmel, Georg, 97, 108, 112–14, 145, 155, 168
Sinclair, Upton, 31, 179
Smith, Adam: beneficiaries and, 4, 66; "capital" defined by, 6; invisible hand and, 38, 52–53, 57–58, 227n47; on production, 59–60; Russian capitalism and, 144
Social Democratic Party (SPD) of Germany, 15, 188–89
socialism: agrarian economy and, 97, 114, 121–22, 145, 194–95; fin de siècle and, 11–12; reform vs. revolution and, 14–15, 22, 25–26, 37, 125–26, 209–10; theorized, 5. *See also* Fabian socialists; Marxism
socialist realism, 64
Sofer, Andrew, 45, 105
Solomon, Alisa, 192
Solovyov, Nikolai, 251n105
Sophia (queen), 101
South Sea Bubble, 26, 28
Soviet Union, 12, 106, 144, 169, 229n75, 243n188. *See also* Russia
Spanish flu pandemic, 192, 202
Special Anti-Robbery Squad (Nigeria), 202
spectatorship: bourgeois theater and, 23–25, 29, 188, 190–93; Broadway, 17, 43; complicity of, 123–24, 128, 132; consciousness raising and, 183–85, 188, 202–3, 208–9; labor of performance and, 29–30; "spectactor," 202–3; of stock exchange, 32–33, 33. *See also* theater
speculation: actuaries and, 131, 134–35; contemplation as, 55–58, 63–65, 145, 156, 159–60, 164, 168; courtship as, 83–86, 88–93, 111, 118–19; deception/moral relativism and, 28–29, 31, 33–34, 46–48, 52, 62, 122–23, 144; erotic desire/capital and, 93, 118–23, 130–31, 141–42; in financial melodrama, 47–50; frenzy/fervor of, 9, 32–34, 33, 118–20, 171–72; vs. gambling, 5, 39, 132–34, 143, 152–54; luck and, 27–28, 66, 144–48, 156, 161; mortgage and, 163–64, 167–70; as perverse, 131–33; poetic, 171–72, 206; potentiality of, 156, 159–60, 170–72, 205–6; prostitution and, 93, 96, 127; theater's reliance on, 30, 124; theatricality of, 32–34, 33, 48–50, 53–54, 66, 143–44, 150–52, 151; women as stock/investments/commodities, 85, 91, 93–94, 136–37, 205. *See also* gambling; investment; stock exchange
Spencer, Herbert, 11
spirituality: antispeculation and, 49–50; Chekhov's focus on, 31, 153–54; economy and, 35; Ibsen's focus on, 15, 37, 58. *See also* Protestant work ethic; Providence
Sprinchorn, Evert, 15–16, 99
Staatsschauspiel Dresden, 176, 192–93
Stalin, Joseph, 126
Stamm, August, 256n94
Stanislavski, Konstantin, 169, 172
Stenham, Polly, *Julie*, 107
Stenport, Anna Westerståhl, 73, 75–77, 98, 219n129, 244n209
Stewart, Susan, 68
stock exchange: architecture of, 32–33, 33; brothel and, 124, 128; divine election and, 53; high-frequency trading and, 153; historical development of, 27–28, 46; marriage market and, 84–86, 88–92, 108, 110, 128, 131; newspaper coverage of, 157; novels of, 31–32; reckless gambling on, 119, 159; stock-jobbers on, 26, 206; stock price tickers, 28, 118, 147; "tainted money" and, 134–35; theater's resemblance to, 5, 32–34, 66, 124; time sensitivity and, 146–47, 149. *See also* investment; speculation; Wall Street
Stone, Lawrence, 108

Strange, Susan, 247n17
Strindberg, August: capitalist modernity examined by, 20, 37, 204–5, 207; on Ibsen's *A Doll's House*, 75–76, 80–81, 99–100; misogyny/protofeminism of, 98–103, 115–16, 123, 205; naturalism of, 99, 105, 176; socialism of, 14–16, 96–99, 102–3, 107
Strindberg, August, works of: *Among French Peasants*, 97; "Bread," 98; *Creditors*, 99, 104, 140; "A Doll's House" (short story), 100; *The Father*, 99, 101; *Getting Married*, 99–102, 115; "Just to Be Married," 115; "Love and the Price of Grain," 115; *The Marauders*, 99; *The Red Room*, 96–97; "The Reward of Virtue," 97–98; *Sir Bengt's Wife*, 99; *Small Catechism for the Underclass*, 97, 115; *Swedish Destinies and Adventures*, 96; *The Swedish People*, 96. See also *Miss Julie*
Strindberg, Nora, 96
Stull, Jay, 210
"success theater," 48
Suez Canal, 28, 46
suicide, 55, 79, 94–96, 136, 139–41, 155, 158, 205
Sumner, William, 97
Suvorin, Aleksey, 161
Swedberg, Richard, 97
Sweden: class hierarchies in, 103–4; Woman Question in, 98–101, 116
Swell's Night Guide, The, 124
symbolism, 162, 165, 245n3

Tawney, R. H., 10–11, 52–53, 58
Taylor, Breonna, 201
Taylor, Frederick Winslow, 181
Taylorization (aesthetic), 34, 180–81
Teixeira, Thalissa, 237n90
Telegrammstil, 198
telegraph, 28, 147, 149, 198
Templeton, Joan, 68, 218n87, 231n107, 232n124
temporality: of daydreaming/contemplation, 156–60; of near hit, 39, 144, 147–48, 163, 167–68, 206; of stagnation, 163–64

textile workers. See labor; *Weavers, The* (Hauptmann)
Thalheimer, Michael, 191
theater: actress and public/private divide, 73, 124, 205; architecture of, 30, 32–33; as bound up with capitalism, 16–19, 26–30, 58, 146, 161–63, 188, 190–91, 207–10; brothel and, 5, 123–24; contemporary, 66–67, 201–2, 204, 206–10; economic experimentation in, 36–38, 41, 67; experience of time in, 163–64; immanent critique rooted in, 24–25, 36–37, 65–66; as income source, 29, 44, 47, 118; jury trial as, 143–44, 146, 149–51, 160–61, 173; labor of, 75, 167, 176, 178–79, 189, 191, 199, 209–10; material conditions of, 5–6, 10, 31, 39, 191, 201, 209–10; vs. novel, 23–24, 29–32, 34, 126–27, 179–80, 186; "of capital," 5–6, 17, 35–41, 65–66, 203–5; political value of, 18–21, 23–24, 45, 202; potentials of, 177; for proletariat, 188–89; vs. stock exchange, 5, 32–34, 66, 124; visible/invisible and, 7, 44–45, 121. See also spectatorship
Theater Mitu, 169
Théâtre Libre, 105, 183, 189–90
Third Reich, 36
Three Sisters (Chekhov): adaptations of, 40; contemplation in, 156, 164; fire in, 154; gambling/speculation/mortgage in, 148, 163–64, 168; mercantile view of, 165–66; "Moscow" as metaphor in, 166–67
Tismer, Anne, 69
Toller, Ernst, 20, 25, 181, 194, 198; *Hoppla, We're Alive!*, 197–98; *The Machine Wreckers*, 177, 187, 195–97; *Masses and the Man*, 197
Törnqvist, Egil, 103
Townsend, Sarah J., 29
tragedy, 26, 35, 45, 58–59, 94–95, 127, 164, 169, 190
Trans-Siberian Railroad, 171
Treadwell, Sophie, 181; *Machinal*, 187, 208
Tretyakov, Ivan, 144

Trilling, Lionel, 233n7
Trollope, Anthony, 31
Trotsky, Leon, 18, 162
Tulip Mania, 28
Turner, Victor, 57

Uncle Vanya (Chekhov), 153, 162–68
unionism, 11–12, 67, 189, 191–92, 209
US labor movement, 11, 189, 191–92
usury, 26, 50, 244n198
utopian performatives, 18–19, 37, 80, 117, 136, 176, 202

Varoufakis, Yanis, 147–48
vaudeville, 160–61
Veblen, Thorstein, 27–28
Venice Biennale, 3, 7
Vercelli, Alessandro, 45
Victorian morality, 127–28, 131–33, 135
Vogel, Paula, 100
Volksbühne, 181, 192

Wagner, Matthew, 164
Waldman, Katy, 23
Wallerstein, Immanuel, 220n142
Wall Street, 6, 16, 32, 118, 204. *See also* speculation; stock exchange
Walrus, Léon, 13
Watt, Ian, 108–9, 238n105, 238n108
Weavers, The (Hauptmann): as catalyzing force for labor, 10, 39, 176, 188–89, 191, 193, 206, 208–9; contemporary productions/adaptations of, 175–76, 181, 191–93; earliest (1890s) productions of, 176, 183, 188–90; expressionist mode of, 176–77, 181, 186–87, 193; German expressionist responses to, 177, 187, 193–97; human labor displayed in, 175–81; as practical counterpoint to Marxist theory, 182–85, 188, 192; Protestant work ethic denaturalized in, 178, 183–86, 188; Reicher's 1915 English-language production of, 6, 175–76, 189–92; source material of, 175, 177, 182–84, 187–88; stage directions in, 175, 177–79, 181–82, 190

Webb, Beatrice, 124
Weber, Bruce, 112
Weber, Max, 5, 21, 97, 185
Weimar hyperinflation, 193
Weinstein, Cindy, 186
Wells, H. G., 144
"We See You White American Theatre," 209
Wesker, Arnold, 208
Whitaker, Chelsea, 17
white supremacy, 17, 24, 106–7, 201, 209
Wickstrom, Maurya, 217n79
Wilde, Oscar, 35–36, 65, 111; *An Ideal Husband*, 28–29; *Lady Windermere's Fan*, 28
Wille, Bruno, 188–89
Williams, Kirk, 177–78
Witte, Sergei, 172
Wolff, Wilhelm, 177, 188
Wollstonecraft, Mary, 85–86, 112
Woman Question: commodification of women, 85, 91, 93–94, 136–37, 205; economic options and, 127, 129–30, 137, 139–41, 166; Fallen Woman and, 95, 111, 134–35, 140, 142; New Woman and, 79, 113, 124, 127, 130–31, 134–35, 197; realism and, 39–40; Strindberg's views on, 98–103; trope of female suicide and, 79, 94–96, 136, 139–41, 205; women's power/independence and, 109–10, 113–16, 124, 134–36, 138–41. *See also* erotic capital; patriarchy
women's work: actuarial, 131, 134–35; art, 129–30, 135–42; copying, 71; factory, 129–30; household/domestic labor, 72–76, 78, 88, 109–10, 112–13, 115, 137; physiotherapy, 139; prostitution, 38–39, 76–78, 127, 129, 135; "sex functions" and, 88; theater/acting, 73, 124, 141, 162, 205; writing, 78–80, 118, 136, 140–41
Wood, James, 155
Wood, Michael, 112

Woodmansee, Martha, 34–35
Woolf, Virginia, 144
World War I, 6, 11–12, 97, 192–93, 202
Worthen, W. B., 39–40, 242n169

Xenophon, 11
Xia, Ran, 245n213

Zangwill, Israel, *A Doll's House Repaired*, 79
Zhdanov, Andrei, 229n75
Zimmermann, Alfred, 177, 188

Zola, Émile, 99, 124, 155, 179; *Germinal*, 179–80; *Money*, 31–32, 119; *Nana*, 33; *Thérèse Raquin*, 27